Savage Beginnings

USA TODAY BESTSELLING AUTHORS

J.L. BECK & C. HALLMAN

To Kelly,

Our beloved editor who has put up with our shenanigans for over a year now.

We love and appreciate you dearly.

XOXO

Your Evil Queens

1
ELENA

Slipping into my nightgown, I sit down on the edge of the bed and finish drying my dark hair while humming some pop song I heard on the radio earlier.

I've asked my father numerous times for a cell phone or laptop, but he swears it's for my own protection that I have neither, so the radio is all I've got. Dropping the towel, a shiver skates down my spine when my long wet hair brushes over my shoulder.

Bending down, I reach for the towel. Before my fingers even touch it, a deafening knock booms through the room. It's so loud and unexpected that a tiny shriek passes my lips.

Who the hell is that?

I glance at the clock on the wall and realize it's after eleven. My father never calls for me this late, and besides him, who could it be? No one, that's who. Since my mom's death two years ago, my dad is the only person I have left. I have no other family and no friends, thanks to my father's overbearing nature.

I wasn't even allowed to go to school because he deemed it too *dangerous* for his little girl. Everything I've ever learned was taught to me through homeschooling. Covering my chest with one arm, I open the door and find Richi, one of my father's personal guards, on the other side.

"Miss Elena, your father wants to see you in his study." There is a strange look on his face, a mixture of fear and remorse. He's never looked at me in such a way. Seeing how uncomfortable he appears to be makes me suspicious.

"Now?" I ask, still a little shocked, given the time. "Is something wrong?"

"Just come with me, please."

Oh no, something is wrong. I can already feel it, something is definitely going on.

"Okay, let me get dressed real quick."

"I'm afraid there is no time for that," a deep, penetrating voice comes from behind the door, filling my ears. Opening the door a little wider so I can see who that voice belongs to, I almost gasp. There's a man in a suit, a man I've never seen before, standing beside Richi.

In the dim light, it's hard to make out the man, but from what I can see, he looks down-right sinister. His gaze pierces mine, and his lips press into a thin line, impatience rolling off of him in waves.

Now I'm really worried, why is a man I've never seen or met before inside our estate, much less outside my bedroom door.

"What's going on?" I try to hide the panic from my voice, but even I can hear how nervous I am.

"Just come downstairs, Miss, enough with the questions," the unknown man orders, and I know there is no sense in arguing. When you're told to do something, you do it, that's what my father always said. If my father has asked for me, then surely this is safe.

Crossing my arms over my chest, I step out into the hallway and grit my teeth at the cold that kisses my bare feet. Goosebumps spread out across my skin as I walk between the two men, wearing nothing but some panties and a thin nightgown. I really wish they would have let me put some clothes on. This is no way to greet my father or any visitors.

The walk to my father's study seems to drag on, but when we reach the heavy wooden door, it doesn't feel long enough. I don't know what's going on yet, but I do know it's not good, and I'm not ready for it. My gut tightens with the unknown. I've had enough heartache in the last few years to last me a lifetime.

Looking up at the door, I don't bother knocking, knowing that my father is expecting me. Reaching for the knob, I pause for one more second, mentally preparing for whatever awaits me on the other side. I'm not sure why, but I glance back at Richi and the unknown guy. Both look at me with blank expressions, which is nothing new to me. My father's men are all trained to look at me like that. No emotions. Feelings get you killed.

Sucking in one last breath, I push the door open and take a step inside.

As soon as I catch a glimpse of what's beyond the door, I want to retreat from the room. It's a reflex, really.

Since I was a little girl, my father had trained me, told me to never listen to him, and his associates talk. To never listen to anything regarding his business. So, when I see him and three men in his office, I have this deep primal instinct to go in the opposite direction.

I shouldn't be here. I can't be here. My fingers tremble against the brass doorknob.

"Elena, come in," my father says, his tone clipped.

He is all business at this point, and even as badly as I would like to run from the room and seek shelter in my bedroom, I know better than to disobey my father, especially in front of his associates.

On shaky legs, I walk further into the office, my arms still tightly wrapped around my chest as if I'm giving myself a hug.

"Take a seat, we have some matters to discuss," he explains without looking at me. I hate how emotionless he sounds and looks, even more so than usual.

Two men I don't know are standing off to the side while a third man is sitting at the desk opposite my father. All I can see is his back from the position I'm standing in, his broad shoulders and thick arms rest against the arm of the chair as he casually leans backward.

Averting my gaze, I keep my eyes trained ahead until I'm at his desk, then I sit down in the free chair, hating how my short nightgown rides up my thighs, exposing even more of my skin. I feel naked and wish now more than ever that I had fought harder to change my clothes.

"Elena, do you remember Mr. Moretti?" My father motions to the man beside me. "Julian Moretti."

Moretti? The name sounds familiar, but I can't pinpoint it right away.

As I glance over to the man in question, my heart thunders in my chest, trying to put a face to the name. Immediately, our eyes lock, his icy blue stare penetrates me like a sharp dagger... just as they did the first time we met.

I remember it well, and I know the exact date because the first time I met this man was at my mother's funeral.

Just as most men I know, he too wears a mask of indifference. His eyes are blank, a carefully constructed wall placed around him, refusing to let anyone see the man beneath.

"You were at my mother's funeral." I simply state.

"Yes."

His voice is deep and smooth, not matching the rest of him. Everything else about him seems rough and jagged. His jaw sharp, his cheekbones angular, and his lips pressed firmly into a tight line. He's handsome in a devilish way, he could even be a model I'm sure. I can tell that he's older than me as he has this air of maturity about him, but I'm not sure how old since he has no fine lines around his eyes, only a permanent scowl between them.

I wonder if this man has smiled a day in his life.

"Elena." My father draws my attention back to him. "I need you to sign right here."

He pushes a piece of paper across the mahogany desk and passes me a pen.

"What is this?" I look down at the document but can't make out any of the words.

"Just sign it," my father orders, his tone harsh. Cruelty isn't something my father has ever shown me, and I can see he's struggling even right now with how to act. He's never been a great father, but that's because of his absence and overbearing nature, not because he is unkind to me. Whatever this is about is weighing heavily on him.

Dragging the paper closer to myself, I grip the pen between my clammy fingers and start to sign my name at the bottom. The room is silent, and I can hear the pen gliding across the paper. I'm not even halfway through signing my name when my hand freezes. My eyes dart from the document before me and up to my father, then back again.

That can't be right.

With the ink pen hovering over the paper, I reread the first few lines of the document.

OWNERSHIP CONTRACT

THIS AGREEMENT CONFIRMS **that as of today, Elena Romero will belong fully and without further stipulation to Julian Moretti in exchange for ten million dollars...**

"WHAT IS THIS?" I question with fervor, dropping the pen as I pull back from the desk.

A knife twists in my chest, the edge digging deeper with every breath I take.

This can't be what I think it is.

"Don't question me. Just sign the damn document," my father growls, slamming his fist down on the desk, and for the first time, he looks up at me. The coldness that reflects back at me makes me shiver. I've never seen him like this, and I don't understand why he's selling me to this man. Julian Moretti.

"I..." My bottom lip trembles and I bite it to stop it. "You can't do this... You can't *sell* me. I'm not signing this." Tears blur my eyes at the betrayal that consumes me. I want to scream, to fight this with all my might, but I feel helpless. There isn't a single person in this room that will help me.

The words have barely passed my lips when Moretti leans over and grabs my hand, engulfing his much larger one with my small one. Heat encompasses my hand, and it's like being burned by fire. I try to pull away, but he only tightens his grip as he forces the pen between my fingers and my hand back to the paper.

"Please... don't do this. You don't want me." I try and tug my hand away with all my might, my hand throbbing as he tightens his grip.

"But I do, Elena." He speaks into the shell of my ear.

With bruising force, he presses the pen to the paper and guides my hand, forcing me to write the rest of my name. A sob breaks free from my lips, and big fat tears of weakness fall from my eyes. The man who now owns me smiles like the devil and releases my hand with ease, placing it down against the paper.

"Father... please?" I pull my hand from the document and press it to my chest.

"The contract is complete," my father says on a sigh, leaning back in his chair. "She is now yours, do with her as you please."

That statement has me blinking back tears.

"Please, don't do this," I whimper, looking up at my father, pleading with him.

How could he just sign me away to someone I don't even know? Sell me for money? It's like I don't even know him. Like he's not my father at all.

"It's business, sweetie, don't take it personal." He shrugs and looks away from me, giving Moretti a get out of here gesture.

My mouth pops open, and I'm shocked, completely shocked. Where is my loving, caring father? The man who taught me how to ride a bike, the man who used to read me stories at bedtime, who held me when my mother died? He wasn't always the perfect father, but I never expected him to do this.

"You can't do this!" I hiss pushing up from my chair while slamming my fists down on his desk, but it does nothing but cause my hand to throb with pain.

He doesn't see me, doesn't care.

"Don't worry, Romero. I'll take good care of her... I mean... I'll break her in gently," Julian says darkly to my father. It's like looking at a shark and expecting it not to bite you. The only difference is this man isn't just going to bite me, he's going to devour me, slowly, piece by piece.

Julian stands, smoothing his hands down his suit. My heart skips a beat, and my eyes dart over my shoulder. I want to bolt for the door, but know I won't make it. Before I can devise an escape plan, his strong arm is circling my waist. He tugs me back against his hard chest and guides me toward the door.

I whimper like a wounded animal knowing the worst is yet to come. I've been sold to the devil, my body, mind, and life bound by an unbreakable contract.

2

JULIAN

Wrapping one thick arm around her waist, I pull her from her father's office, ignoring her tears and small whimpers. There will be many more in the following days.

"You don't want me..."

Her words ring in my ear. Oh, how wrong she is. I more than want her... in fact, I've wanted her for a very long time. *Years.* And now, I finally have her and her father exactly where I want them. I've been watching, waiting, planning to take Romero down for the last five years. The moment he killed my mother, taking from me the one and only person who ever mattered, I've been plotting his downfall.

It wasn't until Lilian Romero's funeral that I knew exactly how I was going to get my revenge. Romero fell off the wagon after his wife's death, his gambling problem multiplying into the millions. He thought he had time to pay his debts, he was comfortable and being comfortable left you vulnerable.

He didn't have shit now—nothing but her.

Now, I finally have her, my prize. My Elena. A dark raven-haired beauty that would soon become my wife. As if she can hear me thinking her name, she shoves at my arm, her nails sinking into the flesh as she struggles to get away from me.

Oh, Elena, there is no getting away now.

Releasing her for a fraction of a second, I grab her by the waist and lift her up, tossing her over my shoulder with ease. The nightgown she's wearing rides up with the movement, giving me a side view of her perfectly shaped ass and a glimpse of her satin panties that hide her virgin pussy. *That too will soon be mine.*

Markus, my second in command and the closest thing I have to a friend, walks ahead of me while Lucca, one of my best and most brutal enforcers, covers my back. We can't be too careful in this place. I did just steal Romero's daughter, after all. And a contract won't matter if I'm dead.

I carry her all the way out to the car while she spends the entire time pounding her little fists against my back. She doesn't actually think she has a chance of escaping me, does she?

When we reach the sleek black SUV, Markus opens the door. Turning around, his eyes fall on Elena, who is still struggling like a cat on my shoulder, her ass cheeks jiggling beside my face. Rage fills my veins, and I forget for a moment that Markus is my ally.

"Look at her again, and I'll gouge your fucking eyes out."

Most men cower in fear when I make a threat like that because everyone knows that when I make a threat, it's not just a threat, it's a promise. Markus is not most men, though, he takes in my words and gives me a respectful nod. If I didn't know him better, I could have sworn his lips twitched up into a smile.

Fucker.

I put her down on her feet but grab her arm before she can make a run for it. Her feistiness only makes me want her more. She covers her chest with her free arm, trying to hide her tits covered only by the thin material. She's beautifully naive, and the fact that she's even trying to maintain an ounce of modesty in this situation proves that.

I give her a quick once over. Her soft shapely legs that I picture wrapped around my waist are on full display, her small body shaking like a leaf either from cold or fear... maybe both. She's short, shorter than I remember her being, and fragile, so very breakable. My gaze moves over her delicate throat, which bobs as she swallows.

Her heart-shaped face is red, and her green eyes are puffy from crying. That raven hair of hers is a tangled damp mess. Still, she is the most beautiful woman I've ever seen. Beautiful and all-fucking-mine.

"Get in," I order.

She merely shakes her head. I stare down at her, knowing full well I'll never be able to hurt her like I've hurt others who disobey me, she is the only person who will ever have my mercy. Though there are other ways of disciplining her.

Pinching her chin gently between two fingers, I force her not only to hear the words I'm saying but also for her to see me speak them.

"Do it, or I do it for you, and believe me, you don't want me to do it."

Her emerald eyes widen with fear, and she must be able to hear the threat in my voice because her body starts shaking furiously. Pulling away, she reluctantly climbs into the car, sliding across the backseat, going to the spot furthest away. There is ample room between us, and I decide to let her have this small space, giving her a sense of control since I just took most of that away from her. I should probably feel bad about how I ripped her from her father's hands, uprooted her without warning from the only home she's ever known.

A good man would feel terrible, but the truth is I'm too selfish to feel any remorse. All I feel is a sense of accomplishment. I've waited for a long time, watching as the Romero family struggled to stay afloat.

"Where are we going?" Elena surprises me with her meek voice, and I look over at her. She's all doe eyes and innocence. Breaking her will be a crushing blow to her father.

"Home."

She wraps her slender arms around her torso like she is hugging herself before turning away from me again to stare out of the window. Her small body trembles, and I can make out goosebumps on her creamy smooth skin.

"Turn up the heat, Markus."

"Got it, boss."

For the rest of the drive home, we sit silently—only the engine's sound and the occasional sob filling the cab.

By the time we pull to the compound, I'm sweating profusely under my three-piece suit. Markus must have turned up the heat to well over a hundred degrees. As soon as Markus opens the door, I slip out of the car.

The fresh air cools me, and I inhale a harsh breath into my lungs. Turning around, I'm prepared for a fight, or at least a struggle and am pleasantly surprised to find Elena sitting on the edge of the seat waiting to get out.

Maybe this won't be as hard as I had assumed it would be.

Eyes cast down, she wrings her hands in her lap nervously. Sliding off the seat, her small feet press against the gravel, and I contemplate picking her up to carry her inside when she winces at the contact. I love how fragile she is and how much I know she'll need me to make it through everything I have in store for her. When I'm done with her, she will rely on me for every single thing she wants or needs.

Obviously, I'm far too trusting because she slips past me like a small mouse. Breaking off into a dead run, she dashes past the car and down the driveway. I'm not worried, though, since there isn't anywhere for her to go.

She doesn't make it far before one of my men grabs her, tugging her by the arm a little too roughly. I grit my teeth, my jaw clenching as I bite back the need to tell him to get his fucking hands off of her. Anger zings through me when he tugs her again, and she loses her balance falling onto the ground, scraping her knees and legs in the process.

"Let go of me!" She screams, sobs ripping from her lungs in quick succession as she pulls against Roger's hold, trying to break free. The strap of her nightgown slips off her shoulder in the process, and she almost flashes a tit at my men.

Fuck no. No one gets to see what is mine.

Walking over to her, I gesture for Roger to let her go, and he does almost as quickly as he grabbed her, retreating two steps back. I'll deal with him later. Right now, I need to get her inside and put her in some different clothes. My men have seen enough of her already.

Looking down at her exposed legs, I see scratches from where she fell, so I'll need to make sure she isn't actually hurt. Reaching down, I grab her by the hips, feeling the heat of her skin beneath my hands and toss her over my shoulder like I did earlier.

A growl forms in my throat as I become aware of how she barely weighs anything.

She doesn't even fight me and rests motionless on my shoulder as I carry her into the house, through the foyer, and up the stairs to the bedroom we will share. Pushing the heavy wooden door open, my shoes slap against the tile as I walk across the room and deposit her on my bed... *our* bed. The moment her butt hits the mattress, she looks up and scoots backward until her back is pressed against the headboard.

Big green eyes brim with fear. I could tell her she is safe here, that nothing bad will happen to her. But that would be a lie. She isn't safe yet, especially not from me.

"Stay here, get comfortable. I'll be back soon," I tell her as I slowly walk back toward the door. I've got blood to spill before I can tend to my new toy.

Looking at my beautiful prize one last time, I close the door and lock it behind me.

I let the anger that I was swallowing down boil up to the surface as I make my way through the mansion and toward the front door.

Stepping outside, I find Edwardo guarding the porch. He turns to look at me, his hand reaching for his gun before he recognizes it's me.

"Is Roger still out here?"

"Yes, boss. He is doing a round over the west lawn. Is everything okay?"

"It will be…" I snap before walking off and into the night.

3

ELENA

Huddled against the headboard, I watch as the door closes, the last sliver of his face disappearing behind the wood and the lock clicking into place. The sound is only a reminder of how trapped I am here, how I was taken from one cage, and put in another.

At least with my father, I knew where I stood. Or I least I thought I did. I knew what was going to happen each day, and I had some freedoms, not many, but not none. Now, I have nothing. No structure, no freedom, no say in anything... not even over my own body.

My life is no longer my own. I've been sold by my father to this evil villainous man.

"She is now yours, do with her as you please."

My father's words replay in my head. I can't believe he did this, sold me to Moretti.

Tears slide down my cheeks as I stare at the door. The room is lavish, manly, and blanketed in grays and dark blues. If the circumstances were different, I might actually be able to appreciate the beauty of it.

After a few minutes of staring at the door, I move off the bed to search for some type of way out of this room.

Walking to the first door I find, I discover an entire closet filled with clothing. I look down at my partially ripped nightgown. Who knew when I put this thing on tonight that it would be the last thing I would have from my old life?

I feel exposed and vulnerable in nothing but this, so I pull it off altogether and throw it on the ground. Quickly, I grab one of the shirts off a hanger.

I'm not sure if he is going to be mad at me for taking his stuff. Will he hurt me if I do? Punish me? Deciding it is worth the risk, I pull it on over my head and let it drift down before shoving my arms through the sleeves. The shirt is more like a dress, and the hem comes to rest against my bruised knees. A shiver snakes down my spine at the size difference between us. This man could easily hurt me, snap my neck, or take whatever he wants. My lungs burn, and I realize I'm not actually breathing.

Calm down. Everything is going to be okay. You can do this, Elena.

Grabbing the collar, I bring it to my nose and inhale deeply, the smell of cotton and soap tickling my nostrils. I do this a couple more times until the burn in my lungs eases.

Walking out of the closet, I go to the next door, knowing it's a bathroom before I even open it. It's clean and organized, but that doesn't make me want to stay here. No matter how lavish this place is, no matter how much he offers me, nothing will ever make me want to stay with him. Then again, who's to say he will offer me anything. He's paid ten million dollars for me, surely, it's me that will have to offer him something.

I curl my hand into a fist; anger and sadness festering like a cancer deep in my gut. I have to get out of here. Going to the door that I know is my only exit, I grab the brass knob, not caring that it's most likely a dead end. I heard the lock click into place. There might not be any escaping this room right now, but that isn't going to stop me from trying.

Taking the chance anyway, I turn the knob and push against the wood as hard as I can. Like I assumed, the door doesn't move, not even an inch. A sob lurches from my throat, and I place my cheek against the cold wood, hoping to maybe hear something. Not sure what I'm listening for, but the unknown surrounding me is worse than knowing what's going to happen. If I knew, then at least I could mentally prepare myself for it.

When my legs grow heavy, I walk over to the single window in the room and sit down on the floor below it. It's as close to escaping as I'm going to get. From here, I can still see the bedroom door, so I can watch to see when he returns. There is no way in hell I'm going to lie down in that bed like a freaking offering.

The darkness outside calls to me, and I twist around and stare up at the stars that hang high in the sky, moving to the glowing moon until my eyes start to grow heavy, and I find myself leaning against the wall, exhaustion sinking its claws into me. Drifting in and out of sleep, I find myself waking at every tiny noise.

My eyes pop open, and my back goes ramrod straight when I hear the lock on the door disengage. Blood rushes in my ears, my heart feeling as if it's being squeezed between two hands. As soon as Julian enters the room, I push to my feet.

I don't want to be on the floor, feeling even smaller and more vulnerable than I am. My throat seems to close up, and a deep-rooted terror explodes within me when he turns toward me, and I see the red splotches of blood on his white button shirt, hands, and neck.

I can't be sure, but I don't think any of the blood is his. The hungry look in his eyes steals the air from my lungs, and I wish the floor would swallow me whole.

He smirks at me. "You waited up for me? How sweet of you."

Turning his back to me, he locks the door and stashes the key back in his pocket before heading to the nightstand and setting a bottle of water on it.

Without another word, he walks into the bathroom. He doesn't close the door all the way, leaving it propped open a few inches. The sound of the shower fills the room, and a moment later, steam starts to come into the space.

Exhaustion weighs me down like a heavy blanket, and I slump back down to the floor. Wrapping my arms around my knees, I pull them up to my chest, wishing I could make myself small enough to disappear.

It takes a lot out of me to keep my eyes open. I'm so tired I just want to go to sleep, but I know that would be too good to be true. I highly doubt he bought me, took me from my home, and brought me to his bedroom for a good night's sleep.

I never thought this would be how I'd lose my virginity. Arranged marriages are normal in our family, so I saw it coming. I had always been aware of the fact that I wasn't going to have a choice in who I would marry, but I was sure that my father would choose a good man for me. Someone who wouldn't hurt me. Someone who'd court me, who I would meet first and have dinner with, not someone who comes and tears me from my home in the middle of the night.

I didn't expect love, but I did expect safety. I realize now how naive I've been.

Resting my head on my knees, I listen to the shower spray, letting it calm my nerves a little. The sound reminds me of heavy rainfall, and I happen to like the rain. I like how it feels on my skin, how it smells, and how it sounds as it pelts against the rooftop and windows.

I'm so disoriented and exhausted that I don't realize I've dozed off again until I feel a heavy hand on my shoulder. My eyes fly open, and I find my captor's large body looming over me. The smell of soap hits me, and as I trail my gaze up his body, I find that he's naked except for a pair of boxers.

"Get on the bed," he orders gruffly.

"No. I'd rather sleep on the floor."

"I didn't ask where you wanted to sleep. I said to get on the bed. I'm not asking."

When I don't move right away, he grunts annoyingly and leans down, ready to pick me up. As soon as his hands touch me, I lose it. I can't let this happen without a fight. I just can't. It's not in me. I won't be a victim.

His hands reach for me again, and I start swinging my arms wildly, kicking out my legs, and flailing my body. I do anything I can to fight him off.

As if I'm nothing more than an annoyance to him, he grabs my upper arms and pulls me to my feet, ignoring my kicks to his legs. In two large strides, he pulls me to the bed and pushes me on the mattress.

In the next instant, he is on me. My chest heaves, terror rippling through me as his much larger body comes down on mine, trapping me against the mattress. Even with him holding himself up with one arm, he is so heavy that I can barely breathe. Placing both hands against his chest, I push with all my might, but he doesn't move an inch.

The terror grows ten-fold, and I find myself spiraling out of control. Before I know what I'm doing, I lash out at him, sinking my nails into the side of his face, dragging my hand down, scratching across his face and neck in a frenzy.

"Fuck," he growls, and snatches my wrists, pinning them above my head. I can't breathe. I can't move. I'm trapped and at the mercy of this horrible man.

Blinking the tears away, I look up at his face, and my eyes go wide with shock. Multiple large scratches are marring his skin. Some of them so deep, blood pools on top of the skin.

I did that. I hurt him.

I look from the gashes and into his eyes, the pale blue is almost gone, his pupils so dilated that his eyes seem black. His whole body vibrates, and there is a distinct vein popping out on this forehead. He is angry, very, very angry. And I'm about to feel that anger.

The only thing I can do now is hope that I make it out of here alive.

4

JULIAN

I can't believe she scratched me. Like an angry little kitten, she showed me her claws. She is a fighter, and I like it. I like how she stands up to me even when she is scared shitless like I know she is right now. She might be frightened, but her instincts still tell her to fight, and that fight is exactly what I need.

Her slim body is shaking beneath me. Her chest rising and falling so rapidly, I think she might be hyperventilating. Leaning down, I let my face hover a few inches above hers. Close enough for me to feel her breath on my skin and for me to inhale her scent into my lungs. Coconut and something exotic, like a tropical island. It's intoxicating.

Her emerald green eyes bleed into mine, an ocean of emotions reflecting back at me. She's vulnerable, so delicate, but she didn't act that way. Not until now. Her eyes fall shut in defeat, and she turns her head away from me. I lean down further and let my lips descend on her exposed neck. I can feel the blood rushing through her veins beneath her silky skin as I place a few open mouth kisses along her throat. I want to taste her, devour her, but I can't, won't. Not yet, at least.

Her body stiffens, and she makes small whimpering sounds, her eyes squeezing tight. I place one last kiss on her jawline before I shift off of her body. All the blood in my body has drained into my cock, the rod so hard it hurts to even move. I want to fuck her, sink deep into her virgin pussy, and send the bloody sheets to her father, and I will... but not tonight.

"Drink the water I brought you and then go to sleep."

Her eyes fly open, and she turns her head to look at me. Her dark brows pull together in confusion. She thinks I'm lying. She probably thinks I'm going to hurt her, take from her, and even though I could, I won't. Not like this anyway. I want her to want me, to need me, and depend on me. That won't happen if I hurt her tonight.

"Drink." I motion to the water bottle on the nightstand.

She scoots over and reaches for the bottle. *Good girl.* I watch her unscrew the cap and take a few large sips before setting the bottle back where it was before.

"Now lie down and go to sleep."

She gives me a questioning look but does as she's told. It isn't out of trust but mere instruction because I haven't harmed her, she's decided not to put up any more of a fight.

Resting her head on the pillow, I grab the blanket and pull it up and over us as I settle down next to her. I leave a few inches between our bodies on purpose, allowing her a tiny bit of space. That's all the space she is going to get though. She will sleep in my bed every night, even if I have to make sure of it.

Watching her out of the corner of my eye, I can tell she is trying to keep her eyes open, but they keep fluttering closed. Her strength is refreshing, but even as she struggles, exhaustion soon gets the better of her.

Of course, the sleeping meds I put in her water might have helped as well. I grabbed the water and pills as a precaution because I wasn't sure if she would be asleep when I got into the room. I want to be able to inspect her from head to toe, and tend to any wounds without her fighting me.

Staring at her, I watch as her breaths even out, and the worry eases from her features.

A few minutes later, she is completely out. Reaching across the space, I touch her face, tracing my fingers along her high cheekbones and my thumb over her plump lips.

Yeah, she won't wake up until tomorrow.

Pushing the blanket off, I get up and go back into the bathroom to get the first aid kit. When I get back, I push the blanket all the way off her body so I can take a good look at her knees. She has some good-sized gashes, some of which still have gravel stuck to them.

I take my time cleaning her wounds, then put ointment on both sides before I inspect the rest of her body. She's wearing one of my plain white shirts, which has a smile tugging at my lips for some reason. I like the way she looks in my clothes and surrounded by my things.

I do my best not to think back on my little obsession with her. I've kept an eye on her since the funeral, which was not easy since her father kept her locked away.

Lucky for me, her dear old dad has a gambling problem, which only escalated after his wife's death. He thought as the head of his family, he couldn't run out of cash, he was wrong. The more money her father took from me, the deeper his debt became, and the closer she got to being mine.

Looking down at my prize, I take her in and smile. She must not have seen the women's clothes I bought for her on the other side of the closet. I highly doubt she would have chosen my shirt on purpose if she knew there were others available.

Pushing up the sleeve on the shirt, I look over her slender arm, and find some bruises forming on her upper arms from Roger grabbing her so harshly. Gritting my teeth, I feel the need to kill him all over again. No one touches what's mine, and no one bruises her flesh. Killing Roger was a warning to my men tonight.

Touch or hurt her in any way, and your life is over.

Pulling the blanket back up, I cover her body once more and put the first aid kit back in the bathroom. Standing at the edge of the bed, I stare down at her.

Romero thought he could kill my mother and that I wouldn't seek revenge. He probably didn't see me as a threat then as I was not interested in taking over the family business at the time. I was young and foolish, letting my uncle run the family after my father died of a heart attack. Romero was a foolish man to underestimate me, and tonight he learned a valuable lesson. He watched me take the one thing that matters to him. His only child. His incredibly naive and sheltered daughter.

I know he's expecting the worst, everyone knows what kind of man I've become since taking over the Moretti family. People know I have no mercy. If you disobey me, if you betray the family, then you're as good as dead. My uncle learned that the hard way. When I killed him.

Just like Elena does, Romero thinks I'm going to hurt her, which was always part of my plan. I'm going to drag out the pain, drive the knife deep, and then twist it. I've had forever to think of this plan, to ensure it goes off without a hitch.

Smiling, I think of what I will do first. Let him wallow in his misery, thinking that I'm doing all kinds of things to his daughter, unimaginable things while he is sitting at home unable to rescue her.

After a few weeks, I will show her off and show him how much control I have over her. I'll marry her and put my baby inside of her. But the icing on the cake will be when I have her wanting me. When she willingly chooses me over him. That will be the final blow, the nail in his coffin. The mere thought of exacting revenge gets my adrenaline pumping.

Romero should be thankful I haven't killed him. *Yet*. I didn't want the bastard to die before he could see what I have in store for his daughter. As if my sweet dark-haired Elena can hear my thoughts, she murmurs something in her sleep, the low sound drawing me out of my thoughts. Tonight has been a very tiring night for my soon to be bride, but tomorrow, I will let her in on my plan.

No matter what, she will become my bride. She'll give me an heir, and she will bend to my will and my rules, or she'll face the consequences.

Crawling back into the bed and under the sheets, I shut the light off and tug her to my chest. As if she subconsciously knows that she needs me, that I'm her only chance of survival, she burrows into my side. Cuddling into me like I'm her salvation.

The warmth of her body washes against mine, slamming into me, blanketing me. Holding women isn't my thing, cuddling or being close. It's personal, too much, but I need Elena to get used to me, and truthfully, I need to get used to it as well.

For a long time, I lie there wide awake. Turning my head, I bury my face in her thick hair. For years, I envisioned doing just this. Inhaling her scent deep into my lungs, sleep finds me, Elena's beautiful face flickering through my mind as I close my eyes.

I've got my bride, and it doesn't matter how much she fights it.

She'll help me get my revenge without even knowing it.

5

ELENA

When I awake I'm sluggish, my mind is a murky pond of water, and I'm trying to see through it to the bottom. It takes only a second for me to remember the events from the night before, and my eyes flutter open at the same time, my body jackknifes upward and into a sitting position. For a fraction of a second, dizziness overtakes me and then fades away.

Frantically, I look down at my body and find myself still clothed. Clenching my thighs together, I don't feel any soreness or pain.

He didn't touch me, at least not sexually.

Looking at the spot beside me where *he* laid before I fell asleep, I find that it's empty. Relief floods my veins, but that relief is short-lived when I hear a throat clear across the room.

"Good morning, Elena." His deep husky voice makes me shiver.

Slowly looking his way, I find he's leaning against the wall, wearing nothing besides a pair of low hanging shorts. His muscular chest is on full display, an assortment of tattoos etched into his skin. I can feel his eyes on me, feel them watching the steady rise and fall of my chest.

When I glance up to look at his face, I take in the scratches I left on his face last night. I still can't believe I did that, and I'm still expecting retribution.

There is a tray of food on the table beside him, and my stomach rumbles loudly as I eye it. I'm hungry, but not starving.

"Hungry?" he asks the obvious, clearly able to hear my rumbling belly. "I had one of the maids bring up breakfast. You should eat while we discuss what is going to happen next."

"I'm not hungry," I lie and tug the sheet higher.

It's like no matter how many pieces of fabric separate us or how much space, I still feel as if I'm exposed, one second away from being completely naked.

Shrugging as if he doesn't care if I eat or not, he plucks a piece of fruit off the tray and pops it into his mouth, chewing very slowly. "Suit yourself. Do you want to hear what's going to happen next, or are you not interested in that either?"

He's baiting me, and as badly as I want to turn in on myself and refuse to play his game, there is nothing like not knowing what your opponent's next move is. It's clear to me that this is a game to him, and I'm the unwilling pawn.

"Tell me."

Smiling, he seems pleased that I've taken his bait. "As you read in the contract, you are mine now. You belong to me, and I can do with you as I please."

"That contract doesn't mean anything. You can't buy a person, and you forced me to sign it. It can't possibly be legal if I didn't willingly sign it."

"I know your dad kept you in the dark, and I know you're naive, but you are not stupid. You know what kind of family you come from, and you know that we don't play by society's rules. You are part of my world, and in our world, that contract is binding till death." His words are like a knife cutting any ounce of hope that I had.

I don't know why I even dare ask my next question, but if I don't, I won't know how to prepare for my next fight.

"What do you want from me then?"

"Everything. Starting with you sleeping in my bed every night. You will live here with me, and there will be no privacy. For now, you will stay in this room. If you want freedom, you have to earn it, and you can do that by following the rules and obeying me. If I tell you to do something, you do it. There will be no fighting."

"Of course," I scoff. "You kidnap me and expect me not to fight when you try and hurt me? You're right... I'm not stupid."

"I didn't kidnap you, and I haven't hurt you..." The words trail off, and his gaze narrows on me. My throat bobs as I swallow around the lump of fear there. I'm terrified and trying my best not to show it. Julian is the type of man that will take a mile if you give him an inch.

"Yet," I add.

"Correct, *yet*. You can keep yourself safe and earn freedoms so long as you obey me."

It's like being at home all over again. Trapped. No freedom. No joy. My stomach twists into a knot, and I think I might puke.

"A month from now, you will become my wife, and then you will be completely mine. In the time leading up to that, I want your complete submission. You will listen to me and trust me without question."

Tears sting my eyes, but I blink them away, fisting the sheets a little tighter. Tears are a weakness, and I don't want him to see how weak I am, how weak I feel. My chest tightens, and anger rips through me.

Why would my father give me to this man? Why would he let him take me without right or reason? This isn't how it was supposed to go. I was supposed to be given to a man that would keep me safe, that wouldn't hurt me. I didn't expect love or even to be equal to my future husband, but I didn't expect to become a rug beneath his feet either.

"Let's see how well you listen." He claps his hands together and walks over to the bed. "I want you to get up and take a shower."

My mind is racing. There has to be a way out of this, but I have nothing to barter, nothing but my body which he already owns.

"Please," I whisper softly, willing him to see me as a human and not an object. "There has to be something else you want. Someone else you want?"

Cocking his head to the side, he stares at me wearily before his entire face goes blank. A moment later, a mischievous grin appears on his lips, and I know I've made no headway.

"I have everything I could ever want. Money, power, status, and now I have you too. I don't want anyone else. There is nothing more in this world that I could want or need." Darkness clings to each word, and I feel my escape slowly slipping away. Spiraling out of control, I need to gain some type of ground. I can't let him win. I can't.

Scurrying off the bed, I make it all of three feet before he's on me. Like a cat, he pounces, his fingers finding, and wrapping around my throat as he shoves me back against the mattress. I land in a heap, the air ripping from my lungs on impact.

All over again, I'm trapped between him and the mattress, this time though, his hand is wrapped around my throat, his grip firm but not bruising, his eyes dark and stormy. He's calculating and fierce.

He holds all the power, and I'm nothing more than a pawn in his sick, twisted game. He has no reason to want me. A man of his stature could have any woman he wants.

"Please," I croak and grab onto his wrist, trying to pry his hand away. I'm afraid he's going to hurt me, take and take until there isn't anything else to take. "Please don't..." I'm not sure what I'm asking him not to do, all I know is that I don't want him to hurt me or rape me. I'm not sure I could come back from that type of pain.

Leaning into my face, his nose brushes over mine, it's such an intimate action that doesn't match his behavior. He watches me cautiously as I tremble. I can't allow myself to fall for his softness. I have to remember he is the one who hurt me, the one who took me away in the middle of the night.

Pulling back an inch, his steely gaze roams my face. I can feel the power he exudes as he holds me to the mattress without barely any effort.

The weight of his body, the steel rod between his legs pressing into my belly, a reminder of what's to come. It's frightening. How he could easily snap my neck with nothing more than the flick of his wrist or steal my virtue while holding me against the bed.

"Then don't make me. Take off your fucking clothes, get in the shower, and listen to what I tell you. I've already shown you more mercy than I should have. Don't force my hand, Elena, don't make me hurt you; I promise you that it won't be something you easily forget. You think I'm a monster now, but you haven't even seen a sliver of what I'm capable of."

I don't realize how much I'm trembling until he pulls away, releasing my throat and taking the warmth of his body with him.

For a moment, I simply lie there, my chest heaving, fear pumping through my veins. My hand moves on its own, pressing against the flesh at my throat where it still feels as if he's holding me, his grasp like a steel shackle.

"Are you going to obey, or do you want to test my patience and resolve?" he whispers, and I decide to swallow my pride, and my need to escape for the time being. There will be other instances where fighting back is more worth my while. I need to save my strength.

Sitting up, I come to stand on shaky legs, cross the room, and walk into the bathroom, feeling his presence at my back the entire time.

Once inside the bathroom, the lights flick on, and my eyes burn at the brightness. I look down at the floor, my fingers shake, and goosebumps pebble my flesh when I grab the hem of his shirt and pull it off. It drops to the floor just like my stomach.

I've never been naked in front of a man. Never shown any of my intimate parts to one, and now I have no option. If I force his hand, I don't doubt he'll hurt me.

"I've never been naked in front of a man before." My cheeks burn at the admission.

"There's a first time for everything. You should get used to being naked in my presence because next month, we'll be married, and I'll be taking that cherry between your legs."

It's hard not to flinch at the words he says, but somehow, I manage.

Looking down my body, I realize that the scratches on my legs look like they have been cleaned. When did that happen?

Julian clears his throat, and his impatient eyes are on me. I know it even though I'm not looking at him. I can feel them piercing into my flesh, branding me, watching my shaky movements. Pressing my lips together, I dip my fingers into the waistband of my panties and push them down my legs. I feel like I'm signing my own death certificate with the motion. Naked, he could easily take from me. He could steal my virtue, not that I think clothes would stop him, but they're another barrier, a security blanket.

Crossing an arm over my chest, I cover my boobs and use my other hand to cover the space between my thighs while still refusing to look at him. I don't want to see the satisfied glint in his eyes. I don't want him to think he's won because the battle has merely begun.

Julian's eyes darken further; emotions I don't understand swirling in their depths.

"Drop your arms," he says gruffly.

Obeying, I drop my arms down to my sides. Shaking with fear, I flinch as he walks closer, nearly touching me as he reaches into the shower behind me and turns it on. I relax but only a little as he reappears at my side, plucking a strand of hair off my shoulder, wrapping it around one finger. Inspecting it like it's a rare jewel.

Leaning to my ear, his hot breath tickling the lobe, he whispers, "Such a beautiful bride you will be. I cannot wait to sink my cock deep inside your virgin pussy and watch as you bleed around me. I'll be your first and your last."

My most basic instincts kick in, and I feel the need to run, hide, but there is nowhere I can go. Nowhere to escape. Instead, all I manage to do is whimper.

"Get in the shower and clean yourself," he orders a moment later, his voice coming out different. Scurrying away from him, I step into the shower, shutting the glass door behind me. I wish it wasn't glass, so I could have a little privacy.

Through the fog-filled glass door, I can still feel his eyes on me, feel him watching me through the glass as I clean myself. I should be thankful, at least he isn't right on top of me, tormenting me with his body, at least he hasn't hurt me. *Yet.* That single word defines everything. If I do as he says, submit, and become a doormat to his needs, he won't hurt me. If I fight, he'll become the devil that I definitely know he is. Though I've always stayed out of my father's business, I know better than to assume Julian is a weak-minded man. He got my father to sell me to him. His men listen to him. He's powerful, cruel, and he'll use his strength to keep me in line. All these thoughts and emotions are giving me a headache.

Closing my eyes, I hold my face beneath the spray of water, trying my best to ignore him and pretend I'm alone. I don't know why but I'm shocked when I reach for the soap and discover he has not only soap for himself but also me.

He had everything planned and ready.

I wonder how long he's been planning this with my father, planning how I will spend the rest of my life. I can never forget what he's done and how I got here. As soon as I let my guard down, he'll hurt me.

Taking my time, I wash my entire body from head to toe, surprised that he's not telling me to hurry up. When I'm done, I turn off the water and spin around, coming to face him again.

This time, I don't look away. I stare at him with the same grim look he's giving me, watching as he leans against the counter, his arms crossed over his bare chest while he watches me like a hawk, his gaze narrowed.

As I step out of the shower, he takes a step toward me. The courage I had moments before melts away. Is he going to hurt me now? The fear of the unknown makes my belly hurt, and my body coil with tension. Reaching for a towel, he unfolds it and holds it out to me.

Gritting my teeth painfully, I step into the towel, unsure of what kind of game he's playing. Steeling my spine, I stand there with my arms hanging down at my sides as he dries me off. Shivering, he touches every part of me without actually touching anything, always keeping the towel as a barrier. His touch isn't sexual or leering. It's gentle, almost nurturing, and that confuses me. When my body is dry, he drops the wet towel and grabs another fresh one.

"Arms up."

I follow his command and lift my arms up, even though everything inside of me screams not to do it. I don't realize what he is doing until he wraps the fluffy towel around my body, tucking it in above my breasts.

"There you go," he says, talking to me like I'm a child. His eyes remain on mine and nowhere else. Obviously, he's gotten his fill. I drop my arms and watch him reach for a third towel. "Turn around."

Confused yet again, I turn around, my whole body stiff with fear.

What is he going to do now?

I relax slightly when I realize he just wants to dry my hair. His actions don't add up. None of this makes sense. Why is he treating me like this? One minute he is threatening me, grabbing me by the throat, the next he dries my hair? What kind of sick game is he playing?

I don't want to find out. All I want to do is get out of this unscathed.

6

JULIAN

After watching her shower and staring at her perfect body covered in soap, it was hard for me to walk away and leave her in that room without fucking her—the heavy swell of her breasts, her smooth belly, and shapely thighs. I didn't get the best look at her pussy, but that was okay. Soon enough, I wouldn't just be getting a look at it, I would be fucking it.

I playback in my mind the way she trembled and reacted to me as I dried her off. She wasn't sure if I was going to hurt her or nurture her, and that was right where I wanted her, straddling the line of fear, anticipating my next move at all times. I want her to crave my touch and want me, but I also need her to obey me, and the best way for that is fear.

I would never actually harm her physically, but she doesn't know that. Some well-placed threats should be enough to keep her in line, and if not, I have an arsenal of punishments that will teach her without actually harming her.

If she behaves, I will reward her. If she disobeys, I will discipline her. Easy as that.

I thought long and hard on how I would punish her if she decided not to obey me. A spanking? Maybe she would enjoy that too much. I probably should think about something more creative.

Locking her in the room is a good start. Isolation will have her craving my companionship, make her want me even though she doesn't. Silence and loneliness do strange things to the human mind.

Markus walks into my office without so much as a knock, stopping once he reaches my desk. "What the hell happened to your face?"

I smirk, remembering the scratches Elena left on my skin. "Played with a kitten last night. That tiny thing has some claws."

Seemingly uninterested in my answer, he changes the subject to Elena's father. "The spy you have at the Romero mansion reported that the girl's father plans to come for his daughter."

Smiling, I lean back in my chair. "Of course, he does. I didn't expect it to be that easy. What's he got planned?" I could easily send some of my best men over to have them end him, but what would be the fun in that?

I want him to watch me ruin his daughter. I want my revenge, and he isn't going to fucking ruin that for me by forcing me to put a bullet between his eyes.

"He didn't have anything else to say but that. I told him to keep his ear to the ground and report back as soon as he heard something."

"Great. I have a meeting at the strip club. Going to collect a debt. Call me if she gives you any trouble."

Markus nods, his face is emotionless as always. He's one of my best men, and I know if I can trust anyone not to hurt her, it's him. He knows the only one who gets to mark her skin is me, unlike Roger, who paid the price. I used him as an example for my men.

Dismissing Markus, I stand and smooth a hand down my three-piece suit. I'm feeling like a million bucks and not just because I stole something precious, something priceless. As I leave my office, I consider walking down the hall to check on Elena. I want to see her trembling, waiting to see what happens next, but more than that, I want her to crave me. Crave my body, my attention. I want her to want me so badly it hurts when I'm not near, and that won't happen if I'm popping in whenever.

This is a lesson and one she must learn.

When I reach the front door, the SUV is parked outside, I slip into the back seat and check my phone for the time, I could send any of my men to do this job. Hell, Lucca would love to spill some blood right now, but sometimes you have to take things into your own hands. Roberto's a long-time associate and is behind on his dues, and if I'm being honest, I'm in the mood to break some bones. The little temptress locked in my mansion is trying my patience, and the tension in my body has to go somewhere.

It's Roberto's lucky day.

The devil is coming to his doorstep.

∼

WHEN THE SUV pulls up at Dimension's, I get out and straighten as does my third in command, Lucca. He's young but has proven himself time and again. His father was an associate of my father's, on his deathbed, I promised I would watch out for Lucca, he wasn't born into this life, but that didn't matter to me. He's earned his spot.

The two bouncers at the door greet us with head nods, and I walk in without speaking a single word to either of them. I didn't get the ruthless reputation that I have by shaking hands and smiling. There were a lot of lives lost, a lot of blood fucking shed for the Moretti family.

If my father were alive, I'm sure he would be proud of the savage way I lead things. He was even more ruthless than I am.

Elena's naiveté and virginity wouldn't have stood a chance against him. He would've taken her without mercy, killed her father right before her eyes. I had more mercy than that; after all, she was an innocent caught in the middle of a war she knew nothing about.

My father always wanted me to take over after his death, but I wasn't sure it was my path, not until after my mother's death. Then everything changed.

Inside, the smell of smoke and sweat permeates the air, clinging to my lungs with each breath I take. The place doesn't open for a couple more hours, so I don't have to worry about any patrons seeing something they shouldn't. Naked women scurry out of my way as we walk through the dimly lit bar and stage area. Roberto's office is just down the hall, so that's where I'm headed.

Reaching the door, I pause for half a second before I twist the knob and shove it hard, sending it flying open. What can I say, I like to make an entrance!

Roberto's beady eyes widen with shock as he scurries from behind his desk, the shock giving way to fear as recognition takes hold. It's not often that I show up personally to collect a due, but today is his lucky day.

"Julian... I... I have your money, sir."

Stepping into the room, I stare down at him. Roberto is a tiny man with a balding head, protruding belly, and seriously bad hygiene. Pigs smell better than he does. His clothes are tattered, his dress shirt barely covering his stomach.

"I would hope so, plus interest."

"Yes... plus interest." Roberto's voice quivers, his eyes darting away, not in fear but something else. Something is going on here, the tightening in my gut tells me so. I reach for my gun at the same time he moves behind his desk.

A drawer squeaks open, and he looks down almost remorsefully at its content.

The organ in my chest thumps loudly.

What is this fucker trying to do? Does he want to die?

"I'm sorry, Mr. Moretti," he whispers.

Adrenaline pumps through my veins. My gun is drawn, my finger on the trigger, the moment he pulls out a handgun and points it at me. I pull the trigger without thought or mercy, watching as the bullet leaves the chamber and enters his chest, the impact of the bullet causing him to stagger back and collapse against the wall. The gun he pulled falls to the floor with a clatter, and I walk over to him, kicking it away. Sliding down the wall, he slumps to the floor. He's making little gasping noises, his eyes frantic and fearful. He's not dead yet, but he will be soon.

"All you had to do was pay me," I tell him disappointedly while pressing the muzzle of my gun to his head.

"I..." The words try to pass his lips, but excuses aren't going to save him. When money is owed, you pay with cash or with your life. You want to operate a business in my territory, you pay your dues. Pulling the trigger, I watch the life bleed from his eyes as his brain explodes against the wall.

Silence blankets the room, and the all too common euphoric pleasure of killing coats my insides like a warm balm.

"Lucca, let the staff know that they now answer to me."

"Yes, sir," he replies, and I can hear his footfalls disappearing down the hall. Leaning against the desk, I look down at Roberto. All he had to do was pay his fucking dues. Shaking my head at the stupidity, I tuck my gun back into its holster and pull out my phone to see if there are any messages from Markus letting me know how my little captive is doing.

I almost frown when I find there isn't.

Deciding to check up on her myself, I log into the app for my surveillance system. As I was putting my plan into motion, I had cameras installed in the bedroom, so I could watch her at any given time. A grainy image pops up on the screen, and I smile, seeing my beautiful soon to be bride perched on the edge of the bed. She's wearing nothing but the towel I secured around her before I left, looking as if she's in shock. I wonder what she is thinking. Perhaps she is thinking of how much she hates me?

Looks as though Elena is behaving herself. I exit the app, and to think I was looking forward to punishing her, seeing her beautiful creamy white ass cheeks a soft shade of pink. Would she cry and beg me to stop, or would she moan and beg me for more?

My cock hardens to steel in my slacks just thinking about it. Pleasure and pain go hand in hand in my mind. Shoving my phone back into my pocket, I walk out of the room and into the hall.

"Any troubles?" I ask once we're in the car. Killing was supposed to make me feel better, but it doesn't have the same effect as it usually does, not now that Elena has taken the spot front and center in my mind.

"No, sir, the bartender is going to run the place until we get someone else to take Roberto's place. I already called the clean-up crew, and they'll be here shortly." I nod. I wasn't worried about anyone saying anything. If they did, I'd send one of my men to get rid of them. Everyone who works here knows the score.

"Take us to the next business," I tell my driver.

The engine roars to life, and we pull away from the curb. As badly as I want to return to the mansion and frighten my little bride, it's important to leave her to herself. The human mind can be your biggest enemy, and I want to make her weak, make her need me. That will be the best revenge against her father, a man who should already be dead.

7

ELENA

It takes me a while to mentally recover from the shower I took with him stood watching me. It was intense, to say the least. Julian is like a ticking time bomb. I don't know what to expect from him. Is he going to show me compassion? Or is he going to hurt me? All I know is that I can't trust anything he does or says, and yet every aspect of my life now forces me to rely on his guidance.

My thoughts twist and turn, the silence within the room is all-encompassing. I feel on edge like he's going to burst through the door any moment now, finishing what he started this morning.

That thought makes me realize that I'm still naked. The only thing covering me is the towel wrapped around my body. I need to find something to wear.

He didn't seem to care that I wore his shirt last night, which has me going back into the closet a little less fearful today. I look through the shirts, running my fingers over the fabric.

At the end of the rack, I discover another completely full rack, but with women's clothes on it.

Baffled, I look through the clothes that range from formal dresses to workout attire. There is an article of clothing for every occasion here.

I pause, unsure what to think. There isn't any way that he bought all this stuff for me, is there? Maybe another woman lived here before me, and this is her clothing? Maybe he bought it for her, and now he's handing it down to me. Grabbing a dress from the rack, I look at the size and almost drop it—size four. There are a lot of women who wear a size four, but what are the chances that his previous girlfriend is the same size as me?

He bought all of this... for you.

It takes me a moment to get myself together. I'm shocked. After a moment, I look through the clothes once more, trying to find the least attractive outfit. Something that will hide my hips and chest. Plucking a T-shirt off a hanger, and a pair of loose-fitting yoga pants, I hope that I've chosen the least sexy combination available. I don't want to draw his attention, I want to lose it entirely.

Going through a couple of drawers, I find bras and panties that are in my size and all matching. My fingers trail over the lacy items. There are red, pink, blue, and black. I go with the white bra and panties because they're the most boring out of the bunch. Not that Julian is going to see me in them.

Not if I have anything to say about it.

Dropping the towel, I get dressed in a flurry, hating how creepily well the clothing fits me. Tugging on the shirt, it's not really form-fitting, but it's not baggy like I would've liked it to be. Whatever it's better than a dress.

Fully dressed, I feel a little less exposed, and I walk out of the closet peeking around the corner, wondering if he's going to pop out of nowhere. Slowly, I walk to the bed and sit on the edge of it, wishing I was at home with my father, or really anywhere but here.

Now that the initial shock of last night has passed, and I've had time to gather my thoughts, I remember where I'd heard the name Julian Moretti before. My father always tried to keep me sheltered, but he couldn't keep everything from me. I'd overheard him talk about Julian, how he was taking over his family business, using methods that others didn't approve of. I didn't even want to know what those methods were.

Time moves slowly when you're confined, what could only be a matter of an hour feels like twenty or more. The sound of footsteps outside the door has me lurching off the bed. Clenching my hands into fists, I force my gaze toward the door, watching as the brass knob twists slowly, and a woman in a maid's outfit walks in.

The air in my lungs stills, and I let out a huge breath when she brings in a tray of food and sets it down on the edge of the table. I don't even think as I rush toward her, grabbing onto her arm, hoping there is a piece of her that isn't corrupted.

"Please, help me. I'm trapped here, and he's going to hurt me."

The maid doesn't even look up or acknowledge that I'm here. Tugging her arm from my grasp, she moves back toward the door, and my hopes once again come crashing back down. I consider rushing her and pushing out of the room, but I don't want to face Julian's wrath. I don't doubt for a second that he would punish me, so I decide against doing that and watch helplessly as she walks out of the room, the door closing, and the lock clicking back into place.

Tears come, but I blink them away as I go to sit back on the edge of the bed.

This is all my life has amounted to.

I've been shifted from one golden cage to the next.

A bird that will never sing, never fly freely...

~

I'M BACK on the floor by the window, my knees drawn to my chest.

My eyes are glued to the door most of the time while I wait for him to return. He left hours ago, leaving me alone with nothing but my thoughts.

Being alone isn't abnormal to me, but I usually have my books or something to do. I could at least roam through my father's house, take a walk outside, or talk to the maids.

Here there is nothing for me, and the loneliness and fear of it all settles deep into my bones. Will it always be this way? Will I always be locked in this room as nothing more than a doll for him to use when he sees fit? I look back to the window, the sun is slowly setting, and I want so badly to go outside. To feel the grass beneath my feet, to feel the warmth of the sun on my skin.

Tears spring from my eyes, and I wipe them away with the back of my hand before they can trail down my cheeks.

Julian says he won't hurt me as long as I obey, but I'm not stupid. He'll hurt me no matter what, otherwise what was the point in taking me.

The longer I sit here, the more I think, which leads me to thinking about how easily my father sold me to him. My stomach churns as I remember the look on his face. I think it will forever haunt me. I squeeze my eyes shut as if that would help me forget. As if my life isn't a constant reminder of the nightmare that is now my reality.

I perk up when I hear footsteps approaching in the hall. A moment later, the lock clicks, and I sit up a little straighter.

The door swings open, and Julian's large frame comes into view. He's huge, taking up most of the doorway. His stormy blue eyes find mine as he steps into the room and closes the door behind him.

"Elena, I hope you had a wonderful day." He smirks, knowing full well I haven't done a damn thing today. When I don't respond, he tilts his head to the side as if he's examining me. "Why are you on the floor again?"

Breaking eye contact, I glance over to the bed. "It's the only place I can look outside. Also, I don't want to sleep in the bed with you."

"Well, you better get used to it." Watching cautiously, he starts undoing his tie, loosening it up before unbuttoning the top two buttons of his dress shirt. "Tomorrow night, when I return to the room, you will be in this bed waiting for me. If not, I will tie you to the bed every day before I leave to ensure you're waiting for me when I return."

I suck in a shaky breath, almost saying something like: you can't be serious. Then, I remember who I'm talking to, a crazed monster. He is dead serious, I have no doubt.

"Now be a good girl and get up," he orders while pulling his tie over his head and throwing it onto the chaise lounge.

My body moves on its own, pushing up from the floor. I'm not sure if I'm just scared or if it's because I'm already conditioned to listen. Either way, I hate it, hate every aspect of this situation. A smile tugs on his lips at my obedience. His gaze rakes over my body, taking in my attire. "I see you found the clothes I got for you."

He points at what I'm wearing, and I nod, hating the way I'm relieved that he did buy them for me. I shouldn't care if they belong to some other woman, but I do.

"Did you eat your food the maid brought up?" He looks around the room, searching for the tray. I didn't finish the whole plate, but I ate what I could with my stomach being in knots. Honestly, I'm surprised I was able to keep anything down at all.

He inspects the half-eaten food and nods, seemingly pleased with the amount I ate. He turns back to face me before taking a step toward me. Instinctively, I try to take a step back, but my back is already pressed against the window.

Closing the distance between us in two large strides, he stands so close, I have to tilt my neck back to look him in the face.

"Give me your hand," he gruffly demands, and again, I obey without thinking. I offer him my hand, and he takes it, engulfing mine with his much larger one.

Without another word, he turns and tugs me along behind him.

"Where are we going?" I ask when he heads for the door, excitement blooming in my chest at the thought that I'll finally get to leave the bedroom.

"Dinner."

He opens the door and pulls me out into the hall. His legs are much longer than mine, and I have a hard time keeping up with his large strides as he drags me through the hallways and down the stairs.

Why is he in such a hurry?

By the time we get to the dining room, I realize that we are completely alone in this large house, or at least I don't see or hear anyone else. Peering at the huge mahogany table that seats twelve, I find that it is already set...for two. There are covered bowls and trays in the center of the table, making me wonder if someone prepared this and left or if Julian made this for us.

He pulls out a chair and motions for me to sit down. When I take the seat, he pushes the chair in and starts to uncover all the food. Steam billows from each dish and an array of savory flavors fill the air.

Before I can stop myself, I ask, "Did you cook this?"

Julian looks like he wants to laugh. "Do I look like a chef?"

"No... I just... never mind," I mumble, my cheeks heating. I feel embarrassed, and all for asking a simple question.

My soon to be husband takes the serving spoon and starts filling my plate with a little bit of everything before filling his own.

"Thank you," I say, more out of reflex than anything else. I shouldn't be thanking him for anything. I should be taking my steak knife and stabbing him in the throat.

Grabbing the fork, I pierce a small potato, imagining it's one of Julian's eyeballs. I don't really feel like eating, but I know refusing is futile. He would somehow make me do it regardless. Plus, not eating will ultimately work against me. I need my strength to escape, so if eating gets me there, then I'll eat.

"Would you care for some wine?" he asks casually.

"No, thanks." There is no way I'm drinking a drop of alcohol. I'm already at a major disadvantage. I'm not going to add anything to make me even weaker.

"Suit yourself. I got you something," he announces, grabbing something from his slack pocket. "Put this on, and don't take it off, *ever*." The tone of his voice carries a finality to it. I look up from my plate, and at the small object he is holding between two large fingers. It's tiny compared to his huge palm—a silver band with a shiny diamond cradled in the center.

"How romantic," I say under my breath while reaching for the engagement ring.

"It's either this around your finger or a collar around your neck? I figured you'd prefer this." He shrugs, and I want to throw the stupid ring in his face.

Instead, I nod in agreement and slide the ring onto my ring finger. Of course, it fits perfectly. How does he do this? Did he have someone measure me from head to toe while I was sleeping? I wouldn't be surprised, to be honest.

Trying not to look at the ring, I continue eating, pretending like I don't find the ring beautiful. The last thing I want is for him to assume I like something he got me.

For a few minutes, neither one of us says anything. I want to ignore him just as much as the sparkling diamond decoration on my ring finger, but I'm not able to do either. His presence is impossible to ignore, and the diamond glitters with every tiny movement. It's annoying, all of it.

"Why did you get me this ring? It's not like anyone will see it."

"*I* will see it," he snaps. Then he continues in a slightly softer tone. "Besides, you won't be locked in the bedroom forever. Just until I can be sure you won't disobey me. How long that will take is purely up to you."

"Of course…"

We eat the rest of the meal in silence. When I can't take another bite, I place the fork next to my plate and lean back in my chair. My stomach is full, and I don't think I could take another bite if I tried.

"Dessert?"

"No, I'm full." The words have barely left my lips before Julian gets up from his chair. Grabbing me by my upper arm, he pulls me to my feet and starts guiding me out of the dining room.

Immediately, I'm alarmed. Why is he so eager to get me back to the bedroom? I thought he wanted to wait until after we were married. Maybe he changed his mind?

"Why are you shaking?" His words take me by surprise as we reach the stairs.

"I didn't realize I was. Why are you in such a hurry to get me to bed? I thought..."

Julian snickers. "You thought I was an honorable man who was going to wait to have sex with you until after we were married?"

"Yes..." I can only hope...

"We'll see."

We'll see? What is that supposed to mean?

By the time we reach the bedroom, I'm shaking even more. I'm completely alone with a man who is easily twice my size. There's no one here who could help me even if they heard me scream. I'm completely helpless, at the mercy of this ruthless man who bought me for ten million dollars.

He locks the door behind us and lets go of my arm. Scurrying backward, I feel like I'm suffocating in his presence.

"Get ready for bed. I'm taking a shower."

"A sh-shower?" I stutter, still shaking like a leaf and a little shocked. I was so sure he was going to rape me, but he's...

"Yes, a shower. Care to join?" The mocking tone he gives me has me snapping out of the fearful fog around my head.

"No," I blurt out, making him grin.

"That's what I thought. Find some pajamas and get in the bed," he orders before turning around and walking into the bathroom. As he disappears into the bathroom, I all but run into the closet. My heart is racing, and my hands shake as I grab a nightshirt and pair of sleep shorts.

Quickly, I peel my clothes off and put my clean pj's on, waiting for him to appear in the closet. He's a cruel monster, and I must always remain alert when he is in the room.

Tiptoeing out of the closet, I walk back to the king-size bed, my eyes catching on the door to the bathroom, which is cracked open. Steam billows into the bedroom, and temptation builds inside of me.

He's seen you naked. Why not see him naked?

Walking over to the door, I peer through the crack and cover my mouth with a hand to stifle the gasp that tries to escape. Water cascades over his tanned, sculpted body, the muscles of his back ripple, but it's not his nakedness that has me gasping.

It's the hand wrapped around the steel rod between his legs, the furious, angry pumping that he's doing with his hand. My cheeks burn, and my throat tightens as I watch him stroke himself. I've never seen a man touch himself, and I become mesmerized. Each stroke is anger-filled, and I can't look away, my eyes roam over his thick thighs that are like tree trunks, his biceps bulge, and with his eyes closed, he looks almost angelic. Licking my lips, I feel a heat creep into my core.

This is wrong. He's your captor.

As if he can feel me watching him, his eyes flutter open, and his dark blue orbs find mine instantly. The air in my lungs rushes out, and I stumble backward from the intensity in them. Shame fills me, and my face burns, watching as his lips tip up at the sides while he doesn't even miss a beat and continues stroking himself.

Rushing from the door, I almost trip over my feet in my escape to get away. Jumping onto the bed, I climb under the covers and press a hand to my chest, trying to get my heart to stop beating out of my chest.

After a while, my breathing returns to normal at about that same time that the water in the shower turns off. Seconds turn into minutes, and I hold my breath while waiting.

Heavy footfalls approach the bed, and then the room falls into darkness. My body is strung tight with anxiety. The blankets are pulled back, and the weight of his body presses into the mattress. I feel like prey hiding in the woods, hoping I won't be discovered.

I don't even get a chance to prepare for his touch, he slings an arm around my waist and tugs my back to his chest, engulfing me in his warmth. Heat zings through me when our skin touches.

"In case you were wondering, I was thinking about you the entire time. Thinking about your tight pussy, the way you'll pulse around me and beg me for more on our wedding night. I can't wait to deflower you." His mouth is at my ear, and I involuntarily shiver at his confession.

He lets out a small chuckle and then settles behind me. I don't say anything and try not to think about his words, but the truth is, I can't get the image out of my mind, and that makes me hate him all the more. He's making me crave something, making me need him, and I'll do anything to prove that I don't need or want him.

8

JULIAN

Working from home is a pain in the ass when you have a beautiful woman right down the hall that you could be fucking. It's also impossible to focus when you keep checking your phone so you can spy on her and see what she's doing. Maybe I should've gone with Lucca today to check shipments, at least then I wouldn't be tempted by the raven-haired beauty.

Last night, she watched me as I beat off to the image of her perfect pussy. Her gaze was full of shock and curiosity. It took me forever to fall asleep, wondering what she would do if I touched her. I never expected her to spy on me, or watch me through the door, but she shocked the hell out of me. Maybe it was a game. Maybe she was trying to test me.

Leaning back in my chair, I think back to this morning and how I tortured myself further. Forcing myself to stand outside the shower and watch as she washed her gorgeous body. She looked like a goddamn angel, and I hate it. Every time I look at her, I see a young woman I want to break and destroy. This is revenge, plain and simple. Any sliver of kindness died the day my mother did.

I see her father standing over my dead mother's body, and I feel shame for not reacting sooner. I feel like a fucking failure for not protecting my mother, and I will never allow myself to feel that way again. Elena is a means to an end, and breaking her heart is inevitable. She will become a casualty of war, and there is nothing I can do about it.

The minutes tick by slowly, and I go over the books one more time, double-checking to make sure that I've received dues from every location in my territory. I'll need to send Markus out to the new businesses so he can let them know how this works. They'll choose either to stay and pay dues or leave.

Grabbing my cell, I call Markus. The phone rings twice.

"Yes, boss."

"There are three businesses that are new on the east side of town. I will send you the names of each of them. I want you to go in and let them know the rules, tell them what they need to do, and show them what happens if they don't."

"Of course." I can almost hear the joy in his voice. Markus doesn't show emotion often, but I imagine he smiles while delivering my messages.

"Let me know if there are any problems," I tell him and hang up.

Logging back into the security app, I find Elena sitting on the edge of the bed cross-legged. She's just sitting there, doing nothing, looking completely unaffected by the fact that she is all alone.

It angers and interests me all at once.

She doesn't seem to be bothered by the silence of the room, and I wonder why that is? She should be going insane, beating on the door, begging for me to let her out.

I knew her father kept her on lockdown in his house, but maybe it was more than that. Had her father locked her up in her bedroom, kept her a prisoner like she is here? Clearly, she's conditioned, which is putting a real damper on my plan.

Checking the time, I realize it's almost lunch. Pushing up from my chair, I walk to the kitchen where Martha–one of the older maids–is just putting everything on a tray.

"I'll take it to her today," I tell her. Her mouth opens to say something, but she quickly changes her mind, closes her mouth, and simply nods instead.

Carrying the tray of food, I walk through the house and up to the bedrooms. I catch myself being eager to get to her, and that thought has me slowing down. I can't have her get to me like that. No one controls me.

I unlock the door while balancing the food with my free hand. When I step inside, Elena jumps up from the bed. Her eyes go wide as she takes me in; clearly, she didn't expect me to deliver her lunch.

She doesn't say anything as I carry the tray to her, placing it on the bed beside her.

"Please don't tell me you were expecting someone else?" I say.

"I just thought the maid brought me my lunch. I didn't know you were here."

"You sound disappointed."

"Just surprised." She shrugs. Without looking up at me, she takes the sandwich from the plate and starts nibbling on it. As I stand there towering over her, I'm burdened with the need to understand her.

"You seem accustomed to being alone."

"Because I am," she simply states. "I would appreciate being able to go out for walks and explore the grounds when I want to."

"Like I said–"

"Yes, I know." She glances up at me, her thick lashes fan against her cheeks. "Listen, obey, behave, then freedom. In that order."

I'm not sure if I'm mad or impressed that she dared to interrupt me. I don't even remember the last time someone did that without dying immediately after.

"Did your father not teach you any manners?"

Her cheeks turn crimson. "I'm sorry."

Her apology is genuine, and I'm not sure what to make of it. Hell, I don't know what to make of any of this. She's nothing like I expected her to be, and I need to get out of this room and away from her. She draws me in, and I won't be made a fool of, least of all by her.

"I'll be back to get you for dinner."

Her lips part, and it looks like she's going to say something, but her gaze darts away, and words never come out. I wonder if she is going to ask me to stay. To talk. Is my plan working so quickly? Is she already starved for my attention?

Not giving her time to figure it out, I leave the room without another word. I close and lock the door behind me before I stare at the door for a second longer than I should. My plan is unfolding nicely, even though not quite as I had planned, she is starting to depend on me, nevertheless. So why am I not happy about it?

∽

My afternoon workload goes just as painfully slow as the morning. Lucca and I discuss a couple shipments of drugs that have gone missing. It's going to cost us big and is a mistake that one of my men will pay for. I have this feeling that someone is trying to stiff me. Concentrating is nearly impossible, knowing Elena is right within reaching distance. Having her here is starting to drive me insane, and I wonder if I can wait until next week to fuck her.

I stop working early and have Martha set the table on the terrace. Elena has been behaving very well, I might as well give her a little reward. I pour myself a glass of whiskey and stare out the huge window that overlooks the lawn. The whiskey calms me, making me warm all over and is just what I need before going to see my bride. Finishing the glass, I leave the office and walk down the hall.

Reaching the bedroom door, I smile smugly while already knowing she listened to me and is waiting like a dog ready to see its owner at the end of the day.

When I unlock and open the door, I find her exactly where I knew she would be—my obedient, soon to be wife. Her green eyes meet mine earnestly, and she stands up and walks over to me. Just like last night, I take her hand in mine, hating the way it fucking feels, and drag her through the house.

I don't want her to get familiar with her surroundings, and I don't want her to see any of the guards or maids unless necessary. Right now, she is my captive, not a guest, and not yet a member of the Moretti family. She will see what I want her to see when I want her to see it.

Her short legs can barely keep up with my steps, and I briefly entertain the idea of picking her up. Mostly because I want to scare her, and partially because I want to touch her. Every time I'm in her presence, I have to stop myself from taking from her, from dipping my fingers into her panties and touching what's mine.

Taking her virginity now or next month doesn't matter much to me, but I'm sticking to my plan. It will help, making her trust me.

That's not to say I won't taste or touch her. I didn't pay ten million dollars, so I could stare at her, and I'm as far from a saint as could possibly be. She's lucky, very lucky, someone far less innocent would've been on her back the first night.

"Where are we going?" Elena asks when we bypass the dining room and enter the French doors off the kitchen.

There's an intake of breath, and I pause just outside the door, looking down and admiring Elena's beauty in the setting sun. I know for a fact that I will thoroughly enjoy fucking her and planting my seed inside her. That's the second-best part of my plan; the first is seeing her father's face when he realizes his daughter actually wants me, maybe even loves me.

Looking out onto the terrace, the outside lights are dimmed, and the table is set for the two of us.

The area is spacious, huge with a brick walkout and small fountain in the center. There's a spot to cook outdoors, and if you walk a little further down, there is a pool. When I bought this mansion, it was because of this space, but since living here, I've used it maybe once or twice, and that's it.

"This... it's beautiful," Elena whispers.

"It really is. This view and this space are the main reasons I bought the house to begin with." I'm not sure why I just told her that but brush it off and usher her to a spot at the table. I take a seat beside her and start uncovering all the dishes.

Elena hands me her plate, and I fill it before filling my own. She takes dainty bites and small sips of her water. I'm famished, so I eat my plate of food and then a second helping.

"Where do you go during the day?" she asks completely out of the blue.

I look up from my plate. "Why do you care to know?"

"Do you always answer a question with a question?" Her remark makes me grin.

"Does it bother you that much?" I answer with a question again, enjoying the frown and tiny eye roll she gives me. "Usually, yes. If you must know, I do business during the day. Sometimes here at the house and sometimes I leave to handle it."

She nods. "My father never told me anything about the *business*. He always said that it was a man's job, and I was meant to be a housewife someday. That I shouldn't be getting my hands dirty or meddling in things I knew nothing about."

"So, your father kept you sheltered then?" I already know this, of course, but I'd like to hear her version and maybe find something out I didn't get from my spies.

Elena laughs, but it's bitter and humorless. "Sheltered is an understatement, but it's not really different from the life I'm living here. I've merely been moved from one cage to the next. The only difference is my gatekeeper."

The blood in my veins heats at being compared to that piece of shit she calls her father. If she knew how he brutally murdered my mother, maybe she would be singing another tune, or maybe she wouldn't believe me at all.

Deciding to change the topic before I get any angrier, I ask, "Would you like dessert today?"

She shakes her head, but looks up at me, her green eyes piercing something inside of me.

"I would like to go for a short walk, though." Those eyes turn pleading, and though I'm tempted to give in to her since she has been so well behaved, I don't.

"No, that must be earned. Your reward tonight was having dinner outside." Her mouth pops open, and it looks like she's going to respond, but I shake my head. "Don't dig yourself a hole that you cannot get out of. Tears and begging do not work on me." Leaning a little closer, I notice the way her breath hitches, my eyes trail over her throat and down her chest. I want her, I want her so badly I can taste it. "In fact, I get off on other people's pain. Tears make my cock hard, and a hard cock leads to fucking. Do you want me to fuck you?" I ask in a low voice.

Elena looks away, and I can see the worry filling her features.

"I saw you watching me beat off. It's okay if you're interested. I won't tell your daddy you want me." *I won't tell, I'll show him.*

"I'm ready to go to bed," she says, ignoring my offer.

"As you wish." I nod and stand, pulling her to her feet in one move. She gasps in surprise at my fast movement but doesn't voice a complaint.

Instead of holding her hand, I tuck her into my side this time, keeping my arm tightly wrapped around her as I walk. She surprises me yet again at how natural she acts—as if she isn't scared of me. She walks with me almost as if she is enjoying my nearness. Like I'm the white knight and not the big bad wolf hiding in the shadows.

Then suddenly, she digs her heels into the ground.

"Wait!"

Instinctively, I pull her closer, holding her to my chest as I scan the space for danger. My heart rattles in my chest as worry overtakes me.

"What?" I growl when I don't see anything out of the ordinary.

She peers up at me through her long coal lashes, her eyes pleading with me. "Can we go in there?" She points her finger at the open door we just passed.

The door that leads into the library. "Please, can I pick one book out? Just one? I'm going crazy in that room with nothing to do. Please…" She begs so sweetly, and I wonder if she would beg this nicely for my cock.

"One book? What would you do for that book?" I question, a grin tucking on my lips.

"What do you want me to do?"

Oh, god, she is so naive. What does she think I want? The first thing on my mind is a blow job, but I know she won't go for that. I could push for some light touching, but I'm not sure that would help my hunger for her. A different idea hits me.

"Take a shower with me. I'll let you pick one book if you agree to willingly step into the shower with me. No cowering and no running."

"Just a shower?" She nibbles on her bottom lip nervously.

"I've already seen you naked. You've already seen me naked," I point out. "What's there to hide? It's just a shower."

"Okay," she agrees reluctantly after a moment, and this time, I can't hide my triumph. I smile.

"Go ahead, then, take your pick."

She hesitantly steps away from me, watching me like I might grab her at any moment to drag her away. When I motion for her to go, she eagerly walks into the library and starts looking through the shelves. She looks like a small child on Christmas morning, and I won't lie, I enjoy seeing her like this. Her smile is much better than her sullen face.

I fully expect her to search the shelves top to bottom to find a romance, thriller, or maybe even a mystery novel. What I didn't expect her to do is stop and browse through my old textbooks. College wasn't something I really needed, but I wanted to do even against my father's wishes. During the day, I took online classes, and at night, I spilled blood. It was the perfect balance.

Watching her curiously, I wait to see what she is up to.

"This one," she announces and pulls out one of the thickest books on the shelf. *Advanced Mathematics.* She can't be serious? This must be a joke.

Arching a brow, I ask, "Are you sure you want to read that? Or did you pick that particular book to hit me with over the head in my sleep?"

"What? No! I do really want this... and maybe a pencil... and some paper?" She bats her eyes even more, and all I can think is this shower better fucking be worth it.

"Fine, but if you try and stab me with the pencil or make me regret giving you any of these items, I'll—"

"Punish me? I know, and I won't. I swear." I give her a stern look at the interruption. Maybe it's her manners that need whipping into shape. Either way, I still walk over to the massive desk in the center of the room, knowing there are some loose pieces of paper and pencils in here somewhere.

I find both items with ease and almost laugh at Elena, who seems to struggle with carrying the massive textbook. Together we walk out of the library and down the hall and into the bedroom. Inside, Elena places the book on the table in front of the chaise lounge. She looks excited, elated even, but before she gets the chance to dig into a shit ton of math problems, she has to pay up.

"It's time for my payment." I grin as I loosen my tie from around my neck and start to unbutton my shirt. Elena nods and stands, the smile wiped clear from her now pale face.

Oh, I'm going to enjoy this thoroughly.

9

ELENA

It's time for my payment.

I have to remind myself that it's just a shower and that he's seen me naked before. Plus, I'm marrying him next week, and then, he will expect more than showers from me. This is going to happen regardless. I might as well get it over with. Grabbing the hem of my shirt, I pull it up and over my head.

As soon as the cool air touches my skin, I shiver. Julian's penetrating gaze is on me, and I feel like a lamb being led to the slaughterhouse.

Nonetheless, I flick the button on my jeans and shove them down my legs, trying not to tremble as I do. Kicking out of them, my panties go next, and then my bra. Lifting my eyes from the floor, I see a hunger like I've never seen before on his face. I almost gasp at the intense look but stifle it at the last minute.

He drinks me in and starts to undress. Chewing the inside of my cheek, I look anywhere but at him. Yes, eventually, we're going to have sex, but I'm still not accustomed to anyone seeing me naked or me seeing anyone else naked.

"Afraid to look? Worried you might see something you like?"

Determined to do this without backing down, I lift my gaze and stare right at him. I look at him the way he looked at me, taking in his well-built physique, the hard lines and ridges, and down to the deep muscled V that leads to his thick penis. His thighs look like tree trunks, his overall body image makes me shiver. He seems even bigger without clothes on, and I'm not sure how that's possible.

"You look... nice." I gulp barely getting the words out.

"Nice?" He chuckles. "I've been called a lot of things in my life, but *nice* isn't one of them." I believe it. I'm not dumb enough to believe he's a good man, or that he's kind.

"I mean, your body is nice," I rephrase.

He doesn't say anything just gives me a strange look and starts for the bathroom. I follow behind him quietly. He opens the glass door, and turns the showerhead on, stepping under it before it can get hot. I wait a few moments until the water is warm enough before I join him.

He turns the other showerhead on, and I almost sigh when I step beneath the hot spray.

It's a large shower, easily made to fit two people, and still, the space feels tiny and confined when sharing it with someone as large as him.

I stare at his muscled back, watching his movements, enjoying the sight before me. Turning, he hands me a washcloth and gives me the soap. I start washing myself, trying to keep my eyes on the tile floor, but I know he is watching everything I do.

Out of the corner of my eye, I see his heavy member swinging between his legs, growing larger and stiffer by the minute. When his penis is so hard that it's curved upward, pointing to his navel, I sneak a glance up at him and find his eyes are glued to me, a hunger like no other reflecting in the blue depths.

It's just a shower...

Nervously, I reach for the shampoo, trying my best to keep some space between us. Unfortunately, in doing so, I shift my weight awkwardly and lose my footing. My feet slip on the soapy tile floor, and I shriek, knowing I'm about to hit the unforgiving floor hard.

Squeezing my eyes shut, I wait for the pain to overtake my body, but instead, Julian grabs me by the arm and pulls me up and against his chest. My hands fly up to press against his chest, and I'm not sure if it's to pull him closer or push him away.

Feeling his long erection pressing up against my belly, I decide it's the latter. I shove against his chest, but his arms tighten around me, pulling me closer. Like quicksand, I'm trapped in his embrace, seemingly sinking deeper with every move I make. My nipples harden as I struggle in his arms, something like fear developing in my gut.

A deep groan rumbles in his chest, reminding me of a grizzly bear. I don't dare look up. Instead, I keep my eyes on his chest, which is rising and falling at a steady rate.

"I want you to do something for me."

"You... you said just a shower..." My lips wobble. Had I been fooled into trusting him?

Leaning forward, his nose skims against my throat, and I feel a trickle of heat in my belly. "I did, but I want more..."

I shouldn't ask. It's asking for trouble, but in reality, do I have a choice?

Swallowing down my fear, I ask, "What kind of more?"

"I know I told you it was nothing but a shower, but having you so close, makes me want to take from you until there isn't anything left. I'm a man of my word, and I won't fuck you until our wedding night, but I want your dainty hand on my cock, jerking me off until I cover the tile in cum."

"Oh... okay," I whisper, not sure what else to say or do. It doesn't sound like he is giving me a choice. Or is he? Do I even want a choice? It'd be easier to tell myself I was forced, but no matter how cruel and horrible a person he is, I can't deny my curiosity, and like I said, this was going to happen, one way or another.

Placing two fingers beneath my chin, he forces me to look up at him. "Do you want to do this?"

Swallowing thickly, I look at the throbbing length trapped between our bodies. The head is an angry red and swollen. It looks almost painful. It's now a choice that he's given, and I find my head nodding without thought. Looking back up, I see a dark gleam in Julian's eyes as he drops his hand and trails it down between my breasts before reaching for my hand.

Anxiety ripples through me, and heat blooms in my cheeks when he guides my hand to his cock, the muscle twitches beneath my hand, and I stare at the appendage in awe. It's soft and thick, and so incredibly warm. It's unlike anything I ever expected.

Placing his hand over mine, Julian guides me, a hiss passing his firm lips at the movement. Biting the inside of my cheek, I wonder if I'm doing this right. My hand is trembling, making each stroke jerky. He's so thick, my hand can't quite wrap around the entire length.

"Harder," Julian grunts, his hand tightening over mine, and I squeeze a little harder, my pulse pounding in my ears. Mesmerized by the movements, I watch as Julian thrusts his hips forward like he's fucking someone.

Like this, given over to the pleasure, he looks more animal than human.

"Faster. I need it fast and hard."

His growl is animalistic, and it frightens me, but it's nothing compared to the way he clamps down on my hand, squeezing so hard I wince. His touch is bruising and pain lances across my hand.

"You're hurting me," I whimper, trying to tug my hand away. His strength is a force to be reckoned with, and I know he'll only release me when he wants to.

It takes a moment for the haze around his head to clear, but as soon as it does, I wish I'd never said anything. He releases my hand like it's fire and turns on me so fast I take a protective step back, my back colliding with the tile.

With clenched teeth, he sneers, "Get the fuck out of here, and go get dressed."

Tears spring in my eyes, and disappointment builds in my chest.

"I... I'm sorry. I didn't... I don't..."

Julian's hand clenches into a fist down at his side, and fear slithers through me. Is he going to hit me?

"Even looking fear in the eyes, even after I told you to leave, you still stand here." Leaning forward, he curls his lip and snarls, "Get out."

I don't think or try to explain myself. I rush from the shower, nearly slipping on the tile in my haste to get away. The bedroom is no better for me because I'm reminded that I'll be in bed with him very soon. Scurrying into the closet, I try and keep my fear and the tears at bay, but they refuse to be pushed down. I drop my nightgown twice before pulling it on, and it takes me forever to balance while putting my panties on.

My heart clenches in my chest, and I don't understand why. Why am I so upset that he pushed me away? Why does it bother me at all? Deep down, I know it's because I wanted to bring him pleasure... I wanted to show him that I know what I'm doing, but all I did was anger him and make a mockery out of myself.

Stepping out of the closet, I walk to the bed and wipe my eyes, willing the tears away.

This night was going so great, and then I screwed it all up. Is he going to punish me for disobeying him? I tried to explain that I don't know what I'm doing, but he didn't want to hear it.

The water shuts off in the bathroom, and the room falls into an eerie silence. The calm before the storm, you could say. Perched on the bed, I crawl beneath the covers as if they could save me from his wrath. Tears glisten in my eyes, and I lick my dry lips.

I stare at the door for a long time, watching, anticipating. He appears in the doorway with a towel slung over his hips, which he drops to the ground when he reaches the bed.

I know I shouldn't say anything, that it's ignorant to even consider opening my mouth right now, but I can't help it. No, I didn't pick him as my husband, and I was bought from my father, like cattle, but he will be my husband. I have to live with this man for the rest of my life, and I can't do it constantly being afraid.

"I'm sorry, Julian. I don't know..." I try not to show how broken up over this I am, but that's harder to conceal. Standing bare-ass naked, he looks at me with barely kept disdain. Like I'm a pesky little bug.

"Stop with the tears. Remember what I told you earlier... your fears make me want to fuck you, and if you thought I was hurting your delicate little hand a short while ago, then you'll be in for the surprise of a lifetime come our wedding night. I won't just hurt you... I'll make you bleed, my naive little wife." The evil grin he gives me promises pain, and I shiver under his inspecting eyes, wishing he never asked me to touch him. This is his fault, and yet I silently sob as he climbs into the bed and shuts the lights off.

I'm marrying a monster, and there is nothing I can do to stop it.

10

JULIAN

I've always known what kind of person I am, a ruthless, cruel, selfish bastard who only cares about power and revenge. There has been a darkness deep inside of me for as long as I can remember, but that darkness was always held at bay by my mother. She was the one good thing in my life, the one person who loved me no matter how fucked up I was.

The day she died, the evil inside of me spread like a fucking cancer, and it hasn't stopped growing since. There are times when I think that's all that is left. Darkness is the only thing remaining, it's all I am and all I'll ever be. Today, I have my doubts about that theory, because right now, I'm feeling something I haven't in a very long time... remorse.

Elena is sleeping in my arms, her body curled up into itself, trying to get away from me even in her sleep. As she should be.

I lost control yesterday, and I broke my word. I told her it was just a shower, but I couldn't keep my lust for her in check. I asked for more, knowing damn well that she couldn't give me what I wanted.

I keep telling myself that I'm angry with her, that I'm angry at how this is messing with my plan, but the truth is, I'm angry with myself. This is on me.

Peeling myself away from her, I move slowly, so I don't wake her up. After the fiasco from last night, I won't make her take a shower this morning. I'll let her sleep in, I don't need the torture of watching her and thinking about how to fix this shit.

Walking into the closet, I get dressed quickly. When I head out of the room, she is still deep in sleep. I stop and take a moment to look at her. Her eyelashes are crusted together, and her cheeks are a hue of red. I know she cried last night, cried herself to sleep while I was holding her.

Shaking my head, I quietly walk out of the room, shoving all those unwanted feelings down. I need to get back in the game, Concentrate on what's important. Her feelings should be the least of my concerns.

Quietly, I close the door behind me and turn the lock. I need to clear my head. Which means, I either need a drink, or I need to kill something. Pulling out my phone, I check the time. It's seven-thirty... too early to start drinking. Killing it is.

∽

BLOOD LOOKS different when it's splattered on the ground, draining from the bodies of your victims. The thrill I get from killing is fucked up, but something I'll never give up. I was only fourteen when I killed my first man. My father placed the gun in my hand and told me to put a bullet between the guy's eyes. I didn't hesitate, didn't second guess myself. I just did as I was told. Since that day, I've grown to enjoy the kill. Enjoy the adrenaline hit I get out of it. It's like doing drugs, but better. What does it say about me morally that I don't even care about the life that I rip from the earth? Killing comes with the job, sure I don't have to do the dirty work myself. I have men to do it for me, but I'm not lazy. I love a good hunt, a chance to sink a knife into some fucker's chest.

Arriving back at the mansion, the endorphin high of torturing my victim all day slowly fades away. Looking down at my blood-stained hands and shirt, I'm reminded that a serious amount of blood covers my hands.

Elena's face pops into my head, and I know if I enter our bedroom dressed like this, there will be a plethora of questions thrown my way.

Business is business, and it has nothing to do with my marriage to her. I'm not obligated to share with her what I do during the day.

Walking into one of the guest bedrooms, I take a shower, washing away the blood, watching as it swirls down the drain. Today was a good day, frustrating because I had to track a shipment of drugs that disappeared but fulfilling when I sunk my knife into the traitor's throat and watched blood spray across the pavement.

Finishing my shower, I feel drawn to check on Elena. Leaving her this morning was hard, even though it shouldn't have been. Drying off, I sling a towel around my waist and grab my phone, entering the app for the security camera on my phone.

I watch the day's events through the camera. She looks like sleeping beauty as she remains in bed nearly a full hour after I left. Then she wakes up, looking around the room, disoriented as if she'll find me lurking in the shadows. Her fear of me makes me smile.

I watch as she pushes from the bed and goes into the bathroom. A short while later, she leaves the bathroom naked, and raw, primal hunger pushes through me at the naked image before my eyes. I cannot wait for the day to come when I take her without care, without mercy.

She scampers into the closet, dresses, and then walks over to the chaise lounge where she remains for the better part of the morning. There is something about her, something I can't pinpoint. She uses the paper and pencil to write out math problems and solves each one back to back. Yesterday in the library, I had fully expected her to go for a romance book, or maybe a thriller, but like everything with this girl, she shocks me into silence.

Her adaption to change, and the way she remains strong even in her weakest moments. She is fierce and bold, and she doesn't even know it.

She does the math problems for a while until Martha appears in the bedroom with her lunch. Elena's face brightens with joy at seeing her, and she gets up, moving toward her. I gave Martha explicit instructions when it came to bringing Elena her lunch.

Don't speak to her, and don't offer her any type of help or you'll pay with your life.

It appears Martha is listening until I see her lean forward, and her lips move slowly. It's subtle, and I almost miss it, but Elena looking down at Martha's extended hand does it for me, and I see her pass the small scrap of something into Elena's hand.

Red hot anger rips through me, and I growl, squeezing my phone in my hand. Nothing is as horrible as a traitor. I find a spare suit in the closet and dress quickly, my hands shaking with pent up rage as I leave the bedroom and head for the kitchen.

Martha has been a long-time employee and one of my father's favorites. Killing her is going to hurt, but there is no way around it. If she has betrayed me, then she cannot live.

As soon as I enter the kitchen, Martha looks up from the pot she is stirring and faces me.

"Mr. Moretti." She looks at the ground as she speaks like most of the staff in this house do.

"Cut the shit, Martha." I crowd her, forcing her back against the counter. My hand is on my gun, waiting for me to draw it. "What did you give Elena when you dropped her lunch off?"

Her lips tremble, and she wrings her hands in her apron before looking up at me. Fear fills her eyes, she knows what's to come.

"It was just a note, sir," she says, and my teeth grind together, my jaw clenching and aching. Her piece of shit father found a way inside and infiltrated my home.

Curling my lip, I circle my hand around Martha's throat and squeeze. "From who?" I ask, even though I already know. I merely want her to confess it out loud.

"Her father," she whispers, her weathered face contouring with shame. "Just a note from her father."

"You know what your betrayal means?" I squeeze her feeble throat a little harder.

She nods. "Yes, sir. It means death."

11

ELENA

I stare at the crumpled-up paper in my hand, reading it for the hundredth time, and still, I'm not sure if it's real or not. And if it is real, what am I going to make of it?

Elena,

I will come for you, sweetheart.

Be strong, Dad

The note is handwritten, the lettering tells me that it is indeed my father who wrote this note. The question is, why? Is he really coming for me? Do I even want him to come after he sold me like an object? I've had days to think about how cruel he was in letting me go, giving me away like I was nothing.

My life here is worse than the one spent at my father's place, but honestly, not by much. I had a few more things to do at home, but not many. According to Julian, I will have more freedom at some point, so being here seems like the better option.

Julian expects things from me, things I'm not sure I can give him, but what are my other choices? If I somehow manage to get back home, I will either be alone for the rest of my life, or my father will marry me off to someone else. Are there any men in my father's world that will treat me differently? I doubt it. Every man is a hardened mafia man with hate and rage burning through his veins.

So, which one is the lesser evil?

Folding the paper until it's only a tiny piece of scrap. I walk into the closet and shove it into the bottom of my underwear drawer, hoping that whichever path my future will lead, I will one day be free.

∽

THE REST OF THE DAY, I busy myself with math. Julian doesn't come and get me for dinner today. Instead, a different maid brings me food to the room. I wonder why he isn't here yet, but I try not to think about that. Instead, I bury my face within the pages of the textbook.

Julian was surprised by my choice, but there was really no question for me what book to take. If I had chosen a romance novel, I would have read it within a few hours. After that, I would have been back to square one with nothing to do.

I don't know if I will get a chance to pick a second book, so I had to make this one count. This book will keep me occupied for a long time.

I have only one issue. Even with me writing as small as I can, the paper is about to run out. I've already used the front and back. Without paper, I can't solve these equations, and I don't want to write in the book.

I fill the last space on the paper, feeling a small wave of accomplishment. That feeling is quickly drowned out by less pleasant feelings.

Putting my pencil down, I look around the room and find that I once again have nothing to do.

Spending most of my life alone, I'm used to being by myself, but this is different. This is next level isolation. I wish I had a radio, at least then it wouldn't be so quiet.

I entertain the thought of taking a shower, but that just reminds me of the shitshow that happened last night. I know I owe him nothing, and yet, I feel like a disappointment, not even being able to give him a simple hand job. I wonder if he regrets buying me yet.

My thoughts and questions are quickly forgotten when I hear heavy footfalls approaching the door. The door is unlocked, and I sit up a little straighter. A moment later, Julian walks inside, slamming the door shut behind him. The loud sound makes me jump, and the knot in my stomach grows.

He is mad, obviously. But why? It could be because of last night. Or he could have somehow found out about the maid, though I don't know how. Maybe he just had a bad day?

Without greeting me or saying anything else, he steps inside the room and drops something on the bed in front of me. Then he twists around and heads into the closet.

Glancing down at what he threw on the bed, I realize it's a book... a notebook, I think.

He bought me a notebook!

Running my fingers over the smooth cover, I'm in awe. It's black leather with golden flower embroidery. It's very pretty, simple with a feminine touch, and something I would have picked for myself.

I flip it open. Empty, lined pages greet me, and I fan through the pages, discovering there is enough to write on for a long time. Setting the notebook down on the comforter, I stare at it. I don't know how to feel about his gift.

On the one hand, I appreciate that he got this for me. It's certainly not something he had lying around on his desk, which tells me he was thinking of me. He went out of his way when he didn't have to, and that means something.

On the other hand, however, he got this to keep me occupied while locked in his bedroom. There's good and bad with this, and I'm not sure what I should expect from him now.

"You like it?" His voice is clipped as if he is fighting to subdue his anger, trying to hold it back. Maybe his anger isn't directed at me?

He walks back into the room a moment later, wearing nothing but a pair of boxers, and my mouth suddenly goes dry.

"Yes, it's beautiful. Thank you..." I'm about to ask him what I have to do in return as nothing in this world is free but manage to bite my tongue at the last minute.

I'm surprised when he doesn't take a shower but slides into bed instead.

When he inches closer, I smell soap on him.

He already showered somewhere else.

Did he not want to shower in our room because of what happened last night? I put the notebook on the bedside table and lie down, turning my back to him.

Suppressing the need to ask him, I say something else instead.

"I'm sorry about last night," I say, knowing damn well it wasn't my fault, but still feeling the need to apologize.

Rolling over to look at him, his face is impossibly close to mine, and my eyes dart down to his lips. The thought of kissing him hits me straight in the chest. I wonder if he would let me.

Who am I kidding? Julian doesn't seem like the type to kiss, nor do I think he would let me kiss him after last night's incident.

His stormy blue eyes roam my face, his features softening just briefly. "Consider the notebook a gift. I broke my word to you last night. It won't happen again," he simply states, and I wonder if that was supposed to be his version of an apology.

"Go to sleep." He gently pushes my shoulder to roll me back on the other side, facing away from him. Then he lowers his hand to my hip and pulls me into his chest.

The position is weirdly familiar now, almost natural. Like we're supposed to sleep like this, which seems ridiculous. I've only been here a couple of days, but we've slept this way every night.

I still have many questions swirling around in my head. I still don't know where I stand with Julian, or if I'm safe, but for tonight, for now, I feel content.

12

JULIAN

"How are things?" Markus asks as he walks into my office, his face a complete mask. If he can see how tense I am, then surely my other men can.

In the mafia, any type of weakness is like a loose thread. Anyone could tug on that weakness until you unravel, spilling all your contents. That's why I've never allowed myself the pleasure of having a weakness, not until the little raven-haired beauty entered my life.

"Things are going well. I need you to find a replacement for Martha. Turns out, she was a traitor." I stretch out in my chair and think back to how oblivious Elena acted last night, and still, I couldn't bring myself to be angry with her.

Yes, she took the note from her father, read it, and hid it, but she didn't disobey me directly, not when I hadn't asked her a single question about it. Plus, after I read the note, it was clear that Elena didn't know anything, she's not trying to escape, and that's really what I would be angry about.

I am, however, curious to know if she would tell me if directly asked. Of course, I could have done that, but it's best for her to assume I don't know, at least for right now. If I tell her I know, chances are she'll put it together and realize I've got a camera in the room. I'd rather she didn't know she is being watched.

The brunt of my anger was passed on to Romero—who will get what's coming to him, I'm keeping count of his sins, I'm a patient man—and the now-dead maid who betrayed me. Hurting women has never been a joy for me, and whenever the job needed to be done, I usually passed it onto one of my men, but Martha's betrayal was personal.

It was me or nothing, so I took my gun out and pressed the barrel to her head. She didn't beg or plead, and it was over in a flash. Life was given and taken in a single breath.

She expected death for her betrayal, and I delivered.

"What do you plan to do with Romero? We knew he was going to reach out to her, and now he has... maybe he's trying to distract us so that he can attack?"

"I doubt it, and we're going to do nothing *yet*. We wait to strike till after the wedding. If he strikes us first, then obviously, we retaliate. I have it all planned. This weekend at the auction, I will show Elena off. Her father will be there, and I will make sure that he sees how much she leans on me, using the moment to rub in his face."

"Then what?" Markus questions, and annoyance bubbles to the surface.

"Then I shove my foot up your ass. Don't ask me stupid questions." I shake my head and thrust my fingers through my hair in frustration.

A smirk twitches at his lips. It's as close to a smile as anyone will ever get.

"It's obvious you're not fucking your soon to be wife, given the tension rolling off of you, maybe consider going to the strip club to blow off some steam."

What Markus doesn't show in emotion, he puts into the tone of his voice.

Blinking slowly, I pierce him with my steely gaze. "Don't mention my soon to be wife, or me fucking her in the same sentence ever again."

Markus is my first in command, a friend, and as close to a brother as I'll ever get, but I'm a possessive asshole, and no one talks about Elena but me, and especially not fucking her.

"I won't, but I think you should still consider going. You've been doing more work than usual, and the men are starting to notice."

Things were changing a little bit. I was spending more time slitting throats and beating the fuck out of people than I ever had before, mainly to stop myself from taking my bride and to put space between us. In her presence, I could grow soft, and I didn't want to do that for a second.

The idea of going to the strip club and finding a whore to fuck wasn't appealing either, not when I had Elena down the hall, but there were very few options right now. I was going to wait until the wedding, but if I was going to make it through the rest of this week and weekend, I needed to let off some steam.

The fact that Markus was right was irritating.

"I should slit your throat," I grumble.

"You could, but then who would be here to bust your balls or tell you that there are whispers among the men?"

"Shut up and get out of my office. Go kill someone or do something."

"Are you going to go to the club? If so, I'll go with you."

Markus never sought out pleasure, ever. If I didn't know him personally, I might even think he was a virgin, but I knew he wasn't.

"What's there for you?" I cock a brow in question.

"A warm hole to sink into."

"I can't remember the last time you went somewhere to get pussy."

"I can't remember the last time you held back on taking something that is rightfully yours." Obviously, he is referring to Elena, and again his comment sparked rage inside of me. He would be lucky if I didn't murder him by the end of the day for insulting me like that.

"I'm still your boss, Markus. I make the rules, and I say what the fuck goes. Or did you forget that?" I hiss and shove from my chair. I wasn't sure I could kill Markus. He was a friend who always had my back.

There isn't an ounce of fear on his face as I walk over to him, my hand on my gun. Markus looked at death the same way I did. Eventually, it would come for us. It was inevitable. The only thing is, you never know when it will happen.

"Let's fucking go before I murder you," I say, pushing past him and out the door.

Calling for the driver, he arrives outside at the same time Markus and I do. We climb into the black SUV, and we drive to Dimension. Markus and I are both silent during the drive, and it gives me a moment to clear my head.

When we arrive at the run-down building, I decide there is no better time than now to check in on the staff.

"Check with the bartender and see how everything is going. Let them know we will bring someone in soon," I tell Markus as I check my phone, my finger hovering over the camera app. Watching her isn't going to sedate my need or help matters. I need to fuck someone, someone who can handle a hard pounding. God knows if I fucked Elena the way I want to, she would break in half beneath me.

Markus nods, acknowledging what I've asked him to do, and we walk in together, the two guards who usually man the doors aren't in place, which angers me. Walking inside, I survey the bar; there are a few patrons in it, and the stage has a couple men sat eye-balling the dancing chick. Music beats through the place, and a stripper works the pole, grinding her ass against it like it's a cock. Stale smoke filters into my lungs when I take a breath, combined with sweat and perfume.

"I'm going to go check the viewing rooms and see if I can find any available pussy," I tell Markus, who gives me a chin nod and heads off to the bar.

The long hall off to the right of the stage is where Roberto's office used to be and where all the rooms are for the private dances that take place, and by private dances, I mean fuck sessions.

Numerous doors lead into different private viewing rooms, and as I walk down the hall, I try and decide which room to walk into.

My balls ache, and my cock has permanently been stiff since Elena arrived. Maybe taking the edge off is what I need.

A door opens, and a dark-haired, half-dressed stripper crosses in front of me, and I don't even think, I just react. Grabbing her by the arm, I harshly tug her back toward the door she just came out of. She lets out a gasp, which she covers with a seductive grin when she realizes who grabbed her.

Women fawn over me, toss themselves at me, begging for me to fuck them, and luckily the women here know just how I like it. Hard and fast.

"Mr. Moretti," she purrs as I open the door and walk inside, her body rubbing against mine like a cat might rub against someone's leg. Releasing her as if her body is fire, I take a step back. She knows why I've grabbed her, and she knows if she does well, she'll get a nice tip.

"Get on your hands and knees," I growl and watch as she complies eagerly, scurrying over to the bed without question, and nothing like I imagine Elena would be if I ordered her to. Knowing how innocent and naive she is, I bet she'd cry, and I'd have to force her.

Annoyance spreads through me like a wildfire at the thought. I want to get my dick wet since I know I'll have to wait till next week, at the very least, to fuck my virgin bride, not be beaten down with thoughts of her while I'm doing it. My annoyance boils over, becoming pure anger. I don't understand why every thought I have leads back to her.

The brunette on her knees looks at me over her shoulder and licks her red lips while batting her eyes.

"I'm going to fuck you hard and fast, and you aren't going to whimper, cry, or say a word. Do you understand?"

She nods her head, and I hate how excitement bubbles up to the surface at her obedience. I stare at her round ass, the globes not quite firm. Her pussy is on full display, her slits glistening in the dim lighting, letting me know she's ready for me, though it wouldn't matter if she wasn't. I'd fuck her dry; after all, she is here for my pleasure and nothing else.

The whore is pretty, but nothing compared to my soon to be bride.

There isn't an ounce of innocence or fear in this girl, and I hate it.

She's waiting for my wrath, welcoming it. *Fuck.* Flicking the button on my slacks, I move to the bed, climbing behind the whore. I take my cock into my hand, stroke the beast, and then pull a condom out of my wallet.

At the crinkling of the package, the woman twists around. "I'm clean, and on the pill. You can fuck me raw if you want."

Chuckling darkly, I grab her by the hip and sink my fingers into her skin.

"I'm a lot of things, but stupid isn't one of them. Now shut the fuck up and put your cheek on the mattress." I'm well aware of how sinister I'm being right now, but here, I can be me, and with Elena, it's like I'm something else entirely.

Letting my eyes drift closed, I will the thoughts of Elena away, but closing my eyes only causes them to rush in. Her cheeks tear-stained, her eyes pleading, her body trembling as I take from her. Memories of the way she whimpered when I simply applied pressure to her hand as she jerked me off appear in my mind.

My cock deflates in my hand, and I know there isn't any fucking point in doing this.

The only person my cock wants is the only person I'm not willing to take from yet. There is a plan, an order, and I need to fucking follow it. Still, her perfectly sculpted heart-shaped face and emerald green eyes haunt me like a ghost.

I'm pissed, burning with rage. I can't even fuck someone without thinking about her. It was bad before, all the times I had to envision her while I fucked others from behind or shoved my cock down their throat.

Now that she's trapped in my web, entirely at my mercy, my body knows I don't have to deny myself, but I am.

Pissed, I take a step back from the woman. "Get fucking dressed," I grit out, wanting to punch something.

"What? I thought you wanted…" She whirls around to face me.

I ignore her question and confused expression and take the waste of a condom off and button my pants back up. Pulling out a hundred-dollar bill from my wallet, I shove the money at her. She looks at me then to the money before snatching it from my hand.

"Are you sure, Mr. Moretti?" she purrs, batting her eyes one last time, and I curl my hand into a tight fist. "I'll let you do whatever you want to me."

The offer is tempting, being that my tastes run rough and a little dark, but making my cock hard for someone other than Elena is going to be impossible. She's cast a fucking spell on me and doesn't even realize it.

"Pull yourself together. I don't want you. The money was for your time. I changed my mind, go find someone else."

Frustrated and annoyed, I walk out of the room, leaving the door open behind me. Elena has captured my complete and undivided attention, and I don't know if that's a good thing for either of us.

13

ELENA

The hours drag on into eternity, and I actually find myself waiting like a dog for my owner to return. It's a horrible analogy, but it's the truth. I watch the sunset through the window, feeling more isolated from the real world than I ever have in my entire life. Worse, I feel myself melting into Julian's touch.

Kindness is what he showed me last night when he handed me that little notebook. It was the kindest thing he's done since I arrived here, and it made me want to see if there is more goodness inside him. It's such a naive thing to assume that a man who kills, steals, and buys a person has any good in him.

Darkness starts to blanket the room, and I move to turn on one of the lights at the same time the door opens. I hold back a little shriek, and I'm almost disappointed when I see it's just a maid entering the room and not Julian. The one that gave me the note hasn't returned since that day. It's been someone new every time, and I wonder why she's never come back. I'm sure Julian doesn't know about the note since he hasn't said anything. If he knew, he would have punished me or something.

He also didn't pick me up for dinner tonight, just like he didn't last night. Why has he stopped?

The maid–which I haven't seen before–sets the tray down cautiously, almost as if she's afraid. Her hair is long, blonde, and braided. Her features are dainty, and she looks young, close to my age.

Briefly, I wonder if I should ask about the other maid but push the thought aside when she starts to head back toward the door.

Talk to her, idiot.

"Hello, I'm Elena," I say.

She gives me a sheepish grin. "I'm... Marie. They told me not to talk to you."

"No one will know that we've talked, just you and me." I smile, longing for some type of friendship or company at this point.

"I have to go. Sorry." She sneaks out of the room and locks the door behind her. Like a balloon, I deflate. My stomach grumbles, alerting me to hunger, so I walk over to the tray and carry it to the bed. As I eat, I envision running through the grass and feeling drops of rain on my skin. I long for normalcy even though the world I live in will never allow it.

As I eat in silence, I become more and more aware of how late it's getting and find myself dressed for bed, beneath the covers with my knees drawn to my chest.

Where is he? Had something happened to him? Was he still working? Worry festers in my gut even though it shouldn't. I shouldn't care for my savage soon to be husband. In fact, I should wish death upon him, maybe I would be sent back to my father, though that's doubtful. I'd be given to a worse evil, I'm sure.

After what seems like hours, and my eyes start to become heavy, the bedroom opens, and Julian stumbles in. His dark hair is disheveled like he's been running his fingers through it, and his tie is loosened, and the first couple of buttons on his dress shirt are undone.

Sleep leaves my mind as he walks in and closes the door behind him. He moves toward the bed, almost falling onto it. Looking into his blue eyes, I find them bloodshot and hungry. I can smell smoke on him from here.

There's also something else, a hint of something feminine, perfume, and that sparks something vicious inside of me. I'm well aware that men have needs, but I'm hurt and annoyed that he sought out someone else, leaving me locked in this damn room while he did it. It only reminds me further of how much of a disappointment I am to him.

"If you have to go have sex with another woman, you could at least have the courtesy to shower before you come in like you did yesterday." I cross my arms over my chest. I don't want to look at his stupidly handsome face, but there is nowhere else to look.

Julian gives me a coy grin. "Jealous?"

"Disgusted is a better word." I know better than to be jealous. My father loved my mother dearly, and even he cheated. I know that in our world, that's simply part of marriage, but that doesn't mean I have to like it.

"You don't look disgusted, you look jealous. Red hot jealous." He pauses and tilts his head to the side as if he's examining my face. "Would it bother you that much if I was with another woman?"

"Yes," I blurt out, shocking myself. "But not because of what you are thinking. I'm jealous of being outside. I'm jealous because you lock me in here while you take another woman out to do who knows what." I don't even want to think about that part. Did he take her to dinner before he screwed her? I think that part hurts the most. The fact that I was waiting for him to have dinner with me while he was with someone else. I waited like a dog at the door for him to show, and he let me down, not once, but twice.

Shaking his head, he starts laughing at me. He freaking laughs at me, and I want to punch him, punch that stupid smile off his face. "I think you have a very unrealistic idea of what I do with women when I *take them out*."

Anger fills my veins. I'm tired of being the naive little girl. Tired of being sheltered and isolated away from the world.

"Then tell me. What do you do? What were you doing while I was locked in here waiting for you? Did you have dinner? Did you... have sex?" My throat tightens as I speak each word. I never expected to marry entirely for love, but I thought maybe, just maybe I'd marry a man who loved me a little bit, that wanted me enough to spend time with me and not lock me away like my father did.

"Wouldn't you like to know."

In a momentary burst of confidence, I raise my chin and stand up to him. "I do want to know. Tell me."

Julian's eyes twinkle, and he trails a finger down the side of my face. His touch is nothing more than a caress, but I feel it deep in my soul. "There are no dates. No dinners. No sweet and gentle sex. There is nothing but hard fucking, deep and fast with the occasional moan."

My eyes go so wide, I'm scared they might pop out. What the hell am I supposed to say to that? Is that what he wants from me?

Suddenly him buying me makes more sense. He doesn't want dates, love, and companionship. He just wants someone for sex... nothing more, and I'm marrying him. I'm being forced into a marriage that is doomed from the start.

"And they... want that?"

He shrugs. "They're whores, and that's their job, so I suppose so, yeah." His tone is mocking and annoying me further. He sought out some whore to sleep with, only to return to sleep in bed with me. I feel sickened, and even though I know I'm not ready to sleep with him, I cannot stop the emotions I have from bubbling to the surface.

"So, you go to a prostitute for sex?" I struggle with my emotions then, realizing that that's what I am. He bought me for sex, so essentially, I'm no different from the women he sleeps with now. My chest aches thinking about it. *Whore.* My mother would be so ashamed and sad if she were alive right now.

"Would you rather me come to you, sweet Elena?"

I know he is taunting me, baiting me to play his game. I should be stronger than this, should turn the other cheek, but at this moment, I'm too hurt already. All I have left is to lash out. It's like everything is weighing down on me at once, being confined to this room, shackled to a man I know nothing about, not even his agenda. I'm alone and tired... so damn tired.

Looking at him straight in the eyes, I gather up every ounce of courage I have.

"You already paid for it, didn't you? You paid for me to be your own personal whore. So why go and spend more money on other women when I'm right here?"

For a tiny instant, I see surprise flash across his face, then the moment is gone. His pale blue eyes turn dark, and before I know it, he is on me. One hand wraps around my throat as he shoves me against the mattress while his other snakes beneath my nightgown, cupping my pussy. My eyes bulge out of my head, and I struggle, gasping for air, panicking that he's going to take me right now. I shouldn't have pushed him. I should've kept my mouth shut. Tears blur my vision. Feral, that's how he looks right now, and I'm trapped in his burning rage.

Leaning into my face, he growls, "Do you think you could handle my dark, sinister needs? Could you handle my cock, owning every hole in your body? Choking on me as I fill your throat with my cum? Is that how you want me to treat you? Like a whore?"

Shaking my head, a whimper of fear escapes my lips when I feel his fingers probing against my entrance. I want his touch. I want him to want me, to see me, but not like this. I don't want his hate, and I don't want this to hurt.

"Please." I barely get the word past my lips.

Coldness overtakes his features, and I feel his fingers move my panties to the side, one finger tracing against my folds. I shudder against him and wrap a hand around the wrist that's between my legs, tugging on it to stop him.

"I could fuck you right now, and you wouldn't be able to stop me." He nips at my earlobe, and I start to shake, feeling fear like I've never felt before in his presence. "Is that what you want? You want me to treat you like a whore? Because I will. I'll fuck you right now–"

"No," I croak, just as his finger presses against my entrance, slipping a little inside. Wincing at the intrusion, I try and squeeze my legs closed, but there is no fighting a man as big as Julian. His strong arms overpower me with minimal effort.

Wetting his bottom lip with his tongue, he says, "Are you sure? Your cunt is wet…"

"Please, don't do this…" I peer right into his eyes, pleading with him like I've never pleaded before. "Please, Julian…"

It's then that he snaps out of it, shaking his head as if he was caught in a trance. He releases his hold on my throat and slowly pulls his hand from my panties, looking down at me with a mix of regret and anger. Scooting back against the headboard, I will my body to stop shaking.

Julian curls his lip and presses his fists into the mattress as he leers toward me.

"Don't tempt me, Elena. I'm not a good man, and if you give me an inch, I will take a fucking mile. I want you, and it doesn't matter to me how I obtain you. But mark my words, next time you taunt me, I'll take what I want, and I won't stop."

All I can do is nod, telling him that I understand. The warning is clear, blinking a bright neon sign. He won't let me get away again if I can't keep my mouth shut.

Curling up, I pull the comforter over me and wait for him to join me in the bed. The only thing I don't understand is why he wants me in the first place? He says he wants rough sex, but also that I can't give him what he wants. If that's so, then why am I here at all? Why does he want to marry me?

14

JULIAN

Thoughts of last night swirl around inside my head like fish in a fishbowl. I shouldn't have touched her, taunted her, or let her get under my skin, but there was no way around it. She is too naive for her own good. All but telling me to take her, reminding me that I paid for her—like I could forget.

Too much pent-up need combined with the alcohol in my system made it hard for me to control myself, and that's why I snapped.

I wanted her, wanted her so bad, and yet I talked myself off the cliff's edge.

All I could see was her fear reflecting back at me. It hit me right in the chest and made it hard for me to breathe. I couldn't bring myself to continue, to hurt her, even though I knew soon enough, I would do just that. But a selfish part of me wanted to continue, wanted to take a taste, even against her wishes.

Sex would come soon enough, and me fingering her, will be the least of her worries.

As if she could hear my thoughts, Elena stirs beside me. Her eyes flutter open, and her head turns to see if I'm here or not. Apart from last night,

I've held her every night since she got here. I couldn't bring myself to do so yesterday.

Turning away, I disappear into the closet to get dressed. When I return, she is still in bed, the blanket pulled up to her chest, and her big blue eyes watching me like I'm a predator who is about to jump her.

She's not wrong.

"Get dressed, we'll have breakfast together on the terrace."

That makes her perk up a little. She throws the blanket off her delicate body and scurries passed me and into the closet. A few moments later, she returns dressed in a casual outfit of jeans and a T-shirt. I'm half-tempted to tell her to put a dress on just so I can see her in one, but that will happen soon enough.

Plus, I don't know that I can handle an argument with her this early in the day.

Taking her hand into mine, I walk at a more even pace so that she can keep up. She walks beside me silently, and when we reach the terrace, she lets out a low sigh. I hear her intake of breath and look over at her, watching as she sucks fresh air into her lungs and smiles.

She wasn't made to be caged, it's obvious, but letting her be free isn't an option in our world. Not right now and maybe not ever.

We sit down, and I can already see her eyeing the fresh papaya I had ordered just for her. I know it's her favorite. My spies kept me well informed about all her likes and dislikes. I wonder if she has noticed that there is always something on the menu that she is fond of.

As I expected, she reaches for the fruit first, then adds some yogurt and granola to her plate. I fill my own up with an omelet before I pour both of us a glass a fresh-pressed orange juice. I watch her take a few small bites, then decide it's time to fill her in on our weekend plans.

"There is an event this Saturday. You will accompany me to it."

The fork slips out of her hand and lands against the plate with a loud clunk. Her eyes go wide as she looks up at me.

"Y-you're taking me out?" I don't miss the excitement and hopefulness in her voice. Something about it pleases me. Knowing she is happy to go out with me means everything is going according to plan.

"Yes, it's an auction. Your father and all of our business associates will be there. Everyone will see you by my side."

Her face falls, the twinkle in her eyes that was there a moment ago vanishes faster than it appeared.

"I see. You want to show off your prize." She leans back in her chair, her eyes trained on something in the yard.

"I thought you'd be happy I'm taking you."

"And I would be if you'd do it for the right reasons," she says without looking back at me.

"Like I said, I don't wine and dine with women. You shouldn't expect that from me."

Crossing her arms over her chest, she turns her body even further away from me. Twisting in her chair like she is physically sick by my closeness.

"I've lost my appetite. Can I go back to the room now?"

"You sure you don't want to eat more? You only took a few bites."

"I'm sure."

"As you wish." I drop my own fork and knife before getting up from my chair. Elena rises at the same time. I take her hand and pull her through the house like I always do, but this time it feels different. This is the first time she wants to go to her room. She would rather spend time alone than with me on the terrace, which enrages me for more than one reason.

"You're hurting my hand." Elena winces. I loosen my grip, not realizing how much I was squeezing her fingers.

An apology sits on the tip of my tongue, but I swallow it down. I don't need to apologize to anyone, not even her.

After locking Elena back in our bedroom, I head downstairs to the gym in the basement. I need to let off some steam, and since I can't do that with my future wife, I have to let the punching bag take my wrath.

I lose track of time at the gym. All I know is that when I'm done, I'm soaked in sweat, and my knuckles hurt. I unwrap my hands and realize they are swollen too. *Shit.*

I take a quick shower, in the bathroom attached to the gym, and get dressed into an extra change of clothes I keep down here.

Unlocking my phone, I check the video surveillance from the bedroom. The feed pulls up, showing me my bedroom. Elena is on the bed, wearing the same clothes from this morning. She is on her stomach, her face hiding in the pillow.

Either she went back to sleep, or she is still pouting about this morning. Maybe both.

I shove my phone in my pocket and head upstairs to my office. I'm not even halfway up the stairs when I hear it. A high-pitched scream coming from the kitchen. Taking two steps at a time, I run up the stairs and down the long hallway leading to the kitchen.

When I enter, I find Lorelei, my cook, on the ground. Her lifeless body still, and her eyes open but completely blank. Marie–the new maid is standing over her sobbing, her hand clutched to her chest.

"I-is sh-she…" She stutters.

"Yes, she is dead." I don't have to check her pulse to know she is gone. The bluish color of her skin and the vacancy in her eyes says it all. "What the hell happened?" I ask as I take out the phone to text Markus.

Me: Get the fuck to the kitchen. Now.

"I-I don't know. She was fine when I left to go to the store. I just got back and found her."

Only now do I notice the groceries spilled out on the floor. The maid must have dropped the bags when she came in.

Markus comes up behind me a moment later. "What the fuck?"

"Maid said she left for a bit, came back, and found her," I explain.

"What was she doing when you left?" Markus implores.

"Nothing." The maid shrugs. "Just eating the leftovers from breakfast." Hiccupping, she points to the nook in the corner of the kitchen.

My gaze falls onto the plate that holds leftover fruit. A half-cut red apple and green papaya peel. Nothing that explains what the fuck happened here.

I turn my attention back to the dead body on the kitchen floor—an awful feeling gnawing in the back of my mind. Something is off, terribly fucking off.

Sucking in a sharp breath, I let the puzzle pieces fall into place. I connect the dots in my mind. Elena, papaya... death.

"Fuck!" I yell before running out of the room.

"What..." I hear Markus yelling after me, but I'm already down the hallway.

My heart is hammering against my ribcage, and my lungs refuse to fill with air as I try to get the door open. I'm probably wrong about this, and completely overreacting. Elena's just sleeping, there can't be a connection between Lorelei's death, and the fucking fruit Elena ate too.

Those are all the thoughts running through my mind as I rush up the stairs and into the room and to her side.

"Elena, get up." I tap her shoulder, but she doesn't react. A feeling similar to the one I had the night my mother died threatens to take me under, and I sink a little deeper inside my mind. If I go back to that place, there will be no coming back.

Grabbing her hip, I flip her over, and that's when I know... my suspicion was right. *Shit!*

Her face is pale, ghostly white with an almost green tint to it. Sweat pearls on her forehead as I move her limp body around. The only reason

I'm not completely losing it right now is the fact that I know she is alive by the raspy shallow breaths she is taking.

Turning her onto her side, she groans in pain before she starts gagging and dry heaving, so I pick her up and cradle her to my chest.

Markus bursts into the room at the same time. "What the fuck?"

"Call the doctor," I growl, heading toward the bath.

I only make it halfway before she starts throwing up, and I turn her in my arms, so she doesn't choke. Her eyes briefly open, but she is so out of it, I don't think she knows what's going on. I have to bend her over the toilet as she continues to vomit. Her whole body convulsing as she does. At least she is getting it out, her body fighting whatever it was that poisoned her.

Thinking of it has a burning rage rising inside of me. Who the fuck dared try to hurt what's mine? I need to figure out who did this, but right now, I need to concentrate on her more.

When the first wave of vomiting has passed, her eyes open again, but they are still unfocused. Her dark hair is sticking against her sweaty forehead, and spit is running down the corner of her mouth. Looking down her body, I see puke is sticking to her clothes and skin.

I need to clean her up.

Carefully, I pick her up and lay her into the garden bathtub, where I start stripping her out of her soiled clothes. Her watery eyes find mine when I pull her bra off, and for a moment, I think she comes to. Her gaze falls onto my chest and mumbled something that sounds like an apology. When I look down to where she is looking, I realize that she puked on me as well.

"It's fine, I've had worse on me."

Once she is in nothing but her panties, I strip out of my shirt, throwing everything into a pile. Turning on the water, I start washing her with a soapy washcloth.

She goes in and out of consciousness while I clean her up, and I silently curse the doctor for not being here yet.

As I rinse her off, I hear the doctor's voice coming from the hall. Markus is there too. I can't make out everything they are saying, but it sounds like he is already filling him in on everything we know.

Grabbing a towel, I wrap it around her small body and pick her back up. She makes a small sound of distress but then buries her face in the crook of my neck.

I put her down on the bed, making sure the towel covers her pussy and tits while two other men are in the room.

"Markus, find who did this. It had to be the papaya I got for her. Someone was trying to kill her. Someone who knew it was her favorite." Of course, there is only one person in my mind right now, but why would her own father want her dead?

"On it." Markus disappears from the room, and I turn back to the doctor, who has already started examining her.

"How much did she throw up?"

"A lot."

"She might not need her stomach pumped, but I'll still give her something to make her vomit more. I'm also going to give her some IV fluids. That's really the only thing I can do right now. I have to run some blood tests to know more."

"Do that then."

Crossing my arms in front of my chest, I watch him work meticulously on Elena. He sets up a makeshift IV before poking her with a needle. He draws some blood and hooks a bag of fluid up to her arm, and the fact that she doesn't flinch is cause for concern. When he is all done, he hands me two pill bottles with instructions.

"Call me if anything changes. She might throw up again, which will be good. I'll be back tomorrow to check on her, hopefully with the result from the blood work."

I nod, even though all I want to do is yell at him to get me the result fucking now. The thing is, doc, doesn't take shit from anyone, even from me. He's been working for the family longer than I've been alive. Not only is he the best at what he does, I know he is doing this as fast as he can.

He disappears from the room, leaving Elena and me alone. She makes a small whimper sound, but her eyes remain closed. For a long time, I just stand there looking at her, unsure of what to do.

For the first time in a very long time, I feel... powerless. The feeling is foreign to me. I'm the head of this family, what I say goes, I'm always in control, always... but I can't control this. I can't take her pain away, I can't make the blood result get here faster, and I can't find out who did this and stay at her side at the same time.

Elena rolls onto her side and almost out of the bed. I move quickly, grabbing her at the last minute, and roll her back over. Her small hands reach for me, her slender fingers wrapping around my wrist to pull me closer.

"Julian..." My name falls off her lips in a breath, soft and quiet, but it hits me like a fifty-pound weight.

"Shh, it's okay. You're okay," I assure her and watch her eyes flutter shut once more.

Her movement made the towel move off her body, and I remember she is still wearing her now soaking wet panties. I pull them off her legs, trying not to look at the valley between her thighs. I don't care how sick she is, she is still beautiful, and I'll never stop wanting her.

Careful not to rip out the IV, I move Elena into the center of the bed, take off my shoes and slide into the spot next to her.

She turns toward me, wiggling her body as she is trying to get closer.

I slide my arm under her body and gently lift her up to lie on top of me. With her cheek flat on my chest, her breath fans out over my skin. Her breathing is still a bit rough, but it's starting to calm down, color returning to her cheeks, and I know she is going to be okay.

Absentmindedly, I run a hand up and down her naked body, enjoying the tiny shivers I draw out of her every time I hit a certain spot on her ribs. For a while, I let her body distract me, let her beauty and sweetness draw me in. I listen to her breathe and watch her sleep, but all too soon, even that can't keep me from thinking about my next move.

I need to find who did this. Who dared try to take her from me. I need to find the person responsible, so I can remind everyone why you never mess with something that's mine.

15

ELENA

My brain feels as if it's been run through a blender. Scratch that, I feel like my whole body has been run through a blender. I don't know what is up or down. All I know is every time I lift my head, the entire room spins. Trying to sort through my memories of the last twenty-four hours, I'm not sure what is real or made up.

What is wrong with me?

I remember Julian holding me in his arms, throwing up on him, him giving me a bath, and the doctor coming. Not all of that had been a dream, had it? Julian holding me against his chest seems like it would be a made-up thought, but I can still feel his arms wrapped around me, holding me securely against his chest. The whole bath thing was probably a dream too.

Blinking my eyes open, I slowly focus on the nightstand, the lamp, the mattress before letting my gaze move around the room at an even slower rate. My stomach is still knotted, and bile rises up my throat, threatening to come out.

My arm throbs like it's been poked, and I peer down at it with one eye open. There is some light bruising, and at that moment, I can't really put the pieces together in my mind.

"You're awake." Marie beams from her spot at the edge of the bed.

How long has she been sitting here? Where is Julian?

"I feel dead." My voice is raspy, and my throat is raw. Reaching for the water bottle I spot on the nightstand, my hand misses, and I reach for it again and miss that time too. "What's wrong with me?" I ask out loud.

Marie moves off the edge of the bed, grabbing the water bottle and handing it to me, "Mr. Moretti said you are sick and told me to stay with you until he returned. Are you feeling better? Are you going to puke again?"

"Not really, and I don't think so. My brain feels like it's been fried."

Marie frowns at my response as I twist off the cap and take a small sip of water. I want to drink the entire bottle, but I just know it'll come right back up if I do that. Putting the cap back on, I sag against the pillows. My skin feels hot and clammy.

"Where is Julian?" I ask, wincing at the sound of my own voice.

"I don't know, but he said he would be back soon."

I nod, or at least I think I do. I can't be sure.

For the next two hours, Marie stays with me while I float in and out of consciousness. My brain refuses to shut down completely, and yet having my eyes open does me more harm than good. What could be wrong with me? Surely, this isn't the flu. I've had that a time or two in my life, and it's never felt like this.

This is different. Like my body is trying to purge something inside of it.

I recall the doctor taking my blood, and telling Julian there was nothing that could be done until tests were run. Or maybe I had misheard that? I didn't know what was real or not? Sometime later, I awake again, feeling only a little better.

When I open my eyes, my head is pounding, but I don't seem as disoriented or like I'm riding a never-ending rollercoaster. Sitting up, I press a hand to my forehead.

"Welcome back," Julian's deep voice greets me, and I find him perched at the edge of the bed, his features hidden in the shadows. He's sitting in the same spot Marie had sat earlier. *Marie.* Immediately, concern for the maid fills my veins.

"Where is Marie?" I croak.

Julian smiles, one side of his lip tipping up. He looks every bit the predator he wants people to see him as. "Probably sleeping since it's well after ten."

"Oh... okay."

"It's surprising that you wonder about her when you were the one lying in bed, half-dead to the world all day."

"All my thoughts feel jumbled. What's wrong with me?"

Julian looks at me, his gaze hardening. "Don't know yet, but you seem to be doing better, that is, after IV fluids and some meds. The doc is going to call and let me know when your blood test results come back. Though we're fairly sure someone tried to poison you."

"Poison! Why would someone want to poison me?" I never hurt a fly in my life. I can't possibly wrap my head around that.

"That's what I'm going to figure out. My cook, who has been with the family for years, was also poisoned. We found her body in the kitchen yesterday morning. She had been eating the leftover breakfast. Specifically, *your* leftover breakfast."

Horror strikes me like a lightning bolt. Someone tried to kill me... and it obviously wasn't the cook since she's dead too. This new information is unsettling and leaves me feeling thankful for skipping out on breakfast that morning. If I had eaten more, I'd probably be dead.

I'm not sure how to feel about that.

Staring at Julian, my thoughts shift... I can't help but see how different he is today than he was the other night. Has me being poisoned changed something in him? Made him more human or maybe made him see how easily I could've been taken from him? I think back to my delirious state, the tossing and turning, and vomiting, the cramps in my stomach. He was there. I remember seeing him, and I'm certain he held me in his arms and told me everything was going to be okay, but maybe he didn't. Maybe I completely made up his kindness. It's not that far-fetched, seeking out comfort when you feel like you're dying.

Still, I have to know if it was real.

"I might've hallucinated it, but I swear you took care of me when I was sick. You held me in your arms... did you?"

Julian turns toward me, his face void of any emotion, and still, something slowly brews in his icy glare. "I hold you in my arms every night when we go to sleep."

"Yeah, but this was different..." More intimate somehow. I'm usually turned away from him, and he has an arm slung around my waist, holding me to him like he is scared I'm gonna run away in my sleep. Yesterday, his hold was gentle, like he was just holding me for comfort instead of keeping me prisoner.

"You're going to be my wife. It doesn't matter how you got here, but me taking care of you is part of the deal. Just like you pleasing me is part of it."

Of course, it is.

Needing space, I toss the covers back. Looking down at my body, I realize I'm in a pair of pajamas I don't remember putting on.

"I dressed you. I didn't want the staff to see you naked." An image of Julian dressing me while I was passed out, pops into my head, but I shake it away quickly. It's too creepy to think about. I can feel Julian watching me, and all I want is to get away from him. He's already proven his point. I'm nothing, an object never meant to be heard and barely seen.

My body has other plans, though, because as soon as I put my feet on the ground and push off the bed to stand, a serious wave of nausea and dizziness slams into me. Knees buckling, I grab onto the nightstand, my nails sink into the wood as I attempt to steady myself, but it's not enough. My legs are weak, and a flash of hitting the floor appears in my mind.

I gasp in shock when Julian's strong arm circles my waist, and he clutches me to his warm chest. My muscles tense, but a part of me feels protected in his embrace.

"You're so stubborn," he whispers into the shell of my ear.

"I don't need your help," I grit out, trying to fight against his hold, but my muscles are like jelly, and my head is spinning like I'm on a tilt-a-whirl.

"If you say so." He releases me, and I start to fall to the floor again.

Chuckling, his hands circle my waist once again, holding me tightly to his chest, and heat creeps through me, slowly trickling into my core.

My cheeks are burning, but I doubt he can see them. It's just the illness, I don't actually like his hands on me. "Looks like you do need my help," he teases.

I roll my eyes, wanting to deny it, but I know the second he lets me go again, I'm gonna be on the floor, no doubt about it.

"I don't want to take a shower with you again. Last time ended horrible."

"My version of horrible and yours are vastly different." He grins, guiding us into the bathroom. Gently, he turns me in his arms and helps me to sit down on the toilet. Then he opens the shower door and turns the water on. I don't bother hiding my body from him and start taking my clothes off without question.

I do my best to avert my gaze as he strips, but it's so hard, literally and figuratively. A man as cruel as him shouldn't be allowed to look so good. Rippling muscle, tone, and tan. He looks like a model.

He's completely naked now while I still have my Pajama pants on. I stare down at my feet and take his hand when he offers it to me, doing everything I can to not look at that mammoth organ between his thighs.

Helping me out of my clothes, he picks me back up, and we step into the shower together, one of his hands remaining on my hip to steady me. His junk presses against my thigh, and I hiss at the touch.

"It won't bite you, Elena."

"Says the owner of the beast." I swallow down the lump in my throat and start washing my body. My movements are sluggish, and it takes me forever to actually wash. The whole time Julian remains beside me, steadying me and doing nothing but making sure I don't fall.

"Here, sit." He guides me to the bench in the corner of the shower, and I sit down, pressing my back against the cool tile.

"Why is there a bench in here anyway? Isn't that for old people?"

A low chuckle rumbles in his chest, a rare sound I could get used to. "The shower doubles as a steam room."

"Oh..."

"I'll wash your hair as soon as I'm done washing myself," he says. I want to object, and I should because I've learned that his kindness always comes with a price, but I'm desperate for someone to care for me, desperate for the man that's going to marry me to actually want me.

My nipples harden painfully as I watch the water cascade down his back. He's absolute perfection, and I'm jealous of the washrag that he uses over his sculpted body.

You don't want him. He doesn't even care about you. I remind myself.

Shivering, I bite my lip, it's at that time, he turns to face me. In that instant, he's both monster and man, his eyes trail over my body, leaving a path of warmth in their wake.

I must be delirious because there is no way this is happening again.

"You're looking at me like you want me to fuck you," he says, swiping a hand down his face. I feel sweat bead against my forehead, and I'm not sure if I should tell him that I want him to touch me or not. I'm not supposed to want him, it's wrong, but I'm so damn lonely, and so tired of fighting.

"I want you... to touch me," I murmur.

Julian grins, and separates the space between us in one step, "You want me to touch you, but not fuck you?"

I nod my head. "Just touch."

"Do you want to touch me too?" he whispers, taking my chin between two fingers. I shiver at the intense need in his eyes and the feel of his fingers on my skin.

"I'm... I don't know," I admit, and Julian looks at me for a long second, and I'm almost sure he's going to tell me to get out, but instead, he releases my chin and takes a step back.

"Spread your legs," he orders, and I obey just like he wants me to. I glance down between my thighs to see what he sees right now. "Eyes on me at all times. I want to see you when you come, and I want you to watch me own your body the way only I can."

A knot of fear tightens in my belly, but I nod my head anyway, wanting to go through with this.

"Touch yourself," he orders while wrapping a hand around his length. Just like the time I watched him in the shower, I'm mesmerized by him. The way his hand wraps around his large penis... the way he strokes himself.

My own hand travels down my stomach and to my folds. I've touched myself before but of course never in front of someone. It feels wrong, too intimate, but also it feels right like I'm sharing something special with him.

"Now, rub your clit for me." His gruff voice vibrates through me as I bring my fingers to my clit and start to draw small circles around it. Pleasure blooms deep in my belly as I watch him stroke himself while watching me in return.

"Mmmh," I moan softly while picking up speed, rubbing my clit more furiously. The pleasure is there, but it's not enough to drive me over the edge. Dropping my hand, I lift my eyes from Julian's crotch to look him in the eyes.

"I don't think I can do this. I want you to touch me," I admit, knowing already that this is a terrible idea.

"You sure?" he taunts, and steps closer again. Leaning down, he pinches one of my nipples between his fingers. The action is painful, but a jolt of pleasure follows, making me chew on my lip to stifle the groan that wants to come out.

Breathlessly, I say, "Yes."

He plucks at my nipple again, and I spread my legs a little wider, beckoning him right where I want him. Chuckling softly, he gets down on one knee, so we are eye to eye. He slips a hand between my thighs, grazing the bundle of nerves between my folds. Something sparks in my belly at his touch, and all I know is that I have to feel it again.

"Again." I look up, pleading into his eyes.

Gritting his teeth as if he's in pain, he swirls two fingers over that magic spot, and I let out a low whimper. Keeping my eyes on him, a slow heat starts to build in my belly, and the faster he moves his finger, the higher it rises. Pressing firmer against that spot, he moves faster and faster, and I build up, my muscles tense, my hips rising, seeking out more until I crest.

"I'm..." I shudder against the bench, every fiber of my body unraveling as pleasure rips through me, overtaking my senses.

"You're coming. Come on my hand," Julian grunts as the orgasm ripples through me.

Pulling away, he stands up. Taking the same hand that was between my thighs, he brings the two fingers to my mouth.

"Open and taste yourself while watching me beat off. All while knowing that only you do this to me. Only you, Elena."

Opening my mouth, his fingers slip inside, and his pupils dilate, the blue becoming almost black. Mewling around his fingers, I taste my arousal on them, it isn't a bad taste, if anything, it makes me hungry for more.

Dropping my gaze to his hand, which is fisting his penis, I suck greedily on his fingers, swirling my tongue around them, listening and watching as he loses himself in pleasure. He works himself hard and fast just as he said, so much so that his movements and grip look almost painful.

Gritting his teeth, the words come out in a rage. "Fuck, I can't wait to be inside you, to blow my load in your virgin pussy. All mine. Every untouched inch of you is mine."

"Mmmm," I say around his fingers.

"Spread your legs. I'm going to mark you," he tells me, and I oblige, wanting to see him unravel and fall apart. He's seen me weak so many times. I want to see him when he gives in to the pleasure—when he's at the mercy of his own will.

Spread as wide as I can, he strokes faster, his eyes darting between my face and my spread legs. Sucking harder, I relish in the hiss that slips past his lips and watch with amazement as he tips his head back, bares his teeth, and the cords in his neck and abs tighten. He looks utterly beautiful, and I want to see him like this again. I crave it, need it.

A moment later, his release comes and spurts of warm white liquid land against my mound in sticky ropes. I stare down at them, feeling not disgusted, but marked, just as he said he wanted to do. Seconds tick by, and he tugs his fingers from my mouth. His chest rises and falls rapidly, matching my own.

When he looks at me again, there is this sedated look on his face, and I smile because I helped put it there. For the first time since arriving here, I don't feel completely useless.

"You were gentle," I say, trying to stand, but my legs are more like jelly now than they were before.

"Stay seated so I can wash your hair and don't assume it will always be that way, you're ill, and I didn't want to hurt you further," he sneers the last part, and I can tell that it's a lie as soon as the words pass his lips. If he wanted to hurt me, he would've. He held all the power in that instant, and all he did was bring me pleasure.

There is this peace that seems to sweep over us. Something has changed, but I can't pinpoint exactly what it is.

The rest of the shower, we're quiet, he washes my hair for me and rinses it. Then he dries himself and me before helping me into a nightgown and panties.

He pulls back the covers, helps me into bed, and I feel a little better after my shower. My head doesn't feel like it's going to explode, and my stomach is settled. Sinking back against the pillows, the sound of Julian's phone ringing causes me to startle.

Julian curses under his breath and walks over to the nightstand, where his gun and phone sit. He looks at the screen and swipes a finger over it.

"I hope you have some information for me," Julian says, suddenly becoming the dark mafia man he is.

Watching intently, his expression changes, becoming murderous as the person on the other line speaks.

"Okay, and yes, she's doing better. It's a good thing she ate hardly any of it." His gaze finds mine, and I look away, the moment feeling too intense. They talk a little while longer, and then he ends the call. He sits on the edge of the bed with his phone in his hand, looking like he could break the thing into a million pieces.

It's none of my business, but I want to know who called him and what they said since it obviously had something to do with me.

"Who was that?" I ask quietly.

"The doc, he confirmed our assumptions that it was poison."

"But who would want to poison me, and why?"

Julian doesn't answer me and crawls under the covers, tugging me into his side. I feel warm and protected, but deep down, there is a nagging fear. Someone wants me dead… and I have no idea why.

"Don't worry your pretty little head. You're mine, and I protect what is mine. Whoever did this to you will pay dearly. I can promise you that." And I believe him, feel the justice in his words moving through me. Julian may be a bad man, but deep down, beneath it all, he is something else, and I'm going to keep digging till I find the person I know he can be.

16

JULIAN

By Thursday, Elena is back to feeling like herself, and I've been asking myself if I made a mistake when I touched her in the shower. Watching her come apart beneath my hand, it was the most exhilarating thing ever. It unleashed a hunger that has yet to be satiated.

Seeing my release on her little pink pussy, it gutted me, made me want to do anything to see it again, and that was a dangerous place to be. I couldn't be developing feelings or growing attached, and yet every day, I feel like I am.

My heart was slowly coming back to life, beating with a newfound joy, and I hated it. I wanted to rip the thing out of my chest because there was no room for it in my life. Feeling was a downfall, and I realized that when my mother died. But when I thought she might be gone, that fear came back ten-fold.

"Are you going to wear that thing for Elena," Markus taunts as he walks into my office, jerking his head toward the dress I had picked out for my soon to be wife.

"Say one more stupid thing, and I'm going to cut off one of your fucking fingers." I grumpily say into my coffee, which I've poured a heavy dose of whiskey into.

I look at the dress hanging from the office door. It's a scandalous scrap of material, and I hate more than anything that I'm going to make her wear it, but it's got to be this way. Her father will be there, and I can't have him thinking his daughter is being treated as anything more than my slave. I want to hit him where it hurts, and unfortunately for Elena, she is his weakest link.

"Do you think she is going to wear that?"

"I guess we will find out, won't we?" I shrug. "Not that I'm giving her an option. It's the dress, or she can go naked."

"As if you would let her do that," Markus teases. Fed up with his bullshit, I get up and walk around the desk. Grabbing the dress from the door, I hold it up and just stare at it. It's barely going to cover her ass.

Fuck. Everything about her lately has been making me possessive. I want her—all the time. In any way, I can have her. But she's too damn soft and naive for my liking. I have the power to break her right in my hand.

"I'll be back," I say to Markus as I leave the office and walk down the hall to the bedroom. Retrieving the key, I unlock the door to find her sitting on the bed, the journal I got for her open, a pen in her hand.

Surprise fills her features, and she shuts the notebook, her cheeks turning crimson as if she's been caught doing something that she shouldn't.

Pride fills my chest. "Were you writing in the notebook I got you?"

She nods, and I can see her throat bob as she swallows. Since the night I touched her, the impulse to do so again has been tugging at me. Something changed between us that night, something that made her trust me more. Like I had anticipated, she is relying on me, trusting me to care for her. I just never expected to develop any type of emotions or feelings toward her. Elena was special, though, refusing to see only the bad in someone. The only problem with that was that she was looking for good in the wrong person.

"What's that?" she asks, motioning to the dress in my hand. The dress I had forgotten all about until now.

"*This* is what you will wear on Saturday night."

Scrunching up her nose, she says, "You can't be serious. That won't even cover my butt."

Gritting my teeth, I do my best to act unfazed. "I'm dead serious, and it will cover all that it needs, but still give everyone a little tease."

Elena's green eyes fill with disappointment. "Why would you want to tease anyone? I thought I was yours?"

My jaw pops, and I wonder if she can sense how annoyed I am, how I really don't want her to wear the fucking dress. There isn't shit I can do, though. "Yes, which is why you will wear it and not complain, otherwise you can go naked. Would you like to do that?" Over my dead body would I ever allow that, but she didn't know that.

Frowning, she says, "I don't want to wear that. I won't be comfortable. It's too revealing, and everyone will be looking at me. Can't I wear something else?"

"No, and that's the point. I'm showing you off, letting everyone know what I have that they don't. I want all eyes on you. I want them to want you and be jealous."

She looks down at her hands and away from me, but I don't miss the dread and disappointment in her features. "Then, I guess I'll wear it. It's not like I have a choice."

At least she's learned that much.

"Correct," I say and place the dress on the bed. "How are you feeling?"

"Fine. Just a little headache today."

Walking to the door, I grip the brass knob and talk over my shoulder. "Good. I'll be back in a little while to get you for dinner."

There is a slight pause, and then Elena clears her throat softly. "Did you figure out... who poisoned us?" she asks hesitantly. She is scared, and I understand why, but she has to know there is no safer place than here.

"I told you not to worry. You're safe with me, and I will make sure whoever did this pays. When I find out more information, I'll tell you." She nods, and I walk out of the bedroom, closing the door behind me. I twist the lock into place and walk back to my office.

Markus is sitting in one of the seats in front of my desk, a smug look on his face. If he doesn't get out of my face, I'm going to rearrange it.

"How did it go?"

"Fine. Don't you have work to do?"

He shrugs. "Probably. I wanted to talk to you, though. See where your head is. This is still all about revenge, right?"

"What else would it be about?"

Markus's eyes narrow. "You're different with her..."

Am I? I'm still a ruthless asshole. I'm making her wear the dress even though she doesn't want to. She is mine... but the need for revenge, to hurt her father overshadows that. I can't push my revenge to the side to spare Elena. It will never happen. I can't allow it. Romero is going to pay for killing my mother, and Elena will just have to be a casualty of war.

"Not really, now get the fuck out of my office and stop second-guessing me. I have shit to fucking do." I seethe, settling into my seat.

"I'm not second-guessing you, just wondering if you've found someone to restart that rusty old thing in your chest."

"Says the almost emotionless asshole in front of me," I counter.

Markus shakes his head and gets up and walks out without another word. With him out of my hair, I think of the event. There will be a major chance for her to escape, and as soon as she sees her father, she is going to try. I just know it.

I need some type of insurance, something to keep her in line, so she obeys. I think of all the different things I can offer her, freedom to roam the house, walks outside on the property. Of course, those freedoms she will gain from getting away as well. I need something that will strike fear in her, make her want to obey me because the consequences will be grave if she doesn't.

Then it hits me, her asking about Marie...

Perhaps that will do the trick.

17

ELENA

*L*ike clockwork, the lock turns, and the door opens at a quarter to twelve. The maid enters the room with my lunch. Carrying a tray of food, she walks all the way up to the bed and hands it to me.

"Would you like me to stay while you eat?"

The tray almost slips out of my hand at the suggestion. "Ah, I'd love to, but..." *Julian might kill you.*

"I'll stay, then," she chirps, taking a seat on the edge of the bed.

"I don't know if it's safe. Julian doesn't like anyone in here." I wonder what she is thinking about my relationship with Julian. She obviously knows that he keeps me locked in here.

"He told me himself it was okay to come in and talk to you while you ate."

"Oh..." That's surprising. So surprising that I'm not sure if I should believe her. Maybe I should tell her to leave just for her safety. On the other hand, if this is true, I would love the company. I already feel connected to her, knowing she was here when I was sick. We didn't talk a lot then since I was mostly unconscious, but there is still a familiarity between us.

"If you're sure, I would love it if you'd stay." I smile. "Would you like some?" I point to my tray. "There is always way more than I can eat, and I would hate to sit here and eat in front of you."

She smiles widely and reaches for the grapes, her fingers barely graze them when an image of a dead person sprawled out on the kitchen floor pops into my head.

"On second thought, maybe you don't want to eat my food. The last person who did, died." I half-laugh even though it's not funny.

"Oh, I'm not worried about that. Mr. Moretti has been having everything tested before it's brought up to you. He doubled all security around the house as well."

"He did?" That makes me pause.

"Yes, he is always very concerned about your safety."

I just nod, not wanting to correct her. He isn't worried about *me*. He is worried about someone taking what's his. If she saw the dress he wanted me to wear, or knew half the story of how I came about being here, I doubt she would think he cares.

For the rest of the lunch, I try to steer away from the subject of Julian and ask Marie about her and her life instead. She tells me about her siblings and her parents, who came to America from the Philippines when she was just a little girl.

"I wondered where you were from, you look so exotic, but you don't have an accent."

"It's because we moved when I was in kindergarten. My parents have very strong accents," she explains while I take the last bite of my sandwich.

"That was delicious."

"I'm glad you enjoyed your lunch. It was nice spending some time with you, but I need to get back to work now."

My shoulders sag in disappointment. I took my time eating, drawing this out as long as I could, but I knew this would end sooner rather than later. "Hopefully, we can do this again."

"I'm sure we can." She grabs the now empty tray and heads out the door. "Bye, Miss Elena." We give each other a little wave goodbye before she closes the door and locks it behind her.

Instantly, I'm overcome with guilt. Is Julian really okay with her coming in? Maybe she was lying, or she misunderstood him? What if this was a test?

Oh, god. What if Marie gets hurt because of my selfish need for company?

∽

I'M SO nervous for the rest of the day, I can't even concentrate on math. I can't shake the feeling that Marie is in danger and that it's my fault.

When Julian finally comes to get me for dinner, I'm on pins and needles. As soon as he walks in, I bombard him with questions.

"Is she okay? Marie, I mean. You didn't do anything to her, right?"

"Why would you ask me that? I told her it was fine to come in."

"I thought..."

"You thought I killed her?" He arches a brow in questioning.

I feel ashamed to admit it, but nod since there isn't any point in lying to him. Julian is cruel, sinister, and I know he wouldn't hesitate to kill someone. Man or woman.

"I didn't kill her... but your concern for her well-being is interesting."

"*Interesting*?"

"Maybe that's not the right word. Convenient would be better."

"What that's supposed to mean?" I'm almost afraid to find out.

"At the event I'm taking you to, I need you to behave. I need you to act a certain way and do things you might not want to do, but you will do them because if you don't, Marie might get hurt." The words slowly enter my mind, and I piece the puzzle together.

"You're using her against me," I growl angrily.

"Yes, but I will not harm her if you behave, and I will reward you. I will give you more freedom. All you have to do is prove yourself to me."

"Prove myself? What does that even mean?" I toss my hands into the air. "I've never done anything for you not to trust me. I've played all your games, never fought you on anything. I let you keep me in your bedroom without complaining. I think I've proven myself enough... maybe you are the one who needs to prove himself to me."

As soon as the last bit leaves my mouth, I regret saying it. Not because it's not true, but because I don't want to provoke Julian.

His crystal blues become stormy, and my eyes move to his hands that curl into tight fists. Sometimes things seem so perfect, and I think maybe I can reach him, and then he says or does something, and I'm back to being hopeless.

"Have I not proven to you that I can be kind? That I'll take care of you? That you can trust me? Have I lied to you? Hurt you?"

"No..." My shoulders sag down, and I turn my head away, unable to look at him longer. No, he hasn't physically hurt me, and he has shown me kindness in his own way, but I can't help but expect more. Maybe that's my problem. I shouldn't expect more from a man who bought me.

Everything he does is to ensure that I behave, and now he is using Marie as extra insurance. I don't like it, not at all, holding another person's life in my hands, but what option do I have? Either way, Marie ends up hurt, and I could never sleep at night knowing that I cost someone else their life.

"I already told you. It's not always going to be like this. You won't always be locked in this room, but I need to know that I can trust you, and this event is going to be the perfect way for you to gain that trust."

"I understand, but I've been here for weeks. I haven't tried to escape... I've listened." Reasoning with Julian is like trying to reason with a bull. It's pointless, and you'll probably end up dead before you get anywhere.

Julian's gaze softens at my words.

"Do this for me, okay? Behave, don't fight, and I will give you freedom."

"Okay," I say, my voice dripping with defeat.

"Are you hungry?"

"Yes, very. It's late." I get up from the bed and grab his hand naturally. I know he only holds my hand when we walk through the house, so I won't run away. He likes me to be anchored to him. So he can control me, but today I'm imagining that he is just holding it because he wants to. It's the one thing that makes me feel like I'm not just his prisoner.

He leads me through the house and into the dining room. It's already dark outside, and probably cold with the sundown. So, I'm not surprised we are staying inside.

The table is set as always with the dishes covered and ready for us to dive into. He pulls a chair out for me, and I take my seat while he takes the one beside me. As always, he serves the food, which is grilled salmon and a variety of vegetables tonight.

Setting my plate down in front of me, he asks, "Would you like some wine?"

"I'm not old enough," I respond.

He laughs and cocks a brow. "You're old enough to marry but not have a glass of wine?"

Deciding to jump out of my comfort zone, I grab the wine glass in front of me and hand it to him. His eyes twinkle with amusement, and I'm pretty sure I like that look more than I like any other he's ever given me.

Popping the cork on the bottle of wine, he pours the smooth red liquid into the wine glass, filling it about halfway before passing it back to me.

Bringing my lips to the rim, I take a small sip, wrinkling my nose at the fruity scent that invades my nostrils. There is a bitter tanginess left in my mouth after I swallow, and I shiver, unsure if I like it or not.

"It takes time to develop a taste for wine," Julian simply says, stabbing a piece of vegetable with his fork and shoving it into his mouth. He eats as viciously as I suppose he kills, and that's not the image I need to be conjuring up in my mind right now.

"It's not bad, but it's different," I say while staring at the red liquid. "I'm not sure if I like it yet or not."

"Drink some more, I'm sure it will grow on you."

Nodding, I drink a little more in between bites of food. With each sip I take, my cheeks grow warmer. In fact, my entire body feels warm, like I've been wrapped in a warm blanket.

Soon the glass is empty, and I look to Julian to see if I may have another.

"I thought you didn't like it?" he teases, and this is the side of him I like most. The side where he shows me glimpses of who he is beneath all the layers of death and vengeance. It's because of this that I can't give up on him.

"I changed my mind." I giggle, the wine helping to ease the tension right out of me.

"Fine, another half glass, and that's it. We have a long day tomorrow, and believe me, you don't want to be hungover on wine."

Smiling big, I hand him my glass and watch as he fills it. I can feel his eyes on me, drinking me in, and I'm curious to know what he is thinking.

I savor that final glass, loving the way it makes me feel... free, like a butterfly.

As I down the rest of the glass, I push abruptly from the table to stand, forgetting that I've never drunk a day in my life before. The world shifts on its axis, and my knees knock together. Grabbing onto the edge of the table, I try to steady myself but am thankful when Julian swoops in, wrapping a protective arm around my waist.

Standing face to face, chest to chest, I crane my neck back to look up at him. I can feel the heat of his body rolling off of him. His eyes are blazing, his cheeks high, and his jaw so sharp you could cut with it. His nose has a slight angle to it, making him perfectly imperfect. My eyes move to his lips, they're full, and I lick my own lips, this strange need to kiss him overtaking me.

Placing my hands on his biceps, he gives me a confused look, and I take that single moment to push up onto my tiptoes and brush my lips against his.

I've never kissed before, and under normal circumstances wouldn't even consider stepping out of line like this, but the wine gives me newfound courage.

A zap of electricity ripples through me, and I squeeze onto his arms, pressing my lips a little more firmly against his. His own lips move against mine, molding to me. I feel so much in that single stroke of his lips, need, possession, and power. I feel like I'm his equal, not a piece on a chessboard.

Then, as if he can sense a change in me, in himself, he pulls away, removing his arm from my waist, and instead, holding me at arm's length.

His eyes become thunderous, and I shiver under their scrutiny. "What kind of game are you playing?"

My lips tremble, aftershocks of the kiss still working their way through me.

"I'm not playing a game," I croak, though for once, I'm not afraid of him. I feel safe in his arms even when I know I shouldn't, even when I'm certain he's going to lead me straight to the slaughterhouse when this is all over. "I just wanted to kiss you..."

Julian shakes his head, his features twist into a peculiar expression. He looks younger now, vulnerable, and I want to etch this moment deep into my mind.

"I don't kiss," he replies softly.

"You just did," I whisper back.

His penetrating gaze roams my face, looking for something I'm not sure of. "You're ruining everything, and you don't even know it."

I'm not sure what that means, and I don't care to figure it out. Julian kissed me, and that's a score in my book.

18

JULIAN

"Come out, Elena," I order, growing more impatient by the second. "Now, or I'm coming in." She's been in the bathroom getting ready for well over an hour. The door isn't locked, so I could easily barge in, but I'm staying out as a courtesy to her. Marie is in there with her, doing whatever girls do to get ready.

"Okay..." The door opens slowly, and I swear my heart is beating out of my chest. Elena comes into view with each inch the door gives way.

I'm already in my tux, it's tailored to me, but suddenly it feels too tight. My chest swells with pride, knowing that she will soon be my wife. Taking her in fully, I can't break my gaze away from her, not even if I tried.

She is wearing light makeup just enough to highlight her natural beauty. Her eyes look larger, and the green in them brighter. Her already full lips are tinted pink, and her flawless tanned skin is even smoother. Her hair falls off her shoulders in dark silky waves, and I have the urge to run my fingers through the locks just to see how soft they really are. I want to tug on the strands, wrapping them around my hand as I... shit, I can't think about that right now. There is no room in this suit for my cock to get hard.

My gaze drops lower to her perfectly sculpted body, a body that is on full display in the dress I'm making her wear. It's an emerald green gown that matches her eye color to a T. The dress has no straps, her tits being held in place by a built-in bustier that gives the swell of her breasts a nice push, though she doesn't need it.

The rest of the dress is form-fitting around her waist and down her legs, but the best part of this dress is that both sides along her ribs and outer thighs are made of a sheer material. A thicker fabric covers her front and back in an hourglass-shaped, which only highlights the shape of her body. But since the sides are see-through, everyone will know that she's not wearing anything beneath.

As if she can read my mind, she pins me with a stare.

"What are the chances that you'll let me at least put some underwear on?"

"None," I grit out.

The frown on her face only deepens, but I already know she doesn't want to do this. I remember the night I took her and how self-conscious she was about the nightgown.

What she's wearing now is even more revealing. I can tell simply from the look on her face and how she wraps her arms around her middle that she is uncomfortable, but I can't help that. She's gonna have to deal with it for one night. She'll survive.

The real question is, will I survive? Am I going to be able to stand by and let other men look at what's mine? Gawk and salivate over her like she's a damn T-bone steak.

I suppose I'll have to if I want to prove a point to her father, though it's not going to happen without serious restraint. The first asshole that asks me if she's for sale, or to spend a couple hours with her is going to get a knife in their chest. I don't share what is mine.

I watch as Elena slips into her high heel sandals, steadying herself on the doorframe.

"I'm going to warn you, I'm not great at walking in heels."

Her warning makes me smile. "Don't worry, I'll be holding your hand the whole night. But... before we go, I have something for you."

"Is it a jacket? 'Cause I would love that."

"No, it's not a jacket, but don't worry, I'll keep you warm. It's this." I pull out the black velvet box from my pocket and flip it open. It's a white gold diamond necklace that I hand-picked for this occasion. As expected, her mouth pops open, and her eyes widen, but I'm not sure if it's with surprise or something else.

"You like it?"

"Is that... a necklace or a collar?"

"It's a choker necklace, but if you'd rather think of it as a collar, we can make that happen. Would you like me to get a leash with it? Diamond studded, maybe?" I smirk like an asshole.

Shaking her head, she holds out her hand like she is going to grab it from me. "Fine. I'll wear it."

"Allow me."

She drops her hands and lifts up her chin waiting for me to move. I grab the choker out of the box and undo the clasp. As I lay it around her slender neck, I drag my fingers along her collarbone on purpose, loving how her whole body shivers under my touch. I wish I could do this all night long, but there are more important things to do.

The clasp clicks in place, and I take a step back to examine my work. The necklace fits perfectly around her slender neck like it's meant to be there. She looks claimed and cared for, maybe a little too cared for. I doubt her father will look that far into it, though, not when he sees her in the barely-there dress.

"Perfect," I tell her, holding out my hand. She takes it, almost trustingly as I walk her out of the room. I walk her through the house, making sure I don't move too fast. She wasn't kidding, she can't walk in these stripper heels for shit.

I'm considering picking her up and carrying her to the car, but it's not like I can carry her around the party. I mean, I could, but then no one would get the full effect of the dress or lack of it. As soon as we step outside, a gust of cold wind rushes over us, and Elena wraps her free arm around herself, clearly freezing. She makes it to the car in one piece, but not without having an iron grip on my hand to steady herself. I definitely won't have to worry about her running off in those heels. I pull her into my side and help her into the backseat of the car before sliding in beside her.

When I let go of her hand, she wraps both of her arms around herself in an effort to get warm. Her lips tremble, and goosebumps pebble her flesh.

"Come here," I say a little too gruffly.

Slowly, she moves across the seat, burrowing into my side. Wrapping a protective arm around her, I hold her tightly to me. Her sweet scent fills my nostrils, sending a zing of red hot pleasure straight to my cock.

She molds to me like she was always meant to be there, the missing piece, and I don't want to acknowledge that, not when I'm about to show her off to an entire room full of blood-thirsty assholes. Not when this cannot be about anything but revenge.

"What will happen at this event?" she asks once she's not shivering anymore.

"It's an auction put on by one of my associates. It's important that you act the part of my wife. Do not speak unless spoken to. Do not look at anyone, eyes always down, and stay beside me at all times. I have more foes than friends in that place. Markus will be there, he is the only other person I trust."

"Okay," she says, her voice shaky.

"If you were to get away from me, and I couldn't find you, some men far worse than myself could get ahold of you, and believe me when I say, they would make me look like a goddamn angel."

"You said my father will be there. I can talk to him, though, right?" Hope fills her features while a burning rage rips through me. Even after all we've been through, what I've done for her, how I hadn't hurt her even when I should've, and still she wants to see the man who handed her to me on a silver platter? Not that he had a choice, though he could've put up a fight, which he didn't.

Gritting my teeth, I barely get a hold on my anger. "No, not even him. You need to remember that what I say goes. You may not like everything I say tonight, or what I do or how I handle you, but you need to trust me. Disobey me and something may happen to Marie and don't think that I'll hesitate to do it. I killed the other maid for simply giving you a piece of paper, and I will kill Marie too if I have to."

Elena pulls away to look up at me, her green eyes brimming with shock. "You killed the other maid?"

Stupidly, the way she's looking at me, all doe-eyed and shocked, makes me want to tell her that it's a lie, but it's not, and I cannot hide who I am from her. Not when I have and always will be this way. I'm a born killer, raised into this life, set to run the family business until the day of my death. A little five-foot-two dark-haired beauty isn't going to change that.

"Yes. I know about the note she gave you from your father. She confessed."

"Why... why didn't you say anything?"

"What's there to say? Your father cannot save you. You're bound to me by a contract, so unless he's going to kill me, which will never happen, by the way, he will never get you back. And you would be good to remember that as well. If you ever run from me, I will find you. There is no place on this planet that you can hide from me that I won't come looking for you."

Elena nods, and I swear I can see her gulp. Deep down, I don't want her afraid of me, but fear keeps people in line, it keeps them from doing stupid shit.

I don't have to let her know it's a ruse. I just have to keep her in line, which is what I plan to do.

The rest of the drive to the auction passes by quickly, and Elena remains beside me. When we pull up to the front door, she becomes stiff as a board next to me, her chest rising and falling rapidly, and her hands are balled up into fists beside her.

She nervously looks past me and out the window at the people–mostly men–walking inside the venue.

"I'm scared," she whispers without looking at me. A small pang of guilt hits my chest, but I shove it away.

"Do what I say, and nothing bad will happen," I say, taking her hand into mine and giving it a gentle squeeze to let her know I've got her.

An irrational part of me wants to take her back home, wrap her up in a blanket, and tell her everything is going to be okay. But none of that would work with my plan. No, I've been waiting for this night for a very long time. Elena might not like this, but she'll be fine. She won't be harmed, and her feelings will pass eventually. What will last is my revenge.

Lucca comes around the car to let us out, and I release Elena's hand and step out of the SUV, adjusting my tux. This is an important event for me. There are arms dealers here, friends and foes, and the selling of flesh. This event is where men join together and rise up. Not showing up wasn't an option, not showing up with her even less of an option, especially with her father being here.

If I'm lucky, I'll show Romero how much his little girl has changed and end up with a deal or two. All I need is for Elena to stay in line.

Reaching for her, I take her hand once more and help her out of the SUV. She stands on shaky legs, and shivers in the cold wind, before smoothing a hand down the rest of her dress. The venue is at an old casino that was newly renovated but not open to the public. Ahead are the only doors that allow entrance into this place, and they're guarded by two mammoth men.

Inside this place, any type of fighting is prohibited, and I feel naked having to leave my gun in the SUV, but I don't need it to deliver damage. There is a reason I work out and why I did illegal fights when I was younger.

Elena leans closer, seeking out the warmth of my body. When we reach the doors, the two men look me over before moving their gazes to Elena. Submissively, she looks down, and the men drink her in, and how couldn't they in the dress she is wearing.

They look a little longer than necessary, and my jaw tightens as I bite my tongue to stop myself from telling them not to look at her.

What the fuck is wrong with me? I'm the one that put her in the dress, the one that wants to draw attention to her. The reason they're looking at her is my fault, and yet, I want to stab every fucker for doing so.

After a moment, they open the door and wave us in. Elena clings to me, looking every bit like the helpless, obedient slave I want everyone to see her as. Peering down at her, my eyes are drawn to the diamond ring on her finger that glitters in the light. *Mine.* All mine. Any man who tries to make an offer on her tonight will die. I'll kill them, not here but afterward.

Walking inside, the smell of cigar smoke filters into my lungs. The place is already crowded, men exchange in quiet conversation while half-naked women walk around the room carrying trays with beverages.

There are a few women with men, but those are few and far between. Most do not bring their spouses to these types of events, women have no real place in our world, except on their backs with their thighs spread. This is a business event, but it's also my chance to show off my soon to be bride.

Anything from the selling of flesh and guns, gambling, and to the arrangement of marriages and illegal fights take place within these walls. This will be Elena's first dip into my dark world, and hopefully, last.

Surveying the room, I see they have it divided into three spaces. A huge horseshoe bar sits at the back of the room, a stage where the auction takes place is at the front of the room, and numerous tables and chairs litter the center, making up the middle. On one of those tables, I spot Markus, he got here early like I told him. Our eyes briefly lock, and he gives me a slight nod, letting me know there is no trouble here tonight.

Walking over to the large bar, I release her arm and pull out a stool. She sits down without question, squeezing her thighs together so much that her legs shake. Keeping her head down, she places her hands in her lap just like I've instructed her to. I long to see her beautiful green eyes but push the thought away.

I take the seat next to her and look around, surveying the space. Of course, most of the people around us are men and looking right at Elena. They openly gawk at her, and with the way she is sitting, most of her legs are exposed, the fabric riding up her legs, so close to her pussy, her bare ass is touching the seat. She is all but naked and fulfilling the job I need her to, but that doesn't mean I like it.

"I don't like this," she whispers beside me as if she can read my mind.

"Don't talk," I brush her off and wave the bartender over. "Whiskey neat, and a water."

"Yes, sir."

Just as our drinks are being served, the first group of men dare to come and talk to me.

It's Boris–a well-known arms dealer in our circles– and two of his men. He's a smug little bastard with a Napoleon complex, but he does have the best guns around, so it's wise to stay on his good side.

"Julian, glad you could make it. And you brought your newest acquisition, I see?" Boris' eyes rake all over Elena, and I fight the urge to gauge them out with my bare hands.

"I figured I paid enough for her, why not show her off? Share her with the world." I take a sip of my whiskey, concentrating on the burn in my throat and the warmth settling in my stomach. I'm going to need much more whiskey to make it through this night.

"Sharing, huh? How much would it cost to share her with me for a few hours?" Boris licks his lips, and I swear I see Elena's chest start rising and falling in rapid succession.

"Let's see what they have for sale tonight first. If there is something to my liking, I'll buy someone new, and you can have this one for the night." Elena lets out an audible gasp next to me, which makes Boris chuckle.

Using my other hand, I grab her exposed thigh and give it a firm squeeze. It's a warning. Anywhere but here, she could have a reaction, but if she doesn't obey, she'll force my hand to keep her in place.

"I'm looking forward to it," Boris exclaims, his beady eyes roaming her flesh one last time.

"I'll let you know soon." The words feel like acid on my tongue.

There is not enough money in this world that would bring me to sell her to anyone, let alone allow them to use her for a night. I've done a lot of fucked up shit, but I'm not selling my soon to be wife to anyone.

"Yes, and maybe we can discuss some weapons."

"Of course," I say before taking another sip of my whiskey.

Boris and his men meander away from us and strike up a conversation with another man who I'm sure is one of his clients, simply from the way he greets him.

"Please," Elena whimpers while tugging on my arm. Her fear is palpable in the tremble of her voice. "Please, don't give me to him. You promised..."

My features turn to stone, and I know she's looking at me. As badly as I don't want to hurt her, it's either me or some other asshole in this room.

"I told you not to talk," I grit out under my breath and grip my glass a little tighter, forcing myself not to glance at her right now. She's making me weak, so fucking weak, and I can't be seen like that. Her fear will have to stay with her because I cannot console her here.

As if she knows my resolve is close to shattering, she tugs on my arm once more.

"You promised no one would hurt me."

Unable to hold it together a second longer, I let the cold, lifeless mask I wear when I'm away from her fall over my face.

Turning toward her, I snap, "Say one more word, and something bad will happen to Marie."

Fear blazes in her eyes at the harshness of my words, and I push her feelings away, push her thoughts, wants, or needs to the back burner. Nothing else matters.

Sucking her bottom lip into her mouth, she nods and casts her eyes down. She drops her hand from my arm, and her shoulders curl inward.

It has to be this way. For her sake, and for mine.

19

ELENA

No matter how much I try to control my breathing, it feels like I'm suffocating. Panic has seized me and is refusing to let go. I hate this place, what it represents, and everyone inside it.

These men, the way they look at me like I'm nothing more than a piece of meat they can buy. I can't look at them directly, but I can see them watching me out of the corner of my eye, and I can feel their predatory gaze on me. Like dogs, they salivate, waiting for a bone. It surely doesn't help me that I'm wearing a scrap of fabric for clothing. Julian wanted me exposed and vulnerable, and here I am.

I think of Marie and his warning, and still, I can't stop the panic from rising up. Even with her life hanging in the balance, I can't comprehend him passing me off to someone else. God, was he serious? Is he going to sell me to that man? Is that why he hasn't taken my virginity yet? Maybe he is planning on selling it, or pimping me out? There is no way I could allow that, and yet, how would I stop him?

Doing the best I can, I try to keep my eyes down but can't help but let them wander around, feeling the need to be aware of my surroundings, and sensing danger nearby.

With my trembling hand, I grab my glass and bring it to my dry lips. Just as the cool water hits my tongue, I look straight ahead, and my eyes find a set of familiar green ones.

My father.

My heart squeezes in my chest, and I find myself squirming against the seat, wanting to run to him. My father is really here. Julian's grip on my thigh tightens, pulling my gaze from my father's, and he leans over, his lips brushing against my ear.

"Don't even think about it—"

"Julian!" Someone calls out, interrupting us. We both straighten up, but I lower my head again and find a spot in my lap to look at.

"Aldo, it's been a while," Julian greets and shakes this Aldo guy's hand.

"And this must be the Romero girl. Maybe if I had seen her in person, I would have paid the ten million dollars you did." He chuckles. "You know he offered me the same deal, but I didn't think any pussy was worth that much. Now that she's in front of me, I think maybe I made a mistake."

"Maybe you did." Julian shrugs. "I can tell you she is well worth the price, though. A little inexperienced, but her pussy knows what to do."

"Mmm, just what I like to hear. So, what do you say, can I have her for a night? See for myself. Of course, I'll compensate you accordingly, and I won't break her too badly."

Bile rises up my throat, and I'm pretty sure I'm going to vomit. Why would Julian say something like that? Act as if we've slept together already. Why is he acting like I'm nothing but a piece of flesh? The questions build, right along with my anxiety.

"You're not the first to ask today."

"Interesting, maybe we can set up a private party? Get some of the guys together and share her? Fuck, we both know Romero will lose his shit. We could even send him a video after, he'd enjoy that."

Oh god. Please, say no. Please, say no.

Wringing my hands together in my lap, I breathe through my nose to stop myself from hyperventilating. I remind myself of what he said when I told him I was scared before we left the car. *Do what I say, and nothing bad will happen.*

"I'll consider it. I'd like to wait a bit to see how many offers I get."

"Wouldn't you say giving Romero a heart attack is priceless?"

He'll consider it?

It's obvious they want to use me to hurt my father, but I don't understand why. All I knew when I was taken was that my father sold me for ten million dollars. I had no idea why, and I didn't think that he had offered me to more than one man. A sourness spreads through my gut, knowing that my father's intentions weren't as pure as I considered. He's proven to me, though, by sending that note that he is going to try and save me, and I'm holding onto that sliver of knowledge with more hope than I should.

"It would, but if I'm going to give away pussy as good as hers after I paid ten million dollars, I want to at least recoup some of my investment."

"I understand, will you at least let me look at her, maybe even allow a little touching?"

My skin crawls like there are tiny insects on it. If Julian wasn't bluffing and was really going to allow this man to touch me, I wasn't sure that I could stand for it. He had explained the rules and promised no one would hurt me, but he never mentioned any of this.

Out of the corner of my eye, I see Julian's steel jaw clench. "Can't you see enough of her? I've put her in that dress, and you can see all I want you to see. If you want more, it's going to cost you."

"Always a businessman first." His friend laughs. "I guess I can't blame you, this is a business after all. I'll go see what the lineup looks like for tonight. Maybe there is something that can keep me entertained until you let me have a taste of her."

"Sure, sure. Take your time. You know how I am, can't get rid of them until I've broken them to my liking." Julian snickers.

"I sure do." His friend laughs again, and I almost sigh against the bar when he retreats away from us.

I don't like how Julian is acting, and I'm not sure if this is his true self or if it's all a show. Part of it has to be a show since we've never had sex before, but the rest, the selling of me, allowing these dirty men to touch me. Is that all for show?

Lifting my eyes just a little bit, I look around the room once more to see if I can spot my father again, but all I see are a bunch of men laughing, drinking, and carrying on.

"I need to go to the bathroom," I whisper under my breath. It's only half a lie. I don't need to pee, but I really need to get out of here, even if it's just for a few minutes.

"I'll take you," Julian growls. He finishes his drink before slamming the empty glass down. He shoves off his seat and motions for me to get up too. His eyes are dark, feral, and I wonder if simply asking to go to the bathroom is the final nail in my coffin.

Apparently, I don't move fast enough because, in the next instance, he is grabbing my hand, tugging me from the stool, giving my wobbly legs and unbalanced feet no time to adjust. One step is all it takes for me to lose my footing, causing my body to collide with his firm back, my cheek resting against the smooth material of his tux.

His entire body tenses, vibrating with rage or maybe something else. I wouldn't be surprised if he truly did decide to sell me at this point.

At least he gives me a moment before he starts walking again. Looking down at the ground the entire way to the bathroom, I make sure not to trip over my own feet again. When he comes to a stop, I realize we've reached the restroom.

He releases my hand and gives me an impatient glare when I look up at him. The coldness in his eyes chills me to the bone, and I walk into the bathroom on unsteady legs, doing my best to keep myself upright.

Sighing in relief, I stand before the huge mirror, resting my hands on the edge of the expensive-looking sink. The bathroom is completely empty, not that I expected there to be many women in here, not when the entire place is packed with men.

Taking a couple calming breaths, I focus on my reflection. My face is put together beautifully, but everything else about me screams, look at me. I want to burn the dress I'm wearing and toss the shoes on my feet into a river. I hate everything about this night, and even more the way it's causing Julian to put walls up and push me out. Tears fill my eyes, but I blink them away. I cannot ruin my makeup by crying because then Julian will know I was in here sulking and not going to the bathroom, and with the mood he's in right now, I don't doubt he would threaten to hurt Marie over something as small as that.

Straightening my shoulders, I'm preparing myself to exit the bathroom when the door opens, and a petite blonde enters. I'm shocked to see her, but I'm even more shocked when she opens her mouth.

"Elena, your father asked me to give you this," she speaks low, low enough that there is no way Julian will hear from the other side of the door. Still, my first instinct is to look at the door and make sure he isn't racing inside.

Glancing away from the door, I look down at what she is trying to give me. In the palm of her hand rests a silver key.

"What is that for?" I whisper.

"The key to your bedroom. Take it." She shoves the key into my hand, the cool silver metal resting coldly and with the weight of a brick on my palm.

The woman looks back to the door before looking at me again. "Your father wants me to tell you that Julian has been trying to kill him. Ever since you were taken, he's been trying to find a way to save you, but he worries that if Julian succeeds in killing him, that you will be next. You need to get away now before it's too late."

"But..."

"No time. Just get away the first chance you get. Good luck." And with that, she spins around on her heels and walks out of the ladies room, leaving me standing there with my mouth gaping open.

What the hell was that?

I look down at the key in my hand, trying to digest everything this woman just told me. How did my father get a key to the room in Julian's house? Why is Julian trying to kill my father when he bought me for ten million dollars?

I have so many questions to ask and no one to ask them.

"Elena!" Julian's gruff, muffled voice filters through the closed door, snapping me out of my own thoughts. I quickly shove the small key into the built-in bra of my so-called dress.

"Coming," I call out.

Rubbing my sweaty palm down my dress, I take one last look in the mirror. *You can do this.* Opening the door, I find an angry looking Julian on the other side.

"What were you doing in there?" He pushes the door open further to look inside.

"I just needed a minute..." I start to explain, but Julian doesn't really seem interested in my answer. He grabs my wrist and starts to pull me away from the bathroom. It's by fate alone that I don't trip over my own feet.

"Moretti," a familiar voice calls, the sound making my chest hurt, and my stomach churn. Julian stops in his tracks, making me yet again bump into him. His hold on my hand becomes tighter, almost as if he expects me to run away.

"What do you want, Romero?" Julian snaps.

"Did you have to bring her here? Wearing this of all things? She's not a whore." My father's voice cuts through the air like a knife dipped in acid. I want to look up at him so badly, assure him that I'm okay, but I remember Julian's words. *Disobey, and Marie will pay.*

"She isn't any of your concern anymore. Ten million says so. In fact, I'll strip her naked, walk her up on stage and throat fuck her in front of everyone if I want to, and there isn't a fucking thing you can do about it."

"Jesus Christ, Moretti, what's fucking wrong with you?"

Julian answers with a chuckle. "Nothing more or less than any other man in this place, including you. Do you know how many offers I got on sharing your daughter tonight? Maybe I'll take some of them. Pass her around. If you're lucky, I'll send you a video." Julian's tone isn't just cold but mocking, and his grip on my hand becomes tighter and tighter until it's hurting.

"I want to buy her back. I've got the money."

"No."

"No? I'm saying I'm giving you back your ten million. You had your fun, now I want my daughter back."

"So you can sell her to someone else?" Out of the corner of my eye, I see Julian shake his head. "Where did you come up with that kind of money anyway? You were pretty broke last time I checked."

"Does it matter where I got it from? I've got it, that's all that matters. Let's go, Elena, we're going home."

My father extends his hand out to me, and my fingers twitch, yearning to grab hold of his, but I force myself to stay still, to keep my gaze trained on the ground.

"What have you done to her?" My father's accusing tone is aimed right at Julian.

"Trained her. She will not speak to you, or anyone because she knows what happens if she does. And your offer means shit to me. She is mine. You knew the type of man you were selling her to when you accepted my offer."

"I will not let you hurt her. She is pure and innocent–"

"Not anymore," Julian interrupts, making my father shake in anger.

"She is not made for this world. Give her back to me."

Julian takes a threatening step forward, tugging me right along with him, and my knees shake. Waves of uncertainty run through me while my captor, and my father, the man who sold me, stand toe to toe.

"She is mine, so if I want to hurt her, I will. If I want to use every hole in her body for my pleasure, I will. Fuck off, and a word of advice. If you try to infiltrate my home again or make any effort to take her from me again, I won't hesitate to come after you. A deal is a deal, Romero. You know how it works. Stand by it, or I'll be forced to draw blood."

Julian doesn't even give my father the opportunity to respond.

Brushing past him, he drags me right alongside him, and my heart feels like it's being dragged through the mud behind me. My father was right within reach, and I couldn't so much as look at him. Tears prick my eyes, and I blink rapidly to stop myself from crying.

When we reach the bar, Julian releases my hand and ushers me back into the stool I was sitting on before. I rub at my wrist, the blood finally circulating back into my hand. The bartender is cleaning a glass, waiting as if he knew we would be returning shortly.

"I need another whiskey and a glass of red wine," Julian says cooly as if he wasn't just arguing with someone.

The bartender gets our drinks, and I grab the glass of wine as soon as it's placed in front of me, taking a small sip, hoping it will calm my chaotic nerves.

"Gentlemen, can I have your attention, please. Momentarily our auction will begin. Tonight, we only have four girls for sale, but believe me, it's quality over quantity tonight. Enjoy, and may the highest bidder win."

Did he just say, girls? I couldn't possibly have heard that correctly. Curiosity gets the best of me, and I look in the direction the voice came from. Horror fills me when I see that there is a huge stage, with four pedestals on it.

This cannot be happening. This is worse than what happened to me... unless the girls are actually here out of their free will. Yes, that has to be it.

A moment later, that thought evaporates into thin air when the girls are brought out on stage. There is a crowd of men congregated around the stage, and the area fills with whistles and loud hollers as the half-naked girls are each placed on a pedestal.

Each girl looks more scared than the next, their eyes wide with shock, their body shaking, but the worst part is that they are in chains. In actual chains. There are collars around each of their necks, and a chain hangs down that's connected to their handcuffed hands, which hang in front of them.

You've gotta be kidding me. How can they just sell another human like this? Tie them up like animals and display them like this is a circus. Rage burns through my veins.

The host starts talking, introducing the first girl, but my mind is in chaos, I can't even comprehend what he is saying. Men start bidding, and I feel like I'm going to be sick. I want to ask Julian how to stop this nonsense but can't get my lips to move.

"Drink your wine," Julian's voice pierces through the heavy fog. He holds the glass of red wine I'd easily forgotten while watching this horrible event out in front of me, and I take it on autopilot. "Drink," he orders as if that's going to help me process what's going on.

"Sold, to number six-o-one!" The auctioneer calls just as I bring the glass to my lips.

"Fucking Christ!" Julian growls, "I need to talk to Markus. I'm going to leave you here at the bar. Do not get up, do not go anywhere, even the bathroom, and do not talk to anyone. I will be within distance and watching you the entire time. If you try and run, I will not only hurt Marie, but I will punish you. Understand?"

Gulping a little more of the wine down, I nod. The fear of being left alone creeps up my spine, making my gut tighten. Even with the auction taking place, I just know someone is going to come over and try and touch me, but Julian doesn't seem to care about what I want. Maybe everything he's said tonight is true? Maybe he'll sell me or let someone take me? I can imagine myself up on that stage.

Yes, being with Julian hasn't been easy, but it's surely nothing like what those girls have been through. I grip the glass of red wine a little tighter and watch as he takes his drink and strolls over to where Markus is standing.

Peeking over my shoulder, I look at where he is standing and to the dark-haired man that he is talking to. I've only seen him twice, including the night I was taken. I think Julian is trying to keep his men away from me on purpose.

They seem to be arguing, Markus's face is completely unaffected even as Julian snarls at him.

When Julian's eyes lift to meet mine, I panic and look back down at the floor, trying to ignore everything that's going on around me. Ignoring that women are being sold, ignoring that men are looking at me like I'm for sale, and most of all, ignoring the fact that there isn't anything I can do about it.

I thought I knew what the mafia was about... I was wrong, so wrong. My fingers tremble against the glass, and I truly feel like I'm going to barf. Julian needs to hurry because I'm not sure how much longer I can keep up this charade.

"Hello, Elena," an unknown voice greets me. I don't answer or even lift my head, but out of the corner of my eye, I see someone taking a seat two spots down from me. "It's okay, you don't need to say anything, just listen." He is just talking loud enough for me to hear, and I'm guessing that's by design.

"You know, I almost had you. I was so close, but Moretti outbid me. Tell me, how tight is your pussy? I mean, is it really that tight and pink? Is it worth ten million, you think?"

I want to get up, to walk away, but I'm reminded of what Julian said.

"Truthfully, I wouldn't have ever paid that much... but for a second, I was so sure I was going to get you. When your father started taking bids, I had a playroom put together for you. I bought chains and whips, and a butt plug so big it would've ripped your tight little asshole apart, but not before your virgin cunt had bled all over my cock."

"Please, go away," I whisper, just wanting him to stop. I don't care if Julian punishes me. I can't listen to another word that comes out of this man's mouth. I feel degraded like dirt beneath his feet.

"She speaks." He chuckles, making me feel slimy and dirty. "Do you think Julian would let me have you for a night? Let me fuck your pussy and ass, let me own your body?" Leaning closer, he whispers, "I mean, he's not here right now, so who's to stop me?"

Something bad is going to happen, I just know it. I can't see his face, mainly because I refuse to look up, but I do see his tattoo-covered hand creeping closer to me. Just the thought of him touching me makes my skin crawl.

Leaning away from him, I try and put distance between us, but he easily reaches me, his fingers almost touching my thigh. I jerk back, twisting in my seat to get away from him, but he just leans in closer.

A scream builds in my throat, but what good would that do? No one would care or try and help me. Here, I'm nothing to no one, not even Julian.

"Playing hard to get, I like it. I love it when they beg me to stop while I fuck them." His fingers graze my skin this time, his nails raking across my skin, digging into the flesh, and that's when I lose it. I don't care what Julian does to me for disobeying. I don't care if he punishes me. Anything is better than this man touching me.

I scurry off the chair, almost getting my heel stuck on the bar stool. The unknown man snickers at my attempt to get away in a hurry, but at this point, I don't care. I turn toward Julian and find him arguing with Markus, so involved in his conversation that he is completely oblivious of the conversation I just had.

My feet carry me to him as fast as I can make them move without face-planting on the floor. All I can think about is getting to him because deep down, even if I'm afraid he'll sell me or give me to someone else, part of me feels protected when I'm in his arms, and that's what I need right now. His protection. For him to tell me it's okay because right now, I'm anything but okay.

20

JULIAN

"What do you mean vacation? You can't just take a fucking vacation! You are my second in command. You're in the mob."

"I can, and I will," Markus tells me, arms crossed over his chest. Of all of my men, Markus is the last person I expected to fucking do something like this.

What the fuck is he thinking, buying this girl, and going on a *vacation*? He is in the mob, we don't go on fucking holiday.

Pinching the bridge on my nose, I grind my teeth and suck in a deep breath. "Markus–" I start, but I'm cut short by someone grabbing my arm. My whole body tenses, and I curl my hands into a tight fist, ready for a fight, but when I look down at my arm, I find Elena's small hands wrapped around it.

Her face is pale, her big green eyes are glassy and brimming with fear. Immediately, I know something is wrong. Her tiny nails are digging into my skin even through my suit jacket. It's like she is clawing her way to me, scared that she is going to lose me or something. I look past her, scanning the area for any danger, but there is nothing, there are just people at the bar, drinking and conversing. Lev, one of the heroin suppliers, also the son of one, Vladimir Volcove, is looking in our direction, but he could be looking at anything. He knows that she is mine, and he wouldn't be dumb enough to touch her.

"What's wrong?" I ask quietly.

"I don't feel well, can we please go home."

She might be able to fool someone else, but she can't fool me. This has nothing to do with her *feeling unwell*. The way she looks right now is how she looked the night I almost gave into my selfish needs and took from her. Did someone try and hurt her? Talk to her? Touch her? Blind rage festers inside me at the unknown.

"What really happened?!" I growl, refusing to accept her lie.

She shakes her head, her eyes bouncing to Markus and then back to me.

I turn my attention back to Markus, knowing full well that I need to get Elena out of here if I want to figure out what the hell happened.

"We will discuss this further," I grit out, and Markus's lips barely twitch.

"There's nothing to talk about. I'm taking some time off. Lucca is more than capable of stepping up."

I want to strangle Markus right now, but that's not going to happen, not with Elena latching onto my arm like this.

"Call the car for me," I order, wondering if it's going to be my last one for a while.

Markus pulls his phone out and calls for the car. Grinding my teeth together, I give Markus a nod before turning all my attention to Elena.

"Let's go."

With Elena clinging onto me, I walk through the crowd as fast as I can manage without making her trip in her high heels. When we get to the exit, and no one is paying us any attention, I lean down to pick her up, so I can walk faster.

Her thin arms come around my neck and shoulder to pull me closer. Burying her face into my neck, she starts to cry, small sobs shaking her body in my hold. What the fuck happened in there? Fucking Markus dropping this *vacation* bomb on me had me distracted for a few minutes. I should kill him, but then I would have to find a permanent replacement for him, which would be even more annoying than finding a temporary one.

Just as I walk outside, Lucca pulls up the car. He jumps out and opens the back door for me. It's not his normal job to be my driver, but I needed my best men with me tonight. Lucca is smart enough not to ask me any stupid questions. He simply watches me get into the backseat while holding Elena to my chest, before closing the door after us.

He gets back into the driver's seat and pulls away from the venue.

That's what I like most about Lucca, always so quiet, never second-guessing me, maybe he will be a great second, after all.

Another sob wracks through the small body in my lap, and my attention is drawn back to her. "Tell me what happened." I try to keep my voice even and calm, but it's hard to do when all I want to do is demand an answer. I'm not used to having to ask or decipher someone's emotions.

"I just wanted to leave."

"Don't lie to me. Something happened. Tell me."

"I stayed quiet like you told me to. I didn't talk until he touched me. I only told him to leave, but he just laughed."

My whole body tightens, every muscle in my limbs flexing, ready to kill someone. "Who touched you?" I grit out.

Instead of answering me, she continues rambling, "I don't care if you punish me, you can do whatever you want to me, but don't hurt Marie, please. I tried to listen to you, but he kept coming closer... and when his nails sunk into my skin..."

"Don't worry about Marie, she'll be fine." It's the guy who dared to touch Elena that's already dead. "Tell me what this guy looked like."

"I kept my eyes lowered on the ground. I didn't see his face." *Fuck.* "But I saw his hand. One of his fingers was tattooed with a crown on it. He also wore gold rings, and on his wrist was a red spider web..."

Lev. I know it's him simply from the tattoo. He is fucking dead.

"I'm sorry..."

"There is nothing to be sorry about. You did great tonight."

As I adjust her on my lap, her legs part a bit and try as I may to avert my gaze, not to be a complete bastard, my eyes glue onto her soft skin where three long red scratches run parallel along the apex of her thigh.

I will kill him. I will draw it out. I will make him pay for touching her. Soothing a hand over her hair and down her spine, I hold her a little tighter, wanting her to know that she is safe with me. Forever safe with me.

Pulling away, I watch as a single tear rolls down her cheek. "Did you... did you mean it? Are you really going to sell me?"

I want to laugh, but that wouldn't ease the tension or worry inside of her, so I choose against doing that. With Elena, I have to dig deep, be gentle and kind.

Cupping her cheek, I turn her face to me. A ragged breath leaves her lips, and it is painfully obvious how much tonight's events have broken her. Her father had been right in a sense. She was not made for this world. She is fragile, and if I'm not careful, I'll break her, and stupidly, I don't want to do that.

"If I didn't want you... if I was going to sell you, do you think you would be in this car with me right now?"

Hiccupping, she shakes her head. "No, but... it sounded like you... like you were going to."

I can't stop my lips from twitching up at the sides. "I told you, you might not like some of the things that I said or how I behaved, but I promised you that no harm would come to you. Did you believe me?"

The answer to my question is obvious, but I still want to hear her say it. Like others, she expected the worst from me, even when I've proven again and again that I didn't have it in me to hurt her. Technically, she didn't fully know that because I needed her fear, for her to be scared of me, to comply, but deep down, I felt like she might feel safe in my arms.

"I didn't know what to believe. I don't know if I'm cut out for this–to be your wife." She sniffled, and her words make the possessive beast that lurks just beneath the surface extend its claws out.

"Whether you are cut out for this world or not doesn't matter. You will be my wife, and there is nothing that will change that." My response is final. I'm not going to let her go, no way, no how. Elena Romero is mine. Mine to corrupt. Mine to claim.

The car comes to a halt in front of the house… *our house*. Lucca opens the door, and I climb out while keeping Elena in my arms. I hold her to my chest, making sure she isn't giving Lucca a show while I bring her inside. She holds on to my neck like I'm her life preserver, and maybe in a way, I am, keeping her afloat and alive in this world of darkness.

"Are you hungry?" I ask her as we pass the kitchen.

"No, I just want to take a bath and go to bed."

Nodding, I carry her all the way into our bathroom, where I put her down on her feet before turning on the water. She sits down on the edge of the tub and slips out of her heels. She looks exhausted, and I want to ease that tension, ease her fears and pain.

What the fuck is wrong with me? Am I growing a pussy myself?

"Can I have a moment? I-I need to use the bathroom."

I almost interject, pointing out that she used the bathroom not too long ago, but I decide to give her a minute to herself. I'm sure she needs a second to gather her thoughts and pull everything together. Stepping into the bedroom, I close the door behind me and pull out my phone to text Lucca.

Me: I need everything you can find on Lev Volcove.

Lucca: Done.

Sighing, I run a hand through my hair before making a fist. Lev Volcove is a dead man walking, and he doesn't even know it yet. I don't care who his father is. What was the fucker thinking when he touched what was mine? Obviously, he wasn't thinking.

A tinge of something foreign and unusual fills my chest. It's an emotion I haven't felt since I was a child. I recognize the feeling like a thorn in my side. *Guilt.* For taking my eyes off her alone at that bar, for letting this happen. I'm not sure how to digest what I'm feeling, so I decide not to touch it at all.

Giving Elena a little longer in the bathroom, I take off my suit jacket and toss it on the chaise lounge. My shoes go next, and I start to unbutton my shirt, feeling better with each piece of constricting clothing I lose. Down to my dress slacks, and my button up shirt, I feel like I can breathe again.

I wait a few more moments before I enter the bathroom and find Elena completely naked, climbing into the tub. The dress she was wearing is on the floor next to the toilet. Picking up the scrap of fabric, I throw it into the trash can next to the sink.

When I turn back to face her, she is just sinking down into the water. I've seen her naked a few times now, but it never gets easier. All I want to do is rip my own clothes off and mount her like a wild animal. Bite her skin and watch her writhe beneath me. The ache in my balls is permanent, and a constant reminder of what I refuse myself daily.

I haven't been able to have sex with anyone else, mainly because every time I tried, Elena's picture popped into my fucking head. She's messing with my mind and my cock. It only wants her, and no one else.

"You did good at the event, and I'm proud of you. I want to reward you. Playing your part wasn't easy, and seeing your father wasn't easy either, I'm sure."

She nods, but there is a hesitant look in her green eyes.

"What is my reward?"

"You'll see when you get out."

I help her wash and rinse her hair, and she uses a washcloth to get her makeup off. Once she is clean from head to toe, I lift her out of the tub and get her dried off. I leave the wet towels in a pile on the floor and lead Elena back into the bedroom.

"Don't put a nightgown on yet. Lie down on the bed, face down."

Elena stops and looks up at me, shock written all over her face, but thankfully, no fear.

"Why?"

"Don't worry. I told you this was a reward. You will like this. Trust me." I motion for her to get on the bed, and she does, even though her movements are hesitant.

I grab the massage oil from the drawer in my nightstand and pour a generous amount into my palm. Her head turns toward me, and she watches what I'm doing with peaked interest. When I come back around to her side of the bed, her head turns again.

Her watchful eyes never leave me, and now curiosity has turned to excitement.

Sitting down on the bed next to her, I rub my hands together to warm up the oil before planting my palms on her back. As soon as I start massaging her shoulders, she lets out a quiet, breathy moan. A sound that somehow has a direct line to my dick. *Fuck.* I must enjoy torturing myself.

Her muscles are stiff, her body tense, but the more I work my fingers into her flesh, the more she relaxes, sinking deeper into the mattress.

"I told you, you were gonna like this."

"It feels really good," she murmurs, turning to putty in my hands.

When her upper body is thoroughly massaged, I move lower to her legs, running my hands over her naked ass as I go. I expect her to tense back up, maybe even squeeze her ass cheeks together, but instead, she moans into the pillow. So trusting, if only she knew the things my hands had done. The death that coated them. Would she still want them on her?

Arching her back, she pushes her perfect globes into my palms. She probably doesn't even realize the invitation she is sending my way, which makes me want her all the more.

"I guess you want a *full body* massage?"

"Mmhh..."

"Is that a yes?" I ask, massaging the insides of her thighs. Her sweet little pussy grinds against the mattress, seeking relief that it doesn't understand, that only I can give it.

"Yes, don't stop," she pleads, jerking her hips as I move closer to her center. The bedsheet is damp beneath her, and her sweet arousal coats the insides of her thighs, dripping like honey from her pussy.

I lick my lips. I want a taste, a bite. I want to devour, to feel her pulse around my tongue. Going down on women has never appealed to me, but I want Elena so bad I can feel it in my fucking bones, feel it in every thud of my heartbeat.

I can't claim her with my cock yet, but I can claim her with my mouth. Using finesse, I grab her by the leg and roll her onto her back.

A shocked gasp slips past her lips, and her green eyes meet mine, a bashful look overtaking her features. I drink her in, her perky breasts, which rise and fall, the hardened dusky pink nipples begging to be sucked and pinched.

"Do you want me to keep going?" I ask gruffly.

The air between us grows heated, and I can feel the electrical current zinging through me. We're two magnets of opposite attraction. We shouldn't want each other, but there isn't any other way. In every way, she is mine.

"Yes," she replies with far more trust in her eyes than she should have. I'd warned her before, told her if she gave me each an inch, I would take everything. Doesn't she know the devil is standing before her or is she no longer afraid?

Moving between her legs, I brush a gentle hand against her knee, pushing her legs up and apart. I can't help myself, the beast inside me has been chained for far too long. My gaze drops to her mound, and my mouth starts to water.

Her pussy lips are mainly bare, except for a small strip of hair in the center. I don't think as I move a hand between her legs and spread her folds, finding the diamond in the center. Her tiny clit begs to be sucked, flicked, and tortured just as it's torturing me.

"What are you doing?" Elena questions breathlessly. Looking up at her from between her legs, I find that she's pushed herself up onto her elbows and is watching me, her eyes big, curious, and dilated. She wants this, and she wants it just as badly as me.

"Eating you. I'm going to fuck you with my tongue like I want to fuck you with my dick," I say, and then bury my face in her pussy.

I lick that tiny bead, flicking my tongue over it, again and again, sucking up every drop of arousal until Elena starts to lift her hips, and her hands sink into my hair, holding me in place, her nails cutting into my scalp, egging me on.

Her muscles clench, and her legs shake, but if she thinks I'm done with her yet, she is very mistaken. I haven't even started.

"Julian," she moans my name, and I swear cum leaks from the tip of my cock and into my boxers. Fuck, it would be so fucking easy to shove my pants down and fuck her right now.

To take her and bring her to the brink of both pleasure and pain. I want it so bad, to lose myself in her soft flesh, to fuck and own her.

Digging my finger into her ass cheeks, I lift her, dragging her closer and plunge my tongue into her dripping entrance. She bucks beneath me like an untamed horse, and I can't wait to learn her body, learn what makes her go crazy.

Groaning into her flesh, the sound vibrates through the room. I dip in and out of her, feasting on her, marveling in her sweet, honeyed taste. There was simply nothing like her, and that was a startling reality that hit me right in the gut.

"Oh god... oh god..." Smirking against her wet flesh, I reveled in how vocal she is, and I want to make her scream from the rooftops with pleasure.

Growling once more, I move faster, my touch becoming bruising, but Elena doesn't seem to care, she is teetering on the edge of complete bliss, and I'm going to deliver the final blow.

Throwing her head back into the pillows, her nails rake through my hair once more, "Please, don't stop..."

Little did she know, I could never do such a thing. Nothing was going to take her away from me. I would burn the world down, kill, and destroy anyone who dared to touch her. Releasing one of her ass cheeks, I use two fingers to pinch her tiny clit, and a second later, she falls apart.

Like cloth being ripped at the seams, she tears right down the middle while coming all over my face, her pussy fluttering around my tongue, my cock beyond envious of the fucker.

I stay between her legs, licking every drop of her release up before pulling away. My balls ache, and my cock is so stiff, I'm not sure I'm going to be able to walk, but I'll take care of myself in the shower.

Sitting up, I stare down at Elena, who's biting her lip, her cheeks crimson. How could she be so shy now when I was just between her legs, devouring her?

Moving to sit up, she asks, "Do I..." her delicate finger points at the prominent tent that I'm sporting between my legs.

"No. Tonight was about you. About showing you that you can trust me, about how much I appreciate what you did."

She nods as if she understands and drops her hand but keeps staring at my cock with big curious eyes.

"On top of this, I'll allow you to choose whatever books you want, and give you some time outside by the pool."

Her eyes widened, and she seemed shocked, which I don't understand. Had she not truly expected me to keep my word? "Really? I get to go outside?"

I nod, and she shivers, reminding me that she is completely naked. Grabbing the blanket, I gently tug it up and over her body, watching her silky-smooth flesh disappears beneath it. I want her so badly, I wanted to take, and take, but her trust was important to me, her wanting me, needing me. I need her to rely on me, and she is almost there. Soon she would be my wife and have no true way of escape unless in death, and I would never allow that to happen.

"I'm going to take a shower," I say and push off the bed.

Space will make this better for me as with my hand wrapped around the heavy organ between my legs. Just a little while longer, and my plan will be complete. The only problem now is will everything I worked toward, built up to, come crashing down once Elena finds out that this was nothing more than revenge?

Will she still want my touch so willingly? Will she still seek out my warmth? She'll always be my wife, but will she enjoy it... be happy? I don't know the answers to those questions, and for the first time in my life, I consider doing something different.

The image of my mother's lifeless body fills my mind, the vacant look in her eyes. He took the only good thing I ever had from me, and so I took her. There is no changing something that was fated. I cannot let her get under my skin. I cannot allow myself to care for her any more than I do because if I do, all will be ruined.

She is a weakness I cannot afford.

21

ELENA

The days pass, and we fall into a new kind of routine. Julian has breakfast and dinner with me every day, he even lets me pick where. Most of the time, I choose the terrace, of course, because the outdoors calls to me.

For lunch, Marie comes and eats with me. Sometimes she stays for over an hour, and we just talk. Julian also lets me pick more books from the library and orders more online from my favorite authors. I have so many that I'm now reading a different romance novel every day. I tried to convince him to let me have an e-reader, but he didn't go for it.

It's a nice distraction from the memories that haunt me from the night of the auction. I don't know what was worse, helplessly watching those girls being sold, seeing my father trying to bargain to buy me back, or having that vile man talk to me and touch me.

I've been trying to forget that whole night, hide from those thoughts the same way I hid the key my father gave me under the bathroom sink. I seriously don't know what to do. I just can't believe that Julian is trying to kill my father, even more unbelievable is him trying to kill me.

He has been kind to me, gentle even. He's never lied to me, at least not that I know of. Every time he gave me his word, he stuck to it. It proved to me further what I already knew, that deep down parts of him are still good.

It's almost lunchtime when I finish the book I started yesterday. Just as I flip to the last page, I hear someone approach the door. A moment later, the lock disengages, and the door opens.

I'm about to greet Marie, but instead, I find Julian stepping into the room. My heart constricts in my chest. He's wearing nothing but dress slacks and a white button-down, the sleeves rolled up, showing off his forearms. My mouth waters, and I clench my thighs together, remembering the things he did to me with his mouth, wondering what other magic he can do.

As if he knows what I'm thinking, his stormy blues narrow.

"Hi!" I squeak.

"You look surprised to see me."

"Because I am. Are you not working?"

"I took the rest of the day off. I want to have lunch with you by the pool, maybe go for a swim before?"

"Really?" I jump off the bed, and without waiting for his answer, I run into the closet. "Do I have a bathing suit?" I yell from inside.

"Yes, probably the bottom drawer, that's where she put my swimming trunks," Julian explains as he leisurely leans against the door frame.

I pull open the last drawer and find there is indeed, a stack of different bathing suits and bikinis. I pull the one on top out, not bothering to waste precious time, I get undressed as quickly as I can, then pull on the bathing suit.

Julian gets undressed as well, not in quite as much of a hurry as I am. I go to his side of the closet and take out a pair of swimming trunks. When he is completely naked, I hand them to him, trying to not stare at his semi-hard penis hanging between his legs.

"Ready?" He smirks after pulling on his shorts. Clearly, he saw me looking. My cheeks feel like they're on fire as I nod my head, yes.

Together we leave the bedroom, and Julian lets me walk beside him at my own pace, rather than tugging me along behind him. I smile, enjoying the new freedom, the words from the bathroom and the key I have stashed, hang heavy in my mind.

If I try and escape, all of this will go away. His kindness, my freedom...

"Is everything okay? You're very quiet," he questions, giving me a guarded look as we walk down the stairs.

"Yes, just thinking how nice this is. Being able to walk on my own and getting to go outside." I beam joyfully. "I love swimming, but my father wouldn't allow it often."

At the mention of my father, Julian's eyes darken, and his lips turn into a frown. Not wanting to ruin this day, I quickly change the subject. "Can I ask you something... about the auction?"

"You can, I can't promise I'll answer though."

"The girls that were sold, what happened to them? They didn't look like they were there out of their own free will."

"I'm sure they weren't. Women hardly ever sell themselves willingly, though I have seen it happen. Desperate times and all. As to what happened to them exactly, I can't tell you. Whoever bought them gets to decide that."

"Have you ever bought a girl?" I ask but look down, too afraid to see the look on his face.

"You know I have." He chuckles. "You."

"Oh, I mean–"

"No, not like that. I only bought you, and I'm not planning on buying someone else if you're worried about that. Markus has got that handled."

"Markus?" I remember him and Julian talking at the auction, their exchange was heated when I interrupted them.

"Yes, he bought one of the girls."

"Wow…" I quickly run every interaction I've had with Markus through my head, which is not a lot to go by. I can't tell if he is the kind of guy who hurts women. "Can I meet her?"

"No. They aren't here, and even if they were, I'm not sure I would allow the girl on the property. Most of the girls sold are…" He pauses, contemplating his words. "Broken, you could say, and who knows her mental state? I won't have some crazed girl running around here."

Frowning, I nod. "Will she be okay?" I ask as we reach the terrace. The sun is hanging high in the sky, and I love the feel of it on my skin. It's like a toasty blanket wrapping around me.

Julian shrugs. "I don't know. Markus is one of my best men. I trust him with my life, and with you, but I don't know his dealings with women, so I can't tell you. The girl should be grateful though, there are worse people that could've bought her."

He's not lying. After the auction, I realized that I could've ended up in the hands of someone far worse than Julian. Thus far has been okay, but we aren't married yet, and I'm still not sure if what my father said was true. I want to ask him, but I can't do that without giving away the key I stashed.

"It would be nice to have a friend," I say. There is a pitcher of lemonade and two glasses on the table where lunch will be served.

"Friends are overrated," he replies dryly, pouring each of us a glass of lemonade from the frosty pitcher before handing me one. "Plus, it seems like you made a friend with Marie."

Immediately, I feel bad for having said that. Holding the glass, I reply, "I do have Marie, and I love spending time with her, but she's working most of the day and is only allowed to see me during lunch. It would be nice to have another friend or at least be allowed to see Marie more."

Julian shakes his head, and a breathtaking smile overtakes his face. "So needy."

We each take a drink, and the lemonade slides down my throat, cooling my insides. Julian sets his glass on the table, and I do the same.

"Since you already pointed that out, I have another question."

"Of course, you do."

"Have you figured out who tried to kill me?"

"Unfortunately, I don't have the answer. We ran into a dead-end, but you don't have to worry. Something like that won't happen again."

"I still don't understand why someone would want me dead. I've never done anything to anyone."

"Don't worry about it," he says like it's no big deal at all. "Come, I want to show you the pool." He grabs my hand, and it's like I've put my fingers into an electrical outlet. Heat zings up my arm, rippling through my body, settling deep in my core. I can feel moisture build with each of my steps, memories of what he did to me the other night, how he gave me a massage, and then made me come with his tongue.

Forcing those memories out of my head, I concentrate on the here and now. Walking down the stone steps from the terrace, the pool comes into view.

"Wow, this is beautiful," I whisper in awe, drinking it all in. The space is magnificent, and the kidney-shaped pool is so clear, you can see your reflection in the water.

Turning to him, I can't help but slowly drag my gaze up to his face, my eyes lingering on his chiseled six-pack that I kinda want to touch.

"Have you gone swimming a lot?"

"Not enough, not worth the cost of the house, that's for sure." Another smile that steals the air from my lungs appears, and I need to get into the water to cool off because something is happening to me. I don't feel like myself.

"Do you think the water is cold?" I ask, moving to sit at the edge of the pool, so I can dangle my feet in the water first.

"No, the pool is heated."

Of course, it's heated.

Tipping my toes into the water, I almost sigh at the perfect temperature. It's not too cold or too warm, simply perfect. Feeling Julian's gaze on me, I peer over my shoulder, shielding my eyes from the sun, so I can look up at him.

"Put your feet in. The water feels amazing."

Julian stares at me like a puzzle he can't find the missing piece to. Then he surprises the hell out of me by jumping into the water, making a huge splash in the process. Water flies everywhere, and I choose then to dip fully into the pool. Sliding off the edge, I sink into the water, shivering only slightly, the lower I submerge myself, the more weightless I feel.

The pool is much deeper than I anticipated, and my fingers grip onto the edge of the pool to stay afloat. When Julian's head pops up from out of the water, I can't help but stare at him, mesmerized by how he looks in this moment.

His hair seems black now that it's wet. Droplets of water run down his perfectly-shaped face, and I have the urge to trace the tracks of those drops, to run my fingers along his cheek and down his jawline. He's like a painting I want to bring to life. Shaking his head, he pelts me with water droplets, and I use my hand to shield my eyes, so I don't get any water in them.

"Stop looking at me like that and come swim."

"Um, I'd rather stay here on the side of the pool. I'm not a great swimmer," I admit.

Puzzled, he asks, "You can't swim?"

"I can, just not well. Like I said, I wasn't allowed to swim often."

"Come on then. Let me see. I won't let you drown."

"You sure?" I tease, while genuinely wondering if he would.

Cocking his head to the side, he studies me, kinda like I was studying him earlier but in a less sexual way.

"Do you trust me?" he asks, swimming closer, looking more and more like a shark.

I think for a moment before answering, my tongue becoming heavy. "Yes."

"You hesitated."

"Can you blame me? It would be very easy to make it look like a drowning, wouldn't it?"

Julian's features become icy as he treads water two feet in front of me. "Spoiler alert, if I wanted you dead, sweetheart, you'd already be dead."

"Okay, but I still don't want to drown."

"Nothing's going to happen to you," he says, and then I feel his rough hands on my bare hips, dragging me toward him. "Let go of the side of the pool and trust me." Looking over my shoulder, I eye my hand, which is slowly slipping from the edge of the pool. *Trust or not trust?* Warm breath fans against my cheek and ear. "Trust me like you did the other night when you let me eat your pussy."

At his crude words, I squirm in the water, feeling them pulse in my center. How does he do that? How can he get me aroused with nothing more than his words?

I push off the side and start kicking my legs out. Using my arms, I push at the water, keeping myself afloat, but barely. I'm sure I look pretty ridiculous right now.

Julian doesn't seem to care though and tugs me closer, lifting me, so I'm not chin-deep in the water. His face is inches from mine, the water beading against his skin, teasing me. Making me want to lick them away. Something about him makes my blood turn to molten lava.

I want him, need him, and that terrifies me so much because the last time I allowed myself to love a man, he sold me for ten million dollars.

22

JULIAN

Her pink tongue darts out over her bottom lip, and I'm tempted to kiss her, to bite that plump flesh. Her eyes are shiny, iridescent, and I know if I stare for too long, I'll get sucked right into their depths.

"What did you think of me the first time you saw me?" I don't know why I ask this question, but I have often wondered the answer. Maybe because seeing her for the first time was such a profound moment for me. It changed the course of my future. In an instant, I knew what I had to do.

"Honestly, I didn't think much when I saw you at my mother's funeral. I don't even remember much from that time, but I do remember you being there. I thought you looked dangerous, but so did all the other men there. Your eyes stood out to me, though. I felt like you could see right through me. I still think you can." Her eyes hold mine, and right in this second, it's like the world around us melts away. It's just us, floating in a pool, no worries, no revenge, no mafia.

"What about you?"

"I knew I had to have you. The very first moment I saw you, I knew." It's not a lie, but I will leave the other part out for now. The part where I wanted nothing from her than to use her for my revenge. Soon she'll discover that all of this was nothing, a facade, and by then, she'll be trapped, married, and bound by a vow and blood. Just like the mafia, there is no out in marriage, there is only death.

I want to ask her what she thought of me the second time she saw me, the time I stole her away from her father and everything she ever knew, but I already know the answer to that. I know she hated me and feared me in equal parts.

She hasn't looked like that at me in a while. Her fear and hatred have turned into trust and calmness. It's what I expected, what I had hoped for, but what I didn't see coming is how much I would enjoy it.

I can't help but wonder if I could somehow have both. Could I get my revenge on her father without breaking her trust, without breaking that fragile bond that has formed between us? The fact that I will eventually kill her father tells me, no, but maybe if she was in love with me, if I turned her against her father completely? I could keep *this,* whatever it is going on between us.

We've floated to the center of the pool. Elena uses me as a life preserver, her fingers wrapped around my biceps. Her eyes dart down into the water, and when she looks up, I see panic at the edges of her eyes.

"If I drown, I will come back as a ghost and haunt you." She smiles nervously.

"Haunt me, huh?" I cock a brow and start to pull away a little. "You have to have more faith in yourself. After all, you're going to be a Moretti, and we never fail at anything we put our minds to."

Her nails rake across my skin as she tries to grasp onto me, but I slip away. She moves her legs a little faster, treading water so she can stay afloat. I would never let her drown, but I want her to trust herself, trust that she can do this.

"I'm not a good swimmer, Julian." She blinks slowly, and I can see the panic inside of her rising up, filling her delicate features with chaos.

"Calm down, focus on your movements, and breathe slowly," I tell her, but her movements become jerky, and soon she starts to sink into the water like a stone, her panicked emeralds finding mine.

Unable to bear watching her another second, I wrap my arms around her waist. I hold her to my chest and guide us back to the edge of the pool.

She clings to me, and it's impossibly fucking hard not to notice her perky breasts plastered to my chest. My reaction to her is instant, and my cock swells in my swim trunks. Ignoring the stiffening rod, I release her, and she clutches onto the side of the pool with trembling hands.

"Are you ready to get out and have lunch?"

"Yes," she murmurs.

A soft little gasp passes her lips when I grab her by the hips and lift her out of the pool, the sound going straight to my cock.

By the time I'm out of the water, Elena is standing, her arms wrapped around her chest. Snagging a towel off one of the sun chairs, I wrap it around her.

"Thank you," she whispers.

Dragging the towel over my face, chest, and arms, I shake my head before tossing it back onto the chair. Turning, I grab Elena's hand to walk us back up to the house but stop in my tracks when I find Lucca standing near the French doors.

His eyes meet mine, and I grit my teeth. He knows I don't talk business in front of Elena, and that's exactly why he's here. I didn't want to have to deal with anything today. As we get closer, he gives me a nod. I release Elena's hand and pull out a chair for her.

She looks between Lucca and me as if she can feel the tension in the air before sitting down.

"I need a word with you, boss." Lucca clears his throat, averting his gaze away from my soon to be wife.

I should've known letting Markus go on *vacation* was a stupid idea. Killing Lev is going to come with a blowback that I'm not sure Lucca is ready to deal with.

Leaning down, I whisper into Elena's ear. "I'll be back in a min."

She nods, and I walk over to Lucca, clamping a hand on his shoulder and guiding him away from Elena and back into the house. We don't stop walking until we're at the end of the terrace, where I know she can't hear, but I can still see her.

Curling my lip, I direct my attention to Lucca. "What is it?"

"You didn't answer your phone."

"I'm fucking busy, and I told you that I was taking the rest of the day off."

Lucca doesn't flinch at my harsh tone. He's been conditioned for violence, pain, for a world that most wouldn't survive in.

"I know, and I apologize, but you'd kick my ass if I didn't tell you that I got word on Lev. He took the bait for the girl and arranged for the services to be completed tonight. He'll be at the hotel at nine o'clock. It's tonight, or we have to wait and set something up."

I wasn't a patient man, and even more impatient when I wanted to spill blood. I wouldn't let Lev slip through my fingers. I couldn't.

"Fuck."

I really didn't want to ruin this evening with Elena, but I didn't have an option. Lev was going to die for fucking with what was mine.

"I'll be ready, good work."

"Of course, sir." Lucca nods.

Dismissing him, I took a moment to gather my own thoughts while leaning against the railing. Killing Lev may cause problems, but it was going to prove a point as well. Word would spread through the mob families that I had killed someone for touching what was mine.

It would bring good and bad with it. Some would fear me further, and others would see Elena as my one true weakness. On top of that, I'm not sure how Lev is with his father, who might retaliate.

Deep down, it would be worth it. Where Elena was concerned, it was always worth it. She was opening my eyes to things. Before her, I saw everything in black and white, and though parts of my life would always be seen that way, the parts with her in it were slowly becoming colored.

Walking back to the table, I find Elena sipping her lemonade. She smiles when she sees me and shifts in her seat.

"Are you cold? We can go inside and eat?"

"No, no. I want to eat outside."

Grabbing her plate, I take the top off the trays and find little sandwiches, bowls of fruit, crackers and cheese, and vegetables with dip. I fill Elena's plate and give it back to her, trying not to let the information I just discovered cloud this time with her.

"Is everything okay?" she asks, popping a grape into her mouth.

"Everything is fine," I reply a little gruffer than I intended to.

Elena flinches at my tone, and I take a gulp of lemonade to stop myself from apologizing. We eat mostly in silence, and when it looks like Elena can't eat another morsel of food, I get up from my seat and offer her my hand.

I don't have much more time to spend with her before I leave, so I'll make up for my sour mood with something more.

Guiding us up the stairs, Elena digs her heels into the floor when we reach the top step. It's obvious she doesn't want to go back into the bedroom, and I can't really blame her, but we're not married yet, and I don't quite trust her to stay put.

"What other rooms are on this floor?" she asks, peering up at me curiously.

"Most are guest bedrooms. There is a bathroom, the library which you already know about, and my office."

Her eyes light up when I say *my office*.

"Can I see it? Your office?"

"I guess, but it's nothing special."

Her curiosity is almost laughable. I've never met someone who asks so many questions. Normally, I would be annoyed, but with her, it's refreshing.

Walking a few more feet down the hall, I stop at the door to my office, retrieve a key from my pocket, and unlock it. The door creaks as I push it open, and Elena releases my hand, walking inside all on her own.

A smile curves at her lips, and her bare feet slap against the tile. Her fingers run along the edge of my desk, and over the armchair, Markus usually lounges in.

"This is where you are when you're working?"

"As of lately, yes, but sometimes I have to go places, and handle business." And by handle business, I mean murder and hurt people.

She nods, and her eyes fall onto the huge window overlooking the front yard. Walking into the room, I come to stand beside her.

"This is the best view in the entire house," she says.

"I thought you loved the terrace the most?" I poke fun at her.

"I do, maybe someday, you'll let me walk the entire estate."

"Maybe, but it won't be without me by your side."

I let her stare out the window a little while longer, and then we leave the room. I lock the door behind me and pocket the key.

"Why do you lock the door if it's just an office?"

"Because I trust no one."

Back in the bedroom, Elena's mood seems to change. She becomes shy, and I'm puzzled by the sudden change in her demeanor. *Was it something I said?* Tugging at the string on her bikini, she saunters toward me, her shapely hips swaying with the movement.

The fabric slides down her chest, leaving her perky breasts on display. A growl builds in my throat, and I clench my hands into fists to stop myself from dragging her panties down her legs and fucking her senseless.

White teeth sink into her bottom lip, and fuck, she looks hot and naive, and so fucking sweet. I want to dirty her up, crack her open, and see what makes her tick.

Her damp, dark locks cascade down her back in soft ringlets, her smooth skin is creamy and begging to be licked. She's a damn goddess, a queen.

"I want you." She bats her eyes softly.

"Is that right?"

She nods. "Yes. I want..." Her fingers slide into the bottoms of her bathing suit, and I swallow my tongue. There isn't any way in hell, she is asking me what I think she is. The bottoms hit the floor, and though there is no sound, the mere action is like a bomb being dropped on top of me.

"I want to have sex."

Shoving from my seated position, I feel the need to get up and move because if I don't, I won't hesitate to take her up on her offer.

"Why wait until after the wedding, I mean… I don't care if you don't care. We've already done… *stuff*."

She's looking at me like I'm her world, and it's exactly what I've wanted to see, hoped to see even, and the fact that I'm going to have to wipe that look from her face angers me. There is no way I can give her what she needs right now.

"I don't have time for this, and I don't have the patience either, not today. I have somewhere else to be."

Why the hell does she have this thought today of all fucking days? I would have gladly done this yesterday, and I would definitely do it tomorrow, but not tonight. My need to kill Lev outweighs my need for sex, even if it's sex with her.

I glance at her face, disappointment, and rejection seeping into each pore. I can't take seeing her like this, it guts me. She is hurt, I hurt her.

Quickly, I disappear into the closet and pull on some dry clothes. I need to leave, get out of here fast before I change my mind.

Without another word or a second glance, I walk through the bedroom and out the door, locking it behind me.

∽

WITH MY GUN in one hand and the key card in the other, I stand in front of the hotel room Lev is in. His slimy voice clearly carries through the thin door, and the blood in my veins reaches a new boiling point. All I can see is Elena's tear-stained cheeks and the fear in her eyes. He hurt her, and now I'm here to hurt him.

I slide the card, push the door open, and step in with my gun raised all in one fluid move. Lev turns to me, looking shocked as hell while the girl we hired looks relieved to see me.

"This is a mistake, Moretti. You're making a mistake."

"You can go now, Lola." At my words, Lev turns pale, his beady eyes go wide, and I know he's quickly putting one and one together.

"Thank fuck, this guy is a real creep." The girl snatches her purse and climbs over the bed instead of walking by Lev to get out. She squeezes past me and scurries out of the room, closing the door on her way.

Alone at last.

"You gotta be kidding me?"

"Funny, that's what I thought when I heard that you touched something that belongs to me. I know you're stupid, but I didn't know you were this dumb."

Lev tips his head back and laughs into the quiet room.

"So, let me get this right. You left a half-naked girl sitting at a bar at a flesh auction, and it's my fucking fault that she was eye-fucking me? It's not my fault your whore can't keep her hands off of me. That she wanted my cock."

Aiming the gun at his kneecap, I pull the trigger. The faint smell of gunpowder wafts into my nose as the bullet flies through the air and hits its target precisely where I intended. A scream that is pure bliss to my ears rips from Lev's throat as he immediately sags to the floor and cries out in pain, grabbing his leg.

"You fucking asshole!" he groans while rolling to his side. "You're gonna die, you bastard! You're gonna die! Everyone is after you anyway!"

What just said makes me pause, but only briefly.

"Who is after me?"

He curls his lip, giving me a half-smile. "Everyone! Romero put out a hit on your ass. Ten million. And to sweeten the pot, he's giving away the whore with it. Hope you didn't use her up, 'cause I'm sure looking forward to–"

I don't blink. I don't even think. Lifting my gun, my finger presses against the trigger, and the bullet leaves the chamber, hitting him right between the eyes, shutting him up for good.

His body stills, his eyes go blank, and blood puddles around his head. I meant to make this painful, draw it out, and watch him suffer, but what he revealed to me changes things.

It means the timeline just got moved up.

23

ELENA

The key seems to weigh ten pounds in my hand. I've been pacing the bedroom for hours trying to decide what to do. I thought Julian and I were getting closer, I thought there could really be something between us, but after today, I'm not sure about anything.

Nothing makes sense. None of his actions line up. He buys me, he touches me, then rejects me in the next instance. Something more is going on, and I can't be stuck in this room any longer doing nothing. What if my father was telling the truth? Julian could be out there killing my father, and then come home to finish the job.

Or maybe Julian simply doesn't want to have sex with me. He mentioned before that he doesn't think I can handle him, handle his sinister needs. What if he went to have sex with someone who can?

Both theories have me in knots. Every thought is worse than the next, and I don't want to believe either theory is true, but what am I supposed to think? Is there even a third option, and would that one be any better? I wish I could call my father. I think if I could talk to him freely, he would tell me the truth, tell me what is really going on. Julian won't allow that, and even if by a miracle, he would agree, it would be under supervision, and my father would never tell me what I want to know with Julian hovering over me.

Then a thought occurs to me. Maybe I could sneak out and find a phone. I think there's one in the kitchen. I saw one of the maids talking on the phone before, and it looked to be a landline. I mean there has to be a phone in this house somewhere.

Looking out the window, I see the orange bursts of light on the horizon.

It's now or never.

Running into the closet, I find a pair of sneakers and slip into them. My heart is racing as I cross the bedroom and stop in front of the door. Bringing the key to the lock, I briefly wonder if it will even work? I still don't understand how my father could have gotten ahold of this.

All my doubt dissipates when the key slides into the lock with ease. I turn it and listen to the lock disengage. My lungs burn as I hold my breath. Twisting the brass knob, I slowly pull the door open. There is a small squeaking sound, but in the early morning hours and the quiet hallway, it seems extremely loud.

This feels like a dream. Like at any second, I'm going to be shaken awake and find that I was only hoping the key had worked, and that I was free of the bedroom.

Sticking my head out the door, I peek into the hallway to make sure no one is coming from either side. I wait for a few more moments, using the time to gather up all my courage. When there is still nothing but silence, I step out and pull the door closed behind me.

On tippy-toes, I move through the semi-dark hallways. The house is huge, but I've paid enough attention to know my way around by now.

I make it into the kitchen without hearing or seeing anything, which makes me wonder if I could be truly alone. Like a needle popping a balloon, that thought bursts from my head when I hear two male voices carry through the house.

Panic claws at me, threatening to petrify my limbs, but I force them to move. Pushing past the fear, I do my best to keep my breathing even and hide behind the kitchen's butcher's block... how fitting since that's where I'm going to be if they catch me.

For the first time tonight, I'm thinking about the repercussions I could face. What will happen if I'm caught, and why the hell didn't I think this through? Will Julian hurt me? He hasn't, but I've also been listening to him. He threatens me repeatedly but says as long as I obey, I won't be harmed.

As the voices come closer, my fear rises exponentially. Curling myself up into a ball, I wish the ground would swallow me. With each passing second, the men grow closer, until they are close enough for me to make out what they are saying.

"I wonder why the boss moved the timeline up?"

"I guess he can't wait to see the Romero family dead and gone."

No! It can't be. My heart stills within my chest, and the beating is replaced by a deep ache. Closing my eyes, I will the tears away, wishing I would have just stayed in the room. Ignorance is bliss, I suppose. I don't know why I thought things were different. Maybe because of how caring he's been? I think back to the way he cared for me after the auction and gave me a chance to spend time outside.

I listen to the men's footsteps as they pass the kitchen and continue walking down the hall, in the direction that I just came.

When everything is quiet once more, and I'm sure they are gone, I pop up and out of my hiding spot, surveying the area. The kitchen is clean, immaculate even, and worst of all, I don't see a phone.

Shit.

Now, more than ever, I need to speak to my father. I need to warn him, and if I can't call him, that means I have to get out of here to warn him.

Rushing over to the terrace door, I unlock it and slide it open just enough for my body to squeeze through. Crisp morning air fills my lungs, and for a split second, I actually feel free.

"Going somewhere?" Julian's sinister voice meets my ears. His tone dark and restrained, promising a world of hurt. A hand wraps around my heart. Squeezing my eyes shut, I curse myself for being so stupid for thinking I could actually get away.

Slowly, I turn to face him. The devil, that's what he looks like. Seconds away from pulling the rug right out from under my feet. I have to think... I have to. Swallowing thickly, an apology sits heavily on my tongue, but I can't suck in enough air to form the words.

"You look like you're scared that I'm gonna kill you now."

Isn't he? Isn't this the whole point? My family dead, including me. There's a giant lump in my throat that won't let a single word pass, but apparently, my legs are still working because in the next moment, my fight or flight response kick in. My subconscious chooses flight, and before I can stop myself, I'm on the run.

Pushing my legs as fast as I can, I dash past him and across the terrace. Hoping that my shorter legs are at least faster than Julian's, I run down the marble stairs, which are wet with morning dew. When there are only three steps left, I jump over them, my heels sinking into the soft grass before I take off on another sprint.

I think maybe I have a chance, but I don't. Not against Julian. I make it about five more feet before his chest bumps into my back, his thick arms circling around me. One moment I'm running, and the next, I'm in the air, headed straight for the ground.

Somehow, he manages to turn us both mid-fall, so I land on top of him instead of the other way around, but the impact alone knocks the air from my lungs.

By the time I'm able to suck a breath into my lungs again, I'm pulled off the ground like a doll and thrown over Julian's shoulder.

"You really shouldn't have done that," he growls as he trudges through the grass and back to the house. I don't even fight him, there is no hope, no point.

Burying my fingers into the back of his shirt, I grip the fabric like it's a life raft, hoping that whatever he has planned for me is going to be quick and painless.

Ha, wishful thinking.

Julian doesn't stop or even talk as he walks through the house, and I think that's the scariest part of all. His silence. It's the calm before the storm because I know what happens next.

He punishes me, or maybe even kills me?

Reaching the bedroom door, I feel myself start to shake. He pushes the door open with his foot and strides into the room, depositing me on the mattress. As soon as my back hits the sheets, I scurry backward.

Julian isn't having it though and grabs me by the ankle, tugging me back to him. I kick and lash out the best I can, but I'm easily subdued by his strength.

Leaning into my face, I can see the betrayal in his eyes. The dark, bleak orbs burn with barely restrained rage.

"Did you really think you could make it off this property without me finding you? Huh? How did you get out of the room? Who helped you? Marie? Did she give you a key?"

Immediately, a different kind of fear fills me. If he hurts her, I don't know what I'll do.

"What? No! No, Marie did nothing, I swear!"

"Who then?"

"My father. He sent a woman to the bathroom at the auction. She gave me a key, I put it in my bra and hid it..."

His stormy blue eyes hold mine, a thousand emotions swirling deep in their depths.

"Why... Why would you try and escape? To go back to him, a man that sold you to me?" His legs hold me in place, and his fingers dig into my arms with bruising force. He looks like he is teetering on the edge of insanity, ready to nosedive into unknown waters. I don't want to know what he has planned for me, but at that moment, I can't think rationally.

Anger and sadness blend together, becoming one, and I snap. "You made him! You forced him to sell me! And what's it matter? Why would I want to stay here with you? How are you any better?"

"You're so naïve—such a stupid girl. Your father doesn't care what happens to you. He would sell you to anyone, the highest bidder, no matter how cruel they were to you."

"You're lying! My father loves me. He wants me back! He said so himself."

"Your father doesn't want you back. He put a hit out on me, promising ten million and *you* as a prize to whoever kills me first. He doesn't care where you are or what happens to you as long as you are not with me."

Shaking my head, I squeeze my eyes shut and try to make sense of what he is telling me, but it doesn't add up. "Why? Nothing you say makes sense."

"He doesn't want me to have you out of spite, he hates me, that's all."

"Is that why you want to kill us? You hate each other so much that death is the only answer?"

"Oh, sweet Elena. Who said I want *you* dead? I have much better plans for you. I only care about killing your father, but not before I make him watch us get married, making you mine completely. He can't stand seeing me with you, not because he loves you, but because I took something from him. I took you, and now you are mine, and I think it's about time you get that into your head."

He moves off me, but retains his hold, pressing me deeper into the mattress. His hands work fast as he undresses me, ripping off my shirt and bra with one hand while holding me down with the other. I can feel the fabric giving away, the cool air against my skin, and for a moment, I'm frozen, then like someone snapped their fingers in front of my face, the cold releases its grip on me. My heart thunders in my chest, each beat rattling me to the core.

"What are you doing?" I croak, fear consuming me.

"You wanted me to fuck you a few hours ago, right? Or was that all a show? Did you think sex would throw me off? Did you think you could use it against me?" He studies me for a moment and continues, "I'm just giving you what you asked for."

"Not like this," I whimper, struggling against his grasps, which becomes tighter the more I thrash around.

"Too bad, you lost my mercy, and my patience when you betrayed me."

"I'm sorry," I sob, shoving at his chest, but he's like trying to move a mountain, and I just don't have the strength in me. Even with me struggling, he still manages to pull my jeans down with ease and rips off my panties like they are made out of paper.

Looking down at my now naked body, he smiles. The look in his eyes chills me to the bone, and I know whatever happens next will change us forever.

"You're not sorry, but you will be by the end of the night."

Fury burns through me with the heat of a thousand suns. "I hate you! I hate you so much! I knew you would do this. I knew you would hurt me, no matter what."

"I haven't hurt you yet, have I? I wasn't going to hurt you at all–"

"Bullshit!" I scream. "You were always going to hurt me. You were just waiting for the right time. Waiting for me to *disobey* like I'm a fucking dog! You lock me in a cage, treat me like I'm an animal, and expect me to have no will and no feelings." I curl my lip. "You are just like him. Just like the man you hate!"

In a split second, his hand is wrapped around my throat, squeezing just enough to warn me. "Don't ever fucking compare me to your father," he says, leaning in, his nose pressed against my cheek. I shouldn't continue, should bite my tongue, and shut up, but I can't. I won't. I'm tired of being treated like a doormat.

"Then don't act like him."

His features twist, and his eyes go vacant as if he's becoming someone else entirely.

"I've warned you. I've been warning you since the day you got here. You think I've been cruel to you? You haven't seen a shred of my cruelty."

He let go of me, but only long enough to flip me over onto my stomach. He shifts his weight off me but keeps a hand placed on the back of my neck, holding me in place. Items rustle together as he reaches for something in the nightstand, but I can't lift my head up enough to look at what he's grabbing.

A moment later, I feel it... the cold, unforgiving metal circling my wrist. Before I can react, it clicks into place. I pull my other wrist away, but he snatches it and slaps the handcuffs on with ease.

He moves completely off me now, but at this point, I have nowhere to go. I'm fully naked with my hands cuffed behind my back. If I wasn't helpless before, I am without a doubt now.

Grabbing my ankles, he pulls me to the edge of the bed, so I'm bent over, my legs hanging down, and my butt jutted out and exposed to him.

I hold my breath as I feel his hand running over my backside.

"Don't do this," I plead, unsure of what he even plans to do.

"There are consequences for your actions. I could hurt you in much worse ways than I'm going to." His gruff voice makes me shiver, and shock rips through me when a moment later, his palm comes down on my ass.

The slap is as painful as it is shocking, and a light sting ripples across my cheek. He repeats the action, and the air expels from my chest at the next slap, my gut clenching. Tears prick my eyes, I don't want to cry, don't want to beg him to stop because I don't want to be weak, but all he's done is spank me twice, and my ass is already burning.

At the next slap, I whimper, and even as pain radiates across my ass, a warmth forms deep in my core. It's sickening that such a heinous act is making me want him more. My treacherous body craves his touch without understanding the consequences. He will break me, rip me apart, take all the good from me, and lock me in a cage and throw away the key. He's already done so, and he'll do worse now that I tried to escape.

I can't even comprehend what happens next. My ass throbs as he gives me ten more slaps on each cheek. It's not meant to bring pleasure; this, I know. The sting and pain running along my ass intensifies further, and by the time he finishes, I'm sobbing into the mattress.

I'm frightened, my ass burning, but there is more beneath the pain, and I hate that I feel it, hate that he brings the worst out in me. I don't want him, this man that plans to kill my father and use my body for whatever he wants, but I do. I still crave him, wanting him to touch me more.

The fragile trust we formed seems to have cracked down the middle, splitting in two. I might have caused part of this, but he delivered the final blow.

Even in the wake of pain, he massages my aching flesh, and I flinch at his touch, trying to ignore the way he cares for me only after inflicting pain.

I feel him move behind me; a shiver runs through me at the thought of what's gonna happen next. His hands are on either side of my butt, kneading the tender flesh. When he pulls my cheeks apart, I gasp, ready to scream, but then I feel his warm breath fanning against my skin.

Before I can ask what the hell he is doing, I feel his hot, wet tongue on my center. I have to bite my cheek so hard I can taste blood just so I won't moan. He drags his tongue through my folds. He starts at my clit and slowly licks up, over my entrance, but he doesn't stop there. He keeps going until he is circling my other hole.

I want to object, want to tell him to stop, but the truth is, I have to force myself from pushing my ass out and into his face. How can something so wrong, so dirty, feel so good?

Shoving my face into the mattress, I pray that he doesn't hear my muffled moan when he pushes the tip of his tongue into the tight ring.

My whole body shudders, begging for release as my core reaches fever-pitch.

And then... he pulls away. Cool air rushes over my heated flesh as he gets up. His hands leave my butt and travel up and over my back until they reach my shoulders.

"This was meant to punish you."

"I hate you..." I growl into the sheets, struggling against his gentle touch. I don't want his kindness. I don't want anything but to be left alone, so I can forget how I was starting to fall for my captor when I should've been trying to run the whole time.

"Do you? Or do you hate that I'm not letting you come?"

"I just hate you!"

"Well, I can't wait to see how much you hate me after this next part." The edge to his voice terrifies me, and when he flips me over, I snarl, kicking my feet out at him to get away.

Chuckling, he easily subdues me and pulls me off the bed and pushes me down to my knees. He grabs me by the chin and forces me to look at him and nowhere else. My lashes are heavy with tears, and my cheeks cold and stained with tears.

My tears and pain don't seem to have an effect on him, though.

"I'm going to use your mouth, and you're going to let me."

Frantically, I search his face, trying to find even a sliver of emotion that I might be able to latch on to, but his mask is firm and in place. The man I've come to know—that I've peeled the layers back on is gone.

His stormy blue eyes are lifeless, his features sharper like the edge of a knife pressed against my throat, he's going to slice me open and watch the blood drain onto the floor.

Reaching for his belt, he quickly undoes it, and then his pants, shoving them down to the floor. He's completely nude beneath, and his steel-hard penis rises like a skyscraper between us. How can he be turned on after hurting me?

"Julian..." His name falls off my lips like a prayer. What I'm praying for, I don't know. More? Less? Both?

"Bite me, and I will hurt Marie." The warning is clear, blinking in bright red neon back at me. I swallow the bile and fear rising in my throat.

"Please," I whimper, my eyes dropping down to the head of his penis. It's swollen, and a bead of white liquid glistens against it. He strokes himself eagerly, and releases my chin, moving his hand into my hair.

He fists the strands, and my scalp burns as he tugs my head forward.

"Open up," he orders gruffly.

My lips tremble, but I do as he says, afraid of what may come next if I don't. Holding my head in place by my hair, he guides himself to my mouth.

His eyes are trained on my mouth, my lips, watching intently as the mushroom head disappears past my lips.

Fear and arousal mix together and spark like gasoline, meeting a match. His soft flesh glides over my tongue, and even though I shouldn't, my lips close around the head, and I suck. I'm not sure what to do. I'm simply following my gut instinct. Pleasing him isn't my priority, and yet, I want to please him so badly it's all I feel.

"Fuck," he groans and tightens his hold on my hair.

He slides forward, pushing deeper into my mouth and in seconds, he's at the back of my throat. I gag around his length, trying to squirm away, feeling as if he's going to suffocate me, but a second later, he pulls back, giving me a chance to breathe, and I gulp fresh air into my lungs.

Tears leak from my eyes, and he performs the same action again, this time a little faster than the first time.

"I'm going to fuck your throat, hard and fast," he warns, frightening me, making me shake. He pulls out briefly, giving me a chance to say something.

"I don't know if I can..." I whine, trying to shake my head, but he doesn't listen.

"You can, trust me." He pushes back into my mouth, his thrusts hard and fast, making it hard for me to breathe but not restricting me completely. I gag around his length and feel saliva dribbling out the side of my mouth and down my chin. He uses my mouth and throat savagely but keeps his eyes on me, and somehow, I feel more connected to him, tethered to him.

Heat blooms in my core, and I rub my thighs together, hoping for the tiniest bit of friction. I hate that I want him to touch me right now, to bring me pleasure like I know my mouth is bringing him.

"Such a warm little mouth," he grunts, "you look so fucking pretty with my cock in it."

"Mmm," I say, around his length, my body reacting without thought.

Julian smiles like the devil he is. "I bet your pussy is throbbing and wet, begging for my fingers to be inside of it. Isn't it?" His thrusts are faster now, his balls slapping against my chin. My own arousal coats my thighs, and I'm ashamed of how badly I want him.

"You're soaked, I know it. Even if you don't want to be, you're enjoying this. Your body knows I would never take more than you could give me."

He is right, even with as terrified as I am, I know deep down, he will not take more than I can give him, and that's the sick twisted part of all of this.

I shouldn't want this punishment, but a dark hidden part of me does.

"Suck," he orders, and I hollow out my cheeks, sucking on him like he's a popsicle.

His head tips back, and his entire body vibrates, all the perfectly sculpted muscles in his body tightening, locking up with pleasure.

Erupting in my mouth, I try to swallow his salty release, but there is too much, and I gag. Gently, he pulls out of my mouth.

"Swallow the rest," he growls, releasing my hair and grasping my chin. I do as he says, and his eyes gleam with joy as he watches my throat work. He studies my features and using his thumbs, wipes away the tears from my eyes.

Licking the side of my mouth, his teeth nip at my bottom lip.

My insides twist and a sob rips from my throat as it all comes back to me, the lustful fog lifting from my eyes. I didn't want this to happen, not really, and it did. I let him use me, let him take and punish me, and worst of all, I enjoyed it.

"Please, let me go," I whisper, wanting to curl in on myself. I don't know what to feel or think, only that this is wrong. What we did, the thoughts swirling around in my head, it's all wrong.

Something reflects in his eyes and back at me. He looks sorry, but that can't be right. He wanted this, wanted me in pain. He wanted to punish me, and he liked it, and part of me liked it too.

Before I can grasp onto the look, his face goes blank again, and he does just as I ask. He lifts me up and deposits me on the bed.

I let myself fall back onto the mattress and curl into a ball. Crawling onto the bed, he takes me into his arms even as I flinch at his touch. His chest is bare now. He kisses my damp forehead and soothes me, holding me tight, and that only makes me hate him a little bit more.

His masculine scent overpowers me, calming me. How can he do this? Hurt me one second, and soothe me another?

"Shhh, you're okay."

"I'm not," I blubber into his bare chest, the warmth of his skin radiating through me. I feel like an iceberg, slowly melting into the abyss.

"I didn't hurt you. I punished you, and I know that you enjoyed it as well." He reminds me again of my treacherous body's reaction to him. His thick fingers run through my hair, making my scalp tingle.

"I hate you," I whisper.

"Sometimes, I hate myself too. You'll be okay."

He holds me for a while longer, whispering sweet nothings into my hair, and I let him. Let him soothe me, hold me, even after what he did. He doesn't let go of me until the last sob has wracked my body.

Setting me back down on the mattress, he climbs off the bed and digs back into the drawer, setting a second pair of handcuffs down next to me. I don't speak or even look at him as he rolls me onto my belly, uncuffs one hand, rolls me back onto my back and brings my arms up above my head, fastening one end of the cuff to the headboard, then repeating the action with the other cuff, and attaching it to my free wrist.

I sag against the pillows as best as I can, my wrists already ache from the position, and my ass cheeks burn against the sheets, but I refuse to let him know that.

We're enemies now, and he doesn't deserve to know how I'm feeling anymore. All he deserves is my hate and anger, which is all he'll get from me.

Ignoring me completely, he walks into the closet and comes out fully dressed a short time later. I pretend to be asleep and hold in the tears that threaten to fall until I hear the door close behind him. Then, I close my eyes, letting the tears fall, wishing things could be different.

24

JULIAN

She betrayed me. I should have seen it coming, but I was so occupied with my revenge that I missed it.

Looking back on the last few days, I wonder how much of it was an act and how much was real? Did she really want me to fuck her, did she really like spending time with me? Did she ever trust me, even one single bit? I don't know, and the truth is, I don't think I'll ever know now.

Walking into the kitchen, I find Marie and our new cook, Celeste, chatting about some kind of new café in town.

"They just have the best pastries and lattes, I don't know what they put in them, but we have to figure it out," Marie chirps.

Celeste–who is about the same age as Marie–claps her hand in front of her in excitement. "I wonder how late they're open, maybe we can go after work?"

"Is breakfast ready?" Both of them jump at the sound of my voice, making me realize how harsh I must sound.

"Yes, I was just about to bring it up," Marie explains, clearly flustered by my presence. She quickly fills the glass on the tray with apple juice, her hand shaking so much that she is spilling half of it in the process.

"I'll take it." Walking further into the kitchen, I grab the food, not missing how Marie flinches at my movement. Good, she should be afraid.

On my way back to the bedroom, my anger about Elena's betrayal only expands. She lied to me, kept secrets from me, and then tried to get away and run back to the enemy. And here I am, still wondering if she would like a fucking pastry from the new café.

This woman messed with my head, got under my skin, and it's time that I turn the tables on her.

Holding the tray in one hand, I unlock the door with the other, then push the door open with my shoulder. Elena looks just as pitiful now as when I left her a few hours ago. I didn't want to leave, wanted to stay, and hold her in my arms, but that would've been counterproductive.

I needed her to stew in her emotions, let her anger simmer a little, and give myself a chance to cool off because I really, really wanted to fuck her and knew if I didn't leave, I would've done just that.

Briefly, she glances up at me before turning her head away.

I sit down on the side of the bed and set the tray down between us. Breaking off a piece of blueberry waffle, I hold it out in front of her face.

"Time to eat."

"Untie me then," she says while still looking away.

"No, I'm feeding you."

"I'm not hungry, then."

"I'm not untying you any time soon. You will let me feed you, or you will not eat at all." I swear she is pushing every one of my buttons just to see if I'll snap again.

She shakes her head but still doesn't look at me directly. "You are sick, you know that, right? That there is something seriously wrong with you?"

"There is something wrong with all of us. Now, are you going to eat, or do you need some more time to calm down?"

"I need to use the bathroom."

Sighing, I shake my head and get out the key to uncuff her.

When her hands are free, she rubs at her red wrists and scurries off the bed, disappearing into the bathroom. She slams the door shut behind her like an angry teenager, and I can't help but smile at the notion.

She returns a few minutes later, and I have to look away because she's naked, and it's doing shit to my head again. I've reached my limit today, and all we're doing now is toeing the line. If I snap again, I'll take her like an animal.

"Can I at least put some clothes on?"

"Suit yourself," I motion to the closet.

"I would choose something comfortable if I was you. You'll be tied up to the bed for a while," I call after her.

"Of course, I will," she mocks under her breath while stomping through the room.

She returns dressed in a pair of yoga pants and an oversized shirt that falls off one shoulder. I can still see her pebbled nipples pressing against the fabric, but at least her pussy is covered now.

"Ready to eat?" I ask, cuffing her back to the bed.

Now that I'm closer, I can see that her eyes are red, the skin around them puffy, letting me know she hasn't stopped crying. I try to ignore the emotion that rises up in me, seeing her like that. She betrayed me, so why is she crying? Because she got caught?

I know what I did shocked her because it shocked me too, but I didn't hurt her. I didn't take more than she could give me, and she never asked me to stop. She was afraid, hesitant, but even as angry as she was, she still wanted it, wanted me to take it from her. The reality of that tells me some part of her trusts me, and I hold onto that fact with both hands.

"I can feed myself," she hisses like a kitten.

"I know you can, but you won't. I told you, I'm feeding you, or you'll get no food at all."

Determination shines in her eyes. "I'd rather starve than let you feed me."

Two can play this game, the question is, how long can she keep it up?

"Then that's what it's going to be." I smile bitterly, hating that it's come to this.

Grabbing the tray, I exit the bedroom, not even giving her a second glance. In the hall, I just stand there, staring at the wooden door. I'm tempted to go back inside the room and shove the food down her throat, but she's made her choice, wanting to do things the hard way. So, we'll do it her way.

Walking back downstairs, I enter the kitchen and place the tray on the island. Marie doesn't look up from whatever she is preparing, but I can see her watching me out of the corner of her eye. I can't imagine what she thinks I'm doing to Elena. Beating her? Raping her? She'll never ask, no matter how curious or concerned because she's far too afraid of what might happen if she does. Still, her accusing eyes make me want to lash out at her.

With everything I discovered last night before taking Lev out, and then the shit with Elena, I haven't had a moment to breathe or think. If I hadn't returned home when I did, who knows what would have happened? Who would have their hands on her? I would have found her regardless, the tracking device I had implanted in her ring would've made it possible, but what if I had been too slow? What if she took the ring off?

The thought of someone else touching her, or hurting her, makes me want to pull my gun and start shooting people. Paint the world red with my enemies' blood. They're all coming for me now. Romero made a colossal mistake putting a bounty on my head because if someone hurts me, they'll hurt Elena too.

I go back upstairs and straight into my office. I haven't slept all night, but there is no way I'll be heading to bed anytime soon.

Closing the door, I walk over to the cellarette, grab a crystal glass, and a bottle of whiskey, and pour myself a healthy amount.

Sinking down into the leather chair behind my desk, I stare down into the amber liquid. Did I make a mistake killing Lev? His family will definitely seek me out to question me, maybe even try and attack me for killing their son. I very rarely doubt myself, but I find it happening now.

I can't imagine not killing the fucker, especially after he touched Elena, but had I put myself out there for no reason, showed my one and only weakness. I'm not sure why I'm wasting so much time thinking about her feelings and wants. None of it matters, not really, or it shouldn't. Shaking the feelings away doesn't work. I'm wrapped up in the dark-haired beauty as much as she's wrapped up in me.

I don't want her to hate our marriage, but I can't have her running away either. I'll do anything to keep her safe and protected, especially from her father, who simply wants to sell her to the next ruthless criminal. Even if it makes Elena hate me, I know I'll still go through with killing her father. He killed my mother. A life for a life is a worthy payment if you ask me.

I can't believe Romero had Elena convinced that I was going to kill her. Part of me understands her need to run, to protect herself. It's courageous and makes her look strong rather than weak, but it's frustrating as hell when there are worse people out there waiting to take her from me.

Sipping my whiskey, I let it warm me from the inside out while contemplating my next move with Elena. I need to tell her that the wedding has been moved up, not that it will matter much to her, I'm sure.

I'm not supposed to fucking care if she hates me or not, but I do. I want her to want me, to crave me, and now for reasons other than revenge. That part changed… or maybe it was always there, just hiding under the surface, hiding under a lie.

Part of her already wants me, but what happened today set us back. Briefly, I wonder what my father would think? What he would expect of me? He loved my mother so much, and while he was a ruthless man, who many feared, he had a very soft spot for my mother.

He taught me compassion and love, but also to never let the enemy win, and Elena by association is the enemy.

A knock sounds against the door, and I turn in my chair. "Come in," I tell whoever is on the other side, knowing it's one of my men.

The door opens, and Lucca walks into the room. It's hard to believe he is so young with the determination, skills, and way he carries himself. If his father was still alive, I believe he'd be tremendously proud.

"We've doubled up on security, and are monitoring the situation with Romero, sir. I'll let you know if anything changes."

"Very well," I say, taking another swig of whiskey.

"A little early to be drinking, don't you think, boss?" He pokes fun, and I turn my steel gaze to him once more.

"It's been a rough morning," I tell him, surprising myself by sharing this bit with him.

"It's going to be hard to see you as a married man."

I look at my ring finger, knowing that soon there will be a band resting there. My father took his vows seriously, and I think he would expect the same from me.

"It will be different, yes, but nothing will change in terms of how I'm running this organization. I'll still be the same asshole I am now. Maybe even worse."

"Yeah? I didn't expect that to change." Lucca snickers.

"Why? Are you worried?"

Lucca shakes his head. "No, you've always been good to my family, and are an honest man who stands by his word. The other men have just wondered if it will change you. Killing Lev might start a war when his family finds out it was us."

"Nothing has changed, and nothing will change. *If* or when Lev's family decides to attack, we will be ready. I'm the capo, and I say what goes, now get out of here," I growl, the frustration mounting. The pressure on my shoulders is immense, and I wonder if I'm doing the right thing. Even if I wasn't, I can't let Elena go.

I've already had a taste of her, and now I want everything, every single inch.

∽

LUNCH ENDS the same way breakfast did, with Elena being stubborn. She refuses to eat and gives me a dirty look, sneering at me like I kicked her dog. I'm tempted to tell her she looks sexy as fuck even angry, but I get the feeling that would make matters worse.

When dinner time arrives, I stroll into the bedroom with the tray, determined to make her eat this time. Even if I have to shove the food down her throat, she is going to eat. As soon as I walk in, her emerald eyes narrow.

"You're not hurting anyone but yourself by refusing to eat."

"I'm hurting you," she says softly with a smile on her lips.

I grip the tray a little tighter, envisioning it as her throat. She's pushing all my fucking buttons, and soon I won't be responsible for what happens.

"No, you aren't. Do you have to use the restroom?" I ask, setting the tray down at the end of the bed.

She nods her head, and I retrieve the key from my pocket. I uncuff one hand and then the other. Taking a step back, I give her room to walk by, but like always, she shocks the hell out of me when she shoves off the bed and comes right for me like a feral animal. Lifting my hands, I try and protect myself and subdue her, but she's like a bucking bronco.

"Why would you leave me here so you could screw someone else?" she snarls.

What the hell is she talking about?

I don't even get to ask because she's attacking again. Her tiny hands might not have much strength behind them, but her slaps sting, and when her nails catch me on my neck, digging into the skin, I hiss. My hands circle both her wrists, and I press them against her chest.

"What the fuck are you talking about?" I growl right into her face, feeling the warm blood on my skin. My cock is so hard it presses against the zipper of my pants, wanting to be unleashed. Her violence only makes me want her more.

Horror fills her eyes as she gazes up at my neck.

Yes, you did that, my queen.

"The other night... you left, were gone all night. You didn't want me, so you went somewhere else."

A light bulb goes off in my head. I can't stop my lips from tipping up at the sides. "Jealousy looks very good on you, and I must say, if it's always going to make you act this way, I may make you jealous more often."

"I'm not jealous," she says angrily, struggling against me.

I laugh in her face. "You are, and that's okay. I like it. It turns me on, makes me want to strip you down and taste you all over."

The fire in her eyes calls to me. "As if I'd let you do that, knowing you were with someone else."

Curling my own lip, I tug her to my chest and grind my groin against her. "If you must know, I wasn't with anyone else. I was taking care of business. No one's pussy has my attention like yours, sweet Elena." I bite her earlobe hard, and pleasure fills my chest when she lets out a soft whimper.

"You weren't with someone else?" she whispers, almost as if she doesn't believe it. I knew when I left that she felt rejected, but I had to leave and get out of the room and away from her before I did something I couldn't finish.

"No. I wasn't. I turned down sex because I had work that needed to be done, and it couldn't wait. I had to force myself to leave this room, so I didn't fuck you straight through the mattress."

I release her wrists when I see her features soften. She really thought I left to have sex with someone else. Taking a step back, she gives me one more look, something close to guilt flashing in her eyes. Before I can latch onto that look, she's rushing into the bathroom and closing the door behind her.

Sighing, I walk over to the bed and sit. Bringing my hand to my neck, I trace the raised marks with a finger and smile. *Great, just when the last scratches had healed up.*

Fierce, determined, and so fucking beautiful. Pulling my hand away, I see the small smear of blood on my fingers.

A few moments later, Elena returns to the bed, crawling up onto it, settling into her usual spot. I feel her gaze on my neck as I cuff her wrists back into place. She hasn't given up, it's obvious, but she's done fighting for now.

"Would you like to eat?" I ask, moving the tray between us.

"Yes," she murmurs.

I nearly grin as I pull the top off of her plate. The savory smell of tomatoes and Italian seasoning fill my nostrils—spaghetti with meatballs.

Elena's eyes glaze over, and she licks her lips. She must be starving. Grabbing the fork, I twirl some noodles and a slice of meatball onto it and bring it to her pink lips.

Eating shouldn't be seen as sexual, but the way that her lips pass over the fork as she devours the food I'm offering her, turns me right the fuck on.

We continue this motion, me feeding her, and offering her small drinks of water in between, with her actually eating until the entire plate is empty. Leaning back against the pillows, she groans. I move the tray and place it on the chaise lounge.

"I'm so full, I think I might explode."

"I wanted to tell you that I've decided to move the wedding up. It will be in a few days, and I hope by then you're behaving better."

"A few days?" She squeaks. "Why have you moved it up?"

"Your father's motives mostly. You'll be my wife by the end of the week."

She doesn't say anything to that, not that her objecting would change a damn thing. I would still marry her even if she begged me not to, though strangely, she hasn't fought me on that at all. Being locked in the room, handcuffed, and trapped, yes, but everything I've asked her to do, she has done.

Stripping out of my clothes, I walk into the bathroom. I start the shower and jump in, washing my hair and body quickly. When I'm done, I walk out of the bathroom without even a towel slung around my hips.

Elena pretends as if she's not looking at me, but I can feel her eyes roaming over my naked form, and I swear I can see her cheeks turning pink even from a distance. She is an enigma. One moment she wants my touch, and the next, she wants to claw my eyes out.

Walking into the closet, I find a pair of boxers, tug them on and return to the bed. I slide beneath the sheets and turn away from her.

"Good night, Julian," she huffs, tugging against the cuffs. "At least one of us gets to be comfortable."

"Be a good girl, and the cuffs might not be needed."

"What do you mean *might* not be needed?"

"They might not be needed to restrain you all the time, only when I want to restrain you."

"There is something wrong with you." She twists and turns, ruffling the sheets with her movements.

"You have a lot to learn, sweetheart," I whisper and turn the light off, blanketing the room into darkness.

"So do you, like this isn't how you get me to listen to you."

Rolling over, I face her, and even though it's dark, I can still make out some of her features. "You ran, knowing I would punish you for it. That sounds like the only person who has a listening problem is you."

She sighs. "I ran because I thought you were going to hurt me, and I wasn't going to run initially."

"Then what were you going to do?"

"I thought you were with someone else, and I was upset. You rejected me, and then I heard your men talking... they said you moved the timeline up. I thought you were going to kill me or do something worse. I panicked."

I wouldn't admit it out loud, but I understood. Deep down, I got why she ran, but that didn't mean it wasn't a slap to my face. Had it been during the day, or one of my men had found her, it would've looked bad for me. Worse yet if she got away.

"I understand, but a punishment is a punishment." Fluffing my pillow, I rest my head on it and do my best to ignore the heat of her body calling to me.

I don't say anything else and let my eyes drift closed. My body itches to bring her closer to me, to hold her in my arms, but lately, she's been feisty, refusing to let me touch her, and I don't want to rehash anything with her. I just want to sleep.

Eventually, her breathing evens out, and I decide to let the exhaustion pull me under.

∼

THE SOUND of someone crying fills my head, lifting me from a foggy sleep. Soft whimpers fill my ears, and I roll over to find Elena with her eyes squeezed close, struggling against the cuffs, her tiny body trembling.

A nightmare. She's having a nightmare.

Gently, I grasp onto her shoulders and give her a tiny shake. A sob breaks from her lips, and her cries get louder when her eyes blink open.

I find myself wrapping her up in my arms, pulling her closer, rather than pushing her away. My eyes are glued to her face, watching as the tears cascade down her cheeks like raindrops on a window. In all the time she's been here, she's never looked as broken as she does right now, and the emotions swirling in her eyes grab onto me, digging their claws into my subconscious.

Her vulnerability is pushing through, and I can't do anything but cup her by the cheek and wipe the tears away. My mouth makes soft shhh sounds, the noises I'm expelling are so foreign, I didn't even know I could make them.

After a while, she stops crying, but I continue stroking her cheek, loving the feel of her skin beneath my hand.

"What was your dream about?" I croak, wondering what could've brought emotions out of her like that.

"My mom," she whispers. "In the dream, I was there again, in the bathroom. When she killed herself... and I found her. There was so much blood, on the tub, on her body, on my hands. I can still see the vacant look in her eyes, feel the coldness of her skin."

I swallow, taking in everything she says. I'm shocked, mainly because that's not the story her father told everyone. According to him, she died in a car accident. Why would he lie about something like that? It gets the wheels in my head turning and reminds me further of what a pig Romero is. He's hiding something, and I'm going to figure it the fuck out.

"I miss her so much, Julian, and I wish she was here now. Wish she was going to be at our wedding." She starts to cry again, and her broken emotions reach inside me, tugging at my heart. "She would've wanted to be here. I know it. She loved me. Far more than my father does." She sniffles before continuing. "After her death, everything changed. I used to be able to go outside, cook in the kitchen, go shopping, and then he took it all away."

Every word she speaks resonates through me. I don't want to be like her father. I don't want to lock her in a cage, but I have to. I can't risk her leaving or someone getting to her. She's reached a part of me no one ever has and as terrifying as that is, I can't let her go. I won't. I'll kill, destroy, and hold her against her will if need be.

She is mine until death.

"Sleep, I will keep the nightmares away," I whisper into her hair, my lips grazing her forehead.

"Will you ever let me go?"

"Untie you from the bed, yes. Leave me? Never. If you ever get away from me, I'll hunt you down, find you and drag you back here. The day you signed your name on that contract is the day you became mine. I will never let you escape me. Never let you go."

Silence settles over us, and even though she doesn't say anything, I know she's still awake. I ignore that fact and hold her until we both fall asleep, wondering if things have to change so much, or if I can keep her like this forever.

25

ELENA

*J*ulian has left me tied to this bed for two days now. My wrists are sore, and my arms ache from being in the same position all the time. I thought after the nightmare, and the way he held me, he would release me, but he didn't.

What's even worse than being uncomfortable is the loneliness. The only person I've seen or spoken to is Julian, and he doesn't stay long when he is here. That probably has something to do with me constantly yelling at him and pushing him away. I hate and yearn for him all at once. Hate what he is doing to me, but also yearn for him, desperate for his touch. The way he held and comforted me has my body confused.

I know that part of it is only because he is the only human contact I have. But I can't help but wonder if it's more than that. The way he touched me, punished me... how he used me. It was... unexpected. Not the part of him acting that way, the part of me liking it.

There must be something fundamentally wrong with me. How can I possibly enjoy what he did to me? How can my body want more of it?

With nothing to do besides think about Julian and what we did, I'm in a constant state of need. My body feels hot, and every time he lets me go to the bathroom, I find my panties soaked.

I turn my head to check the time. He should be back with my dinner soon. Right on cue, my stomach growls.

Watching the minutes tick by, I wait for him to open the door.

When I finally hear him approaching, I curse myself for feeling the excitement bubble up inside of me. *Yes, there is definitely something wrong with me.*

The lock disengages, and the door opens, revealing Julian in all his glory. Like expected, he is holding a tray of food. What I don't see coming is him being in workout clothes.

His usual suit and tie are gone, and he is wearing gym shorts and a T-shirt. Both are covered in sweat and clinging to his muscles like a second skin. I can see every one of his muscles flex as he walks toward me. My mouth goes dry, and my thighs rub together, desperate for any kind of friction. I want him so badly, and I hate that I want him.

"I lost track of time at the gym."

I open my mouth, but nothing comes out. All I can do is stare at his chest, wondering what it would feel like to run my fingers over it.

"You're doing it again." He chuckles, sitting down on the edge of the bed.

"W-what?"

"Looking at me like you want me to fuck you."

"Maybe I do…"

"Don't be a tease, Elena." Julian shakes his head, looking baffled. "Now, be a good girl and let me feed you." Taking the fork, he loads it up with a small piece of chicken and tops it with a heap of mash potato.

I part my lips just wide enough for him to slip the food between them. Then, I close my lips and let him slide the fork back out, leaving me with a savory mouth full of food. I watch him watching me eat. His gaze never leaving my lips.

We repeat the process a few more times, each time feeling more erotic than the next. Who knew feeding could feel so… sensual? Him taking care of me like this, of my basic needs, there is something nurturing about it.

This feeling of him caring for me, and the memory of how he used my body, is a dangerous combination. I have to stop reliving the memory. It was a punishment, after all.

After the fourth bite, I shake my head. Indicating that I'm done.

"You've barely eaten," he says, looking down at the plate.

"I know, I just..." I know this change in conversation is going to surprise him, but I've been thinking about this all day, and I can't keep the thoughts to myself any longer. "Why do you want to wait until after the wedding to have sex?" It's a question I have wondered about for a while. Julian doesn't strike me as a religious man, so he must have some other reason.

"Tradition mostly. That's the short answer anyway."

"I don't want to wait," I blurt out. "I want to do it now. Today."

Julian's eyebrows pull together as he gives me a puzzled look. "Why? The wedding is in a few days. Why now of all the times?"

Lifting my chin, I look him in the eyes. "Because I want it to be my choice." I didn't even realize how true that was until the words left my mouth. Yes, I'm freaking horny, like a cat in heat, but I also want this to be on my terms. "My whole life, every choice has been taken away from me. This time, I want a choice. I want to decide when I'm giving my virginity away."

Tilting his head, he stares at me like I'm a math equation he's trying to solve. "Are you sure about this? I won't untie you for it."

"I don't care. I want this to be my choice."

"Fine, but under one condition." His lips tip up in their signature smirk. "Admit that you liked what I did to you the other day."

Suppressing a gasp, I ask, "What part?"

"Whatever part you liked."

All of it.

Too embarrassed to say it, I opt to say my favorite part. "When you... you know... licked me... there."

"You mean when I had my tongue on your tight little asshole?"

I'm pretty sure my cheeks are bright red, at least, it feels like they're on fire. Looking down at the blanket draped over my lap, I manage to whisper, "Oddly, that too."

I'm ashamed to admit how much I liked everything that we did.

"I think I might need to take back what I said about you before. I thought you couldn't handle my dark and sinister needs. I think you'll be able to handle them just fine. More so, you'll enjoy them."

He gets up and sets the tray on top of the dresser. I'm about to ask him what he is doing. *He better not be leaving again.* My question gets stuck in my throat when he starts to undress, pulling his shirt over his head, he throws it carelessly onto the ground. Then pulls his shorts down and steps out of those as well.

He's not wearing any underwear, and my eyes are glued on his already hard penis, swinging from side to side as he walks back over to me. He pulls the blanket off my legs and dips his fingers into my leggings, pulling them down, along with my panties.

"Are you sure about this? Last chance to back out," he warns as he climbs onto the bed, spreading my legs and moving into the space between them.

"Are you really not going to untie me?"

Grinning, he shakes his head, no. "I like you tied up and helpless."

"Like I would be any less helpless if I wasn't tied up?"

Julian points to his neck. "May I remind you of some deep scratches across my neck? Scratches that your sharp nails put there."

"I was just scared and angry."

"And you're not scared now?" He bends my knees and spreads me even wider, exposing my center to him as much as he can.

I gulp. "Not like I was before." The truth is, I'm still scared, but it's a different kind of fear now. I was scared of being hurt physically before. I was scared of being raped, beaten, and shared between men.

Now, I'm scared of being alone, being cheated on, lied to, and discarded like I don't matter. I'm scared of not being enough, not measuring up to what he thinks I am or who he needs me to be.

Reaching into his pocket, my insides tighten when he pulls out the key to my cuffs and undoes them. As soon as my wrists are free, I lean forward, circling my arms around his neck. I cling to him like a monkey and tug him forward till our lips are almost touching.

"I want you." I breathe against his lips, and lift my hips, trying to guide his tip into my channel. Julian's gaze roams my face for a fraction of a second, and I worry if he's going to pull away and end this, but then he's on me, his lips pressing against mine. The kiss is punishing, teeth, and anger, and lust. A swirling cyclone of destruction waiting to happen.

I'm drowning in the kiss, mewling as his hands move over my skin, touching something inside of me that's never been touched before. I need and want everything he is willing to give me. The things I'm feeling right now are terrifying. It's like standing at a cliff's edge, knowing the only thing you can do is jump.

By some grace, will he save me, or will he be my damnation?

I whimper when he pulls back, and escapes my hold, ducking underneath my arms.

"Don't stop, please." I sound as desperate as I feel, I'm sure.

Julian snickers as he drops to his stomach and tugs me forward, his face is so close to my lips that I can feel the hot breath against them. "Don't plan on it. Not even if you beg."

Leaning back into the pillow, I arch my back and lift my hips as he buries his face between my legs. His tongue moves expertly as he licks me from my ass all the way to my clit and back down again.

He's barely started, and I feel my legs begin to shake, the pressure in my core building with each graze of his tongue.

"Fuck me, you taste so good. I want to live here and eat you until I die." His words only encourage me, and I run my fingers through his dark hair, holding his head in place, loving the control he has over my body. His lips move slowly, nibbling and tasting every inch of my pussy, and when he hums in approval, the sound vibrates right through me.

Arousal coats the inside of my thighs, letting me know just how turned on I am. It's like someone turned on a faucet down there. Caught up in the feeling of his tongue against my pussy, I sink deeper and deeper, my core tightening, a warmth zinging through it.

Sucking my clit between his lips, I crumble, free-falling into the abyss of pleasure. My legs shake, and I float away from my body for a second as my eyes drift closed.

Julian isn't done with me yet, though, and sinks two digits into my tight channel, pumping in and out at a vicious pace.

"Come for me, beautiful, come on my hand, coat my fingers, squeeze 'em, show me what my cock is missing."

The way my body reacts to his touch is shocking, and as he coaxes another orgasm out of me, it feels like heaven and hell are colliding. My mouth pops open, and I thrash against the sheets, a coldness sweeping over me, making my nipples ache.

I need him in a way that I cannot even put into words.

Exploding, I bare down on his fingers, clenching, nearly pushing him out in the process. My breathing is erratic, and every touch is heightened. As he eases his fingers out of me, I open my eyes and look up at him.

It's like two storm clouds hanging above my head. I can see the entire world in those two orbs, see how much I mean to him. The vulnerability within them rattles me to the core.

Pushing up onto his knees, he takes his cock into his hand, and I drag my eyes down at the motion. He's so thick and long. Fear eats at part of my euphoric state, and even though I made this choice, I wonder for a second if I've made a mistake.

"If you're worried about it fitting, I can promise you it will. You're more than ready for me. I've prepared you, and now I'm going to steal the dangling cherry there, just as I stole you from your father."

My entire world spins as if it's been tossed into a snow globe. A soft gasp passes my lips when he moves between my legs, one hand moving, cradling the back of my head while the other guides him to my entrance.

I clamp up, my muscles tightening as he slides the mushroom head through my juices, and over my clit. The touch against my clit ignites a fire inside of me. All you need is a spark to start a forest fire, and Julian is my spark.

Pressing a kiss to my chin, he pushes against my entrance, the thick head of his cock slips inside, and I bite my lip, waiting with bated breath for him to plow into me. I wrap my arms around him, bringing him closer, and he slides in a little deeper.

Air swooshes from my lungs, and our eyes collide. Flexing his hips forward, he slides in the rest of the way, and my nails sink into his skin as my hips lift, my body trying to escape the overly full intrusion.

"So fucking tight and perfect," he murmurs.

Leaning down, his hot mouth circles one of my nipples, and I mewl into the room at the sensations that slam into me. His tongue flicks against the hard peak, and then he nips at it, his teeth grazing the sensitive flesh, distracting me from the pain in my core.

My channel slowly adapts to the fullness, and Julian groans.

"I'm going to start moving." He sighs against my skin. I can see the sweat beading his forehead, his shoulders bunch together, the muscles tightening, giving away how tense he is. He's holding himself back for me, giving me a chance to find pleasure even within the pain, it makes me want to give back to him, to prove how much I want this. I lift my hips, seeking out his thrust as he pulls out and slams back in, his balls pressing against my ass.

Pleasure and pain collide like a cosmic phenomenon, a star being born.

His hand in my hair tightens, and he lifts my head, bringing our foreheads together. Our hot breaths mingle in the space between us, his manly scent surrounding me. His eyes lock on mine, and he growls, upping his pace, rocking his hips forward, owning another piece of me without knowing it.

My lips part and a whimper escapes, this is like nothing I've ever felt before.

A darkness flashes in his eyes, and he starts moving faster, pistoning his hips, pressing me harder into the mattress. The air seeps from my lungs as the pleasure and pain blend together, becoming one.

"Fuck, yes... I can feel you tightening..." Julian curls his lip, and plows into me again and again, swiveling his hips and hitching my leg a little higher, driving his cock deep, so deep that it feels like he's breaking me in two.

An orgasm builds inside of me, but it's just out of reach.

"I need more," I pant, wanting to come badly.

Knowing exactly what I need, he snakes a hand down between our bodies and presses his thumb against my clit. It's just the right amount of friction, and combined with his harsh thrusts, I explode, squeezing his cock so tightly his features fill with pain.

He thrusts through my orgasm, rutting into me until he finds his own release, his eyes bleeding into mine, the intensity within them knocking the air from my lungs. I can see into his soul, and it makes me want him more.

"I... I love you," I whisper the words that just flow out of me like an overflowing sink.

His lips brush against mine, and I feel his sticky warm release dripping out of me and down his length.

"I know," he pants and trails a finger down the side of my face.

Slowly, he pulls out of me, and I wince, shifting uncomfortably against the sheets. Peering down between my legs, he stares, and I look down to see what he's looking at. My mouth goes dry when I see the proof of my virginity, and our combined juices against my thighs and the sheet.

"Come, my queen," he offers me a hand, dragging my attention away from the sheets.

"Your queen?" I place my hand in his.

"Yes, my queen." He places a gentle kiss against my hand, his eyes twinkle like rare jewels.

The air between us is different, and I feel as if I gave him the most sacred part of who I am, expecting him to protect and guard it. Will he guard it? Will he shelter me? I know he'll protect me against his enemies, even against my father, but who will protect me from him?

Julian doesn't love. He just takes, and while I'm left exposed to him, part of him is still hiding. How do I get him to break free and love me back?

26

JULIAN

The last twelve hours have been a whirlwind. When I brought her here, I hoped she would eventually come to me willingly, but I didn't expect it to happen this soon. Once again, she proved me wrong. She not only came to me sooner than I thought possible but gave herself to me completely.

As I replay the memory of her slim body beneath mine, the heat of her cunt as she pulsed around my cock, I try to figure out what her motive is. Is she trying to get me to fall in love with her? She claims to love me, but do I love her? Am I even capable of that emotion? Sure, maybe, but doing so would be foolish. I can't love her, but I'm okay with her loving me. It plays into my plan perfectly. I just have to keep myself in line. As soon as Elena finds out my plan, she will never look at me the same. There is no way she will love me after I am done with her father.

Which makes me think about how she hasn't asked me again about me wanting to kill her father. Did she not take me seriously?

Elena stirs beside me, her body was glued to mine all night, seeking out my warmth, my protection. I won't deny that I love having her beside me, beneath me, and being inside of her.

"Good Morning," I whisper, brushing silky strands of hair off her face.

"Hi," she murmurs, her eyes blinking open.

A knock sounds against the door, interrupting our private moment. That must be breakfast. Climbing off the bed, I run into the closet and tug a pair of boxers on, and then hurry to the door. Marie gives me a wide-eyed look, her eyes sweeping over my mostly naked form before dropping to the floor.

"Here is your breakfast, sir," she murmurs.

I take the tray from her and close the door without another word. She's probably never seen a man naked, or half-naked for that matter.

Bringing the tray to the bed, I survey Elena, who is sprawled out against the sheets, her beautiful breasts on display, the nipples stiff and pink, begging to be in my mouth.

"I can't believe you answered the door like that," Elena whispers.

She sits up in the bed, tugging the sheet over her chest, covering her voluptuous breasts. Directing my attention back to her heart-shaped face, I set the tray down on the mattress.

"It's not any different than wearing shorts." I shrug, wondering if that might've made her jealous. She is just as territorial as me, it seems.

Flipping over the cups, I pour two cups of coffee.

"You didn't tie me back up," she points out.

"Did you want me to?"

"No, I just... does that mean I'm allowed to feed myself again?"

"If you want to. Although, I believe you enjoyed me feeding you as much as I enjoyed it myself."

"Maybe..." Elena reaches for her cup, pouring in a little sugar and cream before stirring it together. It's strange that even the small things she does fascinate me. Absentmindedly, I reach out, tucking a few strands of hair behind her ear. Looking up at me over the rim of her cup, her eyes gleam, and her skin seems to have a new glow to it. She sips on her coffee, the green of her eyes brighter than I've ever seen.

"You know I meant what I said before. I want to kill your father."

"Many have tried…" She shrugs. "I guess I've heard it too many times to get worried."

"You don't think I'll succeed?" I raise an eyebrow.

"I don't want anyone to get hurt. Not him or you. Why do you want him dead? What happened between you?"

"That's a long and gruesome story and certainly not breakfast worthy."

Elena sighs like she is about to keep asking questions, but then just nods. I pull the top off one of the plates and find an everything omelet with an English muffin. I load up her plate first then, mine.

She starts cutting her entire omelet into little squares and puts her knife down. Only then does she start eating, using nothing but her fork. It's odd how these little things, her little quirks fascinate me. I take them in, all of them and file them away, building a database on everything Elena in my head.

"You were gentle last night, during… sex, and now you're looking at me like… well, like you've never looked at me before. Are you sure you aren't growing a heart in that frigid body of yours?"

I chuckle. "There is a heart inside me, but it only comes into play when I need it. Now, eat your food, unless you'd rather have something else for breakfast?" I tease her, dragging my eyes down her sheet-covered body.

Even though the deed is done, and I've had my tongue, cock, and fingers inside her, her cheeks still turn crimson at my insinuation.

She sinks her teeth into her bottom lip, looking a little self-conscious. "It might be a little soon. I'm still pretty sore."

There is a pang of guilt that comes out of nowhere and punches me in the chest. I was gentle with her, but I could've done better. There was no need to rut into her like a wild animal, but as soon as I felt her silky, wet channel strangling my cock, I lost control. I'd never gone bareback before, and I'd never fucked a virgin. Both were firsts for me, and by the time I was all the way in, I became possessed with a need to feel her convulsing around me.

"As expected. I'm just teasing you, I don't expect you to be ready again until our wedding night."

I take the top off the other dish, and we nibble on both plates of food, and the dish of fresh fruit. Elena watches me curiously out of the corner of her eye, those emerald orbs moving over my skin, memorizing all hard dips and planes, I'm sure.

"Are you finished?" I ask once I'm full myself.

"Yes. I feel like since I came here, I've gained ten pounds."

I don't tell her that she's probably correct. That she looked rail-thin the day she arrived. The last thing I want to do is offend her about her weight, especially when I like her body just the way it is right now. I have plans for today, and I don't want them to be overshadowed by anything else.

"The other night, when you had your nightmare and told me about your mom, it made me think of something." I set my cup down on the tray. "I know what it's like to lose a parent, and I know you wished that your mom could be here for the wedding, and since she can't be, I wanted to at least give you something else."

The way she looks at me makes me want to pull that sheet away and fuck her through the mattress. As tempting as it is, doing so would ruin what I have planned, so I swallow down the urge. There's always tomorrow, and the next day, and well, you get the point.

"What is it?" she asks, mystified.

"Go get dressed, and you'll find out." Uncaring to her naked state, she throws the covers back, nearly knocking the stuff on the tray over and bounds from the bed. My eyes gravitate straight to her tight little ass, and an image pops into my head.

Her belly is full of my seed, her eyes bright, and her smile big. She's looking at me like I'm the goddamn world.

The image makes my stomach twist with knots, and a bitterness fills my mouth. *Love.* That's what that image looked like. Shaking the image from my head, I shove off the bed and pad into the closet as well. When I enter, she is half-dressed and bouncing with excitement.

I take my time dressing, wanting to drag out the anticipation. A pout forms on her pink lips as I button the last few buttons on my dress shirt.

"Patience isn't your strong suit." I chuckle.

"Not when you dangle the apple right in front of me. I'm curious by nature, and it's not like you do nice things often."

"Touché." I grin.

Is this the new normal for us? The banter, and dare I say, flirting.

"It's true, and you know it."

I finish getting dressed under her microscopic eyes and unlock the door. Taking her hand, I lead her downstairs. As we pass the kitchen, I hear Marie and Celeste giggling at something. Elena curiously looks into the room.

I didn't plan on stopping, but Elena looking so excited to see Marie has my legs locked in place. Stopping beside me, she looks up at me with a hopeful expression. I know even without asking what she wants. It's been days since she got to interact with Marie, and she's craving the attention of someone other than me.

I shouldn't care, but her happiness means something to me, so I decide to give her what I know will make her smile with glee.

Clearing my throat, I get the two women's attention. Startled, they both stop laughing, spin around, and stand up a little straighter when they realize it's me. Marie's gaze briefly flickers to my side to where Elena is standing, and a small smile tugs on her lips. When I look down at my soon to be wife, I find her waving her hand timidly.

"You two, come with us," I order, and watch as both Marie's and Celeste's eyes grow wide with shock and apprehension. They probably think I'm going to murder them, or god knows what. Without waiting for their response, I start walking away, pulling Elena along with me.

"Where are we going? I've never been in this part of the house," Elena murmurs, with a slight hint of worry in her voice.

"You'll see."

I don't have to look to know that the two women are following us, I lead all three of them to the large sitting room in the east wing of the mansion.

As soon as we walk in, Elena gasps.

"I had planned to pick something for you to wear, but I thought you might want to choose for yourself."

She doesn't say anything, but the twinkle in her eyes says it all. She squeezes my arm, and I walk her inside to introduce her to the older woman waiting next to the racks full of white dresses.

"Margaret is a seamstress, the best, of course. You pick a dress, and she will make sure it fits perfectly on our wedding day."

"Thank you," Elena whispers before getting on her tippy toes and placing a light kiss on my cheek. The notion is so foreign and unexpected, I almost push her away.

"I've got some work to do. I'm going to leave you to it," I say before leaning down and whispering into the shell of her ear. "Don't do anything foolish. This room is heavily guarded, and I'm trusting you."

She nods, my threat not stopping her from smiling widely.

I turn and find Marie and Celeste standing a few feet behind us. "Help her pick out a dress," I tell them as I walk out of the door.

I already told the guards to keep an eye on her, so I'm not worried about her escaping. Still, it feels odd leaving her here. She's done nothing on her own, not so much as shower usually. Anxiety worms its way through me as I enter my office.

Shaking my head, I need to remind myself that I can't keep her locked up in our bedroom forever, no matter how enticing that thought is. I need to at least let her roam the mansion. I guess I didn't know how hard even that would be.

Picking up the phone on my desk, I go through the contacts until Xander Rossi's name pops up. Hitting the green button, I listen to the dial tone.

"Julian," Xander greets me.

"Old friend, just making sure you got my invite."

"I got the first one and the second one." He chuckles. "Why a change of date last minute? Can't wait to put that ring on her?"

"Something like that. I hope you're still able to join us, even with the last minute changes."

"Of course. We're actually thinking about flying in tomorrow. I'd like to discuss something with you, and Ella is eager to meet your Elena. You know how she is."

"Sure, why not." Xander is one of the very few people I associate with that I actually trust. You could say we are almost friends. Definitely allies. The thought of Elena meeting him and his wife is oddly pleasant. Like I'm sharing part of myself with her.

"Great, I'll see you tomorrow."

We hang up, and I lean back in my chair. In two days, I will be a married man, implementing the last steps in my plan for revenge. Part of me feels guilty using Elena, taking away her small chance at finding love or happiness, but then the image of my mother's dead body fills my mind. The stab wounds in her chest and stomach.

Elena's happiness is a small price to pay in the grand scheme of things, and when this is over, maybe I can still give her a sliver of joy, but right now, the prize is Romero dead just like my mother. Revenge will be mine soon, so soon.

27

ELENA

The room looks like one giant mass of dresses, and I can't seem to wrap my head around the kindness that Julian has shown me. I'm half-tempted to ask him if he's sick or if this is some kind of messed-up joke.

I don't realize that I'm standing there with my mouth hanging wide open until Marie walks up to me. "Elena,." She grabs my hand and squeezes it. "This is Celeste, our new cook."

"It's nice to meet you, Elena." Celeste smiles, holding out her hand to me. I take it and return the smile. She, just like Marie, doesn't seem to be much older than me.

"Do you know what kind of dress you would like? Ball Gown? Mermaid? A-line? Trumpet?" Margaret gets our attention and pushes her glasses further up the bridge of her nose. She stares at me like a puzzle piece that won't go into its spot. "You have the body for a mermaid, so if you're undecided, we can try that one first. I want to be certain that Mrs. Moretti looks her finest on her wedding day."

Shocked, I nod, my mouth refusing to work still.

I've only ever heard of two of the dresses she named off, the ball gown and the mermaid, and I know for sure I don't want to look like

Cinderella on my wedding day. Julian might have his sweet moments, but he surely isn't a white knight, which fits since I'm not a princess in need of saving.

Margaret moves through the racks before pulling a dress out. I twist, looking over my shoulder at Marie and Celeste, who look just as shocked as I am.

"The sweetheart neckline will accent your breasts very well, and the overall body of the dress will give your hips a nice flare, showing off your figure."

"Do you want me to strip right here?" I ask.

Chuckling, she nods. "Yes, don't be shy, sweetheart. You don't have anything that I haven't seen before."

I guess she's right. Peeling off my clothes, I strip down to my bra and panties and let her help me into the dress. It fits like a glove, and I stare at myself in the mirror for a long second with tears in my eyes. The neckline draws attention to my breasts, but the dress in itself shows off my body well.

"Oh, my goodness, Elena, it's beautiful," Marie fawns.

"It really is. I don't think you even have to try on another one. This one right here is gold." Celeste clasps her hands together.

I run a hand down the front of the gown, the top of the dress is beaded, and the bottom is a little fluffier made with tulle and some other material.

"They aren't lying, it really does look fabulous on you." Margaret meets my gaze in the mirror, and as much as I like the dress, I decide to try on another.

We go through the grueling process of trying on another mermaid dress, which I like a little less than the first before moving to an A-line, which I think looks hideous.

"I really think the first one was it."

"Okay then, now we just have to pick out the rest."

"The rest? What else is there?"

"Ha." She tips her head back and laughs. "Don't be silly. There are the undergarments, the shoes, the veil, jewelry, the flowers, and maybe a purse or a light fur coat if you get chilly."

"I thought you were just a seamstress?"

"I have many talents, my dear." She winks.

∼

AFTER HOURS of trying on things and making decisions, I am exhausted, yet I enjoyed every minute of it. After being so isolated for so long, these last few hours have been more than great. Hanging out with girls my age is unusual for me, but it's something I have yearned for my whole life. I wonder if Julian would ever let me have a girls' night. Obviously, he wouldn't let me leave, but maybe a movie and pizza night?

I snuff the thought out as fast I think it. I doubt he would ever let me do something like that, but I can always dream, right?

Margaret packs up all of her stuff and promises me the dress will be done by tomorrow. I thank her profusely, and when she leaves, I stay behind in the sitting room with Marie and Celeste by my side. Silence blankets the room, and I turn to Marie, who looks as if she wants to say something but is afraid.

"Is everything okay?" I ask with real concern.

"Yes, I was just so worried. I heard the rumors about you trying to escape, and I wasn't aware that you wanted to leave so badly," Marie admits, frowning at me. "I didn't know what to do or how to help you. I hadn't seen you in days and wasn't allowed to bring the food up. Julian scares me, and I thought the worst, that he would hurt you–"

"You don't have to worry about me. Julian wouldn't hurt me, and I honestly didn't even plan on running away. I thought Julian was with another woman that night. I was angry and mad and thinking irrationally. I just wanted to call my father, and then I overheard the guards talking, and I panicked. I promise I'm fine."

"There is no reason to be concerned about Elena's wellbeing," Julian's deep voice fills the room, startling all three of us.

Marie's eyes drop to the floor, and her tiny frame rattles beside me. Celeste also looks to the floor, but she seems less frightened, probably since she wasn't the one caught talking. Placing my hand against Marie's shoulder, I give her a gentle squeeze. I don't think Julian would ever internationally hurt her, but he's led me to believe he might a few times.

"I... I'm sorry, sir."

"Do not question what I do with my wife behind closed doors. You're a maid in my home, and it would be best for you to remember that."

The stern way he talks to Marie angers me. I bite my tongue, knowing that if I act out, nothing good will come from it. I don't want to disappoint him, especially after all he's done for me today. I won't let this go, though. I'm going to talk to him about the way he acted just now.

"Of course, sir. I apologize." Marie's lips tremble as she talks.

Julian shakes his head, frustration filling his features. He offers me his hand, and I take it, melting into his side as soon as he tugs me to my feet.

"Get back to work," Julian orders gruffly before we walk out of the room.

I frown but let him guide me down the hall and back into the wing of the house where our bedroom is.

"Why were you so mean to her? She was just being a decent human and a good friend. She didn't do anything wrong."

"She works for me, and she is your maid. She can't be your friend, and I will not have her questioning what I may or may not do with you. Your wellbeing is none of her concern." He says coldly, but I can tell he's close to snapping. I shouldn't push the issue, but Marie is important to me, and I won't stand by and let him talk down to her.

Stopping in my tracks, I dig my feet into the floor, forcing him to stop as well. Halting, he looms over me, and maybe before our size differences would've scared me, now his darkness, size, and overall body appeals to me. Placing a hand against his chest, I try not to think of the skin beneath it: the ridges, and dips, and the way his body molded so perfectly to mine.

Jesus... I can feel my core tightening.

"She is the only friend I have. It's not like I can go out and find one that's to your liking. And even if I could, her social standing wouldn't matter to me. She's still a person. She is kind, and she cares about me. I understand that she shouldn't question you and that what happens to me doesn't concern her, but her intentions are pure and come from a good place."

"I won't be questioned by *my* staff." His jaw turns to steel, and his eyes flicker with fury.

"Then don't be, but don't treat her like she isn't a human," I whisper, placing a featherlight kiss against his jaw. "She is loyal to you, doesn't this prove that. Even though she was worried, she didn't act on it. Can't that be enough?"

I don't understand why I feel the need to kiss and touch him so often, but it brings me joy. When he's near, I feel alive. All my life, I've been trapped, and it's like now I've finally broken free. Julian's gaze softens a fraction when I grab his hand once more and let him guide me back to the bedroom.

"Will you stay a bit with me? Maybe just lie in bed with me?"

Julian gives me a questioning look, and I'm one hundred percent sure he is going to say no, but then shocks me when he nods his head.

We both take our shoes off and crawl into bed together. Resting my head on his chest, I throw one leg over his, wanting him closer. I never thought I would feel safe in his arms, and especially not seek out the comfort of his body.

Running a hand up and down my back, he makes me shiver.

"Tomorrow, you will meet someone close to me. He is an ally and has worked with me often over the years. He is bringing his wife. Maybe you can make another friend. Their love story is far more dysfunctional than ours."

"Love story?" I lift my head off his chest and peer up into his calm gaze. "I didn't think mobsters fell in love?"

"Not all mobsters fall in love. Xander is tougher than steel and meaner than fuck. I'm surprised he found someone that could be the light to his darkness."

The light to his darkness...

Maybe that's what I'll become to Julian. Maybe he just needs a little light to dull out all the dark in his life.

"Well, I can't wait to meet her and hear about their love story," I whisper, placing my head back down on his chest. Closing my eyes, I easily slip into sleep, feeling safe, protected, and cherished.

28

JULIAN

The next morning, I find it hard to take my eyes off Elena. She's wearing a sundress with roses on it that ends just above her knee. I can't seem to look anywhere but at her shapely legs, envisioning them wrapped around my middle while I thrust deep inside her.

"What are you thinking?" Elena questions, biting into a strawberry.

I decided breakfast out on the terrace would be fitting for today, but now I'm wondering if we should've stayed in the bedroom, so I could've eaten her for breakfast instead.

"You don't want to know."

She blinks slowly, lust swirling in her depths. "Oh, really? Try me."

Leaning over the table, I trail a finger down her cheek. "You have sex one time, and you think you can handle all my fantasies and the things that I have planned for you?"

Her little throat bobs, and I almost laugh.

"I'm stronger than I look." She leans in, her eyes moving to my lips, determination shining in them. I can't wait to make her eat her words, see her shatter around me, and beg me for her release.

"This is a dangerous game you're playing, my soon to be wife. You have yet to see what I'm capable of." A tiny shiver works its way through her, and I can't even put into words the immense pleasure that makes me feel, knowing that I hold a spell over her, that she's drawn not only physically to me, but sexually.

She licks her lips. "Then show me."

My balls ache, and my cock pushes against the zipper of my now uncomfortable dress slacks. Reaching beneath the table, I slide my hand beneath her dress and over her bare thigh. Her eyes widen, worry, and need swirl together, becoming one.

Moving up to the apex of her thigh, I watch her face as my fingers graze the thin material of her panties, over her damp center.

"You're wet," I whisper, pressing against her clit.

Red fills her sun-kissed cheeks, and I wonder if she's going to stop me. Her eyes dart out onto the green landscape as if she's looking for someone. Like I would ever really allow someone to see me touching her. I'd gouge their eyes out before I let that happen.

Trailing my finger up and down the damp fabric, I watch Elena squirm in her seat, biting her plump bottom lip to stop a moan from escaping.

"If I had the time, I'd stand you up, flip that pretty little dress up over your ass, rip your panties from your body, and bend you over this table and fuck you until everyone in this house heard your screams."

"You'd let someone hear us." Shock coats her words, but curiosity fills her eyes. Someone is into a little voyeurism.

"Hearing, yes, seeing, no. Plus, it's not like they don't know you belong to me already. What's staking my claim and letting the world hear it happen?" I move to the side of her panties, and slip my finger inside, wanting so desperately to lift her up, place her ass on the table and feast on her pink pussy.

"Boss, your guests are here." Lucca's timber voice halts my movements, and Elena's gaze drops to her plate. She isn't good at hiding her facial expressions and looks like a child who got caught with their hand in the cookie jar.

"Bring them out here to us," I tell him and gently pull my hand from between her legs.

Lucca's heavy footfalls retreat, and I place a finger beneath Elena's chin, tipping it upward, forcing her to look at me.

"We will finish this later," I say before giving her a punishing kiss. When I pull away, she looks out of breath, and I decide I like that look on her face.

A few moments later, Lucca returns with Xander and Ella in tow. I stand up to greet him and extend my hand out. Elena stands as well, looking nervous and unsure. As soon as Ella spots Elena beside me, her face splits into a grin.

Ella and Xander are like day and night. Before I knew the story, I always wondered how the dark-haired, brooding man that could kill without mercy, had ended up with the blonde-haired, blue-eyed innocent woman. It was like good and evil collided.

"Xander." I smirk, shaking his hand firmly.

"Julian," he greets, his gaze moving to Elena.

"This is my soon to be wife, Elena." I wrap a protective arm around her and tug her closer to my side. "Elena, this is Xander Rossi and his wife, Ella."

Elena gives both of them a shy smile. "It's so nice to meet you both."

"The pleasure is ours," Xander says.

Ella beams at his side, looking like she is ready to jump Elena. Xander turns to his wife, his features softening for a millisecond as he drinks her in. Who knew the dark king of the Rossi empire could be brought to his knees?

"Why don't you ladies go sit by the pool, so we can discuss some business." Xander smiles, but it's a lot like a shark smiling at you.

"That sounds great," Ella says cheerfully. Elena pulls away from me, her back becoming straighter as she lifts her chin and gives Xander's wife a gracious smile.

We watch them walk away together and down to the pool before sitting at the table Elena I was just having breakfast at.

"Did we interrupt your breakfast?" Xander questions his dark eyes on the table.

"No, no. We were finished. Would you like something to drink?" I offer.

Xander shakes his head. "No, thanks. I'm merely here to see what my dear friend is up to, and of course, to allow Ella to meet your soon to be wife. She was all but jumping up and down when I said we would be attending your wedding."

"It's a wedding of mere convenience," I say, sitting back in my chair, my eyes wandering down to the pool where Ella and Elena are sitting. I know what I've said is a lie, simply by the bitter taste that appears on the tip of my tongue. "I need to know I have your alliance against the Romero family, and I may need your help with weapons."

Xander sits back in his chair as well. "Is that so, it doesn't seem like a marriage of convenience?" Of course, the fucker would call my bluff. Is it that obvious? "And, yes, you have my alliance, and always will, against whomever. You're like family to me, and what is mine is yours. Now, tell me what you need the weapons for?"

"We may be going to war against Volcove. I killed their son the other night after he put his hands on Elena."

Xander grins. "Marriage of convenience, huh? Willing to go to war for her? Sounds a bit more serious than that."

"Tell me you would ever allow someone to touch Ella?"

Xander's features turned dark. "Anyone who ever touched her would die a painful death at my hands."

"Exactly, and you would go to war for her. You killed your father for her." I lift a brow.

"I killed my father because I wanted to, the Rossi empire was meant to be mine." I nod. Xander's a good man, but if you double-cross him, you'll wish you'd never met him.

His power reached far and wide, and if he wanted to destroy you, it could easily be done.

"I'm going to kill her father," I tell him.

"Hmm, are you? Have you let her know this yet?"

"She is aware of it, but I don't think she is taking me seriously. I took her for revenge, that part she doesn't know."

"But she's getting to you, she's weaseling her way under your skin."

I look out to the pool, and this deep fondness pulses through my veins. The organ in my chest thumps loudly, and it's never felt so fucking whole. She fills the spaces that her father's betrayal took from me, and I realize that now.

"It will never work as soon as she finds out why I took her, and that I will never return her feelings, she will hate me even more than she already does."

"I've known you since you were a teenager when you first took over for your father. You don't want to believe it because we're men that aren't meant to feel anything but pain and rage, but I think there is something there."

As if Elena can hear us talking about her, she turns and looks at me over her shoulder. Her green eyes glitter with joy, and I wonder if I could stand to see them filled with bitter rage, pain, and anger all over again.

"I don't know." I shake my head, "I don't want to feel anything for her."

"I think you're past not wanting to feel anything for her. Even though you're doing your best to hide it, I can see that she means something to you. You might have taken her for revenge, but things can change. It changed for Ella and me, the same could happen to you too."

Ella and Xander weren't Elena and me. I may be able to make her happy and give her all the things she wants and needs, but I could never fall in love with her. It would be a slap to my mother's face if I fell for the enemy's daughter.

There was no room for love in our marriage.

∽

"Ella said if it's okay with you, that they would visit us again with their kids next time." Elena beams on the way back upstairs.

"Sure, maybe after our honeymoon."

"Wait, we're going on a honeymoon?" She squeals the words.

"Yes, we'll leave tomorrow after the wedding." *After I kill your father.*

"Where are we going?"

"It's a surprise. You'll like it." I know she will. And the best part is, I can give her more freedom there. She'll be able to walk around the house freely, maybe even on the beach. I know she'll love it, she'll just hate *me* by then.

Pushing all those unwanted thoughts away, I concentrate on the here and now. I soak in her happiness, not knowing when it'll be the last time I get to see it. She is basically skipping along by the time we get to the bedroom. I want one last night with her where there is no hate or guilt between us. Where it is just us, no last names, no contract.

Opening the door, I let her walk in first. As soon as the door closes behind us, I start to unbutton my shirt. All-day, I've thought about this moment, stripping her bare and making her beg for my cock. Now, here we are, the night before our wedding.

"Strip," I order as she turns around to face me.

Her green eyes widen, desire pooling in the depths. She does as I instruct, slowly stripping out of her clothing.

"What are you going to do to me?" she questions innocently.

"What do you want me to do to you?"

"Touch me. Kiss me."

Her reply is soft and sweet, just like her. I cross the distance between us, and trail a hand down her side, enjoying the way her skin quakes beneath my finger. I need her now. Need her honeyed taste on my tongue. Grabbing her hand, I tug her behind me as I walk over to the chaise lounge. She's going to ride my cock, but first, I'm going to taste her sweet cunt.

"Sit on the couch and spread your legs as wide as they'll go."

Nibbling on her bottom lip, she peers up at me before moving to sit on the edge of the couch. Spreading her legs as wide as she can, her little pink pussy comes into view, and my mouth waters. An animalistic urge rips through me, and I drop to my knees, tugging her by the ass to the edge of the cushion. Pushing her legs back against her chest, I bend her to my will, leaving her completely exposed.

"I'm going to fuck you so hard you'll feel me for days, but before I do that, I'm going to make you gush all over my face."

"Yes." She gasps and reaches for me.

Her sharp little nails dig into my scalp, urging me forward. With two fingers, I part her folds and find her clit, unprotected, and begging to be touched. I lick my lips and bury my face between her folds, flicking my tongue against the hard nub.

"Oh, god... yes, please, don't stop." Elena pants into the quiet room.

My hands roam her body, painting a picture of her in my mind as I lap at her pussy, sucking and nibbling. When my hands reach her tits, I roll the diamond-hard peaks between two fingers and relish in the heavy gasps that pass her lips.

Keeping my hands on her tits, I pull back and drop my attention down to her entrance, dipping my tongue inside her, fucking her with it.

"Julian..." She moans, grinding her pussy into my face, and I fucking love it. Love her sweet little moans, her scent, and the way she tastes. It's intoxicating and maddening, and I can only think of making her say my name again.

"If you keep doing that, I'm going to come..."

"That's the plan," I growl.

Pinching her nipples, I lick her down to her puckered ass and press my tongue against the tight ring. A shudder rips through her, and I move back up to her pussy and plunge my tongue inside her. I do this twice more, and like expected, she explodes, her pussy quivers, and her release dribbles out, flooding into my mouth.

"Mmmm," I groan against her folds, lapping up every drop. When I've had my fill, I drop down onto the couch and grab her by the waist, tugging her onto my lap, maneuvering her like she's nothing but a ragdoll. In this position, she looks so unsure but so fucking beautiful.

Her dark hair frames her heart-shaped face beautifully, and her eyes are luminescent with a sheen of pleasure still in them. She looks fucked, but she hasn't been, not yet. Placing her dainty hands against my firm chest, she balances herself as she lifts her hips.

My rock hard cock stands at attention, and I move it into place, the swollen head brushing against her entrance.

"Are you sure? I thought you would be in control still?" She whispers as the crown of my cock dips inside of her.

"I'm always in control, sweetheart," I grit as I grab her by the hips and press her down on my cock—her lips part and form into an O.

I give her a moment to adjust to my length, relishing in the warmth, and the snugness of her pussy. She was made for me, fucking made for me. Even as my muscles ache, and my cock begs to plow into her, I let her bounce up and down on me, taking as much of my length as she wants. Capturing one of her tits in my mouth, I bite at the hardened nipple, and the squeal that Elena emits from her perfect mouth sends me into a tailspin.

I need more.

My fucking balls ache, and this slow, treacherous pace is killing me. I need to fuck her, feel her come apart on my cock. Grabbing her by the nape, I drag her mouth down to mine. I give her a punishing kiss before I wrap both arms around her and hold her tightly to my chest.

She looks up at me, and holds my gaze as I thrust my hips, my cock hitting the end of her channel. Pleasure overtakes her features, and I do it again and again, upping my pace until I'm fucking her hard and fast, using her tight little hole as I see fit.

It doesn't take long for a tingle to build at the base of my spine, and I know I'm close to coming. I grind my groin against her and swivel my hips, watching her face as the tip of my cock hits her g-spot.

"Fuck, come for me. You need to come with me."

Elena doesn't need any more words of encouragement, her eyes drift closed, and her body trembles in my arms. It is then that I feel it, her pussy pulses around me, tightening to the point of pain, and still, I move inside her, fucking her through her pleasure, and finding my own in the process. When I can't hold off any longer, I go off like a rocket, my warm release coating the inside of her pussy. Her tiny little channel can't take all my load, so some dribbles down my length and onto my balls.

"That was…" She pushes up from my chest a little and looks up at me, her eyes sleepy.

"Amazing?" I say, brushing a few strands of hair that stick to her sweaty forehead. The tension in my muscles has eased, and I feel replenished.

She nods. "Yes, amazing, and so good."

I smile. "You've just had a taste of what I want to do to you. Eventually, I'll claim every hole in your body with my cock, and believe me when I tell you, you'll enjoy it thoroughly."

She cocks her head to the side. "How can you be so sure?"

I brush my lips against hers. "Because as fucked up as it might seem, I know exactly what you crave, the right amount of darkness to your light, and I can make even the most painful things pleasurable. You'll see."

She looks at me with wonderment, and strangely, I never want that look to leave her face. I always want her to look at me with need and know that I'll protect her from the dark demons of our world. But I know, come tomorrow, she'll never look at me like that again. I doubt she'll even let me touch her without having a mental breakdown.

Holding her in my arms, I whisper into her ear, "I can't wait for you to become my wife tomorrow."

"Mmmm," she says, nuzzling against my neck.

If only we could stay like this forever.

29

ELENA

Sitting on the bed, I anxiously wait for Julian to return. He said he would be right back, but that was twenty minutes ago. Worry worms its way through me. I hope everything is okay. I'm probably just overreacting. Twenty minutes is not that long. Occupying myself, I think about the time we spent with Ella and Xander yesterday. For the first time, it felt like a normal day, like we were a normal couple. Hearing Ella tell me her and Xander's love story, of how they came to be, gave me hope for Julian and me.

The door to the bedroom comes flying open, and my thoughts evaporate into the air. I jump up from the bed and run my sweaty palm down the front of my sweater.

"Is everything okay?" I ask as soon as Julian steps into the room. His beautiful features are strained, showing how frustrated he is.

"Some guests arrived a little earlier than expected. I had to make sure everyone knows the rules," he explains.

"The rules?"

"No one is to set a foot inside the house. The wedding and reception will be outside."

"Oh, okay. Who is here?"

"The makeup and hair people are downstairs. They are ready for you now." I don't miss how tense Julian is, his body rigid, and his voice a little sterner than usual. Is he worried about the wedding? Is he having second thoughts?

"You're not regretting this, are you?" I whisper the words, hoping he says no.

"What? Marrying you? Never. It's the best fucking idea I ever had," he says, holding the door open for me. The tension inside me seems to ease a bit at his words, and together we walk out into the hallway.

"You seem tense."

"Your father is here."

I suck a harsh breath into my lungs. That explains why he is so tense.

"But, you invited him, right?"

"Yes, but he wasn't supposed to get here until this afternoon. There's no reason for him to be here this early."

"Did he ask about me? Maybe he just wants to talk to me before the wedding?" I try not to sound so eager, but it would be nice to have a small conversation with my father.

"There is nothing to talk about," Julian grits out.

"Julian, I know you don't like him, but he is still my father. I can't help that. You'll need to get along with him, eventually." I need to fix this, need to fix them.

"Let's not talk about that," he almost growls at me. "I don't want to ruin our wedding."

Not talk about it? What's that gonna help? "Why do you hate him so much, anyway? You never told me what happened between you guys."

I can feel the anger coming off of him in waves, and I don't understand why? I'm just asking him a question. We turn the corner, about to descend the stairs when we both come to an abrupt halt.

"Dad!" I gasp, taking in my father, who is standing at the top of the staircase.

"Elena," he greets, giving me a tight smile.

"How the fuck did you get in here?" Julian snaps, pulling me behind him.

"I think the better question is, why haven't you told her the truth yet? Believe me, you don't want to start a marriage built on lies. It never ends well."

The truth? He must've heard our conversation.

"Like I would take any kind of marriage advice from you," Julian sneers back.

"What *truth* is he talking about?" My gaze ping-pongs between them.

"The truth where he only took you from me for revenge. He doesn't want you, Elena. He only wants to hurt me." My father shoots daggers into Julian's face.

"That's not true," I defend Julian, shaking my head. He might not be capable of loving me, but I know he cares for me and that he wants me. In his own way, he tries his best to make me happy, and he wouldn't hurt me.

"Tell her, Moretti, tell her what this is really about. Tell her that it's nothing but revenge for your mother."

"Shut up, you know nothing!" Julian roars.

"What about his mother?" I feel I only know half of the story, and now I'm playing catch up. A second ticks by and then another. "Julian, what is this about? What's going on?"

"Your father killed my mother," Julian grits through his teeth. His hands curl into fists at his sides, the muscles tightening, the veins showing in his hand.

My eyes find my father's, the same shade of green I see when I look in the mirror, greets me. "Dad?" I beg him to explain with that single word alone while hoping that it's not true. I know my father has done despicable things, but I can't see him killing Julian's mother. It has to be a lie.

Worry creases his forehead. "Elena, I loved your mother very much. I never planned on cheating on her, but then his mother seduced me." My father lifts a hand, pointing a finger at Julian accusingly. "She got me drunk and into bed. Tricking me into getting her pregnant. It was the biggest mistake of my life–"

"You're a fucking liar!" Julian takes a step toward him. Feeling like I need to defuse the situation before it breaks out like a forest fire, I grab onto Julian's arm, hoping that my touch will calm him a little.

"It's true! She was nothing more than a common whore, who tricked and used men–"

A gasp escapes my lips when Julian rips his arm away from my hold and pounces on my dad like a lion. Rearing back his arm, he swings his fist and hits my father in the side of his face, making his head snap to the side.

I'm so shocked, I just stand there, watching the whole thing play out in front of me like a movie. Julian's a big guy, but so is my father, and both men are throwing punches at the other, some hitting so forcefully the sounds of bones crushing fills the space... or maybe I'm just in shock and hearing things.

Where are the guards, and why can't I move... or scream for help?

I need to do something, but my stupid body is petrified with fear.

Then I see it. In the midst of them beating each other to a pulp, my father pulls something from his pocket. Between the grunting, the limbs swinging through the air, and the jerky body movements, I almost miss it.

A small silver object, the sharp edge reflected by the light shining in from the window. *A knife! He has a knife.*

In less than a blink of an eye, my body unfreezes, and I spring into action. My father has a knife, and he's about to kill Julian, the man I love. I can't let that happen. I can't let him take this from me. Without fear or concern for my own wellbeing, I lunge a hand between them.

With my eyes on the blade, the two bodies around me become nothing more than blurred limbs. I reach out to grab it, but before I can get close enough, an elbow thrusts backward and hits me in the center of my chest.

Everything happens in slow motion. The impact sends me teetering backward, and I stumble, losing my footing. I take another step back to steady myself, only to realize that there is nothing to step on. I'm at the top of the stairs.

In the midst of the chaos, Julian's eyes find mine, and I see something in his blue depths I've never seen before. *Fear.*

He reaches for me, stretching his arm out, extending his hand. I lift my own, trying to grasp his. Our fingertips touch, but when I close my hand, they slip away, and I grasp around nothing as I fall backward into the empty space.

30

JULIAN

I've been alive for twenty-eight years. Almost three decades, and I can count on one hand the number of times I was scared, truly scared.

Struck with a fear so intense that you can't breathe, that your heart stops beating in your chest, and an ache forms in your gut that is so deep you think it's going to kill you.

Last time I felt anything remotely close to that was the day I lost my mother. I wasn't scared of dying, but I was scared of living a life without her. I was scared of living in a world where no one loved me unconditionally. That was five years ago, and I didn't think I would ever feel this frightened, would ever feel that kind of loss and dread again.

I had no idea how wrong I was.

I feel it now, feel it in my soul.

The moment my elbow connects with her chest, my heart stops beating. Everything happens in slow motion from that moment on. Turning, I reach out for her. Every fiber in my body tells me one thing: *save her*. I have to save her.

My hand extends, my fingers stretch into the air, and I lunge for her, but it's too late. Her beautiful face is riddled with horror.

Her green gaze widens, and her soft pouty mouth opens on a gasp as she falls backward. The organ in my chest thunders to life, beating so fast I swear it's going to escape my chest.

Do something! I scream inwardly.

Forcing myself to move faster, be quicker, stronger, I lunge forward, but it's futile. Fingers grasp onto nothing, and I have never felt so powerless in my life. Not even when my father died. Not even when I found my mother.

Helplessly, I watch with a deep ache as her back hits the stairs, and she tumbles down them. Every step she hits, every limb that twists, and every bump her head takes, I feel it. Feel her pain so deep in my bones, I fear they may crack.

My body moves on its own, and I find myself running down the staircase after her while still watching her fall into the abyss like a ragdoll.

When she hits the bottom step, her body becomes motionless, and I fear the worst. She is so still, too still. My feet make little noise as I rush to her aide.

Only when I get closer, do I see her chest moving. Rising and falling with each breath she takes. A sense of relief washes over me, but it's not strong enough to calm the tsunami of fear. She could still be in danger. Mentally, my brain goes into protective mode. She could have a number of internal injuries, bleeding in her brain, broken bones, or an injured spine... the list goes on, and with each thought, I get more frantic. Just because I don't see blood, doesn't mean there isn't something wrong.

Terror rips at my flesh, tearing me apart from the inside out. All I can think about is how I could lose her, the one person who has the power to make me good, who sees good in me when no one else does, and all because of her father. A man that once already took so much from me.

The coppery tang of blood explodes against my tongue as I grit my teeth.

Kneeling beside Elena, I lift a hesitant hand to touch her, but I'm scared to do even that. What if doing so hurts her more? She needs a doctor, a hospital, not my gentle caress.

Lifting my gaze from her still body, I peer around for my guards and find the hallway desolate. Glancing up the stairway, I realize it is empty as well.

Red hot rage burns through me. Fucking Romero left. He left his daughter. Left her to die on the steps inside of our home.

My hands tremble as I reach for my phone and retrieve it from my pocket. I don't think, I just act as I dial nine-one-one. As soon as someone answers, I tell them my address and yell at them to hurry. I drop the phone onto the marble floor and look down at Elena's pale face. I did this to her. I wanted to hurt her, and now that she's hurt, I can't bear it. It kills me to see her like this. Clenching my hand into a fist, I feel the need to destroy and rip the life from someone's body. Romero will pay.

Footsteps approach from behind me, and a moment later, a handful of guards show up. Their normally emotionless faces are filled with nothing short of fear and regret.

They know what's coming. I'll fucking kill all of them for this.

"How the fuck did Romero get into the house? You had one fucking job! To keep the place secure, and make sure no one got in. Find him!"

They disappear, dispersing in different directions as they start searching the house. I let the sounds around me fall away, the entire world disappears around us.

If there is no Elena, there is no me, and I realize that now.

Holding Elena's hand, I stroke her hair gently, afraid even that will hurt her. I have to do something, anything to make myself feel a little less helpless.

Seconds turn into minutes, and it feels like an eternity until the ambulance gets here. A buzzing fills my ears as the front doors burst open, and three EMTs come rushing to her side. I make space for them by moving out of the way, even though everything inside me tells me to keep holding her hand.

They work over her, their hands moving fast, and every move is precise as they carefully slip on a neck brace and slide the gurney beneath her. They ask me questions in between, and I answer each one like a zombie.

I follow them out as they carry her outside and rush her into the back of the ambulance. For a brief second, I consider getting into the ambulance with them but know I'll only be in the way. My feelings and fear are the least important things right now. I need to make sure Elena is okay, that she is still with me, and that she will make it through this.

Getting into my car, I pull behind the ambulance and follow them to the hospital. With light and sirens, they fly through the streets, and I stay close behind. When I pictured our wedding day, I never expected it to be over before it even started.

Clenching the wheel tighter, there is only one thought running through my mind, like a cassette on replay as I stare at the back of the ambulance.

Please, don't let her die.

~

SINCE THE MOMENT they rolled her back into this room, I haven't taken my eyes off her. They ran every test I demanded them to run, but even I couldn't make the MRI machine work fast enough. Now, I sit beside her, watching... waiting for her to wake, for the doctor to return with the test results. All of this is out of my hands, and I feel like a plane spiraling out of control, nosediving into the ground.

Forcing my thoughts to slow, I look down at Elena's unmoving form. She looks peaceful, her face relaxed, and her head slightly turned into the pillow as if she's simply sleeping. I wish it was mere sleep she was experiencing and that there wasn't a risk I could lose her. The thought leaves a fist-sized hole in my chest.

A quiet knock filters through the door that has me tearing my eyes away from her still body. The door opens, and the doctor steps in, his movements are cautious. He's an older guy with graying hair and dark eyes. Apparently, he's the best the hospital has, and he better hope so.

"Mr. Moretti, I've got your fiancée's test results," he explains. "I'm happy to tell you, her MRI came back good, considering the tumble she took. There are only minor injuries. Her right ankle is twisted badly. We'll keep the foot raised and put a brace on it for a few weeks. Her left ribs are bruised, so we recommend that you keep them wrapped and iced to help with the swelling, aside from that, there is not much more we can do for her.

Her head looks good. No bleeding or swelling in the brain, she does have a concussion, which is to be expected. Again, that is something that will heal with time. It's like a very bad headache. I'm recommending she stay here for observation for at least one more day."

"But she'll be fine? Make a full recovery?" The words rush past my lips.

"Yes, she should be completely back to normal in a few weeks," he confirms, and I suck a deep breath in, oxygen fills my lungs, for what feels like the first time today. "We'll keep her on IV pain medication while she is here, and of course, send some home with you as well. Her body will heal on its own, but she will be in a good amount of pain for the first week."

A deep primal possession rips through me. I'll take care of her. Make sure she only moves if she needs to. She will be taken care of, and her father will pay for hurting her.

"She has all the time in the world to recover," I say, a little gruffer than necessary.

He merely nods and walks out of the room. I return my full attention to the angel in front of me. I stare, my gaze burning into her face. All I want is for her to wake up, for her to be okay. I know the doctor said everything is going to be okay, but I can't believe that until she's awake.

A few moments later, her eyes flutter open, but her vision seems unfocused like she doesn't really see me.

"Hey, everything is okay," I whisper, squeezing her hand in mine as gently as I can.

"Julian..." she croaks, and I cradle her face, turning it toward me.

"I'm here, just relax. You're safe now. I won't leave you, and I won't let anything happen to you either. I'm sorry, Elena."

Her eyes flutter closed once more, and she falls back to sleep.

Over the next few hours, she slips in and out of consciousness. I don't think she knows where she is or that I'm here, but that doesn't mean I'm leaving her side.

I don't care about anything but her right now, and I never thought I would say that.

31

ELENA

There is an insistent buzzing, or maybe it's a beeping, that fills my ears. I can't really be sure which one it is, all I know is that the sound grates on every one of my nerve endings. My throat throbs, and as I try and swallow, it feels like someone has poured sand inside my mouth.

What's wrong with me?

Something similar to a groan escapes my lips, and as I try and blink my eyes open, all I see is white—white ceiling, white lights, white walls. Instantly, I know something is off. I'm not in Julian's house—*our* house.

No wait, we didn't get married yet because… just as I'm about to sink deeper into my thoughts, my head starts to throb like someone is chiseling at the side of it with an ice pick.

Turning my head, I find Julian sitting beside me in a chair. He looks too big for the small space. My nose wrinkles as I suck in a breath and the smell of antiseptic fills my lungs. At the same time, a sharp pain ripples across my ribs.

"Try not to move or breathe too deeply. You've got a concussion, bruised ribs, and a twisted ankle."

Licking my lips, I open my mouth to speak but find there are no words. All I remember is getting up in the morning. The day of our wedding, and then... my mind goes blank.

"What happened?" I croak. My gaze moves down my arm, to where an IV is inserted. Mentally, I think of all the things that Julian just said was wrong. Jesus, was I in a car accident or something? "How long have I been here?"

Julian's gorgeous features fill with anguish. "About a day."

"What happened?" I ask again.

"You don't remember?"

"No, I don't remember anything." I keep searching my brain for the missing pieces to the puzzle, but thinking hurts. I just want to go back to sleep.

"You fell down the stairs."

"Oh..." I visualize the staircase leading to the foyer. I recall walking down them so many times, but I don't remember falling. "I don't remember that."

"That's okay. You hit your head pretty hard. All that matters is that you are going to be okay. The doctor says you'll make a full recovery."

Relaxing into the hospital bed, I feel a little better knowing that. At least nothing that happened will have a lasting effect on me.

"We didn't get married, did we?"

"No." Julian shakes his head, a ghost of a smile curves his lips. "We were walking downstairs to get ready for the wedding when it happened. I tried to grab you, but I wasn't fast enough," he admits shamefully. The sadness and guilt in his voice is like a knife being stabbed into my chest. He blames himself, I know it without even asking him.

"It's okay. It wasn't your fault," I try to soothe him.

His mouth pops open, and he's about to say something else, but we're interrupted by a quiet knock at the door. A moment later, the door creeps open, and a petite nurse walks in. She must be new because she can't be much older than me.

Her eyes immediately gravitate toward Julian, and she clutches onto the clipboard she is holding like it's a protective shield. I'm not sure why, but she's clearly scared of Julian.

Of course, he doesn't help matters as he scowls at her, his eyes dragging up and then down her body like he is sizing her up.

"Hello, Elena," she greets me when she finally tears her eyes away from Julian. She tries to hide the tremble in her voice, but I can still hear it. "How are you feeling?"

"Good, I guess."

"Any pain right now?" she asks as she starts to take my vitals, completely ignoring Julian's presence.

"My head hurts a little, but not that bad."

"We can give you some more pain meds in about an hour. In the meantime, it would be great if you could get some fresh air, maybe go on a walk. I could push you in the wheelchair if you would like–"

"I'll take her on a walk," Julian cuts in gruffly. "Just leave us the wheelchair."

"Of course." She nods and quickly writes down my blood pressure and pulse onto the paper on the clipboard. "If you need anything else, just push the call button."

She scurries out of the room like she's in a hurry to get away. I can't help but wonder if something happened when I was passed out, but it's most likely because of how intimidating he is. He commands a room, and it doesn't matter where we're at, that doesn't change.

Thinking back on the first time I saw him at my father's house, I was scared of him too. Of course, he was basically kidnapping me, so I had a good reason to be frightened. Looking at him now, I'm not scared anymore. I'm the opposite in his presence. I feel protected.

He might not be prince charming, but he always keeps me safe, and I know he'll always give me what I want and need.

"You want to go for a walk?" Julian asks, interrupting my thoughts.

"I'd love that."

Julian gets the wheelchair and transfers my IV to the pole attached to it. Then he helps me out of the bed, and by *helps,* I mean he picks me up and deposits me into the wheelchair.

"I might be injured, but my legs aren't broken," I joke.

"I know, but I don't want to risk you falling." He helps me get situated, locking the leg rests of the wheelchair into place. "You could injure yourself further, and after the last twenty-four hours, the thought of seeing you hurt again..."

There's a faraway look in his eyes, almost as if he's reliving whatever happened. My throat tightens, and my heart lurches in my chest when he reaches for a lock of hair and tucks it behind my ear. It's such a small gesture, but it makes me feel warm all over.

"Don't look at me like that." The gruffness of his voice reaches down inside me and wraps around my body like veins.

"Like what?" I blink, trying to focus on anything but the warmth building in my core. I might be injured, but I'm definitely not dead. Turns out even in pain, he can still manage to make me weak with need.

Leaning forward, he gives me a half-smile. "Like you want me to fuck you. It's not happening... at least not right now." Those full lips of his brush against my forehead, and I shiver as he moves behind me, taking control of the wheelchair.

The warmth slowly seeps from my body as he wheels me out of the room and into the hall. His pace is leisurely like he has nowhere else to be. The silence in the hall is deafening, and I notice a few of his men trailing us. I try and ignore them, but that's hard when I already know they're there.

We pass a few rooms, but it doesn't seem like there is anyone in them, I haven't seen a single nurse or doctor pass by us. I haven't spent much time in hospitals, but from what I remember, there are usually people milling about. I can already imagine him demanding that I'm put in my own private wing, away from everyone else.

"Did you scare the nurses and doctors into giving us our own wing?"

"Of course, I did. I picked the best doctor available to care for you, and two nurses are working eighteen-hour shifts to be there for any and every need you might have."

"Why did you do that?" I croak, squeezing the arms of the wheelchair.

"Because you're a Moretti and should be cared for by the best." The deep growl he emits tells me there will be no arguments about this.

"I'm not your wife yet," I whisper.

"You will be soon, and marriage or not, you're mine. What happened changes nothing."

What happened?

It occurs to me then that he never answered me. He never told me how I fell down the stairs. What was I doing that caused me to fall? Did he push me? Did someone else push me? Panic starts to bubble up, and the pressure on my chest mounts.

No. Julian wouldn't hurt me, but someone else might have.

I recall the time someone tried to poison me. Did the same person come to finish the job? Different scenarios start to breed in my mind like cancer. I force myself to calm and take small shallow breaths, even though my lungs are burning, and my heart is racing out of my chest.

Staring straight ahead, I see we're entering the atrium of the hospital. Huge trees canopy the air, and the sound of trickling water fills my ears. Sun shines in through the glass ceiling, making the space bright and airy.

Julian continues to push me into the massive area, and I calm a little when we reach a small seating area near a giant waterfall that drains into a shallow but large pond. Putting the brakes on the wheelchair, he moves slowly, sitting on the bench beside me.

I stare at the waterfall, watching as the water cascades over the edge, rushing into nothingness without realizing it.

Dragging my gaze from the waterfall, I turn, and my eyes collide with Julian's wild one. His icy blue eyes are mesmerizing, like deep pits that lead to the ocean floor.

"What happened? How did I fall?" I ask, desperately wanting to know what got me here.

Julian's jaw tightens, the angles becoming harsh, his features darkening.

"We will talk about what happened when you're better, and definitely not here." The tight-lipped smile he gives me doesn't reach his eyes, and the sharp edge to his voice is a warning.

This conversation is done for now... but not forever.

"Okay," I whisper, and just then, the throbbing in my head intensifies, and I know he's right. Right now, isn't the time to dive into what happened.

~

THE DOCTOR RELEASES me from the hospital the next day. I get the feeling the nurses are all glad we are gone, which is the way Julian is. They must have been pretty freaked out.

Julian treats me like I'm made of glass. He practically carries me to the car, and then from the car and into the house when we get back to the mansion—our home.

Home. It's still weird to think about this place as my home, but the truth is, it feels more and more like that. When I was living with my father, it never felt like a home, more like a jail cell, and though things with Julian weren't easy at first, things are better here than they ever were with my father.

Julian carries me all the way up the stairs, and I hold onto him, laying my head on his shoulder. When we make it to the top of the staircase, I almost expect to have a flashback, maybe a few memories resurfacing, but nothing happens. The staircase looks as it always has, and I still remember nothing.

We make it to the bedroom, and I'm surprised to find Marie standing inside the room. She greets us with a warm smile, and I'm even more surprised when I take in the rest of the room.

One of the dressers has been moved and replaced with a bookshelf, which is filled with all my favorite books. The bed is set up with cushions and a backrest to sit comfortably with my foot raised. The nightstand has been replaced with a table that looks close to the hospital side table. It's retractable and pulls out and over the bed like a tv tray.

"You'll be more comfortable like this," Julian explains as I take everything in. "Marie will stay with you when I'm busy. You can't be alone right now with the concussion."

"Oh... okay." I can't help but smile.

I don't have to be alone anymore.

Julian lowers me gently onto the mattress, and I sink into the soft cushion with a sigh. There is nothing like being in your own bed. My head is still hurting, and my ribs are killing me, but I try to focus on the good.

"I also got you this," Julian's voice softens, and he pulls something out from under the table and hands it to me. I stare down at the silver iPad in my hands. "It's not connected to the internet, but I preloaded it with movies, music, books, and apps I thought you might like. This should keep you busy while you recover."

"Thank you," I whisper without taking my eyes off the iPad. I'm more than thankful that Julian set all of this up. That he got me this gift and is having Marie stay with me.

But I can't help but shake the feeling I'm having right now. There's this little voice in the back of my mind nagging, telling me that he's doing this not because he wants to but because he feels guilty. I know he feels responsible for what happened, but I can't seem to let go of the fact that maybe it's more than that?

Did he actually hurt me?

The question lingers long after he leaves the room.

Because if he did, I don't know what I would do.

32

JULIAN

Three Weeks Later

SITTING AT MY DESK, I watch the amber-colored liquid swirl around inside the crystal glass. Zeke Black sits across from me. Xander Rossi says he's the best at what he does, and that's exactly what I need. Someone good enough to find Romero without spooking him. I want him brought to me alive.

"Xander tells me you're good at what you do." I look up at him over the rim of my glass.

"*Good* is an understatement, but I don't want to be boastful." His features are stoic.

Zeke is pretty young to have the rap sheet he has, but I guess I'm pretty young myself to be the head of this family. From the little background Xander shared with me, he grew up being tossed from foster home to foster home. He's worked as a hitman for years and is damn good at what he does.

"This is going to be a bit different than what you're used to. I don't want him dead. I want to be the one to deliver that blow. I need you to find him and bring him to me."

"Whatever you want. You know my fee." I nod. "Then we'll be in touch. I'll get to work sniffing around. If you have any information or know anyone who might know where he's hiding, pass the info onto me."

I nod again and peer into his dark gaze. Even as a paid killer, I can see there are still shreds of a soul that lives inside him. He's not as far gone as Xander or me. Not yet, at least.

"I mean it, Zeke. I want him alive. Don't screw this up."

"I won't," he growls and shoves out of his chair. He leaves my office without speaking another word to me, and his attitude is almost dismissive. I don't like being blown off, but I'll deal with it for now.

Even here, in this gigantic mansion, hidden away from the rest of the world, I still don't feel like I can keep her safe.

Since arriving home, we've had two breaches. The men died at my hands, but I still don't feel like their deaths are enough payment. I want revenge, and I won't rest until all my enemies are dead, starting with Romero.

Tapping my fingers idly against the wood, I grit my teeth, rage festering inside me. The fucker could be out there anywhere, and all he's doing is hiding. He hasn't tried to contact me, not even to check and see if Elena is okay. Not that I'm surprised he ran like the coward he is instead of caring for his daughter. Most likely because he knows his end is near and as soon as I find him, I'll be putting a bullet in his head.

I've abandoned the thought of making a big show at the wedding. The need to make him suffer has died down, and all I want now is to wipe him off the face of the earth and move on with my life.

While my need to make Romero suffer is gone, my obsession with his daughter has only grown. I've spent every minute I'm not working with her, tending to her every want and need. I've eaten almost every meal with her, held her every night in my arms, and have taken her on walks around the property every day.

She's recovering well, and I've enjoyed taking care of her for the last three weeks. She has opened me up in ways I can't even put into words. I enjoy her smiles, her lingering looks, and every touch, no matter how small it is.

My need to consume her, to strip her bare, and own her body all over again rises with each sunset, and sunrise. I want her, need her, and as soon as she is well enough, I will have her again. The seconds on the clock tick by as I reach the end of my workday.

Ha, I say that like I'm working in an office and not breaking kneecaps, and laundering money across the country. Bringing the glass to my lips, I down the rest of the amber liquid and let it coat my insides with warmth before placing it back on the desk.

Another day without a single lead on Romero, and another day without my revenge, I try not to let the bitter anger consume my emotions as I shove out of my chair and come to stand. In the end, I still have the most precious thing he owns.

His daughter.

Leaving my office, I lock the door and saunter down the hall, stopping in front of the door to our bedroom. Grabbing the iron handle, I twist it and pull the door open. As I enter the bedroom, Marie jumps up from the chair that's beside the bed.

"Good evening, sir," she stumbles over her words.

"You're dismissed." I wave off her fear. She is scared of me, and rightfully so. I don't like her, but I tolerate her because I know Elena cares for her. They have become friends, and since that makes Elena happy, I'll allow it.

"Okay," she squeaks and scurries out of the room with her head bowed. With her gone, I turn my attention back to Elena.

Her adorable little nose is wrinkled as if she's smelt something bad.

"You don't have to treat her like that. She's my friend."

"I know, and I tolerate that, but she's still an employee of mine, and when I tell her to leave, I expect her to do it."

Crossing her arms over her chest, she says, "I guess. I just don't like how scared of you she is."

I almost laugh. "Many people are scared of me. You were as well once. I don't trust her or anyone for that matter, so it's better to be feared than not because if people aren't scared of you, they think they can get away with things."

For a fleeting moment, our eyes collide, her striking green clash with my icy blues. She is so beautiful, fragile like glass, a fine jewel. Every day, I'm reminded of how precious her safety is, her life is in my hands, and I'll be damned if I let her down.

Soon, she'll be my bride, and then she'll give me an heir.

The day is coming... soon, so very soon.

Breaking the connection, I ask, "Are you ready for dinner? Or would you rather take a walk first?"

"Maybe just a short walk before dinner?"

"As you wish." I nod and help her from the bed.

She loops her arm around mine and uses my body as a brace to stand. She hasn't used the wheelchair in over a week now. The brace on her ankle is enough to let her walk slowly and pain-free, but I still maintain a hold on her. There is always the risk that she could trip and fall and injure herself all over again.

"I think I'll be fine without a brace soon," she tells me as we walk down the hall together. "My ribs barely hurt anymore." The excitement in her voice radiates outward. I know she's ready for me to stop babying her, to do things on her own, but part of me isn't there yet. With her father out there and enemies coming from left and right, her safety and care is of the most importance.

"I'm happy to hear that. I'll have the doctor come take a look and make sure it's okay to take off the brace beforehand."

I might be overprotective, but I don't care. Ahead is the staircase, and in my mind, a flashback of that day replays. Her tumbling down the stairs, the horror in her eyes, and how her father tried to kill me. As if Elena can read my thoughts, she perks up and turns her head to look up at me.

"You never told me how I fell down the stairs," she whispers softly like she's approaching a wild animal. "I know you would never hurt me... I feel safe with you, but... I just feel like there is something you are hiding from me. Will you please tell me what happened? No matter how many times I rack my brain for an answer or a memory of that day, all I get is a black void. I know something happened; I can tell..."

"It doesn't matter now–"

"It matters to me," she almost yells before softening her voice. "Did someone try to kill me again?"

"What? No. You falling was an accident," I assure her.

She relaxes next to me, but the way she looks at me tells me she still wants to know more. I can't hide the truth from her forever.

"Then why are you not telling me how it happened?"

I grit my teeth, my jaw becoming steel. "Your father was here."

Confusion flashes across her face. "My father? He was there when I fell?"

"Yes. He was there, and he saw it happen."

"Why wasn't he at the hospital? Did you send him away?" Her tone grows accusing, and anger rips through me. I can't fucking believe it. She still trusts him more than she trusts me, and that bothers me more than I'd like to admit.

For a moment, I say nothing. I'm caught between wanting to make her see her father for the person he really is and not wanting to hurt her feelings. My desire for her complete submission wins over my need to protect her emotions, and I know what I'm about to tell her is selfish, but it's the truth.

"Your father was there. He saw you fall. He saw your lifeless body lying on the bottom of the stairs, and instead of rushing to your aide like I did, he left. He didn't even check on you, didn't blink, or make a move toward you. One second, he was there, and the next, he was gone."

Her whole body goes rigid, and she stops walking. I almost cringe at the hurt in her eyes. The last thing I want is to see her suffer.

"Did he try to come to the hospital?" she asks, her voice shaky, matching the pain in her gaze.

"No. He left and went into hiding. No one knows where he is..." And then it hits me. "You wouldn't happen to know where he would go to hide, would you?"

"No," she blurts out, a bit too fast, too eagerly.

She's lying.

My self-control is hanging on by a thread, but I don't say another word about it as I lead her outside and into the garden. She doesn't ask any more questions, and that might be her saving grace at the moment. I don't trust myself to say anything right now. My anger is too prevalent.

She's lying to me.

She knows where her father is.

Now, I only have to figure out how to make her talk.

33

ELENA

*J*ulian is oddly quiet at dinner, and that quietness carries over into the evening. After dinner, we retreat back up to our bedroom.

Worry swirls like a hurricane inside of me. He's angry with me. He hasn't said anything, not a single word, but I can feel it. Feel the fury rushing off of him and slamming into me.

Could he tell that I was lying?

Who am I kidding? Of course, he could.

But what am I supposed to do? Tell him where my father is? I can't do that. No matter what my father has done to me, he is still my dad. Telling Julian where he could be hiding would mean certain death to the only family I have left. My father may have betrayed me, but I'm not like him, and I refuse to get involved in their fight.

Like a child, Julian leaves me sitting on the bed as he takes a shower. I slip out of my clothes and down to my panties, then I crawl under the blankets and wait for him.

The bed feels cold and empty when he's not here. I'm so used to sleeping in his arms, I don't think I could fall asleep without him anymore.

The thought is frightening. I never wanted to become dependent upon him, but over time, he's broken down my walls, and shown me a glimpse of who he really is.

The bathroom door opens a few minutes later, and Julian steps into the room completely naked. His dark hair is still wet, and droplets stick to his tan skin. Lowering my gaze, I see he is fully erect. His cock so hard, it's pointing up to his navel.

Three weeks. It's been three weeks since he's done anything, aside from a gentle kiss, or soft caress. Seeing him naked now, ready to fuck me, has my core heating and my breath coming in short heavy spurts.

My pulse races, and not just because of his nakedness. His eyes are dark, his look stern, and his muscles flexed. He radiates anger.

I was right. He is angry.

Like a lion, he prowls toward me, and I cannot deny that the way he's looking at me turns me on even more. It's both frightening and exciting, like riding a rollercoaster, knowing there is a drop coming, but unsure when.

"Why do you protect him? He doesn't care about you, not like I do."

"I'm not protecting him," I squeak as he tugs back the covers, exposing my body. My nipples harden at the cool air that kisses my skin. I instinctively try to scoot back and sit up, but Julian grabs my injured ankle and pulls me back toward him.

"Lies," he hisses through his teeth like a snake.

All I can do is gasp when he pounces on me, his hand circles my throat, squeezing just enough to let me know he is in control. His hot mouth circles one of my hard tips, and his tongue flicks against it before his teeth sink into my skin.

Warmth floods my body, colliding with fear and a zing of pain as he bites down harder. Lifting my hands, wanting to place them on his chest, I hope to regain at least a little control. But he snatches my wrists and pins them above my head with one of his large hands while keeping the other on my throat.

"Julian," I whimper.

"Tell me what I want to know," he whispers against my skin, trailing kisses up my chest and over my throat. My heart races beneath my skin, thundering so loudly it's almost all I can hear.

"I know nothing…" I tell him, and whine when he pulls away and stares down at me. His icy blue gaze pins me to the mattress, and for the first time in weeks, a shiver of fear runs down my spine.

"I'm going to get the answer out of you. Roll over," he orders thickly. I don't even hesitate as I obediently roll over onto my hands and knees. "Leave your hands above your head and jut your ass out."

I follow his order without thought, even though I'm scared of what he is going to do to me. I watch him take a pillow and stuff it under my stomach before he places a hand between my shoulder blades and pushes me down.

I'm surprised when he gets off the bed, but I don't move. I hear him get something out of the dresser. A few moments later, he is back by my side. He takes one of my wrists, and before I know what's happening, my hands are cuffed to the bedposts.

"What are you doing?" I ask meekly.

"Don't talk unless you are answering my questions," he snaps, his voice is gruff, dark, and has an edge to it that has me on high alert. This is not the Julian I trust. This is not the sweet, caring person I seek out for safety. This is the Julian I betrayed, who is willing to hurt me to get his way.

I'm not prepared for what's about to happen. I know the extent he'll go to, to get what he wants. And right now, he wants to get his hands on my father.

Lost in thought, I let out a surprised yelp when he spreads my legs and climbs back onto the bed behind me.

"Such a pretty pussy. It's going to be a shame that I have to punish both of us."

"I don't know where he..." I don't even get to finish the sentence before I feel his back against mine, his weight presses into me, and his hard cock digs into my ass. His mammoth hand circles the back of my neck, and he squeezes my flesh in warning.

"Do not speak unless it is to tell me where your father is hiding," he grits out, giving me a hard squeeze before pulling away completely.

I shouldn't be turned on. I should be terrified. Yet, the warmth between my legs grows, and wetness forms against my folds. He's making me need him, want him, even in the moments when I shouldn't. He's a drug I'll never be able to quit, and I'm ashamed to admit it because wanting him as badly as I do makes me vulnerable.

"Now, let's see how many times I can bring you to the edge before you lose your mind." The darkness in his voice blankets over my skin, and I shiver.

A moment later, he's between my legs, his hot breath fanning against my entrance. Even the sensation that brings makes me pulse and press back against his face, seeking out a release. It's been three weeks. Three weeks without an orgasm, without pleasure.

"I think you're forgetting the lesson here. This is a punishment, if you want to come, then you'll need to tell me where your father is," Julian growls against my folds, and then the world around me fades away.

I fist the sheets and squirm against his hold. His fingers dig into my flesh as he holds me spread open, his mouth devouring me, feasting like a savage beast. His tongue slips inside my pussy, and he fucks me for a few long seconds before moving to my clit. He's merciless, and while I try and hold back the pleasure threatening to swallow me whole, I can't.

My stomach tightens, and the lightning bolts of pleasure start to shoot through me. I can feel myself on the edge of an orgasm, and without care, push back against his face, grinding my pussy against his mouth to get it right where I want it.

That's my biggest mistake because Julian isn't about to let me come. I know this, can feel it as my body shudders against the mattress. A second later, he proves his point and pulls away, leaving me aching and cold.

"Julian," I whimper in frustration, knowing that if I tell him what he wants to know, he'll let me come while also knowing I might as well be pulling the trigger on my father's life.

His mouth is replaced with two fingers, which trace my opening.

"Tell me where your daddy is, and I'll make you come so hard you'll forget your name."

"I don't..."

"If you say so," the words are a whisper, and though I can't see his face at that instant, I know there is a cruel smile on his lips. I'm going to pay for lying to him, pay with my body, mind, and soul.

He traces my opening, sinking the two thick digits inside my already drenched entrance. Like a cat in heat, I push back against his hand, and I'm rewarded with a chuckle.

"It sucks when you want something so badly, and it's within reach, yet you can't have it, doesn't it?"

"You're..." I gasp as he moves faster, making whatever I was about to call him evaporate from my mind.

"Not a liar like you, that's for sure." He moves the two fingers faster and faster, and the pressure in my womb mounts.

"Oh, god," I pant, warning him once again how close I am to coming. It's a stupid mistake because he's not going to let me come.

Like the bastard he is, he stops fucking me with his fingers and slows to nothing more than a stroke, stopping the build-up of pleasure in an instant.

Frustration mounts inside of me, and my head spins. I need to come, want it so badly, I could hump the mattress at this point and get off.

"If you want to come, you know what you have to do." Julian slips through my wet folds and rubs gentle circles against my clit.

"Please... please..." I beg deliriously.

Coating his fingers in my arousal, he trails back to my entrance, sinking the two fingers inside me. He starts to fuck me again, and for a moment, I get lost in the pleasure that starts to build back up. Maybe he's finally going to let me come? Caught up in my own thoughts, I fail to notice the sound of a bottle popping open.

A second later, something cold drips into the crack of my ass. Riding the waves of pleasure coursing through my pussy, I don't realize what is happening until I feel something probing my puckered asshole.

Panic clings to my body, and I tighten up. "Relax..." he soothes, and after a few seconds, I do just that.

With his fingers still inside me, he strokes me from the inside out, making it hard for me to concentrate on his thumb, which gently presses against the tight ring of muscles in my ass. When his thumb slips inside my ass, there is a slight pinch, but aside from that, there is nothing but pleasure, and a deep moan escapes my lips.

Julian removes his hand from my pussy and grabs my hip instead, holding me down, so he can continue playing with my ass.

I wonder how I can be so turned on by having a finger in my ass, but the thought slips away from me before I can fully comprehend it as he starts to fuck my ass with his thumb.

His strokes are precise, shallow, and bring forth a whole new pleasure.

"Your ass looks beautiful with my thumb inside of it. I can't wait to see it stretched from my cock." I don't know how, but his words turn me on even more. Moving his thumb in and out of my ass a little faster, the coil of lust twists tighter in my gut. He pulls out to replace his thumb with two fingers, stretching me even more.

"I'm not going to let you come, no matter how much you beg or plead. Not until you tell me what I want to hear."

He eats his words a moment later because before I can anticipate it, I'm coming, my entire body tightens and snaps like a bow that's pulled too tight.

My core tightens, and I squeeze Julian's fingers tight, holding them inside my body, never wanting to let them go. Pleasure floods every orifice, and I tremble against the mattress. My lids fall closed, and a warm flush blankets my skin.

"Fuck..." I hear Julian grunt behind me. "I didn't expect you to come from me fucking your ass. Guess I'll have to change my tactic then."

For what seems like an eternity, he fucks me with his fingers, making me come two more times. My pussy is barely done convulsing, and he's entering me with his cock while continuing to keep his fingers in my ass.

I'm riding a wave of blissful pleasure, my entire body sags forward, and sweat beads my brow. Twisting, I peer over my shoulder at Julian. The look in his eyes is feral, and I know he's not going to let up. He wants answers, answers I have, and he's willing to fuck me into submission to get them.

"Lean back and bounce on my cock," he orders. I move slowly, my body a puddle of mush. Not moving fast enough, I earn a slap to the ass, which causes his fingers that are in my ass to slip inside a little deeper.

A cross between a moan and whimper passes my lips, and I push back against him and start to ride his dick slowly, my ass slapping against his groin.

"Perfect, absolute perfection. I could fucking come in your tight little hole right now."

"Yes!" I moan.

My folds are sensitive, and my entire body is one big ball of pleasure.

I'm not sure I could take another orgasm, but it looks like I don't have a choice. Every muscle on my body clamps up, and when I feel Julian add another finger to the two already inside my ass, I fall apart, a scream passing my lips.

I'm drunk on pleasure and high on Julian's touch. He fucks me with his fingers in my ass for a little while longer and then replaces his fingers with the mushroom head of his cock.

"You won't fit." I struggle to get the words out as pleasure and pain mingle together.

"I'll fit angel, you were made for me. Your ass will take my cock."

That's the only response I get before he starts to enter me slowly, pushing through the ring of muscles and into my ass. For a brief moment, the pressure is too much, and I whimper, struggling against his grasp.

Placing a hand at the back of my neck, he holds me in place and starts to move, replacing the dull ache with red hot pleasure. All I can feel is him. His scent surrounds me, his body molds to mine. We're one and the same in this moment.

His pace speeds up, and the sound of his balls slapping against my skin fills the room. He grunts, fucking me slowly, even though I know he wants to rut into me over and over again. Bringing two fingers to my clit, he circles the overly sensitive flesh, and I start to shake once more.

"Oh, god…"

"Tell me where he is, tell me, baby, tell me, so I can fill your ass with my fucking cum…" Pleasure becomes pain as he pinches the tiny nub.

"Julian," I whimper, thrashing against the sheets, making his cock go deeper and rub against something incredible in my ass. "I… I can't take it anymore… I can't come again." My body is aching, my core clenching around nothing.

"You can, and you will. You'll keep coming until you tell me; Until you can't walk, or until I've decided you've been punished enough. Now take my cock in your ass." He thrusts harder, and my eyes roll to the back of my head.

With his cock in my ass, and his fingers on my clit, I'm overwhelmed. The feeling is so intense that I don't know how long I can take it.

Then he grabs a fistful of hair and tugs my head backward.

Like an addict, I crave his touch, and when he pinches my clit again, the pain and pleasure collide so profoundly. I come one last time. It's quick and powerful like a punch, but then it leaves my clit so sensitive that it almost hurts.

No, not almost... it hurts. It's too much. I try to pull away, try to close my thighs, but Julian's fingers are relentless. My whole body jerks as if I'm getting zapped, but Julian just holds me down more, his hand on the back of my neck, pressing me down into the mattress.

I feel like I'm about to implode, and that's when I know he's won.

"The beach house... he'll be at the beach house," I cry out.

His fingers leave my clit, and relief washes over me a moment before the guilt hits me.

He crests a moment later, filling my ass with his sticky semen and collapsing on top of me.

Kissing my shoulder, he whispers, "Good girl."

"We used to go there when I was a kid," I admit shamefully. "Please, don't kill him."

"I have to."

"Please, don't, I can't be with the man who kills the only family I have left."

"And I can't let the man live who killed mine."

34

JULIAN

At my words, she goes completely silent. I didn't even mean to say it. My confession just slipped out. That doesn't take away the honesty of my words, though.

Pushing up and off her body, I move to sit on the edge of the bed. My cock is still hard, sliding out of her tight little asshole. She doesn't move as I get up and start undoing her handcuffs. Free, she continues to lie on her stomach even as I go into the bathroom and retrieve a washcloth to clean her up.

She whimpers as I move the warm cloth between her legs but doesn't say anything. When she is clean, I roll her over onto her back, so I can look at her face. Her eyes collide with mine, and I see the whirlwind of emotions reflecting back at me. Inside her depths, I could drown a thousand times over. She wears her emotions like a sweater for the world to see.

Confusion, apprehension, fear. She is digesting what I told her. Trying to wrap her mind around her father killing someone I loved.

"He killed your family?" she finally asks.

"He killed my mother… and the baby she was carrying."

Her big blues go wide and tears well over, cascading down the sides of her cheeks. I watch the droplets, hating that she is crying for me.

"I can't imagine him doing something like that."

Anger rears its ugly head. "I can assure you, he did. He killed her. He even admitted to it." I'm trying my best not to be enraged over the fact that she is defending her father, but it's hard, so hard, especially after the way he ran when she fell, if he was half the man she thinks he is, he would've come to her rescue. "He's not a good man, Elena," I add.

"Neither are you," she rebuts, and I can't argue with that.

"I know I'm not. I've never claimed to be either. Still, there are lines even I won't cross. I would never kill a pregnant woman. There is no point in arguing about this. Your father will die, whether you like it or not, and I'll be the one to end him."

Anguish washes over her face. "Maybe it's a mistake? Or maybe it was an accident?"

"It wasn't. Your father is not the man you think he is. You know he told everyone your mother died in a car crash? He's a liar and a murderer. And don't forget that he sold you to me, a man that he knows hates him."

"Yes, and you bought me! Let's not forget that, either. You bought me like an item on the shelf in the store. Then you locked me in this room and chained me to your bed! You kill people, you lie, and steal. You're just as much of a criminal as he is."

Every muscle in my body quakes, I'm so fucking angry. Angry with her for taking his side. Angry with her father for killing my mother. And angry with myself for letting all of this happen. Unfortunately for Elena, she is the only one here to direct my anger at.

"You can say just about anything you fucking want to me, but do not fucking compare me to him! I'm nothing like your father," I say through clenched teeth. My hands are balled up into fists so tight, my nails dig into my palms painfully to ebb some of the rage away.

Her beautiful face goes ghostly pale, and her mouth pops open like she is about to say something, but no sound comes out. There is nothing for her to say, and even if there was, I'm past the point of reasoning.

"I don't care what you say. I will kill your piece of shit, father. I will marry you, and you will be mine. You will obey me and do as I say, or I will chain you to the bed for the rest of your fucking life. Don't tempt me, Elena. If you want to see how big of a monster I can be, then just try and stop me."

Grabbing my pants off the floor, I slip into them and storm out of the room, slamming the door with a ferociousness that makes the walls shake. My fingers shake, and rage boils over as I slide the lock into place and walk down the hall and away from her. I need a breather to get away before I do something I can't take back.

∼

AFTER POUNDING my fists against the punching bag in the gym for an hour and taking a cold shower in the guest room, I feel somewhat composed.

I was harsh with Elena earlier, maybe too harsh, but I needed her to see her father for who he truly was. I need her to accept that I will be the one to end her father's life, and I refuse to feel bad about that. She should hate him for leaving her lying limp against the floor at the bottom of the stairs, for selling her to me, but it seems she is far more loyal than I ever expected her to be.

In time, she will understand.

Before I go back to the room, I stop at my office and call Father Petro. It's late, and I know my call might wake him, but I don't have the patience to wait until tomorrow morning to call and discuss our union of marriage.

"Hello?" he answers after it rings for what seems like a long time.

"Father Petro, this is Julian Moretti. I apologize for the late-night call, but I need you to come to my estate tomorrow morning. The wedding you were to perform three weeks ago is going to be taking place. It can't wait any longer."

"I understand," he murmurs, and I can almost see him nodding his head through the phone. "I'll be there at nine in the morning, is that good?"

"Perfect. Have a good night, Father." Ending the call, I feel a little bit lighter than before. Scribbling on a sticky note, I head back down the stairs and stop in the kitchen and leave a note for Celeste and Marie to be prepared for a ceremony on the terrace right before breakfast. I already informed Lucca about the changes, which means everything is set in place.

Tomorrow. Tomorrow Elena will become my wife.

She'll be bound to me until death, bound by an unbreakable vow.

I hold onto that thought, letting it calm me when I enter our bedroom a short while later. Elena lies on the bed, the lamp on the nightstand on. The soft glow illuminates the entire room. My eyes move without will to her form, which is wrapped in a blanket.

The washcloth and handcuffs are on the floor next to the bed, a reminder of what I did to her earlier—my cock twitches in my shorts at the memory. I didn't expect her to come from anal, especially since it was her first time, but fuck me if it wasn't the hottest damn thing. It's nothing more but another reminder of how perfect she is.

No other woman will ever be able to compete with her, which is why she will be mine. Forever. Starting tomorrow.

"I know you're not asleep," I say as I strip out of my shorts and T-shirt.

"I never said I was," she snaps without looking up at me. "What else am I supposed to do besides lie in bed if you lock me in the room?"

Smirking at her response, I slip into the bed beside her. Her body stiffens as I pull her into my chest. She actually tries to push me away, but that only makes me hold her tighter. Burying my face in her hair, I breathe deeply, letting her succulent scent ease the rolling hills of anger away. Every time I see her, I think of her father, and I'm reminded that he is out there still living, breathing, and that I have failed to make good on my honor to my mother.

"We're getting married tomorrow, in the morning," I whisper into her ear.

"What? Tomorrow?" She squeaks.

"Yes. You're gonna wake up in the morning, put on your wedding dress, and walk your sweet –not so virgin ass– downstairs and become my wife."

"Is my father going to come?"

"No. No, guests will be here. It will be just us."

There is a long moment of silence, and I'm almost sad that there isn't another fight. The idea of subduing her with sex again makes my cock harden once more.

"Why did you even want to marry me if my father really did kill your mother?" Her question makes everything evaporate, and all over again, I'm on edge. It's too close to the truth. I don't want her to find out, not yet.

"I wanted you from the moment I saw you at your mother's funeral." It's not a lie, but it's not the whole truth either.

"And it doesn't bother you that I'm his daughter?"

"No, I don't care where you came from. I only care that you are with me now. You're a Moretti now, my wife, my queen, the woman who will carry and birth our heirs."

Another moment of silence stretches on before she interrupts the silence with another question.

"Are you still planning on killing my father when you find him?"

"Yes."

"How can you expect me to say my vows if I know this? If I know the man that will be my husband, plans to kill my father?"

"I don't care how you do it, but you will do it, nevertheless. Two things have never been truer. You will become my wife tomorrow morning, and your father will die at my hands. When? I don't know, but it will happen, and if you do anything to try and stop me..." I don't have to threaten her further. She knows what will happen if she doesn't do what I want. I wish I didn't have to force her hand. I wish she would simply say her vows because she wants to.

The only thought that eases my mind is knowing that one day, she will cherish our vows. She will understand eventually that this is the right thing to do.

She will see that I was only doing this for us, for her.

Her father doesn't love her. If he did, he wouldn't have given her to me.

35

ELENA

Staring at my reflection, a feeling of surrealness washes over me. I thought Julian was drunk when he came into the bedroom last night and said we were getting married, but as it turns out, he wasn't drunk, nor lying. Here I stand, in a wedding dress, and I'm about to get married to a man who bought me for ten million dollars. A man, I foolishly thought I could love. He knows nothing of love. This is all revenge, that's all it is. He doesn't want me the way I want him. It's a façade, a mirage. I keep telling myself maybe he'll forget about finding my father, but I know better. He won't stop till he's dead.

"Are you ready?" Julian calls through the closed bathroom door, and my thoughts slip away like grains of sand through an hourglass.

"Yes," I yell back at him. Carefully, I step toward the door and open it just enough to peek through the crack. "Isn't it bad luck to see the bride in her dress?"

"I didn't see you in your dress on our first wedding day, and you saw how well that worked out." He purses his lips.

I guess he's right. What could possibly happen that hasn't already?

Pulling the door open all the way, Julian's entire body comes into view. He's standing a few feet away from me in a fitted tux. He looks sharp, roguish, and dangerous. My mouth goes dry, and I swallow my tongue, afraid that it might slip out like a dog's when it pants. His sea-blue eyes take me in from head to toe, drinking the image before him up.

"You look… breathtaking." He licks his lips, and I'm taken aback by how genuine his compliment is. There's a kind of adoration in his tone that I've never heard before. It's especially surprising after all the things he told me last night and the abrupt way he left and returned to tell me we were getting married.

Sometimes, I think Julian has a split personality. Or maybe he is just a monster inside, and this caring version of him is a façade. Either way, I'm about to marry him. Marry him and all of his sides, the dark one that's front and center and the kind one that no one ever gets a glimpse of.

"Come. Father Petro is waiting for us," he offers me his arm. I close the distance between us and loop my arm into his and shiver when my hand brushes against his.

My stomach churns like I'm on a rollercoaster. I'm about to get married.

Julian leads me down the stairs, holding me extra tight as we walk down the long staircase. When we reach the bottom step, I almost sigh. Marie comes around the corner, and my thoughts shift.

"Oh, Elena. You look stunning," she beams, looking me up and down. "Here, I made you this." She hands me a beautiful bouquet of flowers.

"Thank you, Marie." I smile happily, grateful that she is here. At least I have one friend present at my wedding. One person, I would have invited regardless of when it took place.

Julian dismisses Marie with a wave of his hand, and I have to grind my teeth together to stop myself from saying something to him. I don't understand his distaste for her. Yes, she is his employee, but she is a human as well. Hopefully, with our union of marriage, I will get a say in how things are run around the mansion.

We continue our walk through the house, and it feels very much like we're walking to the cemetery to lay someone to rest. Reaching the terrace, Julian opens the French doors and the cool morning air kisses my skin.

As soon as we step outside, I forget about everything. All my worries, fears, and anxiety over marrying Julian fade away. There is a white woven arch set up at the edge of the terrace, white roses are braided into it. The entire thing is picturesque and whimsical.

Behind it, the sun is sitting in the center of the bright blue sky, illuminating the magical scene. The weather couldn't have been more perfect. Dragging my eyes away from the décor, I find the priest is already standing under the arch, a friendly smile gracing his lips as we walk up and stop in front of him.

I never expected my wedding to happen this way. I always thought my father would walk me down the aisle and give me away. Even though I never imagined it going this way, I have to admit, it's beautiful.

While the priest performs the ceremony, Julian holds onto my free hand with an iron grip while I clutch onto the bouquet with the other.

Father Petro reads a few passages from the bible about cherishing and protecting each other. I wonder if our marriage will ever be that of others. Bursting with love and joy. I hope those things can find their way into our marriage.

After we each say our vows, which are generic ones, we repeat after Father Petro. We exchange wedding bands at the very end, and my fingers shake as I slide the silver wedding band onto Julian's finger. I think I'm going to be sick. I can't believe I'm married.

"I, hereby, pronounce you husband and wife. You may now kiss the bride."

Julian turns to face me, looking every bit as intimidating as he was the night he showed up in my father's office. Turning, I do the same and swallow thickly as I lift my gaze and meet his. He's watching me like I'm his prey, and I guess in a way I am.

Lowering his head, he leans in and presses his lips to mine, sealing our fates with a kiss. The kiss is gentle and kind, completely unlike anything

I would expect, then again, Julian officially owns me now. I am Mrs. Moretti.

"Congratulations." Father Petro smiles as we break the kiss. My lips are burning, and my entire body is trembling.

"Thank you," Julian whispers and grabs my hand, clutching it tightly like he is worried that I'll run away. He guides us down the steps and toward the pool, where I see a table is set up with a variety of fruits, pastries, and other breakfast items.

"Mrs. Moretti," Julian smirks as he helps me into my chair.

"What happens next?" I ask, waiting for the other shoe to drop.

Did he find my father already? Is he going to spring it on me at any second? Guilt gnaws away at my insides. I'm married, and my father wasn't even here to witness it.

"Now we have breakfast and get ready for our honeymoon."

"Honeymoon?" I try not to sound as shocked as I feel. "We're going on a honeymoon?"

Julian smiles, showing off his sparkly white teeth. "Yes, we're staying at a private beach house on a secluded beach, where we will spend the next thirty days together. I want to give you some freedom and let you enjoy yourself. I think it will be good for us and give us a chance to get to know each other a little more as well."

It's like I've woken up in another dimension. I can't believe what I am hearing, and for a brief second, I simply stare at him in awe.

"You seem shocked, perhaps you would rather be locked in our bedroom?"

"No..." I blurt out and reach for the glass of orange juice while Julian grabs my plate and fills it with food. "I'm just surprised is all. After the way things ended last night, I didn't expect something like this..."

"You're my wife, and I want you to be happy. This trip will allow you the freedom you seek, without me worrying about someone hurting you, or you running away."

And just like that, I realize the freedom he is giving me is a false sense of hope. He doesn't trust me, not really. He's giving me freedom but only as much as he is allowing, and it's on his terms. My stomach sours, and the idea of eating makes me nauseous.

"I thought when we married, you would trust me more and give me more freedom?"

"I am and will." He takes a bite of strawberry and hands my plate, which is loaded with food, back to me.

"Only on your terms, though, right?" I scoff angrily.

I was so foolish to think that getting married would make things better. Foolish to think that Julian Moretti, the dark wolf of the mafia underbelly, would fall for me. All he wants to do is control me. Nothing has changed.

"Everything is on my terms, *wife*, you should know this by now. When your father is taken care of, and I have nothing more to worry about, you can be free. Now eat, we have a long day ahead of us," he orders me like I'm a child, and I'm tempted to object, but what good would that do me. Not eating isn't going to hurt anyone but me.

Begrudgingly, I pluck a piece of fruit off the plate and shove it in my mouth. I chew the fruit viciously with maddening anger like it's the person I want to hurt.

A moment later, Lucca comes sauntering up to the table, and Julian excuses himself, leaving me to sit at the table alone, and I hope this isn't a vision of the future. I've already lost my mother, and my father is soon to follow. I'm not sure what I will do if I can't get Julian to see past his vengeful ways.

Is there a future of love and happiness for us, or were we doomed from the very start?

36

JULIAN

I stare down at the silver band on my finger. It catches in the light and feels strange on my finger. I'm a married man. Married to the enemy's daughter. Married to a woman who knows nothing of the truth as to why I took her. A moral man would feel guilt, but I feel nothing close to that. Now, I hold all that Romero cares for in the world in the palm of my hand.

Marie packs our suitcases, and Elena sits on the bed and watches her. She tried to help, but I stopped her. I pay Marie an hourly wage to do the things that I want her to do. Elena needs to come to terms with that.

Leaning against the wall, I watch the two women talk and laugh while I drink a glass of whiskey. The day is still young, I know, but a union of marriage calls for a glass of whiskey. Dressed in a sundress that hugs her luscious curves and shows off the perfect swell of her tits, I have to stop myself from taking my wife into the bathroom and fucking her against the mirror to consummate our marriage properly.

Wife. She is my wife now. It seems surreal, almost as if this morning was a dream.

Marie keeps her head down, her eyes trained on folding the last few items for our suitcases as I stare at Elena. The idea of leaving this mansion and heading to the island makes me nervous, but I know Elena needs this, and a part of me needs it too.

No one will be able to reach her there, and any chance of her escaping is extremely unlikely. Plus, everything back here will be managed and taken care of. Lucca will be holding the fort down, and Zeke is searching for Romero, so I have a little time to relax and focus on us. All will be well.

I'm just anxious to get out of here and to the island. Downing the rest of the amber liquid in my glass, I walk over and set the crystal glass down on the nightstand. The sound causes Marie to jump a foot off the ground, and I bite the inside of my cheek to withhold a smirk.

"Go make sure your things are packed and ready to go. We'll finish up here," I dismiss her. Her eyes dart between Elena and me before she scurries away like a timid little mouse.

"Do you take pleasure in scaring everyone?" Elena questions as soon as Marie is out of the room. The defiance in her eyes glistens in the sun filtering in through the window.

"Do you want the honest answer or the one that will make you feel better?"

"Never mind." Elena rolls her eyes at me.

"Fear keeps people in line. I've told you this before." I step closer to the bed and zip up the suitcase, "Are you hungry? We have an hour-long plane ride, and then a boat will take us to the island. So, it will be a while before dinner."

"Island?" She perks up.

"Is that the only word you heard out of that sentence?"

"Kind of." She smiles widely. "We're going to an island? What kind? Where is it?"

"It's a private island in the Caribbean. We'll fly down to Saint Martin, and from there, a boat will take us to the Island. Have you ever been to the Caribbean?"

"What do you think?" She frowns. "The furthest I've been away from home is Orlando. My parents actually took me to Disney for my eighth birthday."

"You'll love it, and I'll be happy to take you to see the world if that's what you'd like." She gives me an uncertain look like she doesn't believe what I'm saying. "Where would you like to go?"

"I know it's cliché, but I've always wanted to go to Paris."

"Then we'll go to Paris. Maybe in the fall." Her smile widened at my words, and I'm already planning out the details in my head. "Come on, let's get a light lunch before we head out."

Elena gets up from the bed. I let her take the brace off after I called the doctor and confirmed she didn't need it anymore. She loops her arm in mine like she did earlier this morning, but it already feels different now. More natural, more familiar, like her arm is supposed to be in mine... always.

~

I WATCH her raven hair dance in the wind as the boat glides over the water gracefully. I haven't been able to take my eyes off of her all day. Not because I'm worried about her running, but because I've never seen her so happy. Never seen this twinkle of excitement in her eyes or this permanent smile on her lips. Her whole face lights up every time we see something new, and I can't get enough of it.

If I could, I would spend the next hundred years traveling with her, simply to ensure this is how she'll feel every day. I want her happiness, to always see her smiling. It's grown on me, becoming the most important thing next to destroying her father in my life.

"Are you cold?" I ask when I see goosebumps pebble across her bare arms.

"A little, but I'm fine. I want to stay out here. I feel so free with the wind in my hair like I can do and go anywhere."

"We can stay." I wrap my arm around her and pull her into my side. Marie and Celeste are below deck, and I'd rather spend time with my wife alone anyway.

Security is already set up on the island. I'll have fewer men there than I have around the mansion, but since the island itself is secure, and no one even knows where we are, we don't need as many men.

"Is that it?" Elena squeals beside me as the island comes into view. It's less than an hour boat ride from the mainland, but it's far enough away to be secluded. It's not even on a map.

"Yes, that's it. Our home for a month."

"I'm excited..." She looks out at the island in wonder, and I spend the rest of the ride watching her.

Ten minutes later, we arrive at the small dock at our private beach. I help Elena off the boat and walk her onto the shore.

Two of my men greet us and board the boat to get our luggage while I walk to the house with my eager wife by my side.

As soon as we step inside the house, the aroma of fresh roasted chicken greets us. I hired two extra maids, which got here yesterday, to make sure everything was perfect and ready by the time we arrived.

"Are you ready to eat?"

"Yes. No. I mean, I'm starving, but I also want to walk around and look at everything."

"Let's take a quick tour before sitting down for dinner then."

We walk around the house, looking into each room. Elena acts like a kid on Christmas morning, and every new room is a new present she is unwrapping.

"It's beautiful."

"It really is," I say, looking straight at her. "Now, let's eat."

We walk back to the dining room, which is already set for us. A large flower arrangement in the center of the table, with various foods spread out around it.

Our first official dinner as husband and wife.

"Bring us some champagne," I order. A few minutes later, two flutes and a bottle are brought to us. I open it with a pop and pour us each a glass. "Enjoy it while you can."

"What do you mean?" Elena wrinkles her nose.

"You might be pregnant soon, and then you won't be able to drink for nine months."

"Oh," Elena looks down at the table, chewing at her bottom lip. "I meant to tell you. I know it's horrible timing, but when I went to the bathroom on the boat, I realized my period started."

Disappointment slams into me. Partly because we won't be able to have the perfect wedding night like I had planned, but mostly because her getting her period means she is not pregnant yet. I didn't expect her to be after we only had sex a hand full of times, but it still saddens me that I'll have to wait longer.

"I'm sorry," Elena whimpers.

"Nothing to be sorry about. I would be displeased if we had waited, and tonight was our first time together, but since I thoroughly fucked you last night, I'll be patiently waiting to fuck you again in a few days."

Elena's face turns crimson at my words. Not because she isn't used to my dirty talk, but because one of the temporary maids is in the room, refreshing our drinks. Her embarrassment only makes me smile. The maid seems a little flustered as well but is smart enough not to make a sound before scurrying away.

The rest of the dinner goes pleasantly uneventful. When I lead Elena back to the bedroom, I expect her to want to go to bed right away. Instead, she tugs me into the bathroom.

"I want to take a shower." I'm guessing from the way she is pulling me along, she expects me to join. I'll gladly oblige.

I turn on the water and help her out of her clothes before I peel my own off. The shower here is just as large and luxurious as the one at home. There is more than enough room for both of us with the two rainfall showerheads.

Stepping under the spray, I close my eyes and let the hot water cascade over my face. I almost flinch when Elena comes up behind me, running her small hands over my back.

Turning, I face her and open my eyes. She has a mischievous twinkle in her gaze, and for a moment, I wonder what she is up to. That thought, along with every other, disappears when she lowers herself to her knees and wraps her delicate fingers around my already hard cock.

"Fuck," I groan as she leans forward and takes me into her hot mouth. Her soft lips close around my length, and her velvet tongue runs along the underside. I place one hand on the cool tiled wall next to me, feeling the need to brace myself while I bury my other hand in her black hair.

She moves slowly and sensually over my length, taking me deep until I hit the back of her throat before sliding back out all the way. Her hand stays wrapped around the base of my cock as she keeps working the rest like a fucking pro.

It doesn't take me long before I feel my balls tightening and the tingle at the base of my spine.

"I'm gonna come down your throat... you're gonna swallow it," I grit through clenched teeth, barely hanging on.

She moans and nods her head as much as she can with my cock in her mouth. I can feel the vibration of her moan through my entire body.

I try not to grip her hair tightly, letting her stay in control, but when I feel my orgasm rising, I can't resist any longer. I wrap my fingers around her hair and close my fist, holding her in place as I shoot ropes after ropes of my release down her throat.

She keeps sucking until the very last drop, and I'm glad I left one hand at the wall for support because, fuck me, my legs might give out.

Releasing my cock, she gracefully gets back on her feet, licking her lips like she enjoyed herself very much.

"Sorry, my uterus messed up our wedding night." She smiles cheekily.

"I'll take that apology from your mouth every damn day." Straightening up, I grab her hips and pull her close to me, molding her soft curves against my hard ones.

Leaning down, I take her lips, devour her like it's the only thing I'll need to survive. I plunge my tongue inside of her, tasting myself. The combination of our tastes is so intoxicating, my cock roars back to life. Fuck, I'm never going to get enough of her.

Not ever.

37

ELENA

Three days. That's how long we've been on the island. It's strange to wake up in such a beautiful place every day and be able to walk right outside and onto the beach, especially after being locked inside a room, and only being allowed to leave when I'm told I can.

Together we have breakfast in the small nook that overlooks the beach. I can hear the waves as they rush toward the sandy shore. This entire place is beautiful beyond words, but like everything else in my life, it is darkness and control hidden beneath a nicely shaped box. I wish there were no restrictions on mine and Julian's marriage. That I could be free of any chains.

"Are you not hungry?" Julian asks, interrupting my thoughts.

Looking up from my still mostly filled plate of food, I find him watching me. His dark gaze is penetrating as if he can see right through me and into my mind. My eyes catch on the glittering ring that adorns his finger. I still can't believe we're married. That he is mine, and I am his. I'm married to a mobster, a criminal that knows how to bend me to his will.

"My stomach has been a little upset," I say, which isn't entirely a lie.

Julian frowns. "I have some work to do, but I can always work on it tomorrow or later. I do not want to leave you if you're not feeling well." His protectiveness oozes out of him, charging the air around us. Still, I feel like I need to get some time away from him.

"No, no. I want to go for a walk along the beach, check out the island a little bit. It isn't often that I get to go somewhere alone," I tease.

A smile graces his lips a moment before he takes a drink of his orange juice. A man as cruel and dark as he shouldn't be allowed to look so sexy. I find myself always watching him, and my mouth waters at the tightness of his muscles, the way he holds me, his scent, and taste. Everything about him turns me on. I shouldn't want the man who took everything from me, and yet, I can't deny my feelings either.

"You're never alone, no matter where you go, I will always be there. Or at the very least not far behind you." It's not just a statement but a warning. He will be watching me, no matter where I go. I'll never be free.

"Okay, I get it. You're always watching me."

"Yes," his voice drops, and I shiver at the depth of it, feeling the sound deep in my core.

Part of me might be angered how we came together, and while knowing he won't stop at anything to end my father, I can't deny the pull I have to him.

It's like sticking your hand into the flames of fire, knowing it's going to burn while also knowing you have no other option. With Julian, there is no option, no alternative. He holds all the power, and I am a slave to his every move.

"I'm going to explore the island," I say, pushing up from my seat.

The chair scrapes across the tile floor, and Julian's brows pull together. "Are you trying to run away? I'm sure I don't have to remind you that there..."

"Is no way off the island." I finish his sentence, trying not to sound mocking. "You don't have to tell me ten million times. I thought I was your wife. I'm starting to think I'm still a prisoner," I sass.

Julian tosses his napkin down on the table. "Run along, my queen. Just know I'll be watching you."

I resist an eye roll and turn to walk away, but I'm pulled backward, a second later, my back colliding with a firm chest. Julian's hand sinks into my raven hair, and he tugs my head back, making the muscles ache at the angle. His hold is firm, controlling, and I shiver at the power he holds. His teeth skim my ear, and his intoxicating scent surrounds me. Danger and cinnamon, that's what he smells like.

"I hope you plan to change your clothes before you leave this bedroom."

Something inside of me makes me want to tempt the beast, to push back against the steel bars that keep me caged. "And what would you do if I said I wasn't?"

In the blink of an eye, he's released his grip on my hair and twisted me around to face him. The air rushes from my lungs as he shoves me against the wall. The smile on my lips fades when his large hand circles my throat, and our gazes collide. His grip is like that of an iron shackle around my neck. Anyone else would be pissing their pants by now, begging for forgiveness, but somehow, I stand my ground and remain composed. I remind myself that I am his equal, not a doormat he can step on.

Like a feral wolf, his lips curl back, and he snarls his next set of words.

"I would chain you to my side, and never let you out of my sight. That's what I would do."

"Don't you already do that?" I counter, looking him right in the eyes.

Zeroing in on me like I'm prey, his lips nearly graze mine as he says, "You're fooling yourself if you think I've been treating you that badly. Now, change, or I will lock you in this bedroom for the rest of the day. We might be on an island, but my men are still here, and if they see even an inch of flesh they shouldn't, I will put a bullet between their eyes. Do you want to be responsible for someone's death?"

"No," the word squeaks past my lips.

"Then change and get out of my sight before I fuck you until you beg me to stop, and believe me, I won't be gentle."

As badly as I'm tempted to see him do it, I want to explore the island. His lips flutter against mine, and it's the softest kiss, gentle, kind like he is telling me a secret with his lips. I'm frazzled and confused, and my knees tremble, barely holding me up.

"Okay," I mumble, and a moment later, he releases me like I'm a hot branding iron on his skin. Lifting a hand, I rub at my throat while my heart thunders inside my chest. I can still feel his grip there. My lungs burn as if I've been holding my breath, and I sigh loudly into the room.

"One of the guards took Celeste to the mainland for supplies. Only Clyde and Marie are here right now," Julian explains. "If you need anything, I can still text them to pick it up for you."

"I don't need anything," I say, my voice still breathy.

With one last lingering look, I dart across the room and over to the foot of the bed where my suitcase is. It's not like I'm wearing anything overly revealing, a pair of sleep shorts, and a spaghetti strap top, but I'm not going to push him or give him another reason to shackle me to the bed because he will. I have no doubt in my mind that he will do everything possible to remind me of the power he holds.

Out of the corner of my eye, I see him turn away from me. He pulls out his phone, giving the device his undivided attention. Quickly, I change out of my PJs and slip into a pair of shorts and a dressy tank top. Momentarily, I pause and consider putting on a bathing suit but decide against it. I'm not going to be going into the ocean alone, especially not when I can't swim.

Julian has his nose buried in his phone, so I slip out of the room without notice. I'm bubbling over with excitement as I walk through the house.

The island isn't very big, but I plan to search every inch of it. I enjoy being with Julian, but I want more freedom, and I need to see my father. To warn him of what's to come. Eventually, Julian will forgive me for escaping.

The mansion is set right on the beach and is the focal point of the island. Julian claims there is only one way on and off the island, but I don't believe him. What if there were an emergency? With the placement of the house as it is, there is nothing but open concept throughout. Every window you look out of, there is ocean and beach. It's peaceful, and part of me wants to stay here in this bubble of perfection forever.

Rushing down the stairs, I enter the kitchen, which is empty. The French doors that lead outside are wide open, letting the breeze from the ocean in. *Where should I go first?* I walk out the doors and look both ways. I see nothing but the beach for miles.

The air is salty as I breathe it into my lungs, but I love it. Love the freedom that surrounds me, the sound of the ocean, and the way my toes feel in the sand. Randomly choosing, I go left and head away from the mansion.

Walking along the beach, the water creeps closer and eventually washes over my feet. The water is cold, and a shiver runs down my spine. I'm not sure how long I walk before coming to a small area that's overgrown with trees and vegetation. I almost don't see the small boathouse peeking out in between the green leaves.

I consider turning around because the last thing I want to do is go trespassing into something, but there is a nagging at the back of my mind that tells me to investigate further.

Julian said there were no other boats on the island. Was he lying? Or is this boathouse empty? Maybe it's not a boathouse at all?

Curiosity gets the best of me, and I continue walking toward it. My steps are hesitant, and fear coils deep in my gut. It could be nothing just a small abandoned outbuilding, or it could be something bigger than that.

Just a small peek inside, I tell myself. I just want to know what's inside.

As I get closer, walking deeper into the overgrowth, I realize how old and run down this building is. The slats of wood are debilitated, and the paint on them is chipped away by the elements. Smiling to myself, I feel as if I've won a trophy.

I bet Julian has no idea that this is here. I get to the door and tug on the handle, which is barely hanging on. I find it's not locked but cracked open. The hinges creak as I pull the door open and stick my head inside.

My eyes go wide as I take in the motorboat inside the wooden building. I could leave right now, without a word, get a head start. It's what I should do, but deep down, I know I can't.

I can't leave Julian. I want to warn my father, and I plan to, to tell him to leave me alone, that I'm happy where I am, but I can't leave, not yet.

Taking a step back, I let the door fall closed, and feel like I'm betraying myself a little as I walk back through the heavy foliage and onto the beach.

Awareness washes over me, and I realize that I've been gone for some time, so instead of continuing on with my adventure, I head back to the house.

Instead, maybe I'll find Marie, and we can do something together. Make some cookies or watch some tv together? The secret of what I found presses heavily like a stack of bricks on my shoulders. I'm walking up the backside of the mansion, returning the same way I left when I hear what sounds like scuffling in the kitchen. I've not yet reached the French doors to see inside, so I have no idea what is happening, but my heart thunders in my chest, and my legs kick into overdrive when I hear a deep male voice.

"You'll do as I fucking say, or I'll tell Julian that you're a spy..." I know that voice. It belongs to one of Julian's guards, Clyde, I think.

"Please, don't..." Marie softly cries, and I know whatever is happening is bad.

Rushing into the kitchen, my blood is pumping, and I'm ready to destroy. When I spot Marie facing me, her eyes are wide with fear, and tears slip freely down her cheeks.

Clyde is tugging at her clothes like she is a ragdoll.

"I'm going to fuck you, and you're going to enjoy it. Do you understand me?" Clyde's voice is nauseating, and I hate that I have to slow my steps. My eyes dart to the butcher block sitting on the counter near the stove, and I don't even think, I just react.

Darting toward the butcher block, I grab the first knife my fingers touch, which also happens to be the biggest. The blade gleams in the light, and my hands shake while rage simmers just beneath the surface.

Rushing around the island, I lift the knife above my head just as he slips a hand beneath Marie's maid dress. All I see are her tear-stained cheeks, the pain in her eyes.

I put everything I have into that strike, and the knife cuts through him like hot butter and sticks like an ax in a piece of wood in his back.

Immediately, he turns on me, fury in his eyes, his lips curls up, and he roars with rage. I reach for the knife, attempting to tug it out of his back, but a sting of pain ripples across my hand as my palm makes contact with the blade instead of the handle.

"You will pay for that, you little fucking bitch," he snarls, and before I can comprehend what is going on, his fist is flying at my face.

The blow lands against my cheek with the intensity of a house slamming into me, and nearly sends me to the ground. Somehow, I manage to keep my footing, even as pain radiates across my cheek, and blood fills my mouth.

Clyde takes a menacing step toward me, his eyes gleaming with red hot rage. Lifting his hand as if he's going to punch me once more, and my eyes drift closed as if out of instinct.

Oh, god.

The hit never comes. Silence surrounds us, and that's when I open my eyes again and find Clyde on the ground, his eyes vacant and Marie standing in front of me.

"He will blame me for this." Her voice is nothing more than a tremble, and I know she is right. Julian will kill her for this, even while knowing it isn't her fault.

My face aches, and my hand throbs, reminding me of the fresh cut there. Warm blood drips down my fingers and onto the white tile, where an even bigger splotch of blood is forming beneath Clyde's body.

Instantly, I know what I have to do.

Grabbing a kitchen towel, I wrap it around my hand as tightly as I can. "Come on. I'm going to get you out of here. He can't hurt you if you aren't here."

Turns out, my plan to save the boat for another time was a good choice. Marie needs to be saved far more than I do.

38

JULIAN

"There was no sign of him being there. Not recently, at least," Zeke explains over the phone.

"He must have anticipated that Elena would tell me about it." I lean back in the leather office chair. "Keep looking. He can't hide from us forever. If I have to, I'll draw him out of hiding."

"Don't worry. I'll find him. In fact, you'll have him by the end of the week," he promises me.

"I'll be looking forward to our next conversation then," I say before hanging up the phone. I have to say, I'm impressed by his confidence. Let's just hope he can actually deliver. I want Romero dead and gone. I want him out of Elena's life. In my eyes, she will never be safe so long as he's breathing.

Closing the laptop, I push up from the chair. It's almost dinner time, and I don't want to leave my wife waiting. *My wife.* It is fucked up how much I am enjoying this whole marriage thing. When I chose to marry Elena, I never anticipated caring for her, wanting her as deeply as I do. In ways, she's changed me, made me see things in a different light. She brings a goodness to my soul that I thought would never return.

As soon as I step out of my office, a feeling of unease overcomes me. I can't explain why or what or how, all I know is that the small hairs on the back of my neck stand on end. My heart rate picks up, and my breathing becomes uneven.

Fear creeps its way up my spine and settles over my skin like a thin sheen of sweat. I can count on one hand the number of times I've been scared in my life.

Something is off.

The house is completely quiet, too quiet. The silence is deafening.

Frantically, I start moving, racing through the house like a chicken with my head cut off, checking every room. She said she was going to go walking around the house.

"Elena!" I yell into the empty space, but silence still surrounds me. I keep moving until I've checked every room upstairs and find myself rushing downstairs. I'm seconds from calling in the guards when I come around the corner leading into the kitchen and come to an abrupt halt.

My feet and heart stop at the same time as I take in Clyde, one of my guards, dead on the kitchen floor. He's faced down, with a knife stuck in his back, a puddle of blood surrounding him like a black blob of ink against the white tile.

No, no, no. It's like I'm living a recurring nightmare. This can't be real. No one knows we're here. No one could have known.

"Elena!" I scream again, hoping for a different outcome now. Hoping she will walk around the corner and into my arms but the seconds tick by, and she never comes walking into the kitchen.

I'm so shocked that for a moment, I forget about her tracker. Pulling out my phone, my fingers slip over the buttons as I type in the code to unlock it as fast as I can. Navigating to open the app to find her is a pain as the simmering rage inside of me beats to get out. It feels like an eternity until the location loads.

Then it finally pings, and the map lights up the screen, a red moving dot pinpointing her exact location.

Anger floods my veins, rushing through my body like a tidal wave hitting the shore. She is out on the ocean, heading toward the mainland. Someone fucking kidnapped her. Someone took her, and I didn't even realize it.

They took her right out from under my nose, killed one of my men, and escaped the island with her. Failure. I'm a fucking failure. I failed to protect her all over again. Instantly, a million terrible images enter my mind.

Someone else's hands on Elena, hurting her, causing her pain, violating her... killing her. The anger becomes almost unbearable like a knife being plunged into my chest over and over again, and I use it as fuel as I rush outside and toward the boathouse.

My feet pound against the sand, and I almost fall a thousand times as the ocean breeze whips against my face and through my hair. The muscles in my legs burn as I push myself to run faster than I ever have before.

As I get closer to the boathouse, hidden deep in the small patch of trees and tall grass, I can see the door swinging open, and the dreadful feeling in my gut only expands outward. When I get to it, my worst fears come true.

The sand beneath my feet gives way, and I fall to my knees.

The emergency boat is gone.

Elena is gone.

My wife is gone.

39

ELENA

I'm making a mistake.

I'm making a big mistake.

The voice in my head keeps repeating the same thing, but it's too late to turn back now. Marie is right, Julian will blame her and most likely kill her for what happened. She is not safe, and I won't be able to live with myself if something happens to her, not when I was the one that killed him.

Of course, she is still crying, her arms wrapped tightly around her legs while she rocks herself back and forth with the movement of the boat.

"It's going to be okay, Marie," I say softly, trying to calm her down. "Look, we're almost at the mainland. We'll find some way for you to get home, and then I'll go back to the island and explain everything to Julian. Everything will work out."

Her tear-filled eyes find mine, and the fear I see in those depths makes my heart hurt. She is so scared, the fear I see in her gaze rivals anything I've ever felt personally, and there is nothing I can say to her to ease that fear.

Even worse, my husband is the cause of her fear, and I'm not sure even I could stop him from hurting her, which is why we're doing what we're doing now. If I can get her away and get her hidden, maybe there is a chance this can all be okay.

"Ah, I think you better hold on 'cause I'm not sure how to stop this boat at the pier," I warn Marie as we get closer. I shut down the engine and let us float the last bit, but apparently, I didn't do so early enough. Our boat hits the side of the pier with a loud crack. My body jerks to the front, and I barely manage to stay inside the boat.

Marie grabs the edge of the boat and keeps us pulled against the walkway. I climb out first, then help her to get out. Marie ties the boat up while I tighten my makeshift wrap around my cut hand. When we're both done, we have our first good look around.

"Let's head that way," I point toward the road. "That's where we came from. We just need to find a phone, so you can call your family."

"You should just go back, Elena. I promise I'll be fine from here. You need to go back before Julian finds you missing."

I won't lie, the idea is tempting, especially knowing the consequences are going to be dire. "I don't want to leave you…"

"You've already done more for me than I can ever repay you for. Please, head back. I don't want you to get in trouble for helping me–"

"That's them!" A male voice interrupts our conversation.

Both of our heads snap up in the direction the yelling came from. Four men in uniforms are running toward us like we broke some unknown law.

"Police! Stop!" Someone else yells.

All I can do is stand there like a deer caught in the headlights of an oncoming car. They can't be after us. We've done nothing wrong.

Are the police arresting us? A moment later, I get my answer when one of the officers grabs my arms and shoves me to the ground, tugging my arms behind my back and slaps handcuffs onto my wrists. The whole moment is surreal, and I don't even know what to say or do. There is no reaction to what just happened.

One moment I'm talking to Marie, the next I'm arrested, and my hands are cuffed together.

What the hell is happening?

∾

WE'VE BEEN in a holding cell for a while now, and still, not a single person has told us why we were arrested. No one has tended to the cut on my hand either, and I could use some Tylenol and an ice pack for my face, which is still throbbing.

Marie has been crying almost the entire time, and all I can do is hold her and tell her that everything is going to be okay. Thank god they put us in the same cell, at least. I don't know what I would have done if they separated us.

Screams echo down the hall, and I cling to Marie with all my might.

Someone came by and brought us water a little while ago. I asked them for a phone call, but they refused. Told us to wait and shut up. I wanted to say something like if you hurt us, my husband will kill you, but I managed to bite my tongue on that one.

The thought of Julian makes my chest ache. All I wanted was some freedom, and as soon as I get it, I have to get myself into trouble.

He'll never trust me again.

In fact, I bet he'll think the worst. Think I was trying to leave.

Approaching footsteps accompanied by the rattling of keys have me on high alert. Marie and I both stand up, our eyes trained on the door while I refuse to let go of her.

One of the officers comes into view first. Only a second later, does Julian appear behind him. Marie starts shaking in my hold, and I rub my hand over her arm in hopes to calm her, but when my eyes lock with Julian's, I start to shake myself.

I've never seen him like this. His eyes are a deep sea of emotion. Anger, disappointment, and hurt swimming right at the surface, but there is more. Some depth, I never knew existed. There is raw fear, and it's almost as if he was afraid that...

The officer unlocks and opens the metal bar door and motions for us to step out. I'm tempted to dig my feet into the ground because I know when we get back to the island, all hell is going to break loose.

"You." Julian points at Marie, who's shaking only intensifies under his powerful gaze. "Be glad I'm not killing you right now. Get out of my sight. I never want to see or hear from you again. Understood?"

"You don't even–" I start defending her, but Julian cuts me off, his gaze like a razor, cutting through the air.

"And you, shut up. I'll deal with you later." The dismissive tone and raw anguish in his voice are like an arrow being slingshot through my heart. I'm in physical pain, and I'm not talking about my hand or face, I'm talking about my insides twisting with pain.

"Do you understand?" he asks Marie again.

"Yes." Marie nods her head furiously.

I give her one final squeeze before she rushes past Julian and disappears from view. I step up to Julian, torn between wanting to slap him and wanting to fall into his embrace.

The police officer either got paid off, or he doesn't care about the threat Julian just made because he simply locks the cell back up and walks away while whistling.

Julian grabs my injured hand, and I wince at the touch. He starts walking me out of the police station without another word. No one stops us or says anything to us, and I wonder how much money this little charade cost him.

A black SUV is waiting at the curb, and we climb inside without a word. Only when we are settled, and the car starts moving, do I get the courage to speak.

"I wasn't leaving you if that's what you think."

"It sure as hell looked like it," Julian snaps, not even looking at me. "How long did you plan this?"

"I didn't!"

"Where were you going?"

"I wasn't going anywhere!" My voice rises with each word.

"You were going back to your father." He answers his own question, and I'm tempted to tell him he's an idiot.

"Are you even listening to me?" I growl.

The car stops, and I don't think I've gotten any bit of information into Julian's brain. Looking out the window, I discover we are back at the pier. Like a child, he grabs my hand and drags me out of the car. I let him lead me onto a boat and sit down next to him, mostly because there isn't anywhere else for me to go.

We're both angry, right now, and if we're going to make it through this, we need to let each other cool off first. Using all the effort I have, I keep my mouth shut the rest of the way back to the island. I look out at the water and let it calm me, hoping that Julian will be calm by the time we get back to the beach house.

The boat drops us off and turns right back around, leaving Julian and me alone on the beach. My lips part, and I'm about to say something when he leans down and scoops me up, throwing me over his shoulder like I'm a sack of potatoes.

I truly don't understand his need to assert his alphaness on me.

"Julian." I sigh. "Please, listen to me."

He stays quiet, walking inside and heading straight to the bedroom. Kicking the door in, the wood cracks and gives beneath his foot. So much for him calming down. It seems the silence has only made things worse. Walking into the room and over the door's splintered pieces, he throws me onto the bed.

I bounce off the mattress and land in the middle of a pile of fluffed pillows. All I can hear is the rush of my own blood in my ears and feel the heavy thump of my heart in my chest. Fear and anger collide inside of me, and I'm not sure which one is going to win out.

"Julian…" I start again, but it's clear that my words fall onto deaf ears.

He's a volcano, seconds away from erupting, and there is nothing I can do but sit back and watch, hoping the fire inside of him doesn't burn me too badly. Spinning around with a loud roar, he swings his arms and hits the closest wall. His fists go straight through the sheetrock like he is the hulk. He pulls out his fist, just to hit the wall again a few inches to the right.

All I can do is stare, knowing that if I get up and try and stop him, things will only get worse. The dresser becomes his next target. Gripping it by the sides with an iron grip, he flips the whole thing over and kicks it to the side like trash. His muscles bulge, his body oozes rage. One by one, he attacks every piece of furniture inside the room until the whole space is nothing but debris and destroyed beyond repair. Pieces of wood and drywall fall like glitter around us.

Like a statue, I remain sitting on the bed, helpless in the center of the storm.

Chaos surrounds me while I'm completely still, untouched by the disorder.

Then as if the eye of the storm has settled on me, he stands unmoving. Nostrils flare and fists clench. His veins bulge with red hot anger.

His gaze lands on me, and ice skates down my spine when I see the darkness in his eyes. The man I've come to love has been replaced by a beast of a man, and I'm not sure I'm going to make it out of this room without being ripped to pieces.

"We can talk about this. Let me explain..." I start, but the menacing look in his eyes steals the air from my lungs, and I find the rest of my words get lodged in my throat.

Separating the distance between us in three huge strides, he stands before me as if he is a Greek god. I have enough common sense to keep my mouth shut and thank god because something tells me Julian wouldn't hesitate to strangle me.

Fear zings through me with the intensity of a lightning bolt, and the hairs on the back of my neck stand on end. When he leans forward and grabs a fist full of my shirt, tugging me to the edge of the bed in the process.

Gritting his teeth like an animal, he sneers, "I don't want to talk... I want to hurt you."

His words stir a fire of desire and anger inside of me, and without thinking my actions through, I lift my hand and slap him across the face. A sting of pain kisses my palm, and Julian's face cuts to the side from the impact.

What happens next is something I never could've expected. Instead of hitting me back or hurting me, he kisses me. His lips press against mine with a hateful heat. It's teeth and the coppery tang of blood explodes against my tongue when his own enters my mouth. I swear I feel every drop of pain, anger, and fear in that kiss.

It's like he's trying to suffocate me with it. The kiss becomes something else entirely when the world around us starts to fade away, and we start tugging at each other's clothes. Fabric tears and buttons fly, and I'm only vaguely aware of my naked state when Julian pushes me back against the bed and climbs on top of me.

One large hand circles my throat, as he pins my naked body beneath his. My sex clenches and nipples harden as he squeezes my slim throat a little tighter, his eyes never wavering from mine. He's pushing me, looking to see how far I will go.

"Hurt me. Do it. I know you want to." I push the words out through my gritted teeth. Even as angry as I am with him, I'm turned on too. I lift my hips even though they're pinned to the bed by the weight of his body.

"I do... I want to fucking strangle you for being so stupid. For thinking you could leave, and I wouldn't find you," he hisses and leans down, pressing his nose flat against mine. His nostrils flare like a bull that's ready to charge. I want to push him, to anger him because at least when he's like this, I can see how much he cares, see that he does want me even if he doesn't always say it.

"If it wasn't for the police, I could have. I'd be long gone by now." It's the wrong move and one that could end up burning me in the end, but I want to feel him right now, feel his fear, feel the love I know he refuses to admit for me.

Like a branch swaying in a storm, he snaps. In an instant, he's lifting me and reversing our spots. The world around me spins for one brief moment, then he's regaining his hold on my throat as he situates me on top of him.

Squirming against his thick cock, I mewl into the air, there is a thick, primal need frantically clawing up my spine.

"You want my cock, don't you? Want me to fill you up? Touch that spot deep inside you that no one else will. You think you can run, but you would come back. There is nothing like what we share, and if you think I would let another man touch what is mine, you're just as crazy as me. I'd kill him, and then fuck you right beside his still-warm body. You're mine. All mine. Every fucking inch of you, and I'm going to punish your tight hole. Remind you of who it is that owns you, my wife."

There is no warning as he tightens his grip on my throat, and enters me in one swift move, his cock sliding all the way home. The muscles of my core quiver, and even though I'm slick with raw need, there is a tinge of pain that follows.

The pain fades to nothing when he starts moving, fucking me with an edge that makes me wonder if he will actually strangle me. His stroke is precise, like balancing on the edge of a blade, knowing that one slip will draw blood.

"Mine!" he growls into my ear, squeezing my throat even tighter.

The air in my lungs is cut off, but the pleasure spiraling through me is all the oxygen I need. Julian fucks me like he hates me, and it's the most exhilarating thing in the world. My toes curl, and my spine stiffens as every bounce on his cock sends me to a new height of pleasure.

I'm close, so fucking close, and then he pulls out. Like a savage, he lifts me and tosses me down onto the bed. I whimper at the loss of his cock inside of me but moan with ecstasy when I feel him move behind me, and his cock slides deep inside of me once more.

"Say it. Say that you're mine." I can all but see the cords in his neck tightening, the grip he has on my hips is bruising as he forces his cock inside me over and over again.

When I don't answer fast enough, he grabs a fist full of hair and tugs my head backward, and somehow, the movement drives his cock deeper inside of me.

He's all I can feel, smell, and taste.

"Fuckin' say it. Tell me who owns you. Whose pussy is this? Whose body is this? Say it, Elena. Say it, so I can feel that tight pink pussy quiver around my cock."

Gritting my teeth, I try to fight off the orgasm, rising up with each penetrating stroke. I try and ignore his hot breath against my skin, his deep, dangerous scent that fills my nostrils with each breath I take, but there is no escaping him. Julian Moretti owns me. He owns my body, my heart, my mind, and my soul.

"Come on, baby, say it, so I can let you come..." His teeth nip my ear hard, and I tighten around his cock. "Yes, just like that. Tell me who owns you. Otherwise, I'm going to pull out and come down your throat."

The idea of not coming is deterring enough and is the last push I need to admit that I'm completely taken by this man.

"You. It's you. You own me," I cry into the demolished room with my head tipped back, my neck aching, and my fingers clawing at the sheets. A moment later, Julian releases his grip on my hair. His hands find my hips, and he fucks me right into the mattress. I grab onto the sheets to keep myself in place as the headboard crashes against the wall over and over again.

Crumbling, my orgasm slams into me fiercely, stealing the breath from my lungs. My eyes drift closed, and all I can hear is the thundering beat of my own heart. As the pleasure washes away, I find Julian is still fucking me. He continues owning me, forcing me to orgasm three more times before he allows himself to come, painting the inside of my womb with his warm release.

Sagging against me, I feel his sweat-slicked skin against mine, and a warm sensation works its way through my limbs. In his arms, nothing in the world can reach me. He is my protector, and my savior.

For a short time, we both lie there, trying to catch our breath. Rolling off me, he falls onto the mattress beside me but then drags me over his body. He makes me lie on top of him, my head resting on his chest as he draws circles against the small of my back. All the anger that was consuming him an hour ago has vanished now.

"I wasn't trying to run away. Clyde was trying to hurt Marie. He had her pinned against the counter with his hand up her dress. He was going to rape her if I didn't stop him," I whisper, turning my face to rest my cheek against the mattress on the other side, so I can see his face. "I didn't think. All I did was react, and when I saw him dead on the floor and Marie started crying, saying you would kill her. I knew she was right. I had to get her off the island."

"Do you think that low of me? That I would kill her for saying no to one of my guards?"

Do I? He isn't all that fond of Marie, and his men are above the maids and cooks.

He sighs. "I can tell by the look on your face that you believe I would've killed her."

"I'm sorry. You don't exactly like Marie, and I was afraid for her. I wasn't leaving you. I swear. I want to be here with you."

There is a long moment of silence, and I wonder what he's thinking. Running a hand through his sweaty hair, he stares at me, his gaze penetrating. "You should've come to me and told me what happened. All that leaving did was put you in danger. What if I hadn't got a call? I never would've found you, and god knows what could've happened." The anguish in his voice clings to my skin.

"I know. I'm sorry," I apologize almost shamefully.

"I know you are. I can see it in your eyes, and that is the only reason you're not shackled to the bed, and I'm not spanking your ass until it's pink and sore. I understand that you were afraid, but I am your husband, and enough bad things have happened to you recently. I can't risk losing you. You're more important to me than you think. When I discovered you were gone... betrayal sliced through me, and I felt like I couldn't breathe."

Reaching for his hand, I grasp onto it and squeeze. "I wasn't leaving, Julian."

"I know..." he brings my hand to his lips and brushes them against my knuckles. "Do not do something like that again. I'm not sure I'll be able to withstand it."

"I'm not sure our furniture will withstand it either. Look at this room."

"They are just things. I do want to look at you. Your hand and your eye to be more specific."

"It's fine. It's just a cut and a bruise." My hand stopped bleeding a long time ago, and with everything going on, I totally forgot about it. "It doesn't even hurt anymore."

"You know if Clyde wasn't already dead, I would have killed him from touching you."

"I know..."

40

JULIAN

We left the next day. The honeymoon was tainted, and there was no way either one of us could enjoy the rest of it. She said she didn't intend to leave me, and I believe her, but she still didn't trust me enough to protect her and Marie from my rogue guard. She put herself in danger to protect her friend, and I wasn't okay with that. It made me feel inadequate as a husband.

We flew back home, and now we're settling in as newlyweds.

Elena is still mad at me for firing Marie, and I'm actually thinking about rehiring her just to make my wife smile again.

As promised, I gave Elena some freedoms, but not nearly enough to keep her happy. I let her walk around the house as she wishes but only with two guards or me by her side. She uses that freedom to spend a lot of time in the kitchen, watching Celeste cook, chatting with her about music, movies, and desserts. She lacks the spark of joy that makes her who she is, and I can see it from a mile away.

I know Elena is seeking normality. She just wants to act and live like a normal person, but unfortunately, this is not something I can easily give her. I can't have her be unprotected, ever. Her father is still out there, and just like any criminal, I have a long line of enemies waiting to find my one true weakness.

Like most days, I find her in the library after I'm done working for the day. She is curled up on one of the chaise lounges, her nose buried deep in a book. It's usually a romance novel that she prefers to read, but occasionally, I'll see her with a thriller. Her need to read and expand her mind only makes me want her all the more.

When she notices my presence, she closes the book and drops it on her lap while her lips turn into a frown like she is disappointed to see me. I would be offended if I wasn't sure it's fake. Even when she is pissed at me, she seeks my body, cuddles into me at night, melts into my touch, and moans when I steal a kiss. Part of the way she acts is fake, but part of it is real too. She misses Marie and wants to be free, but she never will be.

"Don't pout, my wife. A smile becomes you much better."

"Then give me something to smile about," she quips. "Take me on a date."

I raise my eyebrows at her. "A date? You know I don't do those."

"Then, I have nothing to smile about," she says almost dramatically. Her frown deepens, and I almost roll my eyes at her. She is showing her young age right now, and I'd laugh if I knew I wouldn't get a book thrown at my face.

"Fine, I'll take you on a date," I agree before I can come to my senses.

Now it's her eyebrows that are shooting up with surprise. "Like a real date? You're going to take me on a real date, like the kind that a normal couple would go on?"

"I don't know what you consider to be normal, but yes, if that's what will make you happy–"

"Yes!" She jumps up from her seat and rushes forward and into my arms. "Can we go right now?"

"I guess now is as good a time as any." Worry worms its way through my body, and I have to tell myself to calm down. It's just a date. What the hell could possibly happen?

～

THE HOSTESS LEADS us to a secluded table in the darkest corner of the restaurant, just as I asked. I keep Elena's hand wrapped up in my own, pulling her close to my side. I've got two guns strapped to the inside of my jacket, and a knife at each ankle. I might be overly prepared, but if something does happen, I want to know that I can protect us.

Elena is beaming, smiling from ear to ear. She chose a simple but elegant dress for dinner, and I haven't been able to keep my eyes off her.

"Does this match up with your idea of a *date*?"

"Yes! It's perfect." Her eyes gleam with joy, and I find my own lips tipping up at the sides.

The waitress comes over, and I order food for both of us, along with a bottle of wine. When she walks away, leaving us alone, I turn my attention back to Elena.

"I thought if it would make you happy, maybe Marie could return to the mansion, and work for me. I know you miss her, and if it makes you return to your normal self."

Elena giggles, and the sound zings straight to my cock. "Are you bargaining with me, husband?"

"It's not a bargain. All I want is for you to be happy. She obviously makes you happy. Therefore, I will have her brought back to the mansion."

"I would love that. I won't lie. I was really angry when you ended our honeymoon and sent her away." She peers down at the tablecloth as if she's too ashamed to look at me.

"I'll make it up to you," I promise, and the waitress walks in with the bottle of wine, then. She pours us two glasses and leaves the bottle sitting in a bath of ice on the table.

"To new beginnings," I toast, staring into Elena's dark green eyes.

Our glasses clink together, and my gaze is drawn to her full pink lips as they touch the rim of the wine glass. I want to taste them, bite them, mark her, so everyone knows she is mine. The possessiveness I feel toward her is something I doubt will ever fade.

My need to lock her up and keep her away from everyone outweighs all logical thinking. Every part of me says lock her in the cage and throw the key away, but in doing so, I take the very things I love so much about her and squeeze the life right out of them.

When it comes to Elena, I know I would do anything to keep her by my side. Is that love? Or is what I'm feeling just an abnormal need for control?

I know she loves me now, but will she still love me when I end her father's life?

When all the dominoes fall, and the blood of my enemy is shed, will she still want me? I guess only time will tell. It doesn't matter. I'll never let her go, never let her leave me.

"This is nice, normal. I wish we could do this more often," she whispers, taking another sip of her wine.

"As soon as your father is taken care of, we can. After the incident on the island, I thought someone had gotten to you. I was reliving the moment you fell down the stairs at the mansion. I never want to feel that way again." I reach for her hand without thought and cling to it.

"It doesn't have to be that way. I can tell my father to leave us alone, tell him that I want to be with you and to stop trying to take me away."

I almost laugh. "It doesn't work like that. Your father is as determined to get you back as I am to keep you. This will only end in bloodshed. There is no other way around it. Your father never should've gone back on our agreement."

Elena's face sours. "I don't want either of you to get hurt."

She doesn't know how horrible of a man her father is. The difference between him and me is that I don't pretend or hide what I do from Elena. She knows I'm a killer, a criminal that has done horrible things. Her father spent his entire life sheltering her.

The waitress interrupts us, bringing our food to the table, stopping me from responding to what she's said. Then again, maybe the waitress appearing isn't such a bad thing. I don't want to ruin our date any further with talks of her father.

"Let's eat. We can talk about this later." I force myself to smile.

Elena nods, and we dig into our homemade ravioli. Stuffing our faces, eating, and drinking, the conversation slowly slips from my mind. By the time we're finished with our meal, I am ready to return to the mansion and cuddle up beside my wife in bed. I feel satisfied with the choices I've made today, taking her out to dinner, and even offering Marie her job back.

Things should return to normal for a short while, or at least until Zeke finds Romero, then everything will explode again.

I pay for our meal and leave a tip on the table.

"On the way here, I saw this little ice cream shop that was about a block away. Could we walk over there and get a scoop?" Elena pleads, batting her dark eyelashes at me.

"You still have room inside your stomach for dessert?" I ask astonished.

Elena's lips curve into a grin. "I always have room for dessert. Please? Pretty, please?" Her voice drops to a seductive tone on the last please, and I hear the word in my cock. Holy hell, when we get home, I'm tying her to the bed and fucking her into submission again.

"Fine, we can get ice cream," I finally agree, acting as if she twisted my arm backward to get me to go.

"I'm so excited. I haven't had ice cream since I was a child." In an instant, an emotion I'm unaware of slams into me, and I swear I'll do anything in the world to keep her happy, to make sure she has everything she wants and needs.

Taking her hand in mine, I lead us out of the restaurant. I don't realize how careless I am as we leave the restaurant and start down the street to the ice cream parlor. I'm so caught up in the joy on Elena's face and the happiness radiating from her, that I don't notice the man following a short distance behind us, not until he is almost on us.

As we pass a dark alleyway, I grab Elena by the arm and drag her down it, hoping to shake the guy off us.

"What's going on?" Elena asks, her voice a whisper of worry.

"We're being followed," I grunt and glance over my shoulder to see if the fucker is still following us. Every nerve ending on my body is in defense mode. I'll protect Elena, or I'll die trying. Her father is not going to get his hands on her. She is mine.

Reaching inside my jacket, I pull out a gun. A soft gasp escapes Elena's lips when her eyes catch on the shiny metal from the fluorescent streetlight above.

Footsteps slap against the pavement behind, us and ahead, I spot a dumpster. I shove Elena into the corner and place a finger over my lips to let her know to be quiet. She nods, her slim body trembling with fear or maybe adrenaline. I don't know which. I catch a glint of excitement flicker in her eyes, and for a moment, I can't believe that I'm really seeing it.

She can't really be excited about me killing someone because that's what's going to happen if this person doesn't turn around.

Shielding her body with mine, I press her against the brick wall and listen as the footsteps grow closer. The blood rushes to my ears, and I let everything around me fade to darkness. At this moment, there is just me, the hunter, and the prey.

My finger moves to the trigger of my gun, and when the person pops up around the corner, I lift my weapon and fire a bullet into each of his kneecaps. Like a doll, he falls to the ground with a scream, his own gun slips from his hand and hits the pavement.

Rushing toward him, I'm obsessed with the need to make him pay. He didn't even do anything, simply followed us, but the fact that he had a gun and was after us is enough intent for me. If given the chance, he would've hurt Elena.

Grabbing the fucker by the front of his shirt, I lift him off the ground and growl into his face, "Who sent you?"

Pain lances his features, and yet, he still manages to smile like an asshole. His smile pisses me off, and so I rear my fist back and punch him right in the mouth. His head falls to the side with the blow before turning back to me. His yellow teeth are coated in blood now, and as I scan his face and neck, I find he has a tattoo on the side of his neck.

It's the family crest for the Romero family.

Fuck.

"Did Romero send you?" I question but already know the answer.

"You might as well kill me because I'm not telling you a fucking thing," he sneers, and my patience is thin enough. I could have my men come and get him and take him back to the house to torture him, but there would be no point.

"As you wish. If you don't want to talk, then you're useless to me." Lifting the gun, I press the barrel to his forehead and pull the trigger. His eyes go vacant instantly, and I pull away from him and come to stand.

Turning, I peer over my shoulder, and I find Elena watching me with caution and curiosity, nothing like the worry or fear I expected to see in her eyes. I'm surprised, shocked even. Maybe she is growing more used to this life.

"You killed him?" she whispers. Looking between the dead guy and me. I expect her to be terrified, shaking, or crying, but instead, she just looks surprised.

"Yes." I place my gun back in my jacket and grab my cell phone from my pocket. "You're taking this pleasantly well, better than I thought you ever would."

Her eyes gleam like jewels. "I never thought I would get to see you in action like that. I mean it's terrifying, but it's also exciting. How do you know he was after us?"

"When we came down the alleyway, he followed, and he had a gun. Plus, the tattoo on his neck tells me all I need to know. He's one of your father's men. Sending someone so sloppy is really an insult."

Worry festers deep in my gut. If someone could attack us out in the open like this, what could happen at the house? One trip outside the house, and I had to kill a man. It also tells me we're being watched, and if we're being watched, it's only a matter of time before the next attack.

How can I protect Elena when we can't even leave the house for a simple dinner? There is no other way around it. She won't be safe until my enemies, and her father are taken care of. I will kill them all to protect her.

41

ELENA

Since the night in the alleyway, Julian has been more vigilant. He keeps me within his sight almost always now and has been working from the library or our bedroom more than the office. While he works, I usually sit next to him and read or watch a movie on my iPad.

Security has been tightened, and more guards are patrolling the house, which I'm guessing has something to do with the attack on our dinner date.

Thankfully, Marie has returned to the mansion, and I have someone to spend time with, the times he does have to step away or leave.

I wish things with my father and Julian would end already. I won't deny that seeing my husband kill to protect me, excited me more than it should have. I'm pretty sure there is something wrong with me, why else would I be turned on by blood and bullets?

Shoving my lunch around on my plate with my fork, I look up and find Marie staring at me from across the kitchen. She smiles when I catch her staring. "Maybe we can go in the pool for a swim this afternoon?" I suggest.

"I'll take you," Julian's voice booms through the kitchen, startling the hell out of me.

"Hey," I greet him, catching my breath. "Are you done working?"

"To see you in a bikini? Yes." He winks, and a smile spreads across my face.

"I can bring your lunch out to the terrace," Marie offers quietly. She is still afraid of Julian, even though she was very thankful to have her job back.

"Yes, do that," his voice turns sharp as he talks to Marie, then softens again when he turns his attention back to me. "Come on. Let's get wet."

We never make it to the bedroom to get changed because on the way up, Julian's phone rings.

As soon as he answers, his playful demeanor changes, and instantly, I know something terrible is going to happen.

"What do you mean he is with the Volcoves'? Is that where he has been hiding out this whole time?" Julian's eyes cut to me, and all the puzzle pieces fall into place.

Oh, god, no... he found my father.

My heart races in my chest, and I feel like it's somehow getting harder to breathe. He found my father. He found my father, and he's going to kill him.

"Yes, I agree... don't go in alone. I'll get a team together. Wait for my call." Julian ends the call and stuffs the phone back in his pocket. "I'm sorry. I'll have to take a raincheck on the pool." He grinds the words out through his teeth.

His entire demeanor has changed now. Before me stands a man of power, of ruthless violence, and he is going to bring down the world around me.

"You found my father, didn't you?"

"Yes." At least he isn't lying about it. "He's been staying with the Volcoves'. Do you know who they are?"

I shake my head, no, mainly because the words won't come.

"Lev Volcove was the man who scared you at the auction. The one who scratched your leg."

A shiver runs down my spine just thinking about him. Why would my father surround himself with those people?

Julian's next set of words shock me to the core. "I killed Lev for touching you. His family knows. Your father allied himself with them because they want my head on a pitchfork." The seriousness of the situation hits me like a freight train.

"Let me talk to him, tell him that I'm happy here," I plead, doubting he would even consider it. "The last thing I want is for something to happen to either of you."

Julian pulls away as if I'm crucifying him with my words. "Nothing you say or do is going to change my mind. If your father truly loved you, he would've stayed and made sure you were okay, but instead, he tucked his tail between his legs and ran. There is a price to pay for hurting those that I care about, and his hourglass has run out."

Tears well in my eyes, and I know that this is going to end badly. It feels like my heart is being ripped in two. I love Julian, but I love my father, too, even if he sold me to the enemy. You can't help who you love, and I'm caught on a teeter-totter between the two most important men in my life.

"I'm going to end this today." The darkness in his voice bleeds outward like a blot of ink on paper. It takes everything in me to remain standing before him, and when he turns his back on me and starts to walk away, something inside of me shatters. It's like all over again, he is choosing his need to make my father pay over me. His need for revenge outweighs any love he has for me, and I know I have to do something, warn my father, tell him to end this before Julian gets the chance to.

As soon as Julian is out of sight, the wheels in my head start to spin in motion. I consider my options. There are not many. Leaving the grounds to search for my father will put me in more danger and cause bigger issues between Julian and me. I have to do something, though, because I can't stand here while he puts a group of men together to scour the countryside for my father.

Turning on my heels, I rush out of the room but stop once I reach the door jam. It hits me then. I can't leave, but I can call him. I can warn him.

The only phones in the house are the guards' cell phones, but I'd bet anything there is a phone in Julian's office. I could use it, that is, if the door is unlocked. Tiptoeing out of the bedroom, I look both ways down the hall.

Seeing no one, I dart into the hall and rush toward the door that is Julian's office. Praying like I've never done so before, I grab onto the cold iron wrought door handle and twist it.

I'm half expecting someone to jump out into the hall and find me or the door to be locked, but neither happens. A breath passes, and the knob continues to twist, the door creaking open as I give it a light push. My heart is galloping like a horse in my chest as I slip inside the room. I can't imagine the punishment I will receive if Julian finds out what I'm doing.

The fear of being caught doesn't outweigh my fear for my father. I will take whatever punishment is given to me if it gives my father a chance to escape.

Walking toward the massive desk, I locate the phone, the single landline in this place after Julian had the one in the kitchen removed. My hands shake violently as I grab the receiver and bring it to my ear. The dial tone fills my ear, and I push the buttons and dial my father's number.

Worry wells like a molehill inside of me. The phone rings, and rings, and rings, and just when I think he won't answer, I hear his soft tone filter into the receiver.

"Hello?"

"Daddy!" I cry, "You have to stop this. You have to stop coming for me, trying to save me. I'm happy here. I love Julian."

"Don't say that. You can't love him. He has you brainwashed, he only took you for revenge, that's it. He doesn't love you, Elena. You need to escape. Find a way out, and I will find you, wherever you are."

The muscles in my throat tighten, making it hard for me to breathe, to swallow. "Revenge? He took me as revenge?" I can't seem to wrap my head around his words. I know Julian believes my father killed his mother, but still... me as revenge?

"Yes, he doesn't love you. He only took you to get back at me. I'm coming for you. I'm going to right all that I've done wrong. Soon, you'll be free, sweetheart. Free of the cage he's put you in."

My heart shatters in my chest, and I feel the deep lashes his words have left across the organ. "You're lying. Julian might hate you, but he loves me. He loves me. This isn't revenge."

"It is, and I'm sorry you were dragged into this."

Before I can respond, the door creaks behind me, and I whirl around and find Julian in the doorway. His gaze is dark, penetrating, but with the reeling emotions inside of me, I'm as far from afraid as it gets. I'm angry, sad, and shocked, but more than anything, I'm hurt.

I hang up the phone and turn to give him my full attention. Lips trembling, I ask, "Is it true? Did you take me for revenge? Was this all about getting even with my father?"

He takes a step toward me, and I automatically take one back, trying to keep as much distance between us as possible.

"Yes... it's true." As the words reach my ear, I can feel my heart cracking in my chest. Broken, I feel broken.

"Everything was a lie? Our marriage is a lie..."

"No. I took you for revenge at first, but I really do want you to be my wife. You are more than revenge to me now," he tells me, and I almost believe him... almost.

"If you gave up revenge, and I do really mean something to you, then prove it. Don't go after my father. Don't kill him."

"I can't do that. He needs to die," he says without even thinking about it. It's the confirmation I need to know my father was right. Julian doesn't love me. He only cares about revenge. I was just too stupid to see that until now.

42

JULIAN

Guilt grows like a cancer, rushing through my veins, and pumping into my heart. I feel guilty for hurting Elena. She hasn't smiled, leaned into my touch, or sought out my company in two days. It's a one-eighty from what she was like a few days ago, and I hate it.

I feel like I'm losing her, and that has me more on edge than the fact that Zeke and a team of my best men are attacking Romero tonight.

"Our marriage is a lie..." I can hear the words in my mind still as if she said them right this instant. My need to make her father pay has cost me the last important thing in my life: her.

I thought having Marie back would help things, lighten the mood for when the shit hit the fan, but it seems Elena has closed in on herself further, and I'm not sure how to reach her. She's fading every day, pulling away from me, sinking into the sand.

It's maddening what her silence does to me, and I'm even considering letting her father live to prove to her that things have changed, that I do love her, and that our marriage is real.

At first, revenge was the driving force behind me wanting her, but it hasn't been for a long time. Since almost losing her, I've only wanted her father dead. Not only for revenge but also to protect her. To ensure that neither of us would ever have to look over our shoulders and wonder if something was going to happen. Now, I only have to make Elena believe me.

She's been hiding in the library, I know she doesn't want to be anywhere near me, but I'm done pretending like there isn't an elephant sitting on top of our marriage.

"I want you to stay posted outside every room that she goes in and comes out of, regardless of whether I'm inside it," I say before heading to the library.

"Yes, sir," Lucca responds. He's done well as my second in command, but if I'm honest, I can't wait for Markus to return. I can't wait until everything goes back to normal.

I've tried my best to give Elena some space, but it's hard letting her out of my sight while knowing Romero and Lev's family are working together and after us. Hopefully, that will end tonight, in the meantime, I will be on high alert. Especially today, when I only have a few men guarding the house. Call it paranoia if you want... I call it protecting what is mine.

The Volcove compound is well fortified, and it's going to take a lot of men to take them down. I wanted to be there, but I decided it is more important to stay with Elena.

When I step into the large library, I find my wife sitting in the windowsill. Her attention is drawn to the book in her lap while mine is drawn to the way her hair shines in the sunlight. She's beautiful as sin, and I should've known the day I forced her name on the dotted line that she would become my demise.

"Did you have a good day?" I ask when she finally looks up from the book in her hand.

"Mhhh." She nods her head and closes the book.

She won't even look at me, let alone talk.

"Let's go to dinner, I want to talk to you about something."

She gets up from the windowsill and lays her book face down as if she is going to come back to read it later, walking over to me, she stops right in front of me.

Her eyes are lowered, cast down at my chest. I know she is doing this because she's hurt, but two days of this behavior is all she is going to get. I've had enough. My guilt is being drowned out by my ever-rising anger, and her dismissiveness is not helping. I want my wife back, hurt feelings, or not.

"Look at me," I order, but she shakes her head in defiance like a small child refusing to follow directions.

Grabbing her by the chin, I force her head upward, so she has no other option but to face me. She glares at me like she is about to lash out, maybe scratch me again, but as I wait to give her a chance to do so, she doesn't make a move.

"Enough of your pouting. I don't like how you've been acting lately."

"Really?" She scoffs and crosses her dainty arms over her chest. "Does me not loving you not go along with your revenge plan? Poor you..." She patronizes, and even though I admire her bravery, I will not stand for it. I don't let my men or anyone talk to me like that. I will not let my wife do so either.

"Your behavior is unacceptable," I snap, tightening my grip on her chin. "I've already told you things have changed. It's time for you to remember your place... which is by my side as my wife. Now, let's have dinner on the terrace, so we can talk some more."

She nods her head as much as she can while still in my grip, and I release her. Taking her hand, I start our descent down the stairs. She doesn't hold onto me in return, refusing to wrap her fingers around mine. Her slender hand just lies flaccid in my larger one.

I feel like a volcano that is ready to erupt. She is my wife, and yet, she acts as if she is disgusted by my very presence.

We walk in silence, and I use that time to let what I'm planning to say marinate in my head. I know I'm taking a leap of faith here, but if that's what it takes to keep her by my side and happy, I'm willing to do it... ready to say the words I haven't since I was a little boy.

Arriving on the terrace, I pull out a chair, and Elena sits down in it almost immediately. An image of Elena in her wedding dress flashes before my eyes as I look over at the spot where our wedding arch stood only a few days ago. I wish I could go back to that day.

"What is it you want to talk about?" Elena asks, her cold demeanor cracking slightly as I hear a touch of defeat in her voice.

"Elena, you are my wife because I want you to be. I didn't lie to you, not really. When I saw you at the funeral, I knew the instant I laid eyes on you that I had to have you. Yes, I told myself that it was for revenge, and maybe that was part of it, but it wasn't the sole reason. And now, revenge has nothing to do with me wanting you. I want you because of you. Because you're the most important thing to me."

"If that was true, then you wouldn't still want to kill my father."

"And I wouldn't if he wasn't actively trying to kill me and take you from me. What do you think would happen to you if I was gone? There are others, far worse than I. He sold you to me. I imagine he would sell you to someone else if I were gone. Someone like Lev."

Just like that, the mask of anger and defiance Elena had carefully placed over her face slips away. Leaving behind nothing but acidic fear and grief.

"I don't want you to die," she admits, and the dread I've felt since that phone call finally starts to lessen. "I don't want anyone to die."

"You are my wife, and I will protect you at any cost. Even if that means doing something you don't like. I will never stop making sure you are safe, and as long as your father is out there, you are not safe. He doesn't care about you. What about when we have children? Do you think he is going to stop trying to come after me?"

"I just don't understand." She shakes her head, still not ready to admit her father's fault.

"Elena, I..." The words are on the tip of my tongue. *I love you.*

Before I can find the courage to speak the words out loud, I hear glass shattering off in the distance. I'm up and out of my seat before I hear the first shots ring through the air. The chair clanks against the ground, and my insides twist at the sound.

Fuck! Where the hell is Lucca? Where are the guards?

I grab my gun from my holster and pull Elena up with my free hand, tugging her behind me. In that instant, my only thought is her. I need to get her somewhere safe. On the patio, we're out in the open, and in the worst spot when under attack. *Fuck!*

"Stay close!" I bark over my shoulder and start walking inside.

Elena fists the fabric of my shirt as if she is afraid, her body's close to mine as we make our way back into the house. I need to get her to my office. It doubles as a safe room, it's fire, and bulletproof. I just need to get her inside–

We don't even make it to the bottom of the stairs before the explosion hits, rocking us right off our axis. One second we are heading to the stairs, and the next, we are thrown to the ground from the shockwave of the explosion.

My ears ring, my head throbs, and my lungs burn, but all I can think about is Elena as I frantically try to regain my bearings. Searching around me, I'm desperate to find her, to hold her, but she isn't there. I can't reach her.

Where is my wife?

I can't lose her too.

I have to save her.

43

ELENA

Complete and utter chaos ensues around me. Before I know what's happening, I'm thrown to the ground, unable to keep my grip on Julian. My hands reach for him but grasp nothing but air. I'm reeling, trying to get my bearings, but it's like being on a boat, my body swaying back and forth with the ocean waves.

Then there is a tug on my arm, and I'm being pulled to stand. I immediately know it's not Julian, simply by how the man's fingers dig into my skin painfully and the way he carelessly jerks me around, not caring if I get hurt.

It takes me a moment to regain my bearings, shake away the ringing in my ear, and be stable on my legs. When the dust around us settles, and the room becomes visible again, I realize this is even worse than I could've imagined.

Julian is on the ground just now pushing himself up to his feet. My father is standing on the opposite side of the room, his eyes trained on Julian.

My gaze swings around the room, I don't know most of the men, but all of them have their guns out and pointed at my husband, which tells me they're the enemy. I twist around to look at the man who has a death grip on my arm, which sure enough will leave a lingering bruise. I've never seen this man either, but he looks at me like he knows who I am, almost like we have unfinished business.

"You'll pay for what your husband did to my brother. I'll make you pay, and I'll make your pitiful excuse of a husband watch." He chuckles, but it's anything but a joyous laugh, and I know who he is—Lev's brother.

My instincts kick in, and I tug my arm back to get away from him. I recoil just from his touch alone. Dread swirls like an impending storm above my head. I want to get away, but his grip just tightens to near pain, and the reality of the situation slams into me.

"Daddy," I try to get my father's attention. "Please, stop this." My pleading falls on deaf ears, and the ground beneath my feet trembles.

"You can have her. Consider it as a gift. A life for a life. She is no longer useful to me." My father dismisses me without a single look. I hear his words, but I don't understand their meaning. My brain can't comprehend what he is saying. Only when the man holding me starts pulling me away, does everything begin to sink in and make sense.

"What do you mean I'm no longer useful to you?" The words rip from my throat, and it's like he's shot an arrow into my chest.

He doesn't even look at me as he speaks, he looks at the spot beside me, but not into my eyes. *Coward.* "I don't need you anymore. I've got Julian right where I want him. You were merely a pawn to keep him in place."

Curling my hand into a tight fist, I want to slug him.

"You weren't supposed to fall in love, but you did. I thought you were stronger than that, more resilient." The bitter laugh that he emits makes me want to lunge at him. "You did this to yourself."

Julian was right. This whole time, he was right. I was just too stupid and naive to see it. My father was playing his own games, and I was just a pawn. Another piece on his chessboard that he could move exactly where he needed and sacrifice when the time came.

"Thanks, Romero, I'll have a lot of fun with this one."

"No!" Julian's voice booms through the room with an authority that has everyone stopping in their tracks. All eyes are on him, including my own. "Don't fucking touch her!"

Julian lunges toward us, and everything after that happens in slow motion. Out of the corner of my eye, I see my father lift his gun and fire the first shot without hesitation.

"No!" I scream, but no one is listening to my pleas. It's as if no one can hear me, and I'm tired of it. Tired of being in a cage, tired of being shoved around, and tired of not having control of my own life.

Julian drops to his knees, clasping his shoulder with one hand. His white shirt soaks with blood in seconds, and all I want to do is run to him and tend to his needs, but instead of getting closer, I'm only being pulled away further.

I struggle as much as I can, kick, scream, and scratch like my life depends on it because it does. If I don't break free and get away, I might as well put a bullet between my eyes. My father no longer cares for me—his words. The only person in the world that matters now is the man on his knees.

Suddenly, I'm free. Cruel hands disappear from my body. Twisting on my heels, I find Marie on the man's back, her slim arms are wrapped around his neck, and it looks like she's trying to choke him.

I know what I have to do before I even realize it. Reaching for his gun, I spin around with it in my hand and pull the trigger.

Time slows down. I can almost see the bullet flying through the air and entering my father's chest.

For the first time tonight, his eyes find mine, and he actually looks at me. I don't know what I expected to see when our eyes finally met. Maybe guilt, sadness, fear? I don't find either. All I see is shock. Like he can't believe I shot him and that this is how his life will end. Not at the hands of his enemy, but at the hands of his own daughter.

I keep staring into his eyes, unable to look away, I watch as the life leaves him. I watch until the eyes so similar to mine go blank. His body drops to the floor, and my mind clears.

This is not over.

I reposition myself and point the gun toward one of the other men. My hands are shaking and fear like I've never felt before blooms in my chest. I could die, but I'd much rather die than be taken from the man I love.

Everyone else moves with me, pointing their guns at me instead of Julian. Julian uses that to his advantage and grabs my father's gun off the ground. Two more shots are fired, and then it's all over.

All the men who were threatening our lives are on the ground, dead... including my father.

I glance to where Marie was struggling with Lev's brother and find him on the ground while Marie and Celeste are standing over him. Celeste is holding a bloody knife in her hand.

She looks at me and smiles, literally smiles.

"No one messes with my family."

I want to go hug her and tell her how much I love her, but Julian is all I can think about. I hurry to his side and start applying pressure to his wound. He groans and clenches his teeth, pulling out his phone.

"We need to call an ambulance," I say, hoping that's what he's doing.

"No, I'll have one of our doctors come and stitch me up. We can't go to the hospital for a gun wound. Too many questions."

"Okay." I nod. I don't like it, but I understand. "Where are all the guards?" My eyes dart around the room as if they will appear out of thin air.

"I don't know," he grits out while dialing the number for the doctor.

"Hello?" A deep voice I recognize comes through the receiver.

"Doc, I need you now. Got shot."

"On my way…"

As soon as the line goes dead, Julian calls Lucca. It rings for a really long time. So long that I don't think he'll answer. If I wasn't so consumed with worry for Julian, I'd probably be worried about Lucca.

"Hello," he finally answers.

"Where the fuck are you?" Julian screams into the phone.

"I'm sorry… I had no choice."

"You fucking betrayed me! You let them in, didn't you?"

"I'm sorry," Lucca repeats. "They have someone I love."

"That's no fucking excuse! You vowed to protect this family. You vowed to protect Elena with your fucking life! You took an oath, Lucca, a fucking oath."

"Long before that, I vowed to protect someone else–" The line goes dead, and Julian throws his phone across the room. The device collides with the wall and shatters into pieces.

"That bastard is going to pay for this. I will kill him for betraying us, for endangering you."

"It's okay. You'll be okay," I whisper low into his ear, my voice trembling as I keep my hands pressed to his shoulder.

"Fuck, I'm sorry." Julian shakes his head. "Are you okay? Are you hurt?" His eyes scan over my face and then slowly drop down to the rest of my body.

"I'm fine. You're the one who got shot."

"It went straight through. Clean shot. I'll be back to normal in a few days. I'm only worried about you," Julian confesses, and for the first time since the night he took me, I believe him wholeheartedly.

Celeste appears next to us with clean towels and a first aid kit. I look up expecting Marie to be here too, but I don't see her anywhere.

"Marie is waiting at the door for the doctor," Celeste explains. "If it's okay, I'll go and wait with her."

"Yes, go ahead. I've got this," I tell her, and she sprints toward the door.

Using the towels she brought, I cover up the wound and apply as much pressure as I can. I glance over to where my father's dead body is sprawled out on the floor.

"I wish you hadn't done that," Julian confesses, and I know what he is saying. He didn't want me to kill my father. Part of me thinks maybe because he just wanted to do it himself while the other part thinks he might be worried about the guilt I may feel someday.

"I thought you wanted him dead?"

"I did, and I'm glad he is gone, but I didn't want you to be the one to pull the trigger. I've never wanted you to have to kill someone, especially not someone you loved. I didn't want you to carry that kind of guilt around."

I think about his words and what I've done.

Maybe it's because I'm in shock, but right at this moment, I don't feel guilt. I don't feel guilty about killing the man who sold me, treated me like cattle, and discarded me like trash in the very end. I don't feel guilty about killing the man who was supposed to love me and instead cared about nothing but himself.

"The only thing I feel guilty about is not believing you sooner. Everything you said was true. He never loved me." The truth weighs heavily on me. He never loved me.

"*I* love you." Julian's deep voice interrupts my thoughts, but it's not his voice that has me hanging on by a single thread.

"You love me?"

"Yes, I love you, Elena. I should have told you sooner. I love you. I have for a long time, and I was a coward not to admit it before. I was convinced I could make myself fall out of love with you. I was so afraid of falling for you, of becoming vulnerable, that I didn't realize I already was." My heart soars to life in my chest.

Leaning down, I press a kiss to his lips.

"I love you too, so much, and I'll never doubt you again. I'm your wife, and from now on, I'll behave like it. I'll be by your side, always."

Always.

EPILOGUE

Elena

I stare down at my small rounding bump. *I'm pregnant.* I still can't believe it. Not long after the shootout with my father did Julian and I discover we were having a baby. And every day, I stare down at my belly with wonderment, watching as it grows each day. It's still shocking that Julian and I will be parents in six months. Me, the princess from the ivory tower who found freedom with her captor. Him, the mafia made man, that shows only strength and never weakness.

To imagine him with our children, wrapped tightly around their tiny fingers. It makes me giddy with excitement. I know he will be an amazing father, even if he doesn't yet believe in himself.

"You've smoothed your hand down the front of your sundress ten times now. Is something wrong, beautiful?"

I shake my head. "No, nothing is wrong. I'm just not used to the bump or the way my body is changing. Somedays, I feel huge, and others I don't feel like I'm pregnant at all."

Julian crosses the space between us and wraps his arms around me. His hands come to rest gently on my belly, and my stomach flutters as if there are a thousand butterflies inside of it.

"Personally, I would like it if you lost the dress and walked around the house naked, but unless you want me to kill every person in this house, I don't think that's a good idea."

Whirling around in his arms, I look up at him. "I agree. There has been enough bloodshed on these floors as of lately."

A shadow crosses Julian's face. Ever since Lucca's betrayal came to light, he's been even warier of his men. I know he feels that if Markus was here, my father never would've gotten in, but then he wouldn't be dead either. We'd still be looking over our shoulders, wondering when the next attack was coming. He says Lucca is a traitor, but I understand why he did what he did. I can't fault someone for protecting someone they love.

I would do the same, would I not?

"I will always be here to protect you. Nothing will ever happen to you or our child."

"You can't protect me from everything, Julian."

"I can, and I will."

All I can do is roll my eyes. "Where are we going for dinner?" I ask, wanting to change the subject and divert it away from us.

"Our favorite spot, of course." He winks and leads me outside to the terrace.

As soon as we walk out, I gasp. The table is decked like usual, but there are candles placed all around the table and along the rail. The outside lights are shut off, so the only light is coming from the hundreds of candles.

"How romantic. I didn't think you had it in you." I grin.

"I had help. Plus, it's a special night."

"Is that so?"

"Yes, sit down, and I'll tell you." He pulls out a chair for me, and I take it, wondering what he could possibly want to talk to me about.

"What is it, Julian? Is everything alright?"

"Yes." He takes the seat across from me. "I realize that I've always made choices for you, and before that, your father did the same. I know you have been longing to be free, and even though I can't give you all the freedom you deserve, I do want to ask you… What do you want, Elena?"

For a moment, all I can do is stare at him. *What do I want?*

Those words are foreign to me. No one ever asks me what I want. So, what do I want?

"I want to be with you."

"And that will never change." Julian gives me a knowing grin. "But what about beyond that? What do you want for your life? Do you want to go to school? Study? Do you want a career, or will you be content being a wife and mother? I don't want you to feel trapped, and I don't want to control every part of your life. I want you to have hopes and dreams, be free as much as I can let you, without risking your safety."

"I don't know what to say…" Seriously. I'm speechless. "Honestly, I've never thought about it."

"Good thing, you have all the time in the world now."

Julian's phone rings, interrupting the moment. He curses under his breath and shakes his head.

"Of course, he would choose now to call…" he growls. "Nice to hear from you, how is your…" He pauses, and the voice on the other end fills the phone. "What are you talking about? Wait… I see. Yes, I suppose I can help." Julian hangs up the phone and turns to me, a devilish glint in his eyes. "That was Markus. He needs help, killing someone."

THANK YOU FOR READING SAVAGE BEGINNINGS!

Curious about Markus?
Read Violent Beginnings Now!

ALSO BY THE AUTHORS

CONTEMPORAY ROMANCE

North Woods University
The Bet
The Dare
The Secret
The Vow
The Promise
The Jock

Bayshore Rivals
When Rivals Fall
When Rivals Lose
When Rivals Love

Breaking the Rules
Kissing & Telling
Babies & Promises
Roommates & Thieves

***

Also by the Authors

DARK ROMANCE

The Blackthorn Elite
Hating You
Breaking You
Hurting You
Regretting You

The Obsession Duet
Cruel Obsession
Deadly Obsession

The Rossi Crime Family
Protect Me
Keep Me
Guard Me
Tame Me
Remember Me

The Moretti Crime Family
Savage Beginnings
Violent Beginnings
Broken Beginnings

The King Crime Family
Indebted
Inevitable

The Diabolo Crime Family
Devil You Hate
Devil You Know

***

STANDALONES

Also by the Authors

Their Captive

Convict Me

Runaway Bride

His Gift

Two Strangers

ABOUT THE AUTHORS

J.L. Beck and **C. Hallman** are *USA Today* and international bestselling author duo who write contemporary and dark romance.

Find us on facebook and check out our website for sales and freebies!

www.bleedingheartromance.com

Copyright © 2020 by Beck & Hallman LLC

Editor: Kelly Allenby

Cover Designer: C. Hallman

Photographer: Wander Aguiar

Cover Model: Dina

All rights reserved.

No part of this book may be reproduced in any form or by any electronic or mechanical means, including information storage and retrieval systems, without written permission from the author, except for the use of brief quotations in a book review.

Printed in Great Britain
by Amazon